FOUND
IN THE
WOODS

FOUND
IN THE
WOODS

A NOVEL

Glory Ralston

Palmetto Publishing Group
Charleston, SC

Found in the Woods
Copyright © 2018 Glory Ralston
All rights reserved. No part of this book may be reproduced in any form or by any
means without written permission from the author.

This is a work of fiction. Names, characters, places, and incidents are the products
of the author's imagination. Any resemblance to persons, cities, places, business
establishments, or events is entirely coincidental.

Printed in the United States

ISBN-13: 978-1-64111-305-2
ISBN-10: 1-64111-305-7

For Reta Austin

Who always says yes when I ask and occasionally tempts me away from the ocean and the forest with promises of grand adventures in the high deserts of Arizona and Nevada. Without her, life would be less exciting, and I would have fewer stories to tell.

It is the primal awe,

Shaking us from the stupor of our daily lives,

Reminding us what matters,

As it quietly, persistently demands to be noticed.

To ask what is nature is to ask what is everything.

—Dylan Berman, "What, you ask, is Nature" (2017)

(1)

Olive-Sided Flycatcher

Screened by the brush, he watched the woman and the dog. To him they were separate parts of a single animal. Their strides matched, their smells mingled. He lifted his nose and sniffed. Ears forward, he listened. He would need to make his move soon.

Susan stopped. She heard a branch breaking and a slight rustling of leaves. Something was moving in the brush. She turned her head and listened. Now there was nothing. The forest was unusually quiet. The only sound was that of Chance's panting.

"Chance, down," she whispered. He dropped down, whining softly, never taking his eyes off her.

"Quiet." Again she gave the command in a whisper. Chance stopped whining and lay still.

Far off an olive-sided flycatcher cried out. Its unique call had been echoing through the forest all morning. Determined to take pictures again, to reclaim at least a little of what she had lost, Susan brought her camera along. But the bird's call had distracted her. She remembered the first time she had heard the flycatcher.

———◆———

Bill, the smell of him, his voice, the pressure of his arm across her shoulder. Waves of reflected heat off the weedy pasture, the old bedsprings, the rusted car bumpers. The beautiful, dilapidated farmhouse, graying and peeling.

"Hey, that bird's giving away beer," Bill said.

"What?" she asked.

"Listen. Quick, free beers," Bill said in an almost perfect imitation of the bird's three-syllable announcement. "It's an omen. We can't say no to free beer."

Against the advice of friends and family, even against their own good judgment, they bought the land and the house. They were young and strong; they could do anything.

There was the long drive out to the abandoned lumber mill where they had heard that free lumber was available if they were willing to haul it off. Bill gripped the steering wheel so tightly that his knuckles turned white as the truck bounced over the dusty, pot-holed road. Susan clutched the armrest on the passenger door with one hand and braced herself against the dashboard with the other.

"Damn," Bill said after hitting a particularly deep pothole. "I think I just lost a filling."

"Yeah, right," Susan said, releasing her hold on the dashboard long enough to punch his shoulder. He smiled at her, revealing his perfect teeth: he never had a cavity in his life.

At the mill, they found hundreds of weathered redwood boards scattered about. They gathered the best of the longer planks together and tossed them into the bed of the pickup. Bill sang snatches of Hank Williams's songs the entire time.

They began building the goat barn early the next morning, using the reclaimed wood. The gray boards felt like smooth leather in Susan's hands. Her first carpenter's belt hung heavy and unfamiliar around her waist. Bill's belt was also a first for him, and he was so proud of it. Every time he made a trip to the hardware store, he bought another tool to put in the belt's many pockets or to hang from the outside loops: hammer, nail punch, tape measure, tri-square, and the world's smallest nail puller.

It took them three weeks to finish building the six-stall barn and milking stanchion. Bill hammered in the last nail on the stanchion late one afternoon while Susan swept the remaining sawdust off the barn floor. When done, they both stood back and admired their work. Bill put his arm around Susan's shoulders and said, "Would you look at that. We did that." It was a small barn but well built. It would keep their future goats safe and dry at night and during the long rainy winters to come.

The vegetable garden was next, another first for them. Bill shoved the ancient, sputtering and smoking rototiller over a quarter acre of ground close to the house, the only place on the property that had full sun in the spring and summer. The scent of the earth, sharp and tangy, drifted up from the soil. Later, Susan crawled next to the long rows she had hoed up, burying the seeds. The rich, dark dirt crusted on her fingers and the knees of her jeans.

Then there were all those long months spent getting the house in shape: stripping the worn linoleum and laying hardwood flooring in its place, redoing all the electrical wiring and plumbing, and replacing the roof shingles. After that came the painting. Susan painted each room inside a different variation of tan, ranging from pale mushroom to light brown, with ivory trim. These were safe colors, nothing risky, nothing clashing. The one exception was a wall in the bathroom. She painted this olive green in honor of the flycatcher. She and Bill worked together painting the outside of the house, the siding a soft shade of yellow, the trim white.

Winter shadows fell across the place from November to March, keeping the house and pasture wet and dark even on those rare days when it wasn't raining. They hauled truckload after truckload of firewood to keep the house warm and free from mold. Most of the garden's topsoil washed away in the winter rains. They spent every spring toting wheelbarrow loads of mulch and manure to build up the clay soil again. And of course there were the legions of slugs, relentless in their determination to eat everything Susan planted.

One gray and sodden November day, Bill stood at the kitchen window and said, "You know, Susan, this is a hard place to live."

"Yes, it is hard, but I like to work hard," she said, coming to stand behind him. "This is our home, where, if luck is on our side, we're going to spend the rest of our lives."

———

A sound of movement in the brush pulled Susan out of the past and back into the woods. Once again the sound stopped. Now it was so quiet that Susan could hear the rhythmic whoosh of her heart beating in her ears. Even the flycatcher had stopped calling. Everything seemed to be waiting. But waiting for what? What was out there?

She pulled the camera case forward on her shoulder and lifted the camera out, hanging the strap around her neck. If she was ready, she might be able get a picture of whatever was out there. She unwound a short leash from around her waist and hooked one end to Chance's collar. The other end she clipped to her belt. The camera bumped against her chest as she moved. Susan steadied it with her hand.

Chance cocked his head and listened. Susan scanned the edge of the trail. Off to her left, the gunshot snap of a branch broke the silence, followed by the sounds of loud cracking and thrashing in the underbrush. Something large was coming their way.

Chance sprang up, growling deep in his throat. Susan signaled with her hand, palm facing the ground, the sign she used to remind him to lie down and stay. He stopped growling but stayed standing, his eyes focused on the thick undergrowth on the left side of trail.

The noise stopped. Silence. Susan held still, listening. The hot, dry air closed in around her. Sweat coated her forehead and the palms of her hands. Chance stood beside her, his muscles quivering, his hackles raised.

A tall stand of pampas grass on the edge of the trail moved as if a soft breeze stirred through it. Susan lifted the camera, checking for light and focus.

Suddenly out of the brush came an explosion of movement and power, a rippling of muscle and fur, a bolt of awkward speed. Susan took in a quick breath and reached out with one hand as though to touch the bear as he ran by. Then he was gone.

Chance sprang forward, jerking hard on the leash, causing Susan to stumble and almost fall. The camera flew out of her hand and flung back at the end of the strap, banging against her chest.

"No! Down!" she yelled at Chance. He lunged again in the direction the bear had gone, snarling and bristling. Susan grabbed onto the leash with both hands. She set her feet firmly on the dry trail and leaned back against Chance's weight. Powdery, gray clay swirled up around them as Chance dug in with his nails, straining against the leash.

"Settle down," Susan said, yanking back hard on the leash. Chance stopped pulling, but he continued to growl, making a low, threatening sound. Susan brought him in close to her on the leash and said, "Chance, that's enough now."

Her hands shook as she replaced the camera in the case and slid it back over her shoulder. She looked around. Was it safe to keep going?

"Let's head back," she said. She kept Chance hooked to the leash until he relaxed into an easy pace beside her.

She relived the encounter with the bear. In the confusion of Chance's yanking on the leash and the speed of the bear, she had caught only a glimpse of him before he disappeared into the brush. But she had felt his strength and smelled the oily scent coming off him. Susan was sure he was a male bear because of his size—he was huge!

Now everything appeared brighter to her, each leaf and branch clearly defined, every small sound loud and close. Her skin tingled with that same thrilled-to-be-scared sort of feeling she had experienced years ago while riding the old wooden rollercoaster on the boardwalk in Santa Cruz: the metal safety bar cold in her hands; her heart beating, beating; Meagan screaming in her ear; hot wind racing by; the rails clanking, shaking, thundering.

Susan's first rollercoaster ride had happened to appease her daughter. "Ride with me, Mom, please," Meagan had begged countless times until Susan gave in.

What had surprised everyone in Susan's family, including her, was that as the day wore on, scaredy-cat Susan became a rollercoaster junkie. She rode the jarring dips and hills so many times that she worried her bones might shake loose. One more time, she kept telling herself that day, and I will conquer my fear of this thing.

Looking back, she didn't remember it as a day of fear. It was a thrilling day. She realized now that the need to overcome fear wasn't what had motivated her to ride the rollercoaster over and over again. It was fear itself that had drawn her in. She felt more alive rocketing down the hills and banging around the curves of the rollercoaster than she had at any other time in her life until now.

Seeing this bear today gave Susan that same rush of fear and excitement. But the bears in the woods weren't like the rollercoaster. The rollercoaster was a machine designed specifically to scare people. She could have ridden it all day long if she had wanted, endlessly being frightened right up to the edge of her tolerance. The bears were different. They weren't here to scare people. They were living creatures, with lives of their own that had nothing to do with her or Chance, or anyone else for that matter.

In Susan's experience, wild bears stayed away from people as much as possible. This was only the second time she had seen a bear in the woods in all the years she had been walking here. The first time was a few weeks after Bill's funeral. That day, she had been lost in grief, not fully aware of anything around her until Chance took off after the bear. The sound of Chance's barking caused her to look up in time to see the bear running away through the trees with Chance hard on its heels. Being that close to a powerful, wild animal brought Susan out of the grief she had been struggling with since Bill died. In that short minute, she became again part of the forest, her forest, where she had always felt she belonged.

Susan had been walking in this section of timber company lands for more than twenty years, once in a while with Bill, but mostly by herself or, in these last few years, with Chance. Nothing unexpected ever happened, just birds and deer scattering when startled, and now these two bear sightings.

Recently, though, she had been having this feeling that there was more here than she could see, something important that she was missing. More than once she had the sensation that if she turned at the right moment, she would see what it was, could reach out and touch it.

That day shortly after Bill died, as she watched Chance and the bear disappear into the brush, the feeling came to her again, only stronger. Could the bear she had seen then be the same one she saw today? Could it be that this bear was always there, unseen, watching her, learning about her? Was it from this bear that she would finally discover the purpose of her life, even learn the meaning of Bill's death?

Susan shook her head. No. There was no meaning to life or death, no purpose. Life happened. People died. Bill had died. This bear didn't hold the answers to any of that. He wasn't anything more than a big, clumsy-looking bear. There was nothing special about him other than he happened to be there when she and Chance were. Possibility both times, but that was a coincidence. Nothing more.

Still, there was this—

"That's enough," Susan said out loud, causing Chance to look up at her. Susan reached down and absentmindedly ran her hand over the top of his head.

What was the matter with her? She didn't believe in any sort of psychic connection, especially not with a wild animal. She had to get control of herself. What she needed was something else to concentrate on, not this crazy notion that a wild bear was the link to understanding life.

She laid her hand on her camera case. Could she photograph a wild bear? That would be worth doing, and she might be able to accomplish it. Even if it turned out that she wasn't successful, the process of figuring out how to photograph a wild bear was a way to fill the emptiness that threatened to overtake her since Bill died.

In truth, Susan had carried around a vague sense that something was missing from her life for as long as she could remember, but that had nothing to do with Bill's death or this bear. That was about how shy she was and how uncomfortable she was taking any sort of risk. She knew this about herself and knew that she couldn't change how she was.

Susan looked at the forest around her. Why couldn't she change? She didn't have to stay the way she had always been, not now. Maybe she could do this one brave thing. Maybe she could capture this bear on film.

She had never been able to photograph any of the animals who lived in the woods. In fact, she hardly ever saw them. When an animal did show itself, it offered only a fleeting impression of sound and movement. There was never time to think, let alone focus the camera and shoot a picture. What would she need to do in order to photograph a wild bear? Should she build a blind close to where the bear spent time? This was about the same place she had seen the bear last time. Could she hide here and wait for him to come again?

She searched her memory for anyone locally who might be able to help her figure out how to do this. A year or so ago there had been an article in the paper about a professor at the college in Crescent who had done extensive research on coastal black bears. Next to the report on his research was a sidebar about two bears at the local zoo. The professor was part of a project involving those bears, but Susan couldn't remember what the project was. He might have taken pictures of wild bears as part of his research. Even if he hadn't, he must know how to get close enough to a wild bear to photograph it. He would be the best person to talk with about her idea.

Susan stopped on the trail. What was she getting ready to do? Just thinking about going to the college and talking to this professor tied her stomach in knots.

She had never attended college. When she was younger, she had toyed with the idea of getting a degree in animal behavior, but one thing or another got in the way. The farm took up all her spare time, and then Meagan was born. Shawn followed four years later. She had spent the last twenty-four years raising children. She had no idea how to talk to a professor, how to ask for his help. He would probably think she was deranged. He might be right.

"Derange," Susan said out loud. To upset the arrangement. Yes, that described her to a tee, an upset arrangement, all loose ends and scattered dreams. Photographing a wild bear wasn't going to fix that. Maybe nothing could ever fix it, but it was something to do. Right now, more than anything else, she needed a way to fill up her time.

He stopped running when he could no longer hear the dog. Head up, he sniffed for traces of the woman and the dog. He had known

them almost all of his life. He had been traveling with his mother the first time he smelled them.

———

It had rained the night before, and the air was heavy and wet. He was in front of his mother, moving down a well-worn trail, slipping in the spongy mud. The scent of a dead deer hung in the moist morning air. His mother's hunger was strong on her, and he knew they were heading for the decaying animal. This was the longest journey he had ever taken. Excitement tingled through him. He scampered ahead and back to his mother several times, rubbing against her damp, warm body.

At the top of a small hill, his mother stopped and sniffed, moving her head from side to side. When he began to run to her, she lifted her front paw, warning him to stay back. Confused, he started for her again. She charged at him, swatting the ground, her mouth partway open, her lower lip flared out. He ran up the trail, searching for a tree, a way to climb to safety. There were no trees close, and tangled blackberry vines blocked both sides of the trail.

Afraid, he ran again to his mother. He longed to nuzzle her fur and to feel her lick his face. She charged him, knocking him off the trail and into the berry vines with a strong swipe of her paw. He lay hidden, crying quietly. She stepped away and moved down the trail. She rocked from her heels to her toes, her muscles tense.

He could smell her fear and anger and an animal scent he didn't recognize. He crept out of the vines, crying louder in his need to be by his mother. She clicked her teeth together and blew out a deep warning. He sank back into the berry vines and waited. The unfamiliar scent grew stronger, more distinct, imprinting forever in his memory. Then it grew weaker until it was gone. His mother was all that he smelled now, the stench of fear still strong on her.

She shook her large head and came to him. She licked him, lifting the fur up along his spine. With his mother taking the lead this time, they started again toward the dead deer. The odor of decay grew stronger as they went. He looked back over his shoulder and cried faintly.

———

Susan found Professor Sharpton's office by asking a young woman who was standing at the entrance to the Wildlife Building. The woman, really not much more than a girl, didn't even glance up from her textbook when Susan spoke to her. She merely pointed down the hall and said, "Room 124."

Susan tried to come up with an interesting comment or a question that might catch this young woman's attention if only for a moment, but she couldn't think of anything. She had been struggling more than usual since Bill's death with her innate shyness. She muttered, "Thank you," and went into the building.

She checked the numbers printed above the office doors until she found the correct one. The door was open and she looked in.

David Sharpton sat behind a large wooden desk, leaning back in a chair with his feet propped up on the edge of the desk. He held a phone's receiver to his ear with one hand and twirled a pen between the fingers of his other hand. Susan stood outside his open doorway until he nodded at her and pointed the pen at an old leather chair across the desk from him, indicating she should sit. The aged leather creaked when she sat down and again when she bent to lay her briefcase on the floor. Susan curled her toes inside her boots and concentrated on holding still so the chair wouldn't keep making that noise.

The office was small and smelled faintly of musty paper. It was crammed full of teaching and research paraphernalia. Books and folders were stacked on every available surface, and charts and graphs covered the walls, many hanging at odd angles from single thumbtacks.

Susan's tongue felt dry and thick. She desperately needed a drink of water. She chewed on her bottom lip and wished she were back home. She didn't belong here. How was she going to explain to this man why she had come?

That morning she had looked closely at her reflection in the bathroom mirror for the first time in months. Her face appeared leaner and more angular than she remembered, her amber-colored eyes larger over prominent cheekbones. Her skin—the tan color of her father's Italian ancestors—was still clear, but now there were new wrinkles at the corners of her eyes and mouth. Her wildly curly, dark-auburn hair had grown down to her shoulders and gray strands showed in places. Her tall, slender body was almost too thin and sinewy. Many years of working around the farm and countless hours of hiking had kept her lean and hardened her muscles. She had lost weight since Bill died, making her muscles and tendons even more noticeable.

When she was younger, Susan had become accustomed to men watching her when she entered a room. She had never thought of herself as beautiful, but nonetheless she had drawn those looks. Now she no longer noticed men's eyes following her as she walked by. They mostly looked past her like she wasn't there. She had to admit this hurt her ego a little, but there was a certain freedom in it. She no longer felt the need to spend much time or energy on her appearance.

She tucked a stray curl behind her ear and looked out into the hallway. There, entombed in a glass case, stood a black bear. How had she missed this when she was waiting out there? The bear wasn't much bigger than the Newfoundland dog her neighbor Jean used to have, but its teeth were enormous, its claws thick and pointed. The bear's mouth was open, its lips curled back in a frozen snarl.

"So, Ms.—" Professor Sharpton said. Susan turned to him. He came from behind his desk, holding his hand out to her.

"Susan. Susan Campton," she said, standing up to take his hand. He was tall, an inch or two taller than her five foot eleven, and had the look of an aging athlete—still fit but with a little too much weight around the middle. Judging from how tan his face and hands were, and from the web of fine lines on his checks and around his eyes, he spent a great deal of time outside in the sun. It was his eyes that held her. They were an unusual shade of gray and had an intensity that was hard to look away from.

"David Sharpton," he said, "but David will do. How can I help you?" He stepped back and leaned against the edge of his desk, facing her, his legs stretched out in front of him.

"I'm hoping you'll be able to answer a few questions concerning local bears." The leather crackled as she sat back down and folded her hands in her lap.

"Having trouble with a bear?"

"No." Susan's voice sounded harsh even to her. She cleared her throat and started again. "No, I'm not having trouble with bears. I want to learn more about them, their habits, what they eat, how they live, if they hibernate in this area."

"What are you going to do with this information?"

"Find them," she said.

"Find them?"

"Yes, and photograph them. Record them doing what it is they do."

"Why?" David asked.

"Why?" Susan repeated softly. On the way here this morning she had practiced what she wanted to say. Now she couldn't remember most of it. It was important for her to be honest about her intentions in wanting to photograph a wild bear. Still, there was no way she was going to tell this man, this professor about how she felt a connection to one bear in particular, the one she had seen the other day.

Start at the beginning, she told herself. Tell him what led up to wanting to photograph a wild black bear. Leave out the rest of it. She took a breath and began, "A couple of years ago I was walking in the woods by my house. My dog and a friend of mine were with me. Chance, my dog, was out ahead, running and playing. He was a year old at the time, a black Lab, and full of energy." After a short pause, she asked, "Do you know much about Labradors?"

David shook his head and said, "No."

"Oh. Well, they're known for being wildly energetic." David nodded.

"Anyway," Susan said. "It was a wet spring morning, right after a rain. I noticed bear prints on the trail. There were two sets of tracks, one large and one smaller, much smaller. I figured we were following behind a mama and her cub."

Susan stopped, giving Professor Sharpton a chance to respond. When he nodded again without speaking, she continued, "We kept seeing the tracks. I noticed one of the larger prints was filling with water. I turned and saw that water was also seeping into my boot prints. We had to be very close to the bears. I wanted to turn around. I was worried about my dog running out front with a mama and her cub that close. My friend Shirley, Shirley Stiles, is not comfortable in the woods to begin with, so she was happy to go back."

"Good decision," David said.

"That's what my husband said. When Bill got home that night, I told him about the footprints and how we'd turned around to avoid running into this bear and her cub. He said we did the right thing because it's hard to predict what a mama bear with a cub would do. The truth is, I don't know what any bear would do. I've seen their tracks and scat many times, and I've heard stories about them getting into people's garbage, but other than that I don't know anything about them. Then Bill died and...." She trailed off, not knowing what more to say.

"And you need a project," he finished for her.

"No," Susan said, louder than she intended.

"No?" David asked, raising his eyebrows.

Susan thought about how to explain what she meant. "Not a project like knitting or gardening, but yes, I guess you're right. It is a project. A project about the life that surrounds us."

"You're a photographer?"

"No, not really," Susan said, smiling. "Years ago I took a few photography classes. I've mostly taken pictures of our farm, the gardens, the trees, the things I see every day. Occasionally I've been lucky. I've been able to capture the feelings in a scene, the textures and movements." She shrugged. "Usually they're just pictures of things. Snapshots."

"What would you do with the photos, assuming you were able to photograph a bear?"

"I don't know for sure. Many people are afraid of bears. A few act like they hate them, threatening all kinds of things if they catch them in their garbage. If people could see bears in their natural environment, maybe they would come to appreciate them more." This was part of what she had practiced on her way here this morning. She knew it sounded a little childish, but she needed to have a reason why she wanted to photograph a wild bear other than that she felt compelled in some inexplicable way. This was all she could come up with.

She was now clasping her hands so tightly in her lap that her fingers were beginning to cramp. She opened her hands and stretched them out on top of her thighs. Without thinking, she said, "I owe it to them."

"Why?" He seemed to fling the question at her.

"Why what?" Susan asked. His abrupt manner was throwing her off. Did he want her to explain again why she wanted to photograph bears?

"Why do you owe something to the bears?"

"Oh." She glanced again at the glass-encased bear in the hallway. How in the world was she going to explain this without sounding totally crazy? She looked back at Professor Sharpton and began, "Right after Bill died, my children came home, but they couldn't stay more than a couple of weeks. Meagan has a job she needed to get back to, and Shawn can't afford to take much time away from his college classes."

Even as she was talking, Susan wondered why she was telling him all of this. He didn't need to know this much about her or her family, but now that she had started, she couldn't seem to stop. "For a while both Meagan and Shawn phoned me every day to see how I was doing. I was able to pull it together and pretend I was doing fine, but I wasn't fine. I was lost in sadness. I did only what I had to do to keep Chance and me alive.

"One day I came out of it long enough to notice that Chance was also grieving. He'd spend most of the day asleep on his pillow. He had lost Bill, and it must have felt to him like he had lost me, too. Bill used to roughhouse with him every night, and I walked him in the woods almost every day." Susan's eyes met Professor Sharpton's and she smiled. "Bill and I used to tease each other that Chance was our empty-nest dog, our other son. That's how he got his name. Bill said he was a new chance for me to be a mom."

"Pets can be good friends, and good company," David said.

"Yes," Susan said, relieved to have found one point of agreement. "I realized that the least I could do was give Chance back our time in the woods. So I took him for a walk on an old logging road close to our house, one of our favorite places, but I couldn't focus on where we were. I followed along behind Chance without noticing much of anything. Then Chance started barking, and I looked up in time to catch a glimpse of a bear running off through the brush with Chance right behind him. I yelled for Chance to come, but he didn't stop. After what felt like an eternity, he finally came back to me, panting and wagging, looking excited and happy."

She slid forward on her chair, gripping her knees, her shyness forgotten in her eagerness to describe her feelings. "I was scared but also excited. I felt alive. I noticed that the sun was shining, that it was a hot summer day and the woods smelled liked berry pies cooking. The sight of a bear, the thrill of being that close to a big, wild animal, brought me out of my grief, at least for a little while. I felt like I could breathe for the first time since Bill died."

She stopped, wondering what to say now. She looked directly at Professor Sharpton and said, "I owe the bear something for that. I owe him gratitude and respect."

"Gratitude and respect," David repeated softly. Then, "You must know that there has already been extensive research done on black bears, including photographs. The most common practice these days is to use food to bait the bears to a specific location where researchers set up a blind from which to observe the bears. In a few studies, the researchers attached radio collars to the bears to track them. One group of wildlife biologists had good success using both techniques, food to bait the bears in so they could study them up close and tracking collars to follow the bears from a distance when they left the baited area."

Susan shook her head. "That isn't what I had in mind. I don't want to interfere with the bears in any way. I want to be able to photograph them doing what they normally do when people aren't around."

"I wasn't suggesting that you use either food or collars by yourself," David said. "You couldn't do this on your own. You would need help from a biologist who has experience with wild bears."

"I'd like to try to do this by myself without anyone else being there," Susan said.

"In that case, you could set up a trip wire on your camera and use a flash in the general location that you've seen bears. This hasn't been all that successful because bears tend to either shy away from areas where there is an odd or unknown smell—apparently cameras smell odd to bears—or they investigate the cameras and in the process destroy them. And one flash of the camera and the bear will run away. But if you're planning to do this on your own, this is your best option."

Again Susan shook her head. "No, I don't want to use a remote camera. I want to be there. I want to do this myself."

"I don't think you appreciate the seriousness of what you're proposing," David said. "Going into the woods alone is never a good idea. Trying to get close enough to a wild bear to photograph it is most certainly ill advised."

"But I wouldn't be alone. I'd have Chance with me."

"Chance, your dog?"

"Yes."

"A dog? You're planning to take a dog into the woods stalking bears? You can't do this with a dog. He'd bark. He'd chase the bear. He might try to attack the bear. You can't do it. That's all there is to it."

Susan stared at him, at his eyes. They seemed to change from light gray to something darker, more threatening. She sat deeper in the chair. How could his students possibly take notes with his eyes changing color as he lectured? It was unnerving.

"I could teach Chance to stay by me, to be quiet," she said. "He's a good dog. He understands what I want of him. Since Bill died, he's been with me most of the time. I couldn't do this without him. I couldn't leave him behind."

"Let me make it perfectly clear to you how dogs and bears react when they unexpectedly come together," David said. "Black bears are not usually aggressive. They stay away from humans, unless they've learned to eat garbage. If they hear you coming or smell you, they will normally move away as quickly as possible. That's why it's always a good idea to make a lot of noise when you're in their territory, so that they know you're close. If you startle them, corner them, or in any way threaten them, there could be a problem."

He waited, checking her reaction. Susan merely nodded. David continued, "Dogs usually help by letting a bear know you're there, either by barking or by smelling like a dog. It can even be helpful if the dog chases the bear, provided he'll come back when called. If the dog keeps chasing him, the bear will eventually realize he's running from an animal much smaller than he is. There's a chance he'll turn around and chase the dog, more than likely right back to its owner. This could be trouble, serious trouble."

"Good," Susan said, leaning toward him. This is what she had come here to learn; she wanted to know all there was to know about black bears.

"Good?" David said, his mouth caught between a smile and a scowl.

"Not good for the owner of the dog, of course," Susan said. "You're right. That could be bad. But that's the kind of thing I came here to find out. I want to know how bears behave, what they eat, where they go in the winter, how they choose a mate." She took a notebook and pen from her briefcase on the floor.

"All right," David said. "I'll talk with you about your project, but first I want you to read this research." He lifted a large manual off a bookshelf so full of textbooks and papers it seemed on the verge of collapsing. "And you have to promise me that you won't go searching for bears until you've read this from cover to cover, and we've talked about the details of what you're trying to do."

Susan closed her notebook and took the manual Professor Sharpton held out to her. She could feel warmth creeping up her face. Had she really believed that he would tell her about his entire life's work during this first meeting? In the next fifteen minutes or so? Susan pictured how foolish she must look, sitting there with her notebook in her lap, getting ready to write down everything he knew about bears.

"And be sure to leash that dog of yours if you go into the woods," he said.

"Right," Susan said, not meeting his eyes. She looked down and got her briefcase from the floor. She shoved the notebook and manual inside and stood to leave.

David followed her to the door. She stepped into the hallway and stopped to look at the encased bear.

"She looks like she's snarling, doesn't she?" David asked, coming to stand beside her. Susan nodded. "That's Hollywood fiction. Black bears never snarl. If this bear were threatened or startled, she would chomp." He clicked his upper and lower teeth together noisily. "And blow out blasts of air through her mouth." He opened his mouth and blew out four or five times, making a deep coughing sound. Susan tried not to smile or, worse, laugh at how downright silly he looked and acted.

"You'll know it if you ever hear it," David said. "Black bears have quite an assortment of vocalizations. Depending on the situation, they might grunt, moan, or purr, but they don't growl or snarl. Nothing that dramatic."

"They purr? Like a cat?" Susan asked.

"Yes, a bit like a cat but deeper, more rumbling. They do it when they feel particularly comfortable and safe, or while nursing or eating a tasty treat."

Susan had many more questions about black bears, but her cheeks still felt hot with the embarrassment of thinking she could learn everything he knew about these bears in less than an hour. Plus she had already taken up too much of his time. She held out her hand to him and said, "Thank you for your time, Professor Sharpton."

He took her hand in his, gave it a quick shake, and said, "Call me David. I save the professor part for students who need a reminder that I know what I'm talking about."

Susan smiled and nodded, thanked him again for his time, and walked away. She tried to picture herself calling him David, but it was close to impossible for her to imagine calling a professor by his first name.

That night Susan sat propped up in bed with Professor Sharpton's manual on her lap. "David's manual," she said, trying it out. No, she decided. She couldn't call a professor by his first name, not until she got to know him better anyway.

Chance was snoring on his pillow on the floor beside the bed. Susan began to read: Black bears are one of the most intelligent animals. They are able to grasp simple concepts, have excellent long-term memories, and....

Before she reached the end of the sentence, her eyes closed and her breathing slowed. With the manual across her chest, Susan dreamed of a black bear, one much larger than any she had ever seen. In the dream, she and Chance were walking through thick brush. Without making a sound, she pushed hanging redwood branches and berry vines out of the way. Chance walked low to the ground close beside her, searching for a scent. It grew darker and the undergrowth thinned as they moved deeper into the forest: tall second-growth Douglas fir and redwood trees kept most of the sunlight from reaching the forest floor. Large ferns growing out of old fallen logs stroked her arms as she moved past them. With a sense of increasing urgency, she reached up and brushed a large branch back from her face. There, in a clearing right in front of her, stood a massive black bear. He was facing away from her, absorbed in rolling over a rotting log with one immense paw. Susan gave the signal for Chance to stay quiet. She silently slid the strap attached to the camera case off her shoulder. The bear faced her. Their eyes met and held.

Susan jerked awake, cold with sweat and gasping for breath. Chance whimpered and touched her arm with his nose.

"It's all right," she whispered to him. "Go back to sleep. It was a dream. That's all." But she couldn't sleep. Behind her closed eyelids, she saw the bear's eyes staring directly into hers.

In the morning, Susan returned to the woods. Ignoring Professor Sharpton's warning about keeping Chance on a leash, she let him run free. She had always let Chance run here, and there had always been bears.

Susan rolled her shoulders and shook out her arms, trying to relax. She kept seeing the bear from her dream last night—his head slowly turning until his eyes met hers, his mouth open, the tips of his huge teeth showing. It was a dream, she told herself. Nothing but a dream. Still, she couldn't shake the feeling that something was out here watching her and Chance.

Chance romped ahead of her, slowing now and again to sniff the trail. His nose practically touched the dirt as he breathed in a swirl of invisible smells. Even though he had never seen many of them, Chance knew every animal who had been on this trail by the scent they left behind. Susan envied this ability. Occasionally, she had the urge to get down on her hands and knees and sniff right alongside him. She never told anyone this, but once she had gotten down an inch from the ground and taken in a deep breath through her nose. She hadn't smelled anything different from what she had expected to smell. It had all smelled like dirt to her.

The trail narrowed through a section of thick brush. Chance stopped. He widened out his chest and lifted his nose, his nostrils flared. Susan squinted in the bright sunlight and peered into the dense foliage on the side of the trail. There, camouflaged in the undergrowth, was a large doe. The doe stood stock-still, her head up, her ears forward, her dark eyes fixed on Chance.

Susan made a grab for Chance's collar as he leaped with all four feet off the ground into the brush. With one loud stomp, the doe fled. Chance was right on her tail.

"No!" Susan shouted. "Chance, come!" His excited barking faded in the distance.

"Chance, come," she yelled again. Now it was silent, no barking, no twigs breaking, nothing. Again she called his name and then listened. At last, she could hear him in the distance. His loud panting grew closer until he broke through the brush next to her. His mouth was open in a wide, impish grin, his tongue hanging out one side. He wagged his tail ecstatically and bounded up to her. Susan took his head in her hands and looked into his eyes. "You are going to have to stop doing that," she said, "if I'm ever going to be able to find a bear and photograph him." As a small prayer to any god who might be listening, she added, "Please don't make this impossible."

Early the next day, Susan and Chance made their first trip to the small zoo in Crescent, twenty minutes from her home. A thick layer of fog hung over everything, obscuring the highway, the trees, even the animal cages at the zoo. Susan introduced herself to Julie Wells, a short, gray-haired woman dressed in a navy-blue wool skirt and matching sweater. A nametag pinned to her sweater identified her as the zoo's curator.

Susan explained that she was working on a photo project of local bears. Since her dog would be going with her into the woods, it was important for him to learn to be calm around bears. She thought that spending time close to these bears at the zoo would help with that. She promised she would keep Chance on a leash and stay back from the bear enclosure. Julie hesitated. She looked from Susan to Chance, frowning.

"I'm working with Professor David Sharpton," Susan blurted out. She felt an instant stab of anger at herself, mixed with a bit of guilt for resorting to using Professor Sharpton's name. She had no right to use his name as leverage to get Chance into the zoo. She also didn't want to rely on his reputation to help her with this project. She was willing to ask for his advice and knowledge about black bears, but ultimately she wanted to do this on her own.

"You're working with David?" Julie asked. Susan nodded. "Then of course you may observe our bears as often as you would like. You probably know this already, but without David's input on the design of the bear enclosure and his help raising the money to build it, we wouldn't be able to take care of these bears. At least not like we can now with this new habitat."

"And my dog?" Susan asked.

"The dog," Julie said, staring at Chance. He sat looking up at her, his tail thumping on the sidewalk. "I guess we could give it a try, as long as you keep him quiet and out of the way of other visitors. If there is any trouble or someone complains, you'll have to leave."

"He'll do fine," Susan said. "He's a good dog. Chance, say hello to Julie." Chance lifted his right front paw and waved it in the air. Bill had taught him to do this, saying every dog should have a trick or two up his sleeve.

"Oh," Julie said with a smile. "Well, hello to you too, Chance." To Susan she said, "I'm not that fond of dogs, but this one seems polite. He's a Labrador retriever, isn't he? Is he big for his breed?"

"Yes, he's a black Lab. He's about average size for a Labrador, close to seventy-five pounds." Mostly to get Julie's mind off Chance, Susan asked, "How long have these bears lived here in the zoo?"

"They were brought here as cubs. A hunter didn't see the cubs until he had already shot their mother. They're from the same litter, brother and sister, although they might have different fathers. Female bears often mate with more than one male during a breeding season. Let's see now. Yes, it was five years ago that they came to live with us here at the zoo.

"The original plan was to return them to the forest once they were older, but it didn't take more than a few months for us to realize that wasn't going to work. They quickly got used to humans taking care of them and weren't equipped to survive on their own. They didn't even have the skills needed to find food by themselves. Once we realized they were going to stay here with us, we had both of them neutered so there wouldn't be a chance of them mating with each other and having cubs."

"I see," was all Susan could think to say. She kept her eyes trained on Julie's back while she followed her through the narrow, winding paths to the bear enclosure. Susan didn't like zoos, never had. She couldn't get past the sadness that came with seeing animals living on display in cages. She had brought Meagan and Shawn here only once, years ago. Afterward she had felt like crying or going back and staging a jailbreak. If there had to be zoos, though, this was a good one. It was small and clean, and all the animals were well cared for.

Chance cowered and growled softly as they neared the bear enclosure. "No," Susan said with a firm tug on the leash.

Julie looked at Chance and then at Susan. "Are you sure this is going to be all right?"

"We'll stay back here for today," Susan said, taking Chance with her to the far side of the sidewalk, opposite the bears.

Both bears were sleeping on a cement rock at the edge of a pond in the center of an open area. They weren't large bears, not when compared to the one she saw in the woods the other day or the black bear in her dreams, and these two had shaggy, brown fur. One was slightly larger than the other. The larger bear, the male, was lying on his side. The female was partway on her back, her jowls falling away from long, yellow teeth.

Chance growled and the hair all along his back bristled. Susan gave a sharp tug on his leash and said, "Down, Chance." He lay down on his chest, his head up, his eyes on the bears.

Julie frowned at Chance. "I'm not sure having your dog here is a good idea."

"We'll be fine," Susan said more sharply than she had intended.

Julie looked hard at Susan. "Okay, if you're sure you can handle this, I need to get back to work. Just don't get any closer to the enclosure, and if your dog starts to growl again, you'll have to leave." With that, she turned and walked away. When she reached the first bend in the path, she looked back at Susan over her shoulder.

Susan smiled and waved in a way that she hoped made her look confident and in control, although she didn't come close to feeling either confident or in control. She felt stupid and unprepared and completely out of her element.

She seemed to have fallen into the habit of either doing nothing or jumping in before thinking it through. She had no idea how Chance was going to handle being this close to these bears. She hadn't considered the fact that he might be frightened, or worse, become protective of her or aggressive toward the bears. Until now, he had never shown any signs of being either protective or aggressive. That is if you didn't count those two times he had seen a bear in the woods. And there was that deer yesterday, but that wasn't aggression. That was part of Chance's natural instinct to chase prey animals. All dogs would chase a deer, given a chance. Wouldn't they?

Susan slumped down on the sidewalk next to Chance. She ran her hand along his back. When he settled down and rested his head on his front paws, she breathed a sigh of relief. Maybe this was going to work out after all.

No one walked by. They appeared to be the only ones at the zoo on this foggy morning. The bears hadn't moved from where they were sleeping. Susan's mind drifted. She wondered what Bill would have thought about her plan to photograph a wild bear. He had never worried about her spending time in the woods, but this was different. She wasn't going for her usual walk in the woods. She was planning to stalk a wild bear, to get close enough to photograph him. Bill might have pretended that he wasn't worried about her doing this, and he certainly wouldn't have told her not to do it. He would probably have said he knew that she could take care of herself. Nonetheless, he would have been worried. He might have asked if he could come with her. Or maybe he would have hatched a crazy plan to follow her without her knowing he was there. Susan almost laughed out loud at what a ridiculous idea this was. Bill would never have done that. If he worried for her safety and wanted someone else to go with her, he would have told her so. He wouldn't have snuck around behind her. Still, she smiled at the thought of Bill following her, tiptoeing along and ducking down next to trees and bushes so that she wouldn't know he was there.

Then the fantasy of Bill trailing her in the woods vanished, and he was gone. She saw herself alone with only Chance for company, and not just in the woods. Everywhere she went from now on, she would be alone with no one knowing or caring where she was or what she was doing. She tried to swallow but couldn't: her throat was tight and her mouth had grown dry.

Now that Bill was dead, would anyone ever feel protective of her again? Would anyone ever love her like that again? Oh God, why did Bill have to die and leave her alone? She wrapped her arms around her waist and swayed slightly.

Don't do this, she told herself. Pay attention to where you are now. Now she was here, sitting on this cold, hard cement watching two sleeping bears. Her knees and lower back ached. She was getting too old for this. She stood up and stretched her arms over her head. As she moved, the male bear woke up. He rolled to a stand and shook, then opened his mouth in a toothy yawn.

Chance raised his head, stiffened, and sprang to his feet. He lunged toward the bears, dragging Susan with him, barking ferociously, saliva flying from his mouth.

"No, Chance! Stop!" Susan yelled. She set her weight and pulled back hard on the leash with both hands.

Chance snarled and pounced closer to the enclosure, his chest wide, his front legs stiff, his tail high. The female bear opened her eyes and looked around as if trying to determine where all this noise was coming from.

Both bears appeared bewildered by this unseemly ruckus. They looked at each other and then at Chance. The male rocked forward, shifting his weight from his hind legs to his front legs. He clacked his teeth together repeatedly and then blew out a series of what sounded like throaty coughs. The image of Professor Sharpton imitating this behavior flashed through Susan's mind.

Chance pulled harder on the leash, dragging Susan closer to the first of two fences that separated the bear enclosure from the sidewalk. Susan again yelled at him to stop.

The male bear rose up on his hind legs and lowered his head, staring right at Chance. Chance snarled and lunged at the fence, getting closer with each strong pull. The bear dropped on all four legs and charged, covering the distance from the rock to the inside fence in three bounds. He swatted at the ground and blew aggressively.

Susan shoved her hand under Chance's collar and pulled him away from the fence. She hauled him around the corner and out of sight of the bears. Chance kept his head turned back in the direction of the bears, growling, until they were almost to the gate leading to the parking lot.

Inside the exit gate, Susan slumped down onto a bench next to the prairie dog pen. She took in a deep, shaky breath. She could still smell the wild scent of the bear as he charged the fence, could still see his brown fur rolling over fat and muscle. She could also smell fear and adrenaline, and something else, something deeply animal, coming off Chance.

"That's it for today," she said. With a firm grip on the leash, she led Chance out to the parking lot and loaded him into her van. Her hands trembled as she held the steering wheel. "It's okay," she said. "We're okay now. Let's go home." She repeated, "It's okay. We're okay now."

That night the bear came to her dreams. He was much larger than the ones in the zoo. His coat was black, shining in the diffused light coming through the trees. The dream was silent except for the sound of her breathing, which grew faster as she moved the last branch away from her face. The bear was rolling a log back and forth with one paw. Slowly he turned his head toward her. Susan could see the patterns of light moving and shifting on his large neck. He held his paw in the air above the log, his thick claws hanging down, his eyes again meeting hers.

Susan woke up, gasping. The full moon bathed the room in a soft light. She kicked the blankets aside. Heat radiated off her skin. Sweat covered her legs and stomach and glistened in the curve between her hipbones. Her menstrual flow used to coincide with the full moon, but she had gone months now without a period. How long had it been—four or five months? This was more than a bout of intense dreams: she was starting menopause. So now I'm officially middle-aged, she thought. Or was this the beginning of old age? She didn't feel old. She felt hot and sweaty and unsettled by the dream.

Out of a habit formed from years of having sleeping children in the house, Susan slipped soundlessly out of bed. She put on her robe and went to the kitchen. She held a glass of cold water against her face and stared out the window above the sink. The pasture shone white in the bright moonlight, cut through here and there with deep shadows cast by the wild rhododendrons and redwood trees standing along its edge. The darkness between the trees appeared to move as she watched. Susan leaned over the sink and strained to see into the shadows.

"Are you out there?" she whispered. The only reply was the gentle sway of branches as a soft wind moved through the trees. She set the glass on the counter and went back to bed. A short while later she fell into a restless but dreamless sleep.

He moved cautiously, keeping to the shadows at the edge of the grass. He didn't like being out at night, but this part of the forest was safer after sunset. The smell of humans was everywhere here. Best to stay clear of them. This lesson came from his mother, and it stayed with him.

One of the places that smelled strongest of people was visible through a break in the trees. He rocked forward, sensing movement. He rose up on his hind legs and sniffed. Nothing was close, nothing to fear. He dropped onto all fours and headed deeper into the forest.

In the low fog of early morning, Susan crawled between the long rows of peas, beans, and corn, pulling weeds with her hands. She never used a hoe. Bill used to tease her about this. "Hoes are for lazy gardeners," she had told him. "You can't get the weeds' roots out with a hoe."

Susan had tried to teach her children this technique, with varying degrees of success. When they were very young, long before they could tell a weed from a carrot top, Meagan and Shawn had loved helping her in the garden. More times than not, all three of them would abandon any pretense at weeding and spend the rest of the day building dirt castles and digging long tunnels around the vegetable rows. These were some of Susan's most treasured memories: slippery, fragrant mud all the way up to her elbows and covering each child from head to toe; her children's giggles and squeals of joy; their damp, tired bodies snuggled close to hers after a warm hosing off—the hose having been uncoiled and left in the sun earlier in the day to heat the water.

By the time Meagan and Shawn were old enough to offer real help with the weeding, they were no longer interested. Other than on rare occasions when they inexplicably felt the urge to kneel in the dirt and tug out a few weeds, Susan worked in the garden alone.

It was the middle of September, the end of this year's growing season. The peas had stopped making new pods months ago. The last ones hung on the vines, wrinkled and tough, and the corn was almost ready to harvest. She didn't need such a large garden now. Even when Bill was alive, they had grown more than they could eat. Bill had tilled the garden soil each spring anyway, saying they could give what they didn't use to the neighbors.

When John had come by on his tractor in May this year and offered to turn the soil in the garden over for her, Susan had set aside her impulse to refuse and told him to go ahead and plow it. She knew John felt the loss of Bill as much as she did. Bill and John had been more than business partners. They had been best friends since they were in high school together. Susan had tried over the years to like John, or at least

33

tolerate him, but something about him made it impossible. She could never quite figure out what it was.

The memory of that day in May when John had finished tilling the garden played over in Susan's mind. Again she saw John standing on her front porch, his tractor idling in the driveway behind him. He held his dirty, Pacific Lumber Yard cap in his hands, turning it over and over until Susan felt dizzy from watching it. His face was lined and streaked with dirt, his rusty-brown hair flat and dark with sweat. Susan pictured herself reaching up and gently touching his cheek, teasing him a little, saying how silly he looked, inviting him in for a cold glass of iced tea. What stopped her was the memory of John telling her how he had knelt next to Bill after the accident on the day Bill died. Even though she knew there was nothing John could have done to save Bill's life, in some dark corner of her mind she blamed him for Bill's death. She couldn't stop thinking that if Bill had never met John, never gone into the construction business with him, he would still be alive.

With John there in front of her, Susan closed her eyes and saw Bill: his hair damp with sweat, his face streaked with dirt, and that lop-sided grin of his. That was how it was supposed to be. Not this. Not John with his hat in his hands.

She opened her eyes to John saying, "You know, Susan, this shouldn't have happened to Bill. If I had been there, maybe I could have prevented it." Susan didn't reply. There was nothing to say to this. John shoved his hat on his head, gave her a curt nod, and turned away. He climbed up on the tractor and drove out of the driveway. Susan stood in the open doorway until she could no longer hear the tractor's engine.

Now, alone in her garden, Susan pictured the day Bill had died. It had been unusually warm for April. She had washed the sheets that morning and hung them outside to dry in the sun, something she rarely did in the moist coastal weather. This was supposed to be a special treat for Bill because he so enjoyed the smell and feel of laundry that had dried outside. For Susan, the smell of sun-dried sheets would forever bring back the memory of that day.

———◆———

The warm dampness of the sheets, the snap of the clothespins, a puff of wind, the slight scent of laundry detergent drifting around her.

She was coming in the back door, wiping her damp hands on her jeans, when she saw John's pickup pulling into the driveway. She didn't want to have to deal with him now on this otherwise beautiful day. Bill must have forgotten one of his tools. She forced a smile out of her tight lips and went out on the front porch to greet John. Then she saw his face, white and wrinkled up in a sick parody of his normal crabby expression. She knew immediately that Bill was dead. It was as if she had been waiting for this moment most of her life.

As far back as Susan could remember, she had feared she would lose someone she loved. She never understood where this feeling came from. It was simply there as a type of background noise to her life. To quiet this, she planned every event carefully and didn't take any unreasonable risk with herself or her family. But no matter how hard she tried, she could never get completely away from the knowledge that life was fragile and could be gone in an instant. First she lost both her parents to cancer within five years of each other. And now she had lost Bill.

There on her porch, even before John spoke, she almost said, Yes, I know. She said something, or maybe she cried out. She couldn't hear anything other than a shrill ringing in her ears, couldn't think of anything except that Bill was gone forever. She went into the house, to the kitchen window, and stared out at the white sheets floating in the breeze.

John followed her and stood behind her, talking to her back, saying Bill must have fallen from the scaffolding. John told how he had called for an ambulance and started CPR, but it had been too late. Bill was already dead. John's voice broke, and he put his hand on her shoulder. Susan shrugged him off and leaned away from him until she felt the counter's edge pressing hard against her stomach. The image of Bill lying at the bottom of the scaffolding, his neck twisted at an impossible angle, came to her as clearly as though Bill were dead on the grass right outside the window. The thought of John bending over him, trying to breathe life into his dead body, made her sick. She gripped the edge of the counter and swallowed hard to keep from vomiting into the sink.

John backed away from her, saying he needed to call Shirley. He sank down onto the chair by the phone table. He held his hand over his face, his shoulders shaking with silent tears. Susan watched him from across the room. Crying didn't suit him. He always had too much self-control for such a childish show of emotions. Only intense grief could make a man like John cry.

Susan started toward him, but stopped. She couldn't bring herself to touch him, let alone offer him any form of comfort.

John rubbed at the tears on his face with the palm of his hand. He put the phone's receiver to his ear and dialed his home number. When Shirley answered, he spoke quietly, asking her to hurry, saying Susan needed her.

Later that night, with Shirley sitting beside her on the couch, Susan wanted to know every detail of Bill's death. She needed to be able to visualize the last few minutes of his life.

"Did you see him?" she asked Shirley. "How did he look? Did John say?" Shirley was Susan's best friend, had been ever since John and Shirley had married fifteen years ago. Susan could trust Shirley to tell her the truth about Bill's death.

"No, honey, I didn't see him. John came to you first after the ambulance left. He called me from here, remember?" Shirley took Susan's hands in hers and ran her finger over the wedding ring on Susan's left hand.

"Did John say what happened? I really need to know."

"Of course you do, but John hasn't said much. He told me that when he got to the job site Bill had already fallen from the scaffolding."

"There must be more to it than that. There must be a reason he fell. He worked on tall scaffolding all the time. He was comfortable working up high. It doesn't make any sense."

Shirley's face was white, her brown eyes darker than usual. Earlier she had been unconsciously combing her fingers through her hair, fluffing her perfect bob into messy strands of light-brown curls. Now she held Susan's hands firmly in hers. "John said the same thing. He couldn't figure out how this could have happened to Bill. There's no way to know what happened. We'll never know."

———

Susan never talked to John about Bill's death, never asked him the questions she had asked Shirley. Every day since Bill died, she thought about what must have happened up on that scaffolding; many days it was all she thought about. She wanted to ask John about that day, but it was almost impossible for her to talk to him. She and John never talked about much of anything. They were polite to each other, mostly because of their shared love for Shirley, but that was it. Their relationship never got any further or deeper than that.

Why had it always been so hard for her and John to get along? Susan thought about this now as she weeded between the garden rows. John wasn't particularly pleasant to be around—he was a natural-born grump—but he was never unkind. Even so, Susan often felt he was judging her, making note of all her imperfections, and he was always so sure he was right. He never seemed to question any of his decisions or opinions. She found this particularly annoying. Maybe she was jealous, wished she had his confidence.

Relationships could be so confusing and complicated. Her fingers pried into the soil, loosening the roots and pulling the weeds free. Weeding was simple and easy. It required nothing beyond physical effort. She enjoyed it for that reason.

Finished with the last row, Susan stood up and gazed out at the big pasture surrounding the old goat barn. This is where she and Bill had kept their goats during the five years they had tried to realize the dream of running a small farm. The goats had given them milk and cheese but not meat. They had planned to butcher a few of the bucks, but Susan couldn't do it. She had knelt, holding the young buck in her arms and crying while Bill stood by with his rifle over his shoulder. In the end, he shook his head and walked away.

Selling goat's milk and cheese paid for the goats' feed and vet bills but not much more than that. Susan's memories of that time were collages of joy, loss, and backbreaking work. She had loved the sweet smell of the nannies when she milked them at sunrise and sunset. She would lead each goat in turn to the milking stanchion. Most jumped up willingly. A few pulled their heads back and rolled their eyes before settling in. Once securely clipped in place, they would chew alfalfa pellets and grunt with satisfaction. Their teats were warm and full in her hands. The first of the milk squirted and pinged on the bottom of the stainless steel pan, steam rising off it.

She could still feel the crisp bite of the early morning or evening air and the weight of Meagan in the baby backpack. Meagan would lean over and lay her small head on the goat's neck and grunt, their voices joining together in a chorus of contentment. Then there were all those long, demanding hours of cleaning out the goat barn, the endless washing and sterilizing of milking and cheese-making equipment, and the frustration and heartache of dealing with sick or dying goats.

Things began to change when Bill and John decided to start a construction business together. Most nights Bill would get home from work long after dinner had grown cold. Practically the minute he was in the door, Susan would start an argument with him about how he was never there to help with Meagan or any of the work around the farm. She tried not to, but she couldn't stop herself. They fought almost every night. She felt both overworked and abandoned. Taking care of Meagan and all the farm work was too much for her to do alone.

Bill had promised her the late evenings wouldn't last long. Once the business got going, he would work more regular hours and help more on the farm and at home. One terrible night, in a fit of rage, she had yelled at him to get out, to go live with John since he was spending most of his time with him anyway.

———

The hot edge of anger; the sound of her voice, shrill and coarse; tension, frustration, and disappointment circling like a dark cloud in the room.

Bill sat on the edge of the bed, his shoulders hunched, his hands laced tightly in his lap. "What is it you want?" he asked. "I'm trying to make a good living for us, for you and Meagan. What more do you want from me?"

"I want you," she said, her voice full of resentment. "I want our farm. I want my life the way it used to be."

"I don't want the farm anymore," Bill said softly.

"What?" Susan yelled. Then struggling to regain control of her emotions, she asked, "What did you say? I couldn't hear you."

Bill sat up straighter and spoke clearly and without anger, "I don't want to farm. I like construction. Building houses is what I want to do. You need to let go of the idea of having a small farm. Either that or find someone else to help you around here. We can afford to hire some- one, if you want. I won't live out this dream of a farm any longer, and it's clear that you can't do it alone." He reached his hand out to her, palm up, and then let it fall back to his lap.

It was this gesture that stayed with Susan and finally convinced her to sell the goats. It spoke of Bill's sadness and frustration over having to argue with her about being able do the kind of work he wanted to do. The farm had been her idea from the beginning. He had gone along with it to appease her. Susan had seen it as a way to earn a living and still be home to raise their children. Now it wasn't working. In truth, they had never made enough from the proceeds of the farm to pay all of the bills, let alone handle an emergency.

Less than two months later, in November, they sold the goats. Susan's favorite—a sweet-natured, French-alpine nanny named Flora—was the last to go. Susan watched, holding baby Meagan in her arms and fighting back tears, while Flora's new owner loaded her into an old flatbed truck and drove away.

By March the farm was all but gone, only the vegetable garden remained. Bill and Susan agreed that she would stay home with Meagan. Neither of them wanted strangers raising their children, and Bill was now making enough working in construction to support the family.

Without the goats to tend to, Susan felt lost and useless. To keep from going stir crazy, she began taking photography classes through the adult education program at the local high school. Soon she was bringing her camera with her pretty much everywhere, especially when she went into the woods.

———

Now Susan saw how overgrown with weeds the pasture had gotten. What grass remained was tall and gone to seed. If she didn't cut it down before winter set in, she would never be able to push the mower through it.

"Where are the goats when you need them?" she asked the empty field. She wasn't sure why she bothered trying to keep this place up. She could sell it and move to town where life would be easier. But this had been her and Bill's home, where they had raised their children. She wasn't ready to give it up.

Susan lugged the mower out from under the overhang attached to the storage shed. The mower was a grimy mess. She must have mowed at some point during the summer, otherwise the grass and weeds would be up to her knees by now, but she couldn't remember doing it. Much of what happened in the months after Bill's death was lost to her.

A matted layer of dried grass and oil from a leak it must have had all summer clogged the mower. Susan used a stick to scrape off as much of the oily grass around the blades of the mower as she could. She then pulled on the starter rope until her shoulder hurt and her shirt was sticky with sweat, and the mower still hadn't started. She kicked at a tire and shouted, "You stupid thing!" Cursing under her breath, she walked away, massaging her shoulder.

She slumped down in the long grass, her legs crossed under her. Unshed tears stung the backs of her eyes. "I don't want to do this alone!" she yelled. "Damn you, Bill! Why did you leave me alone? Why did you leave me so soon? I'm not ready to be alone."

Chance moseyed over tentatively. He dropped his ball in her lap and touched her hand with his nose. Susan wiped her eyes with the sleeve of her shirt. "You think it's time to play, huh? All right, let's do it. Then I'm going to get this damn mower started one way or another."

Susan threw the ball for Chance for a while and then went back to trying to start the mower. It took nearly twenty pulls and a lot of frustration, but the old mower did finally kick into life. Susan mowed until it was almost dark. Chance danced along beside the mower, his ball in his mouth, asking Susan to play. Eventually he gave up and fell asleep in the shade next to the shed.

Done mowing, Susan hosed off the mower and rolled it back under the overhang. In the fading light, fog swirled through the tops of the tallest redwoods at the edge of the pasture. The air had the grassy smell of freshly mown hay. Somewhere over by the garden, maybe near the old watering trough, a single frog croaked. Hunting out of season, Susan thought. This was the wrong time of year to find a mate. Chance woke up, yawned, and stretched. "Time for dinner," Susan said, and she and Chance headed for the house.

After dinner, Susan stretched out on the couch with Professor Sharpton's manual open on her lap. She read: Usually shy and afraid of humans, the black bear (Ursus americanus) can at times show signs of aggression when hungry, feeding, approached or woken unexpectedly, injured, or with cubs. The next ten pages dealt with the black bear's food preferences and territory choices. The text stressed that, given a choice, wild bears prefer large stands of berries, nuts, and grasses to human garbage.

Susan laid the manual down and got up to add another piece of firewood to the woodstove. She gazed around her living room, taking in the muted gleam of the oak floors; the brightly colored satin pillows on the couch (those frivolous pillows she had spent weeks making); and the long, mahogany dinner table. Bill had worked on the table for over a month when she was pregnant with Meagan, sanding it until it was as smooth as glass.

Despite the furniture and the pillows, the room was too empty and quiet. Was this going to be her life now—cleaning, gardening, and eating alone? She imagined herself growing old here, rattling around alone in this house, becoming increasingly fragile and bad-tempered. She would become one of those eccentric people neighbors steer their children away from, saying things like, "Don't you be going around her house. It's not safe. She's gotten a bit odd in her old age."

"Odd," Susan said, smiling. Maybe someday but not yet, not odd like that anyway. "We'll have to find a way to make this thing with the bears work out," she said, stroking Chance's head and neck. "There's something I need to know about the bears in the woods, and I want you there with me when I find out what it is."

Susan revisited the zoo the next day and every day after that for three weeks. For the first four days, she stayed away from the bears. Instead she walked Chance by all the other animals: the monkeys with their loud screams; the inquisitive pygmy goats; the prairie dogs, chattering and popping in and out of their holes; the varied, multi-colored species of birds. Chance showed little interest in any of the animals. He sniffed the sidewalk, hunting for spilled popcorn and wagged his tail at anyone who walked by. On the fifth day, Susan took him past the bear enclosure, walking by without stopping. Chance growled low in his throat and slunk back. "No," Susan said, giving a sharp tug on the leash.

For several days, Susan walked by the bears until Chance no longer growled. "You ready to try again?" she asked him near the end of the second week. She gave Chance the hand signal to lie down by the bear enclosure. He lay facing the bears, sniffing the air, his chest barely touching the ground. Again the bears were napping on the rock. Susan stood firm and steady, keeping a strong grip on the leash. After a couple of minutes she said, "Chance, stand," and together they walked away.

Each day Susan and Chance stayed a little longer watching the bears sleep. Within a week, Chance relaxed and lay on his side, breathing evenly while he gazed at the bears. "Good dog," Susan told him. "You're a good dog."

A couple of days later, Julie Wells joined them. She sat down on the edge of a planter next to them. She crossed her legs at the ankles and tucked them back, her skirt draping over her knees. "I brought coffee," she said, offering Susan one of the two Styrofoam cups she carried. "But if you prefer tea, I have some back in my office. It's such a cold morning, I thought maybe you could use a hot drink."

"Coffee's perfect. Thank you," Susan said, taking the cup. "You're right, it is chilly this morning."

"I guess if we wanted it dry and sunny all the time we wouldn't live on the north coast," Julie said. "Oh, I almost forgot." She reached into the pocket of her sweater and took out a large dog biscuit. "This is for Chance," she said and held the biscuit out to him. He snatched it and ate it down in two bites. Julie laughed. "Apparently he liked it."

Susan laughed right along with her. Here was a surprise: this little woman, who appeared so formal in her dress and demeanor, was carrying dog presents in the pocket of her sweater. What would she pull out next? Tug toys? Balls? Rawhide chews? Julie, the traveling dog magician.

"Chance seems to be doing fine close to the bears," Julie said.

Susan lifted her head. She had been staring at Julie's pocket, the one with the secreted treats. "We had a tough beginning, but now things are better. We're both getting more comfortable around the bears."

"What is the goal of your project?" Julie asked. "You never said."

"To be honest, I'm not entirely sure. After this, the first step will be to see if I can photograph a wild bear in the woods. If I'm able to do that, I'd like to use the pictures to help people better understand bears. Most people don't know that much about them, only that they get into their garbage and damage their fruit trees. Until recently, I didn't know more than that either, other than coming across their footprints and scat in the woods."

Julie gazed at the sleeping bears. "I've always hoped that seeing these bears would help people learn to appreciate them, but not many people come to the zoo. In the last several years it's been mostly children on school field trips, and they don't stay long enough to learn how these bears behave. Teachers these days are always on such tight time schedules, rushing from one place to the next."

Susan nodded. In her experience, this wasn't anything new. The field trips she had taken as a chaperon with her children's school classes had always felt like some sort of endurance contest. They spent the day hustling the kids from one exhibit to the other with little time given for questions or anything other than a quick stop at the drinking fountain or a bathroom break.

"You're working with David on this project?" Julie asked.

"Not exactly," Susan said, deciding it was time to be honest about this. "I've consulted with him, but I'll be taking the photos by myself."

Julie nodded as if she had already guessed this. "And Chance? Is he going to help in some way?"

"No, I don't think he'll be any help at all." Susan scratched the top of Chance's head and chuckled. "He'll be a hindrance, if anything, but

I want to take him with me. He loves being in the woods. I don't want to leave him behind."

Julie looked at Chance, her brow furled. She raised her eyes to Susan's and asked, "You've talked to David about taking Chance with you on this project?"

"Yes, he knows," was all Susan said.

"Excuse me if I'm prying, but David agreed to this plan?"

"No, but…." Susan was getting ready to say that this wasn't Professor Sharpton's project, it was hers. She stopped herself before the words were out. The last thing she wanted was to be rude to this woman who had been so welcoming to her and Chance.

Julie studied Susan's face. "I'm sorry. I was prying. What you and David talked about is none of my business."

"It's okay," Susan said. "You weren't prying. Professor Sharpton made it clear that he's against me taking Chance along, but I'm still going to take him and hope that it all works out."

"I see," Julie said, sounding like she was a long way from understanding why Susan would take her dog with her to photograph wild bears. She took the last sip of her coffee and stood up. "Will you let me know how this goes for you? I feel like I'm a little part of this project now, and I'm going to worry about you and Chance until I hear from you."

"Yes, of course I'll let you know, but please don't worry about us. Chance and I are used to being in the woods."

Julie nodded. "Well, that's good, at least. Now I'd better get going. I'm supposed to be working on a fundraiser for the next Chamber of Commerce meeting." Julie smiled at Susan and started to walk away.

"Thank you for the coffee and the treat for Chance," Susan called to Julie's back.

Julie turned and smiled again, a big open smile that made the lines around her mouth deeper. "You're welcome."

As Julie rounded the corner and was out of sight, the male bear rolled over and stood up. He licked his nose with his long tongue. Chance raised his head, alert. He looked from Susan to the bear and back at Susan. "Stay down, Chance. Good dog. Stay," Susan said. She knelt beside him, took hold of his collar, and gently petted his head.

The bear shook himself awake and turned toward them. He held motionless, his eyes locked on Chance. After a long minute, he sat, lifted a back paw, and scratched lazily behind his ear. Chance watched closely but didn't move. The bear yawned, lay down on his side, and went back to sleep. Susan exhaled a long breath. "Good dog. You're a good dog," she told Chance, scratching him under the chin.

(2)

Belted Kingfisher

Susan walked right by the coat rack next to the front door without seeing Bill's old sweater hanging there. It was too stained and tattered to go to the used-clothing store where she had taken the rest of Bill's clothes a few weeks after his death. Every time Susan saw it she thought about throwing it away, but she couldn't do it. She had reached for that sweater more times than she cared to count but each time had brought her hand back empty. Seeing it hanging there allowed her to pretend, if only for a little while, that Bill was alive. She could picture him coming out of the bedroom, pulling on his old work sweater, giving her a big kiss and hug, and heading out to start his day as he had done hundreds of times before. Today the idea of eating breakfast at Penny's Eatery, with nothing but greasy food to choose from, was distracting her.

For years, Susan and Shirley had gone out to breakfast together on the second Tuesday of every month. It was an odd day to pick and hard for Susan to keep track of, especially now that she was living alone. Without Bill or the children's schedules to ground her, she mostly wandered around with no idea what day of the week it was. Lately she had taken to marking off the days of the month on the calendar as they went by to remind her of various commitments, including this one with Shirley.

It was Shirley's work schedule that had originally decided what day was set aside for their monthly breakfast together. Before Shirley and John's girls were born, Shirley worked full time as a paralegal for a law firm in Crescent. The first and last week of the month and every Monday were always the busiest times at the law office, leaving Shirley little time for a leisurely breakfast out. So Susan and Shirley had settled on the second Tuesday of each month for their breakfast dates.

Once her girls were born, Shirley had started working part time at the same law firm. In addition to that, she had endless commitments with the girls' sports and school events. Nonetheless, she rarely missed her breakfast date with Susan. They took turns choosing where they would eat. This month it was Shirley's turn to pick, and she had picked Penny's because, she said, she couldn't stand any more of Susan's whole grain food choices.

At least this was something that stayed the same. Even at Bill's memorial service, Shirley had complained about the food, telling Susan that people needed fats and sugars during times of sorrow.

The memorial took place at the old Town Hall in Farhaven. Susan had taken on the job of contacting the caterer while Shirley, Meagan, and Shawn handled all the other arrangements. The day of the memorial, Meagan and Shawn had been in the main room greeting friends, giving Susan and Shirley a few minutes alone in the kitchen before the service began.

———◆———

The scent of Pine-Sol and mildew, murky light refracted through old windows, muffled voices coming through wood-paneled walls, the creak of cracked linoleum.

"What were you thinking, girl?" Shirley asked, inspecting the trays of vegetables the caterer had dropped off. "Good thing I roasted a couple of chickens and a ham and had John pick up rolls at the bakery. People can't grieve on carrot sticks and celery. Haven't you ever heard of comfort food?" Shirley held up a decoratively carved carrot stick as proof of her point. Susan laughed at her friend's exaggerated look of disgust, and then she pressed her hand to her lips, her eyes clouding with tears. "I shouldn't be laughing," she managed to say.

"Oh, honey, don't cry," Shirley said. "There are times when laughter is all we have left." She wrapped her arms around Susan's waist, laid her head on Susan's shoulder, and began to sob.

When they stepped apart, wiping their eyes with the backs of their hands, Shirley pointed to Susan's blouse and said, "Oh, no." She put her hand over her mouth to stifle a laugh, but it did no good. She was giddy from the stress of the last few days, and from lack of sleep. She began laughing so hard, she couldn't talk. All she could do was point at Susan's blouse.

Susan looked down and saw two black blotches on her blouse right below her left shoulder. Shirley applied mascara to her eyelashes every single morning no matter what, even when she was home in bed, sick with a cold. Now here it was, rubbed into Susan's blouse, looking like two tiny bats had lost their ability to echolocate and collided with her shoulder.

Susan looked at Shirley wide-eyed, and then she too started laughing. She took Shirley's hands in hers, and together they laughed until they could hardly breathe. They didn't stop until Shirley caught her breath and said, "Okay. That's enough. We need to pull ourselves together and get out there and let all those people tell you how sorry they are for your loss."

———◆———

What would I do without Shirley? Susan wondered. After Bill's death, most of their friends had gradually disappeared from Susan's life. Death made people uneasy, unsure of how to behave. She had done her best to be gracious when people showed up on her doorstep offering their condolences, but she never succeeded.

The irony of these visits was inescapable. These kind-hearted people would sit in her living room, glum-faced, sharing their sadness over Bill's death and offering their help and their frozen casseroles. Meanwhile, Susan would rush around, trying to make them feel comfortable. She would provide coffee or tea and ask about their children, their jobs, their pets, anything she could think of to shift the focus of the conversation away from her grief. More times than not, right in the middle of one of these visits, she had wanted to laugh out loud at what a pathetic social mess she was.

Why couldn't she have met these people at the front door, received their precooked meals, thanked them and assured them that she would call if she needed help? Then softly but firmly closed the door behind them? This would have been preferable to her clumsy attempts at being polite once they were inside the house. No wonder most everyone she knew had stopped coming around: she had worn them out with her frenzied perkiness.

Shirley often teased Susan about her lack of social skills, but it was a gentle chiding based on a mutual understanding and an appreciation of the differences between them. They were about as different as two women could be, from the types of foods they enjoyed to how they chose to dress and spend their free time. Nevertheless, there was a natural bond between them.

Penny's Eatery aside, Susan was looking forward to seeing Shirley today. She needed to have some fun, to be normal and lighthearted. Chance stood by the door wagging his tail, expecting an adventure. "Oh, all right. You can come," Susan said. "We can stop by the beach on the way home."

Susan started up the old van. Once the engine warmed up, she pushed the heater lever all the way over to high. A blanket of cold fog obscured much of the Jacoby River and drifted up over the bridge. Across from the mouth of the river, a belted kingfisher sat on a power line.

For as long as Susan could remember, this same kingfisher, or its ancestors, had perched in this spot, patiently watching the river below. Curious, she had done a bit of research on these birds. She learned that belted kingfishers usually built their nest at the end of a tunnel they carved into an overhanging bluff close to a river. There, in complete darkness, kingfisher nestlings hatched and grew each spring. Both parents, mom and dad, dove for fish at the mouth of the river and carried them back to the nest in their long beaks, at times flying full speed into the tunnel. A few weeks after hatching, the fledglings would make their way to the mouth of the tunnel—sometimes thirty or more feet up the cliff face—hesitate, and then leap into space for their first flight.

What would it be like to stand on the edge of the cliff and make that leap, counting only on a genetic code to provide flight? Were the baby birds afraid or did pure instinct drive them, leaving no room for fear? Susan wondered if she had a form of primal instinct that would allow her to make a leap into the unknown. She doubted it. She hardly ever did anything without considering every possible outcome first. Even now, with her plan to photograph a wild bear, she was consulting an expert, reading about black bear behavior, spending time getting Chance used to being around bears, covering every conceivable possibility.

Somewhere within her a voice whispered, "Ah, but there is always the inconceivable." Susan quickly dismissed this. She had been in the woods by herself hundreds of times and nothing dangerous or risky had ever happened. Besides, she would plan ahead, be prepared. She would be safe.

She checked the clock on the dashboard of the van. There was plenty of time to stop at the blueberry farm in Kenville. Even this late in the season, there would still be blueberries available. Her plan was to surprise Shirley by setting the little basket of plump berries on the table right alongside Shirley's usual breakfast of bacon, scrambled eggs, home fries, and a double order of sourdough toast. That way Shirley would get a little something healthy with her breakfast.

On the two-lane road leading to the blueberry farm, Susan rounded a corner and saw the flashing red lights of a school bus warning her to stop. Mothers hovered in the fog, clutching sweaters closed across their chests and waving goodbye to their children. Susan watched them from behind the windshield. She gripped the steering wheel hard, a deep sense of emptiness growing inside her.

When Shawn had left for college two years ago, four years after Meagan had moved out, the house felt too big and silent and cold. Susan and Bill circled like dogs, trying to get the scent of one another.

They were unsure of how to be alone together after more than twenty-four years of raising children.

Susan would find herself crying at odd times during the day. Late one afternoon, she held a shirt Shawn had left in the laundry basket up to her face, breathing in the smell of him and weeping. Later that same week, tears ran unchecked down her cheeks while she pushed the vacuum in Meagan's old bedroom, transformed into an office for Bill years before. She spent one entire day going through photo albums and crying until she felt sick. Bill never knew of these episodes. By the time he arrived home from work, Susan would have gotten control of herself, appearing normal, even cheerful. If he guessed at the depth of her sadness, he kept it to himself.

Gradually they both grew used to being without their children in the house. Susan spent more and more time during the day in the woods with Chance. She and Bill began to enjoy their freedom, going out to the movies and dinner or spending evenings at home chatting about their days, reading, or watching television. Bill grew kinder, gentler, more like the carefree boy she had fallen in love with. Now he was gone, too.

Tears blurred her vision. She swiped at them with the back of her hand. "Stop this," she said out loud, but she couldn't stop the flow of tears. She pulled the van over to the curb, shut off the engine, laid her head on the steering wheel, and wept.

Finally she was able to take in a slow breath. She wiped her eyes and blew her nose on a paper napkin she found in the glove box. Outside the van's windows, sunlight was slanting through the fog in long, misty streaks. The trees on either side of the road were dark and laden with moisture. Susan stared at them. Then, without fully realizing what she was doing, she fired up the van's engine and cranked the steering wheel all the way around to make a U-turn. No longer thinking about going to the blueberry farm or breakfast with Shirley, she drove with one thought in mind—to reach the woods.

At the entrance to Smith and Sons Timber Company lands close to her house, Susan pulled the van off the side of the road and set the parking brake. She hung her camera case across her shoulder and opened the back door for Chance. He dashed ahead of her into the woods. He sniffed the ground and the air, stopping here and there to bury his nose in a clump of grass, snorting loudly before running on.

Susan walked fast, inhaling deeply, breathing in the cool, damp air. Her normal habit was to watch the trail for animal tracks, checking to see which creatures had been there before her. Today was different. She stepped right over the double-crescent tracks of deer hooves that weaved through and around the long-toe prints of raccoons without noticing them.

Huckleberry and salal bushes, heavy with ripe fruit, grew on both sides of the trail. Chance lagged behind, pulling berries free from the bushes with his front teeth and swallowing them whole. When he had eaten his fill, he raced ahead, sounding like a horse as he thundered by to regain his position as the leader of their little pack.

Susan touched the fat, juicy berries without picking a single one. She walked in the long strides of someone used to being alone in the woods, instinctively stepping over roots that had risen in the trail and pushing whip-like alder branches away from her face.

This was her forest, her sanctuary for more than twenty years. A little over fifteen years ago the logging company had cut this section of the forest, stripping it of all but a few trees. This opened the canopy, allowing sunlight to reach the forest floor for the first time in many decades. Pampas grass, an alien to the redwood forest, now grew in all the open spaces between the berry bushes.

When Susan and Bill first started coming here, the trees had been undisturbed for more than a hundred and fifty years. Near sunset in the dark shade of those tall, silent trees they had seen the stretched bodies of flying squirrels, their front legs reaching out as they jumped and glided from tree to tree on wings of skin. Once, on a hot summer day, she and Bill had seen a pygmy owl. Its fierce, yellow eyes blinked at them from the shadowy branches of a massive, old Douglas fir.

Today, moving deeper into the forest, Susan passed clusters of small third-generation redwoods and a few larger Douglas firs that dripped moisture from branches covered in lichen and moss. Only in a narrow strip of land bordering Woolly Creek did a trace of ancient forest remain. This is where Susan was headed.

She kept a fast pace, leaning forward up the steep grade that led to a ridge above the creek. Occasionally, Chance would crash through the brush on the side of the trail, following a scent. Susan didn't stop to wait for him or bother to call him back.

Around a bend in the trail, the sun broke through the fog, changing the day from gray to bright yellow green. Moisture hung suspended from the ends of every leaf, each droplet a rainbow prism. In the warm air, smoke-like swirls of mist twirled off the tree trunks and floated along the trail. Susan continued to climb, pulling her sweater off and tying it around her waist as she went.

She hiked steadily uphill for close to an hour when the trail dumped into a clearing above Woolly Creek. Here the air was alive with dragonflies. They darted high into the sky and tumbled close to the ground in a primeval insect dance. The deep blues and greens of their bodies changed to silver as they dipped and spun around each other, their double transparent wings beating the air with an intermittent *whirr-r.…*

"Look at this," Susan said, raising her hand into the air. After touching her hand and flitting away a number of times, a dragonfly landed on her fingertip, weightless, all wings and fiber. It stayed for a frozen second before lifting off to rejoin the flight. Susan had been holding her breath. She let it out slowly, feeling the tense muscles in her neck and shoulders relax.

On the ridge above the creek, she followed what might have once been an old logging road but was now nothing more than an overgrown trail. From there she could see the tops of Douglas firs and redwoods rooted in the creek bed a hundred feet below. She watched the edge of the trail for a path she had seen weeks before that led down to the creek. When she found it she stopped and peered down.

The path dropped straight down the side of the embankment through a patch of salal. Susan started down but stopped.

I'm afraid to do this, she thought. She looked back the way she had come and again at the nearly vertical path. The creek murmured at her from far below.

"We can do this," she said to Chance. "It can't be that hard." She looked down the path once more and then whistled and pointed for Chance to go ahead of her: the last thing she needed was for him to run into her from behind.

The first part of the path was exceptionally steep and covered with loose leaves and stones. Susan sidestepped, digging in with her heels. In two of the steepest places, she slid, her feet skidding out ahead of her. To keep from falling, she grabbed onto branches until she could regain her footing.

Chance waited on the path below, his sides heaving, his tongue hanging out. When he saw her coming, he turned and ran on. Susan heard him splashing in the creek long before she saw it.

When the path leveled out, Susan rested against a large second-growth redwood tree. The air was damp and clean. The branches of the tall trees on each side of the creek overlapped to form a thick curtain, effectively hiding the creek from above.

Chance dropped a stick at her feet and barked in a high-pitched yelp that echoed off the steep canyon walls. Susan flinched and then laughed. Chance wagged and pawed the stick. "Oh, all right. I'll throw your stick. No more yelping, though. It hurts my ears."

She threw the stick along the creek bed until Chance flopped down in front of a large rock, panting heavily. Susan sat down next to him, leaned back against the rock, and closed her eyes. She fell asleep listening to the gurgling and lapping of the creek.

———————————

Susan woke up with the rock cold and rough against her back. The canyon was speckled in sunlight coming through the dark trees. Chance was breathing peacefully beside her. She idly fondled the hair on his neck and gazed around. Clusters of sword ferns grew along both sides of the creek, their long fronds reaching out to each other across the water. A group of tiny, fluorescent-orange mushrooms grew out of what was left of a decomposing tree that had fallen in front of the ferns. The edges of the mushrooms rolled up, forming a ruffle around their tops, making them look like fancy teacups left after a doll's tea party.

Not too far down the creek bed was a large redwood tree, charred halfway up its trunk. At its base was a hollow cave where the heartwood had burnt away in a fire at some point in the past. The tree continued to grow despite the damage it had suffered. Something had scraped away the redwood and fir leaves at the mouth of the cave and scattered them in piles on either side.

"What could have done that?" Susan asked. She stood up and rubbed her neck and arched her back. Chance also stood up and stretched, doing a perfect downward-facing dog. "Chance, lie down and stay," Susan said. "Let me see what this is before you start charging around."

Chance lay down and watched her. She walked close to the hollow tree and bent to see inside. It smelled vaguely familiar, almost like a wet dog. A mat that looked like it was made of short, black fur covered the cave floor. Susan stepped back. Something's here, she thought, looking around her. No, not here now, but an animal lives here. What kind of animal would live here?

Susan had started again for the tree cave when she saw three dark clumps of animal feces on the ground. "Bear," she whispered. She scanned the canyon walls and then moved closer to the feces. They were deep purple and full of berries. She examined more of the forest floor. All around her were clumps of bear scat. A layer of fuzzy, gray mold covered most of them, but a few were fresh-looking and full of undigested huckleberries. The bear must have been here recently, maybe even earlier today.

She turned in a circle, checking for movement along the walls of the canyon. "Where are you?" she asked. She tilted her head and listened. All she could hear were the soft babbling sounds of the creek. Out of the corner of her eye she glimpsed her camera case next to the creek where she had left it.

She took her camera out of the case and knelt as close to the cave's mouth as she could without stepping on the cleared space. Chance whined and inched toward her on his belly, army style. "You stay," Susan said. She focused the camera lens on the cave opening and snapped the picture. She shifted her position and refocused, taking four shots from different angles. She took three shots of the bear scat and one more of the cave tree from a few feet back. She then moved around the clearing in a circle, snapping pictures of the creek bed as she went, automatically winding the film forward after each shot.

Chance whined again. Susan put her hand out to remind him to stay. He was lying in front of the rock where they had slept, his long body stretched as far in her direction as he could get without moving from where she had told him to stay.

"I wonder…" Susan said. She skirted by Chance and crouched behind the rock. A large, fallen redwood tree lay over the rock, making a kind of lean-to. Susan crawled under the tree. The ground was soft and dry. Around the edge of the rock she could see the cave opening and much of the surrounding area.

"Chance, come. It's time to go," Susan said, crawling out from under the tree.

Climbing up the path was much more challenging than going down, but Susan barely noticed. She crab-walked on her hands and feet up the steepest parts, grabbing onto low branches to heave herself upward and to help keep her balance. She was anxious to get home and call Professor Sharpton, to talk to him about what she had found here.

Could she do this? Could she stay by the cave and photograph the bear who lived there? Was it possible, or was she crazy to even think about it? Maybe she was crazy, crazy as a moose in heat, as her grandma used to say. Grandma would always follow that up by saying there was nothing wrong with going a little crazy once in a while. Right now, Susan could use some craziness in her life, some risk. She hadn't taken many risks, not ever. Safety first had always been her motto. Look both ways before crossing the street. She felt that now she had nothing left to lose: Meagan and Shawn were doing fine on their own, and Bill was dead. If she was going to take a risk, this was the time to do it.

Susan had just made it through the front door when she noticed the answering machine was blinking, indicating new messages. She stared at the machine. John had given it to them as a gift. Bill had hated it. He would go on about John and his obsession with new-fangled devices, how he didn't know a single person who owned one other than them and John and Shirley, how people didn't understand them and nobody other than John and Shirley wanted to leave a message. These messages had to be from Shirley. Bill had been right, hardly anyone except John and Shirley left messages, and John hadn't phoned here since Bill died.

Susan's heart sank. She had forgotten all about her breakfast date with Shirley. How could she have forgotten? She didn't bother taking off her boots. She went right to the machine and pressed the Play button and listened to the first message. "Susan, where are you?" Shirley's voice asked. "I've been waiting for over forty minutes. We did say Penny's, didn't we?"

Susan slumped onto the chair by the phone table and touched the button to play the next message. It was Shirley again. "Now I'm starting to get worried. I went by that garlic and wheat grass place you like, thinking we got our restaurants crossed. They said they hadn't seen you. I'm on my way to your house now. If you get this message, wait there for me."

And the last message: "Susan, if you get this message, call me right away. I drove up to your house to see if you were all right and saw your van parked at the entrance to the timber company's land. Now I'm really worried. You know how I am about the woods. I'm not going in there by myself, but I've called John. He's going to come home from work as soon as he can, but he said it wouldn't be until this afternoon. If I haven't heard from you by then, he's going to see if he can find a few neighbors to help search for you, so call, okay?"

Susan sighed. She picked up the phone and dialed Shirley's number.

"Hello?" Shirley answered on the first ring.

"Hey Shirley, it's me."

"Oh thank goodness. Where have you been? You scared me to death. Are you all right?"

"Yes, I'm fine. I was walking."

"Walking? You were walking?" Shirley asked, her words clipped, her voice harsh. "You can't believe how much terrible Penny's coffee I drank waiting for you. Did you forget it was Tuesday?"

"No, I didn't forget, not at first. I was on my way when I…." How could she explain what happened? She glanced around the room. Her eyes came to rest on Bill's gray sweater hanging on the coat rack. It was definitely time to throw it away.

"When you what?" Shirley all but shouted into the phone. "Do you have any idea how frightened I was? When I saw your van, I was sure you had broken your leg or been eaten by a mountain lion. For the love of God, Susan, John's on his way here now. He's already phoned some of the neighbors to round up a search party to go find you."

"I was on my way," Susan repeated, "but I had to stop behind the school bus, and I saw the children with their moms. I don't know. I'm not sure what happened. I felt alone. Not just lonely, but completely alone." Her throat tightened and tears formed at the corners of her eyes. She rubbed at them with the back of her hand and swallowed hard. "I was in the woods maybe an hour, maybe two before I realized where I was. I'm sorry."

Shirley exhaled into the phone. "It's okay. It's been a while since you let yourself have a breakdown day. But I swear I'll never drink another cup of Penny's coffee. Maybe that was your plan, huh, making me not want to go to Penny's ever again?" Shirley laughed, a thin, joyless laugh. "You want to try tomorrow? I could take a few hours off work. We could go to the whole earth place."

"I can't tomorrow. I have an appointment."

"What?" Shirley snapped. "What kind of appointment?" Then, in a calmer voice, "No, listen, forget it. You don't have to tell me. Just come on over. I owe John a good dinner after dragging him away from work, and I think you should be here."

Susan looked down at her muddy boots and dirty jeans. All she wanted now was a long, hot bath. She could picture steam floating around the ceiling above the bathtub, could all but feel the warm water on her aching muscles. But she couldn't say no to Shirley, not after today. "That sounds great," she said, trying for a bit of enthusiasm. "Let me take a shower and feed Chance, and I'll come right over."

Next Susan dialed David Sharpton's office number. "Sharpton here," he barked into the phone.

"Hello, Professor Sharpton. It's Susan Campton."

"Susan, how are you? And it's David, remember?"

"Yes, right, David. I'm fine. I was wondering if I could make an appointment with you for tomorrow. I've read your manual, and I have a few photos to show you and a few questions to ask."

"Let's see. I have a couple of free hours tomorrow morning starting at ten. Will that work for you?"

"Yes. Good," Susan said. "I'll be there."

"Looking forward to it," David said and hung up.

"Not big into goodbyes, I guess," she said and set the receiver down.

At the dinner table that night, Susan sat between Amanda and Mary Ann. John and Shirley sat across from her. The girls giggled and chattered almost nonstop about their teachers and friends at school. Shirley smiled and nodded and at times told them to hush and eat their dinners.

As usual, John said very little. When he did speak, it was in response to something one of the girls had said. Susan caught Shirley glancing at him throughout the meal.

When the girls left the table, John looked at Susan and said, "Shirley told me you were walking in the woods today."

"Yes," Susan replied.

"Weren't you supposed to meet her for breakfast?"

Shirley put her hand on John's arm. "You and I talked about this already. It's okay."

"No, Shirley, it's not okay. I want to hear from Susan why she left you sitting at Penny's for hours. Why I had to leave work early."

"I'm sorry," Susan said.

"Sorry? Shirley was half sick with worry. She'd already decided you were seriously injured or dead. I had to let the crew go home early so I could go search for you. Half the neighborhood was getting ready to join me. And you're sorry?"

John cleared his throat and then cleared it again. When he spoke this time his voice was calmer. "Please Susan, just this once, talk to me about what's going on with you. I want to understand."

"I..." Susan started but stopped. No matter what she said, John wouldn't be able to understand what had happened. She didn't understand it herself.

John watched her for a long minute, then he scraped his chair back and stood up. Quietly, almost kindly, he said to her, "You need to get on with your life. It's time. Bill would want that from you."

"John," Shirley said, reaching out to him.

He rubbed his hand over his face. To Shirley he said, "I'm going to take a walk. I'll be back." He turned and left the room. He took his baseball cap from the rack by the front door and went out, shutting the door behind him.

65

"Susan, I'm—" Shirley began.

"No, don't apologize," Susan interrupted, shaking her head and holding her hand out, palm facing Shirley. Her fingers trembled slightly. She pulled her hands down under the table and fisted them in her lap. "John's right. I was wrong. That was a terrible thing to do, to go off and leave you waiting, not knowing where I was. He's also right about my needing to get on with my life. It is time."

"John said that because I was so worried," Shirley said. "I couldn't stand it if I lost you. You're my best friend, even if you are a bit crazy at times."

Susan touched Shirley's small, soft hand and noticed how big and rough her own was in comparison. Shirley was from Georgia. She told people that the main thing she had learned as a child was how to be a lady. She had laughed about this with Susan, making fun of herself, saying she couldn't go out without doing what she called dressing up. "For me," she once said, "dressing up means ironing my clothes and doing my nails so that I look respectable while weeding the garden." Susan often felt like a shabbily dressed giant next to her friend.

"I made blackberry cobbler, if you want," Shirley said.

"Thanks, but I should go home. It's been a long day."

"You can say that again," Shirley said with a weak smile.

Clumsy with fatigue, Susan began to pick up the dirty dinner plates and stack them together.

"Leave those. I'll get the girls to help later," Shirley said.

At the front door, Susan faced Shirley. "It felt good to be in the woods today. It helped me calm down, to feel better. I feel like I belong there."

"That's good. We all need somewhere we find peace. For me, it's out in the flower garden. For you, it's the forest. Be careful, though. I don't like you being out there alone."

"But I wasn't alone," Susan said. "I had Chance with me."

Shirley shook her head. "You can be so weird."

Back in her own living room, Susan curled up on one end of the couch with Chance at the other end, his head resting on her legs. She stroked one of his ears between her fingers. The scene with John at dinner had bothered her more than she was willing to admit. She forced her thoughts away from John and back to the woods, to Woolly Creek. At first she had been at peace there. Then after seeing the cave and realizing that it was most likely a bear's den, she had felt nervous, even a bit frightened, but she had also been excited.

She sat up abruptly, causing Chance to lift his head with a groan of protest. She knew now what she had been trying to explain to Shirley. It wasn't simply that she felt more comfortable in the woods without other people around her. It was also about that jolt of fear mixed in with excitement whenever a deer or a bird startled out of the brush. The expectation that there was a wild animal just out of sight made her feel more alive, more real. More awake.

Susan got up and walked to the window. There, reflected in the glass, a dark figure, almost animal-like, gazed back at her. She touched the cold pane, traced the shape with her fingertips, running them over the wild, tousled hair and around the thin face. She leaned closer, her breath fogging the glass, and smiled at the thought that she was changing into a wild animal.

"Time for bed," she said to Chance. "We've had enough excitement for one day."

As she turned, she saw Bill's tattered sweater hanging on the coat rack. "Okay," she said. She lifted the sweater off the hook and—folding it carefully, holding it up to her face one last time—carried it to the trashcan under the kitchen sink.

That night she fell into a deep and dreamless sleep.

Nose up, scenting. The smell of the woman and the dog was all along the trail, drifting up from the ground in unseen threads. His nose quivered in an effort to pull any trace of them from the air. Were they still here? He listened. There was no sound of them. He moved forward, his nose low, following their scents up along the creek bed, across the clearing, and around the rock.

This smell had been part of the forest most of his life. He had followed it along the trails or caught it wafting in the air, but never here, close to his home.

Muscles tense, he walked around his den, breathing in fast huffs. He stuck his head into his den and pawed at the ground. He lay in the dirt outside his den and rolled, grunting, covering their scent with his own, erasing them from this place. But the memory of them was not gone. Nose lifted in the night air, he snorted once before crawling into his den to sleep.

Early the next morning, Susan headed for *Erick's Photos*, eating a piece of whole-wheat toast spread with peanut butter as she drove. She knew Erick would be there already: he was always in the shop by five in the morning.

Erick had been processing her film for years. He understood things like shading, color saturation, and composition better than anyone else she knew. As their business relationship had evolved into a kind of friendship, Erick had started allowing Susan to help while he printed her pictures. She was one of a select few who saw the inside of his darkroom.

The bell above the door chimed when Susan entered the photo shop. Erick came out from the darkroom, wiping his hands on a paper towel. He was his usual rumpled self, with his hair plastered to one side of his head and his shirt and pants wrinkled. Susan suspected that he slept here, although she had never seen a bed or other personal belongings to support this idea. It could be that he wasn't concerned about his appearance. She could relate to that. She never spent much time on how she looked, either. A clean pair of jeans and shirt were good enough for her, and she wore her hiking boots just about everywhere.

"Hey, Susan, how're things? Haven't seen you around lately," Erick said, gazing over Susan's shoulder and then at her feet. Over the years, Susan had become accustomed to his habit of never looking directly at her when he spoke.

"Things are fine. Do you have time to develop a roll of film and let me help with the prints this morning? We can skip the proofs because I want all the negatives printed."

"This morning? As in now? How soon do you need them?"

"I'll need them for an appointment at ten."

Erick's eyebrows shot up. "Ten? Whoa. Okay, give me time to develop the film and dry the negatives. Then we can work on the prints together." Turning away, he muttered to himself, "That'll work. I can do that."

When the negatives were ready, Susan and Erick stood side by side behind the enlarger.

"Could you sharpen this one up?" Susan asked. It was a view of the cave opening from a few feet back.

"Sure. Maybe a bit more contrast will do it. This whole series here, are they a panorama?"

"Yes, I took them as I turned in a circle."

"Interesting. Not your usual close-ups. And this," he said, after sliding the next negative into place. "What is this? It looks like bear shit."

"That's what it is."

"To each his own," Erick said. "Sort of a new nature thing, huh?"

"You could say that."

At five minutes after ten, Susan stood with David Sharpton in his office, the photographs spread out on a table in front of them.

"These are good, very good. Look at this." David pointed at a spot on one of the photos.

"What am I looking at?" Susan asked.

"Here, partway up this tree. Those are teeth marks, and above them are claw marks. It's called a bear tree. Bears do that to mark their territory. This bear wants other bears to know that this is his home. Judging from the height of the marks, I'd say this is a large boar. If it's a sow, she's unusually large."

Still studying the photo, David asked, "Did you go into the den?"

"No. I took these from about four feet away."

"Good. And your dog, was he with you?"

"Yes."

"Did he go into the den?"

"No. I made him stay back." Chance had probably been sniffing for the bear all over the place before she got down to the creek, but she didn't want to tell David that.

As they spoke, David walked around the table, carefully examining each photograph. "How long did you stay by the den?"

"About an hour, maybe longer. I threw a stick in the creek for Chance, and later we both fell asleep beside the creek. This was before I saw the den."

"So you were all over the area with your dog?"

"Yes, but not right up to the tree with the cave in it."

David looked at her with those disturbing eyes of his. "This bear will smell you. He'll smell your dog. They have an incredibly acute sense of smell. A bear can detect the slightest trace of a scent from over a mile away. It's remarkable, really. He may not stay here again. Whether he stays or not will depend on how he feels about you."

"Let's hope he's not bothered by our scent, because I can't do anything about it now," Susan said. She pointed to one of the photographs. "There's a place behind this rock where a fallen tree forms a small shelter. I could conceivably photograph the bear in his den from there. I could get to know his habits, when he sleeps, when he wakes up. He must drink in the creek, maybe even fish. I'd be able to photograph all of that."

"The goal would be to become invisible," David mused. "Not an easy feat with an animal who has the sense of smell and hearing of a bear."

"I'd like to try," Susan said.

David frowned at her, shaking his head. "I was speculating as to whether this could be done in theory, not suggesting in any way that you could or should do it. It's risky. As I stated in our first meeting, black bears are not usually aggressive. They would rather run than fight, especially with a human, but they can be unpredictable. They're wild animals, powerful wild animals. In addition to which, being in the woods for long hours carries its own significant set of risks—falling trees, slippery trails, any number of things."

"I know you're concerned about me," Susan said, "and I appreciate that, but I'm going to do this with or without your help. I don't need your permission." She felt heat rising up her face. She breathed out slowly. "It's important to me. I'm used to being in the woods. I'll do whatever you suggest to be as safe as possible, but I'm not going to go home and forget this."

David looked at the array of photographs. Susan was unable to read his expression. "Okay," he said. "I'll work with you on this project, but you have to take precautions. Do you have someone you can call when you're going into the woods? Someone who could look for you if you don't return in a reasonable length of time?"

Shirley came to mind, but Susan couldn't ask her for help with this, especially not after how worried Shirley had been yesterday when Susan hadn't shown up at Penny's Eatery as planned, not with how angry John was because of this. "No, not really," Susan said.

"Then I'll be that person," David said. "Let me know every time you're going into the woods, and phone me when you come out, day or night. I'll give you my home number." Susan nodded.

David reached for a piece of paper and a pen on his desk. "This is for your protection," he said over his shoulder. "Someone needs to know where you are in case you get into trouble."

No longer able to contain her excitement, Susan grinned widely. Originally she had feared he wouldn't talk to her at all. When he had given her the manual to read, she figured that would be all there was to it—just the facts about bears. Now he was offering his help.

David turned from his desk and caught her smiling. "Now you're happy, but you may not be after spending ten hours in the cold and dark, waiting for a sleepy bear to wake up."

"I was sure you'd tell me that what I was trying to do was insane and send me on my way," Susan said. "I've been hearing a lot lately about how crazy I am."

"You might be a little crazy. Many people who have a strong desire to do something important, especially when it requires courage and stamina, are a bit crazy. In addition to that, you made it perfectly clear that you are going to do this with or without my help." He stopped and looked directly into her eyes. Susan wanted to look away but didn't.

David shrugged. "I'm not going to do much. You'll be the one out there with the bear." David checked his watch. "I need to eat before my next class. Would you like to join me? We could talk about the specifics of your project over lunch."

Susan agreed. They strolled side by side to the center of the college's campus, where off the main quad there was a small restaurant above the bookstore. Susan was struck with how beautifully landscaped the campus was, with sweeping lawns bordered by large stands of rhododendron and azalea shrubs, some of the former as big as trees. She had been here only once in the spring when these plants were blooming. It was truly a spectacular sight. Even now, when the rhodies and azaleas weren't in bloom, their dark-green foliage set off the original mission-style buildings and gave the campus a stately elegance.

As they walked, David said, "You are aware that black bears move around within their territory regularly, and that this bear may abandon his den at any time?"

"I read that in your manual, but from the looks of it he's been there for a while."

"Every bear's different. Maybe this bear is a homebody."

At the restaurant, a waiter showed them to a table by the window. Without consulting the menu, David ordered the soup-and-salad special. "The soups are always good here, made fresh daily," he told Susan, "and the salad greens come from the gardens right here on campus." Susan followed his advice and ordered the special.

David asked for coffee with a pitcher of cream. Susan opted for mint tea. The last thing she needed right now was a shot of caffeine. Being here with this man was making her jittery enough. She hadn't eaten in a restaurant with a man other than Bill for decades. She was as nervous as she had been on her first real date as a teenager.

After the waiter left, David's expression turned serious. "One thing I forgot to ask, were you on Smith and Sons lands when you took these photos?"

"Yes. I've been walking there for years."

"For years," he repeated, the barest hint of a smile playing across his face. Susan nodded. "You do understand that I can't officially sanction trespassing? That if you're caught there, you're on your own?"

Susan nodded again.

"With that said, let's talk about what you'll need to take with you and how to get into a position to take your photographs." Pen and notebook in hand, Susan sat poised to write down every word he said.

"First, it might be best if you went alone. You have an advantage. Your scent is already all over the area. He's either decided it isn't dangerous or he's left. If he stays, he won't be as fearful if he smells you again. The scent of someone new may be all it would take to cause him to leave."

"And Chance? He's been there, also. His smell is everywhere mine is."

"Right, your dog. What's to keep him from barking or chasing the bear?"

"Oh, we've been working on that." Susan told him about her time in front of the bear enclosure at the zoo.

"Interesting approach. How'd you come up with the idea?"

"I'd read about the zoo's bears in the paper. I figured that if Chance could spend time up close to them, he'd get used to staying calm around bears."

"Might work," David said, nodding. "Okay, let's get down to business and make a list of the supplies you'll need." He pointed at her notebook. "Warm clothes are a must, in dark colors, either dark green, brown, or black. They won't be as visible under the trees. You'll need a light waterproof tarp, a rain jacket, and waterproof pants, also preferably in dark colors. Bring a small flashlight and a good compass. You do know how to use a compass, don't you?"

"No. I haven't really needed to use one. I've spent so much time over the last twenty years walking in these woods that I know my way around out there."

"You'd be surprised how many people get lost in the woods, even when they're familiar with the area," David said. "If you have to move fast at any time, you can become disoriented, and your usual landmarks can look very different at night. Get a good compass and a book on how to use it. It's not that complicated. You'll also need a map, one that shows in detail the exact area where you'll be. A topographical map. On this, find the longitude and latitude lines closest to the bear's den. The people at the outdoor store in town will be able to help you with that. Call me with the numbers when you find them."

"All right," Susan said, adding these to her list.

"Pack snack foods in plastic sacks and seal the sacks up tight. Bring foods that don't have a strong odor and aren't crunchy or noisy to eat, and don't open the sacks or eat close to the bear. Also, bring a large bottle or canteen of water and maybe a thermos of tea or coffee. Photography is not my field, so I'll leave all that up to you." Susan wrote quickly, glancing up at him from time to time.

When their order arrived, Susan set the notebook and pen down beside her bowl of soup. She ate slowly, pausing to take notes. David ate with gusto and talked with equal enthusiasm. He was quiet only when he needed to chew or swallow. At one point he looked at his bowl of soup and said, "Damn, this is good."

Susan smiled at his childlike enthusiasm, but she agreed that the soup was remarkably good, thick with fat, slippery noodles and simmered carrots, tomatoes, broccoli, and celery. The salad was equally tasty, made from an assortment of crisp vegetables and croutons seasoned with rosemary. Even so, Susan could hardly eat. She couldn't stop thinking about how she was sitting here having lunch with a man other than Bill, and a university professor on top of that. Every movement she made, every bite of food she took seemed to her to shout out how awkward and incompetent she was. It took all her concentration to keep her mind on what David was saying and to ask somewhat intelligent questions.

"Now that we've covered what you'll need in the way of supplies," David said, "let's discuss the specifics of getting into position to take your photographs. You should get set up before dusk. Most bears travel through their territory during the day, hunting for food, and return to their dens at night. If they live close to people and come into contact with them frequently, they'll often reverse this pattern, roaming at night and sleeping during the day. You were there during the day and this bear wasn't, so we can assume he comes home at night."

"And if he smells me?" Susan asked.

"If he smells you or hears you, he will most likely go away. The worst possible situation would be if he realizes you're there after he's gone to sleep—if you make a noise, say, or the wind picks up and he gets the scent of you. Bears are not at their best if disturbed when sleeping. There's the remote possibility that if this were to occur, he would try to defend his home with force. This is why I want you to have a way to protect yourself."

"A gun? No. No guns," Susan said, setting her spoon down with a loud clink and shaking her head.

"I'm not asking you to hunt bears," David said with a bemused grin. "I'm asking you to be prepared to defend yourself if things go wrong. Many scientists who observe bears carry a canister of pepper spray with them, one made specifically to deter large animals."

"Oh. Yes, I see. I'll add that to my list." Susan lowered her eyes to the notebook, her cheeks hot. Of course he wouldn't want her to shoot a bear. What had she been thinking?

"Most of the time when a bear charges," David said, "it's a false charge. As I said before, black bears don't like to fight. If this bear charges you, the odds are he just wants you out of his territory. You should move away from him. Don't turn your back and don't run. Running can make him see you as prey, and he can outrun you. A lean bear can run as fast as thirty miles an hour. Instead, back up slowly. You can even talk to him, but stay calm."

"Talk to him?"

"A friend of mine told me he says, 'Good bear, nice bear,' as he backs up from a charging bear." David paused, seemingly lost in thought. "I was charged only once, and truthfully it was frightening, but when I backed up, the bear moved back as well. When we were far enough apart that I was no longer seen as a threat, she went back to chomping grass."

"So why do I need the pepper spray?"

"That's for the bear who doesn't follow the usual pattern. These are large, wild animals. Unexpected things can and do happen. And you'll have that dog with you. We have no idea how this bear will react to a dog."

"I see," Susan said, looking straight at him. She wasn't going to let him scare her into leaving Chance behind.

"Evidently you can be stubborn at times," David said.

Susan wasn't sure how to react to this. She didn't think of herself as stubborn. She saw herself as shy and practical, but maybe he was right. Maybe she was stubborn when it involved something she cared a great deal about.

When she didn't answer, David pushed his empty soup bowl and salad plate aside and rubbed his mouth with his napkin. "Okay," he said. "Let's talk about this rock you found. How far is it from the den?"

Susan wasn't quite half finished with her meal, but she also pushed her bowl and plate aside. She was too excited to eat more. "Thirty feet. Maybe a little more."

"No. That's way too close," David said, shaking his head. "I had no idea you were planning to get that close to this bear. There's no way you should be that close. I can't in any fashion support that. You'll need to find a place twice that far away, even farther would be better—far enough away that any small movements you make won't alarm the bear, and you'll have some escape room if needed. I would advise going one more time to find a good spot to set up. It should offer a reasonable amount of shelter and protection from the bear, similar to this one behind the rock, except much farther away from his den."

"I can go tomorrow."

"Yes," David said. "Tomorrow would be good, while your scent is still in the area. Go at the same time as you did yesterday. The bear should be gone, if yesterday is an example of his usual pattern." He gestured at her bowl and plate and asked, "Are you finished?"

She glanced at what was left of her meal. "Yes," she said, feeling a tinge of regret that she had been too nervous to fully enjoy how good the food was.

David came around to Susan's side of the table. He waited while she gathered her things, then he raised his hand to the waiter and ushered Susan toward the door.

"I haven't paid yet," Susan said.

"It's my treat. They keep a tab for me." When Susan continued to glance at the waiter, he said, "Don't worry. It's all tax-deductible. A work expense."

Back in David's office, he took four small glass jars from the bottom drawer of his desk and handed them to her. "Use these to collect scat samples from around the den. We don't need more than one sample of those with berries in them. We already know he's eating berries this time of the year. I mostly want the older ones. I'll have them analyzed to see what he eats when berries aren't available."

Susan stuffed the jars into her bag and prepared to leave. She thought about what to say, and finally settled on, "Thank you for your help, and for lunch."

He nodded and said, "My pleasure."

Susan was reaching for the doorknob when he asked, "You will remember to call me when you come out of the woods tomorrow?"

"I will," Susan said.

Out in the hallway, Susan put her hand on the glass front of the bear case. "Don't you say a word. Not a word," she whispered, looking at the bear's fixed gaze. "It wasn't a date. It was a business lunch. That's all." She started down the hallway but turned and again met the bear's eyes. "Okay, you're right. It did feel a bit like a date, but it wasn't. It was a business lunch. It was tax-deductible."

Susan sat in her van and checked over the list of supplies, determining which items she already had and which ones she would need to buy. She made a new list of the latter. She then drove to the outdoor store.

"Going camping?" the fellow working behind the counter asked when Susan handed her list to him.

"Yes." She answered without really listening to what he had said. She was staring at a book on the counter titled *North American Black Bear Attacks.* The cover showed a bear with his mouth open in a vicious snarl. Susan started to put her hand up to the book but stopped.

"That's a great book," the clerk said, "full of these incredible stories of black bears attacking people. I've always heard they were wary of humans and unwilling to attack, but, as this book points out, that's not always the case. It's worth reading. You interested?"

"No. No, thank you," Susan said, shaking her head.

"I asked because I see you have bear pepper spray on your list. I figured you might want to learn about how and why bears attack."

"The spray, oh yes, well...." Susan glanced around the store. She didn't want to explain to this guy why she needed the spray. He couldn't be much older than sixteen or so. How could he understand her desire to photograph a wild bear? She didn't really understand it herself. "First, I need to find a compass and a book on how to use one. I'll also need a map of the forest behind Farhaven. Do you have maps showing the latitude and longitude of that area?"

"You mean topographical maps. Sure. What section do you need?"

"The area around Woolly Creek."

After three tries, they found the map Susan needed. She marked the area by the bear's den and made a notation of the longitude and latitude. She looked at every compass in the store before choosing a Silva brand and a book with simple instructions on its use. She selected the rest of the items on her list, adding a knitted hat with earflaps to keep her ears warm on cold nights.

While the clerk rang up her purchases, Susan couldn't take her eyes off the book about bear attacks. The cover showed the bear in mid-charge, his head to one side, his mouth wide open, his huge teeth showing. She again heard David saying, "Unexpected things can and do happen."

On the drive home, Susan repeated, "I won't be afraid. Fear is a choice. Animals can smell fear. I won't be afraid."

(3)

Common Murre

Susan stood inside the doorway of the storage shed behind her house. This had been Bill's shed. It had always been a place too full of unwanted clutter, a source of continual irritation to her. Even with Bill dead, when she was no longer supposed to care about such trivial annoyances, she felt a hot rush of anger at the amount of junk stored here. How was she ever going to find the camping gear? Couldn't he have at least labeled some of these boxes?

After an hour and a half of searching through containers of plumbing parts, broken construction tools, and old electrical wiring, she found a large box marked **CAMPING** in Bill's bold, block printing. Why had he labeled this box out of all the others? There must be more boxes out here that held things other than construction cast-offs. Did he harbor some hope that they would head off on camping adventures again, maybe when he retired from working construction? He had never said anything about wanting to go camping when—

"When he retired," Susan said softly. They had planned for Bill to work about six more years. After that they would—

Susan stopped, her eyes scanning the cluttered storage shed one more time. "Okay," she said, and she reached down for the box.

She maneuvered the box out the shed door, dragged it through the back door of the house, and into the living room. She sat down on the couch and began to sort through the camping supplies. She found her and Bill's backpacks and sleeping bags (they had given away the children's bags years ago); a thin, waterproof canvas tarp; and a daypack. Near the bottom of the box, she found a small flashlight that had an adjustable beam and four quart-size water bottles. A layer of dust covered everything. None of these things had been used in years, not since Meagan and Shawn were in elementary school and they had taken a few backpacking trips together as a family.

Susan took both the sleeping bags and the tarp outside and gave them a good shaking. She was glad this was a canvas tarp. It might be slightly heavier than a plastic one, but it would make less noise under the sleeping bag that could alert the bear to her presence. Next she rinsed out the water bottles and wiped off the backpacks and the daypack. She put Bill's backpack and sleeping bag back in the box, letting her hand rest gently on the top of the sleeping bag for a moment before closing up the box.

In the utility drawer in the kitchen, she found new batteries for the flashlight. Once these were in place, the flashlight worked perfectly.

The next thing on the agenda was to decide what kind of food to take that didn't have much of an odor and that was easy to carry. She had purchased a small bag of trail mix at the market the last time she was there. That would be the best choice for her, especially for this quick trip tomorrow, but what about Chance? Not long ago one of her neighbors had told her a story about a bear who had stolen a fifty-pound bag of dog food off her back porch. Most everyone living in bear country knew to keep their dog's food locked up because bears loved dog food and would steal it given a chance. For this in-and-out trip tomorrow, Chance could eat in the morning before they left and again at his usual time when they got home in the afternoon. This should be okay for an overnight trip, also. He could go a day without food, especially if there were still some ripe berries for him to snack on.

The daypack was the right choice for carrying what she needed tomorrow, but Susan wanted to practice getting her backpack ready for when she would be spending the night. She put everything in the backpack that she had purchased at the outdoor store along with her sleeping bag, the tarp, a change of clothes, the water bottles, and the flashlight.

When all her supplies were stowed in the large pack, she checked her camera equipment. She slid the tripod and monopod into long, narrow pockets on either side of the backpack. She packed her camera case with her Minolta, the 300mm telephoto and 50mm lenses, the cable release, and six rolls of high-speed film for action shots or those taken in low-light situations: a strobe flash would be out of the question around a bear.

She also decided to bring the Nikon camera with the 50mm lens that she had purchased a few years ago at a garage sale. The Minolta had been an anniversary present from Bill last year and was her favorite. But if the bear moved away from his den she might need a second camera, one that wasn't attached to the tripod. If need be, she could use the monopod with the Nikon. She put the Nikon under the sleeping bag in the backpack.

She squatted and fitted her arms through the backpack straps and hefted it on. She draped the camera case over her shoulder. She then tested the release clip on the waist belt of the backpack. Bill had insisted that she and the children practice this. He had said that if they fell or had to move fast for some reason, they needed to know how to get out of their packs quickly.

Susan closed her eyes and was back there lying out in the open through those long, dark nights. Bill and the children would fall asleep as soon as they crawled into their sleeping bags, but she would be awake for hours, listening to the unidentifiable animal noises coming from somewhere out there.

She took a quick step back and sat down hard on the arm of the couch. What was she getting ready to do? She shouldn't be doing this kind of thing. She wasn't sure what she was, but she certainly wasn't an outdoor adventurer. During the day she felt at home in the woods, but she had never spent even one night alone outside.

What would it be like to be in the woods at night, alone, sitting on the damp, cold ground with a bear lumbering toward her, sniffing the air? She saw herself frantically hunting for the can of pepper spray while Chance growled and surged against the leash. She felt the bear charge, his heavy body shaking the earth as he ran at her.

"Stop!" she cried out loud. Chance looked up at her, his tail down. "No, not you," Susan said, stroking the top of his head. "You're fine. It's me. I'm either going to do this thing or I'm not, but I'm not going to be afraid. Let's go for a walk." She shrugged the backpack and camera case off her shoulders and reached for Chance's leash and the keys to the van.

She loaded Chance into the van and drove to Farhaven Park. The forked trail from the picnic area meandered down to meet the beach on the left or followed Waterwheel Creek to the right. From the creek, the trail twisted up through a forest of Douglas fir, alder, and spruce trees, ending on a bluff above the ocean.

Susan followed the trail to the right, heading for the bluff. Shortly after making the turn, she crossed a small wooden bridge over the creek. Large maple trees grew on either side of the bridge, their leaves starting to change from green to golden brown.

Past the bridge, the trail made a bend to the left and headed up a steep hill. There it leveled off and snaked around the bluffs above Hidden Cove, a spot famous for nude sunbathing. This part of the walk reminded Susan of the forest in *Snow White and the Seven Dwarfs*. Douglas fir and spruce trees shaded cotoneaster bushes, their branches growing dark and deformed in the deep shadows of the larger trees.

The trail ended high above the ocean at Deer Head Bluff. Below, the waves crashed onto large rock islands on Susan's left and slammed into the sand walls of a cliff on her right. In front of her, gray seals lay sunning themselves on flat rocks, just out of reach of the churning surf. At times a wave would break over the rocks, causing the seals to arch their backs and lift their heads and tails out of the water.

Farther out on one of the large rock islands, Susan could barely make out the brown-and-white upright shapes of the common murres. There was only a small group there now. Most of the birds had already left to spend the winter out at sea.

Years ago, Susan had taken a guided bird tour here during the murres' mating season. Through the guide's spotting scope, she had seen these birds covering every available ledge, standing shoulder to shoulder. They resembled small penguins, bobbing their heads and shuffling their feet. Susan had wondered how they kept their eggs from being stepped on or knocked off those narrow ledges. It looked like there were thousands of birds, all milling around on tiny ridges sixty feet or more above the ocean. Even from this distance, she had been able to hear their unusual murmuring and purring sounds.

Susan would not be there to see the chicks become fledglings, but the guide had told her that they would leave the nest before they had flight feathers. She could imagine the small, awkward birds standing on the rim of the rock, cocking their heads and peering at the ocean that churned far below. The fledglings would sidle up to the edge and then move back, calling out in loud, befuddled voices. After a few false starts, they would leap off, rolling and sliding down the rock face to land in the cold Pacific waters.

Today, a flock of brown pelicans swooped above the water, their long necks bent, scanning the ocean for fish. The entire flock banked and flew in a large circle, dipping close to the water and lifting up again.

Susan sat on the bluff and watched the surf while Chance slept beside her. She breathed with the rhythm of the waves breaking below. All the nervous energy of getting ready for a night in the woods was now gone. This peaceful, almost magical place had always seemed to exist outside of time, untouched by the encroaching needs of people. Over the years, Susan had come here often to enjoy the ever-changing tempo of the sea.

With dusk settling in, Susan rose to leave. "Come on, Chance. It's time to go home and get dinner." At the word dinner, Chance bounded up, wagging happily.

———————————

That evening Susan read the compass book while she ate dinner. After cleaning up her few dishes, she unfolded the map of the Woolly Creek area on the table and practiced taking readings with the compass. She had to refer to the book often, but before long she began to understand the principle of how to find a specific location using a map and a compass.

As she drifted off to sleep that night, her mind kept practicing what she had learned, leading her back into the woods. There, in her dreams, the bear came to her. Again, he turned his head until he was staring right at her. Again, he held his paw above the rotting log. His jaw hung open, the tips of his white teeth gleaming in the dark forest. He held still for a long moment, and then, blowing ferociously, he lunged at her.

Susan startled awake with her mouth wide open. She lay there, breathing hard, wondering if she had been getting ready to scream or say good bear the way David's friend had done when charged by a bear.

The bedroom clock read five a.m. Unable to return to sleep, Susan got out of bed and went into the living room. She added wood to the small pile of coals smoldering in the woodstove. Mid-October, and already it was cold enough to have a fire every morning and night.

She sat down on the couch and opened the cedar chest that served as a coffee table and contained the family photo albums. The last time Susan looked at these photos was right after Shawn had left for college, a little over two years ago. Some of the albums were bound in black, others in red. Susan selected one at random and opened it in her lap.

The first page was full of snapshots taken when Meagan was six and Shawn was two. One photo was almost completely out of focus, but in her mind Susan could see her children clearly. They were wearing slick, yellow rain jackets over their pajamas, their feet bare, their heads covered in elaborate headdresses made of colorful construction paper.

The picture was taken on a rainy day in the middle of May during the wettest spring in recorded history. The morning had started out badly and things had gotten worse as the day progressed. Both the children were cranky from having been inside for days on end. They never bothered to change out of their pajamas and had been squabbling with each other on and off for hours.

In a moment of desperation, Susan had pulled out the construction paper and suggested they make headdresses in the shape of their favorite birds. Shawn had chosen a parrot and Meagan a Steller's jay. Susan had decided on a barn owl, a less flamboyant bird, for sure, but nonetheless one of her favorites. They spread the paper and glue around them on the living room floor and set to work.

The project had taken most of the afternoon, but it was worth the time and effort. The results were fantastic, even though none of the headdresses had the faintest resemblance to a bird. Shawn's stood up on his head like a tall crown of pink, green, blue, and red paper feathers, all flopping and bending as he moved. Meagan's lay flat across her head, stretching out about six inches past her ears in a long sweep of blue and gold paper. Susan's was dull in comparison, a brown and black cap, with a touch of yellow representing the owl's eyes.

It was Susan who had suggested they go outside to see if they could dance the sun out. She knew the paper headdresses wouldn't survive the rain, and there wasn't the slightest chance of seeing the sun that day, or for many days to come, but none of that mattered. What did matter was playing outside with her children on this rainy day.

The three of them, squealing with glee, had run and circled in the pasture. Susan had left the dance long enough to snap a roll of film. Most of the photos had not turned out. The one she had put in the album was a blur of movement, color, and water. Only Meagan's face—her sparkling, green eyes; her damp, pink cheeks; a swirl of her blond hair—was in focus.

Toward the end of the album, every picture of Meagan showed her dressed in black. This was the year she turned thirteen. Susan smiled, remembering the day close to the end of that year when Meagan had come out of her bedroom one morning wearing a brown shirt and a gray pair of pants. Bill had looked up from his breakfast and, with his normal dry humor, said, "We must be coming to the end of the funeral procession."

Susan closed the album and selected another one from the stack. It was full of pictures taken on a warm, sunny June day, the day Meagan and Peter were married. The wedding ceremony and reception took place in the pasture. On the day of the wedding, the pasture was dotted with tables and chairs set up for the reception. A white linen tablecloth covered each table, and a vase of multi-colored flowers sat in the center. Susan and Meagan had picked all the flowers from the border along the fence around the vegetable garden. There, over the years, Susan had planted a variety of perennials, including foxgloves, both white and purple; red columbines; pink bleeding hearts; and a collection of old roses. In the morning the day of the ceremony, Susan had gathered a basket of rose petals and tossed them around the yard. When the guests stepped on them, the air filled with the pungent aroma of roses.

Susan liked the old-fashioned photo albums, the kind with the black corner triangles that held the pictures in place. She touched each corner with the tips of her fingers. In the center of one page was a photograph of Bill and Meagan walking across the pasture. Before the ceremony, Bill had been fidgety in his new suit, fussing at the collar and cuffs, but in the picture he looked proud and happy. He had his arm linked through Meagan's; his eyes fixed on hers; his lean, handsome face creased in a wide smile.

Late that day, after the reception, Susan had slipped away to the quiet of her and Bill's bedroom. She sat alone on the bed, crying, ruining the makeup Shirley had insisted on helping her apply for the occasion. When Bill found her there, she couldn't tell him why she was crying. She didn't know why. She just was. Bill sat with her on the bed and held her hand without speaking. They stayed like that, holding hands, until the last of the daylight faded from the room.

Over the last couple of years, Susan had become neglectful about keeping up the family albums. Then Bill died, and she had stopped doing almost everything she used to do. The last picture she had pasted in was one of Shawn and her standing by his car. His old Ford sedan was packed full of things he was taking with him to college. Shawn was leaning against her, his arm around her shoulders, his cheek touching her hair. He had inherited his father's strong, wiry body; dark-green eyes; and fair complexion, but not Bill's straight, blond hair. Meagan had her father's hair, but Shawn had a dark mop of wild curls like his mother's.

The photograph showed them smiling. Shawn held one hand up in a relaxed wave. Susan had accompanied him on the twelve-hour drive to Santa Barbara, his loud music playing most of the way. Within an hour of leaving the house, she had wanted to scream and throw his case of tapes out the car window. On the plane ride back to Farhaven, listening to the drone of the plane's engines, she would have given almost anything to arrive home to music blasting out of his bedroom one more time.

Susan shut the album and set it on the table. She stood up and stretched. It was starting to grow light outside. She checked the clock on the kitchen wall: seven o'clock. Meagan would be getting ready for work. Susan picked up the phone and dialed Meagan's number. She could see her daughter clearly—her long, blond hair clipped back in a ponytail at the nape of her neck, her green eyes, so much like Bill's. Both of the children more closely resembled Bill than her.

When Meagan answered, Susan went through their new ritual of her reassuring Meagan that everything was fine, that she had phoned to chat, not because there was an emergency of some sort. Then she listened while Meagan told her about how busy her life was, how demanding her job was, how complicated everything was.

Meagan finally slowed down enough to ask her mom what she had been doing. Susan told her that she was working on a new photo project, although she left out the part about the bear. She was sure she shouldn't mention the bear, especially about trying to photograph a wild bear close to his den at night. No, she definitely didn't need to tell Meagan that.

"What type of project?" Meagan asked.

"It's in the woods. Pictures of the trees and, if I'm lucky, some wildlife."

"You shouldn't go into the woods alone. It isn't safe." Meagan hadn't worried about Susan spending time in the woods alone before Bill died. Now she seemed to worry about so many things, including Susan's safety. This had become almost an obsession with Meagan.

"But I won't be alone," Susan said, going for the cheerful and confident approach. "I'll have Chance with me."

"Oh for heaven's sake, Mom. Chance won't be any help at all if you fall or a wild animal attacks you. You shouldn't be in the woods unless someone else is with you, another person, not your dog."

Susan didn't know how to respond to this. Meagan was always quick to form opinions and not shy about saying whatever came into her mind, but she had never been this harsh before, not with Susan anyway.

Meagan was still talking, saying something about Shirley going with her into the woods. Susan pressed her fingers to her lips to keep from laughing out loud at this. Shirley hated walking anywhere that didn't have a paved path and a bench here and there to rest on if need be. "I'll talk to her about it," Susan said, knowing there wasn't a chance in the world she would ask Shirley to go with her into the woods to photograph a wild bear.

There was a short, awkward silence. Then Meagan said, "I was going to call you this weekend. I wanted to let you know that Peter and I won't be able to come home for Thanksgiving this year. He wants to spend it with his grandmother in Nevada. She's getting old. After Dad…well, Peter wants to spend time with his grandmother while he can. We'll be with you at Christmas, though." Meagan's words ran together in one long sentence, as if she wouldn't get them said if she stopped even to breathe.

"Oh," Susan said, looking around her living room. "That's fine. I mean I understand, and Christmas isn't that far away." She could hear Meagan moving and pictured her pacing or rocking from one foot to the other. Meagan could never hold still. Even as a baby, she had been busy discovering her toes and ears and squirming under Susan's hands while having her diaper changed.

"I'm sorry, Mom," Meagan said.

"Don't be sorry. It's fine. Really." Susan hoped Meagan couldn't tell that she was lying. How was she ever going to get through this holiday alone?

"What about Shawn? Will he be coming home for Thanksgiving?"

"No. He only gets two days off from classes, and he has to work on the weekend. It's such a long drive. We decided he should wait until Christmas to come home."

"So you're going to be alone?" Meagan asked.

"I'll go over to John and Shirley's. They've already invited me." She didn't even blink at the lie. She could go there if she wanted. Shirley would ask her to join them if she knew that Meagan and Shawn wouldn't be coming home for the holiday, but after the other night, Susan wasn't sure that was a good idea.

"I'm glad you won't be alone. I wish we were coming there, this year especially, but Peter has been talking about this for some time now."

"I understand, Sweetie. It'll be fine."

"Well, I don't understand it. Not one little bit," Meagan said. "Why do we have to go to Peter's grandmother's this year?"

Susan didn't know what to say to this. All the reassuring and polite things that she would normally have said about someone else in this situation wouldn't come. This wasn't someone else. This was her, and she was going to be alone on Thanksgiving for the first time in her life.

Before Susan could come up with some sort of response, Meagan announced that she had to go or she would be late for work. This, too, had become a part of their relationship: Meagan would abruptly end the conversation by announcing that she had to get off the phone to do one thing or the other. At first Susan had found these sudden dismissals hurtful, but now she had grown used to them. She told her daughter that she loved her, said a quick goodbye, and set the phone's receiver down in its cradle.

Susan gazed out the living room window, her hand still resting on the phone. After Bill's death she had felt adrift. At unpredictable moments the house would tip and sway, leaving her to grasp onto the doorframes or the backs of chairs for balance. "Unbalanced." Susan said the word softly, testing the feel of it. She lifted her hand off the phone. Now it was time to go.

———————

The morning was sunny and crisp when Susan and Chance entered the forest. Over her shoulders were her camera case and the daypack containing trail mix, water, and the collection jars David had given her.

There was a thin coating of dew on the dark-green huckleberry bushes lining the trail. Susan ran the berry stems through her hand, letting the ripe berries fall into her palm. She loved their tart taste. Of all the wild berries that grew on the north coast—huckleberries, blackberries, Himalayan, salal (as far as she could tell, only Labrador retrievers and black bears ate these), salmonberries, and thimbleberries—huckleberries were her favorites.

The air was alive with birds fluttering about and singing, more than Susan had ever seen in one place before. Every branch jiggled with a smorgasbord of small birds. Bill used to call these birds LBJs (little brown jobs) because it was close to impossible to tell one from the other. She felt as though she had wandered into some type of bird convention, full of a little business and a whole lot of gossip. Susan laughed in delight at the chaotic movement and sound. Chance ran ahead with a stick in his mouth, not seeming to notice the birds at all. True to his breed, he was mostly interested in fetching for his people. To him, these birds had nothing to do with Susan, so they were insignificant.

On the ridge trail above the creek, Susan began looking for a new way down into the canyon. Her plan was to follow the creek in the direction of the cave tree until she found some type of shelter a safe distance from the den where she could set up to photograph the bear.

The canyon walls were steep here, way too steep to descend. Susan walked along the ridge, examining the edge. Eventually she found a narrow opening through the brush, heading down at a severe angle. After a short hesitation, Susan stepped over the lip of the canyon.

Within yards, the canyon wall dropped off sharply, and Susan lost her footing. She slid feet first, grabbing onto any exposed root or branch she could get hold of to keep from plummeting to the bottom. At one point she lost control and skidded and bumped along until the canyon leveled off and she was able to come to a stop.

She got up, breathing hard. She rubbed leaves and dirt off her pants and inspected her hands for cuts. Chance ran to her and pressed his nose against her leg. Susan stretched her arms over her head and shook out her legs. To Chance she said, "It's okay. I'm fine. But we're not coming this way again."

After making sure her camera equipment had survived the fall, Susan started down the creek bed. She hadn't gone far when the creek widened out, cutting into the hillside on one side of the canyon and flowing up against a vertical rock face on the other. She either had to climb up the bank to find a way around or wade through the water. Wading seemed the fastest and easiest choice.

The frigid, calf deep water ran like ice into her boots. Jagged, slippery rocks lined the creek bottom. Susan sucked in a gulp of air and kept going, her arms held out to her sides for balance. To make matters worse, Chance was frolicking up and down the creek, splashing her with each pass.

"Chance, stop that," she said. This isn't going to work, Susan thought. Next time, we're going the other way. I don't care what that bear thinks about it.

At about the same time the creek narrowed and she was able to walk on dry ground again, she caught a glimpse of the cave tree in the distance. Susan began searching for a place to set up. She stopped next to every large tree and rock and looked through the telephoto lens on her camera. In each case, either another tree or a rock blocked the view of the den. If she went past the den and down the creek the other way, she would be on the wrong side of the den's opening. In front of her was the shelter behind the rock she had found last time. David had said it was too close to the bear's den, but what if it was her only choice?

When Susan reached the rock, she ducked under the fallen tree and lay down on her belly. She stretched out around the rock far enough to see into the clearing. In this light, she could see inside the den. The bear wasn't there.

She called Chance to her and gave him the command to lie down and stay. She moved away from the rock to check if he was visible from the other side. He wasn't. She walked toward the rock. It wasn't until she was almost behind it that she was able to see Chance. Even then it was difficult to see him in the shadows under the tree.

The possibility of the bear seeing them wasn't the real problem. He was more apt to hear or smell them. There wasn't much she could do about that other than to stay as quiet as possible and hope the wind currents didn't give them away.

Susan scrunched in close to Chance under the fallen tree. It was a tight fit, but it would work for one night. "We'll be nice and warm at least," she told Chance. He licked her face, one long chin-to-cheek tongue swipe. "You silly dog," she said, scratching him behind his ears. He stole one more lick. "Stay," she told him. She scooted out from under the tree and got the collection jars from her pack.

She was squatting beside one of the older piles of scat when she noticed the light had changed. She lifted her head and saw that the sun had moved over into the tree line on the lip of the canyon. She checked her watch. It was almost one-thirty. The hike here had taken longer than she had realized.

If she was going to drop the samples off at the college before David left for the day, she had better hurry. Susan quickly finished collecting the samples, snatched up her camera case and the daypack, and, with Chance ahead of her, started up the path out of the canyon.

They reached her van in record time, and she drove straight to the college. It wasn't until she found David's office door locked that Susan remembered that this was the day he had classes all afternoon and evening. Disappointed, she was turning to leave when she noticed a small bulletin board attached to the wall next to the door. A message was pinned to it instructing students to drop papers off at the department office, room 107.

Susan found the correct room number and asked if she could leave a few sample jars and a note for Professor Sharpton. A woman with short, curly gray hair; thick glasses; and a round, cheerful face squinted up at her from behind a typewriter. "Right over there, Hon," she said, smiling and waving toward a cardboard box marked with David's name.

Susan picked up a pad of paper from the counter and, using a pen tied with a long string to the edge of the counter, wrote: David, here are the samples of bear scat you asked for, and the longitude and latitude numbers that are closest to the bear's den. I found a good observation spot and will be going back there tomorrow to set up for the first time. Wish me luck, Susan.

She placed the note and the jars into his box. She felt a slight twinge of guilt for not mentioning her plan to set up behind the rock. David disapproved of that location, so the less said the better. She could always tell him later. Besides, this was her project, not his.

The next morning Susan woke up before sunrise, too excited and on edge to sleep. She opened the camera case to reassure herself that she had enough film and that the Minolta and both lenses were in good shape. She then emptied her backpack and checked each item against her list. She repacked meticulously, again putting the Nikon under the sleeping bag to cushion it and making a mental note of where she placed everything else. She didn't want to be fumbling around in the dark trying to find something.

She added a small amount of kibble for Chance. She would feed him before they climbed down to Woolly Creek. He shouldn't have to go without food all night after such a long walk. On the other hand, she didn't want dog food in her pack when they were close to the bear. She also packed a cheese sandwich and an apple for her lunch. Trail mix would have to do for the rest of time she was in the woods, but she wanted more than that before she headed down to the creek.

Her pack ready, Susan ate her usual breakfast of oatmeal and then washed her few dishes. By now the sky had lightened. From the kitchen window she could see the vegetable garden. The pea vines hung over the wire trellis, brown and limp, and the corn was way past its prime. It was time to put the garden to bed for the year.

The old freezer in the garage already contained more vegetables than she could eat, and there were rows and rows of canned beans and beets in the pantry left over from last year. It would be a waste of time to harvest and husk bushels of corn to have it sit in plastic sacks in the freezer until she tossed it all in the compost next year. Why not skip the freezing part and throw the corn, ears and all, in the compost now?

Susan pictured herself madly yanking corn stalks out of the ground and tossing them onto the compost pile, her wild hair flying around her face. What would Bill think? She had always made sure they used or gave away every bit of food they grew, but things were different now. Everything was different now.

"Maybe I'll let the ravens and the coons have the corn this year," she said out loud to nobody. Then to Chance, "We should go. We need a day in the woods."

Susan entered the woods feeling that something wasn't right. The weather felt wrong somehow, too hot, too quiet. The yellowing leaves on the alders fell from their own weight in the humid morning air. She willed herself to be calm. She didn't need her imagination running away with her now. Carrying both the backpack and the camera case had to be what was making her feel uneasy. She was used to carrying the camera case, but the backpack was way too heavy and uncomfortable. She kept fiddling with the waist belt and shoulder straps, trying to get them adjusted correctly.

An hour into the hike, Susan was already hot and sticky. A thin coating of dust clung to the sweat on her arms and face. She laid the pack and camera case in the shade and joined Chance as he ate huckleberries. The berries were still juicy, but there weren't as many as there had been a week ago. She had learned from David's manual that a good berry and nut crop would keep bears close to their home range. During years when native foods failed, most bears would leave in search of food, especially in the fall. A male bear could wander more than a hundred miles from his home territory. Susan hoped that the bear in Woolly Creek was fat and happy and would return home at dusk.

She stopped once more on the ridge above the creek. She fed Chance and ate the sandwich and apple she had brought for her own lunch.

Early in the afternoon they reached the original path they had taken down to the creek. A hot breeze had begun to blow, drying the sweat on her face. The tops of the tallest trees swayed in small circles. Susan's skin prickled. The warm wind bothered her. Years ago on a hot, windy October day—a day much like this—fire had swept through a section of wooded land north of Farhaven. Since that day, warm winds in the fall always made her think of forest fires. She ran her hands through her hair and looked once more at the treetops before motioning for Chance to go ahead of her down the path to the creek.

At the bottom of the path, Susan hooked one end of the leash to Chance's collar and clipped the other end to her belt. She skirted around the bear's tree, staying as far away as possible from the den entrance. The bear wasn't there and most likely wouldn't return until just before dark. Susan removed her pack, and with Chance close beside her, climbed behind the rock.

Even though the large trees shaded the canyon, the air was still unusually warm. In her shelter under the fallen tree, Susan smoothed out the canvas tarp and unrolled her sleeping bag on top of it. She put the small flashlight, the pepper spray, and the Nikon close to her sleeping bag where she could reach them easily. She fastened the Minolta with the telephoto lens to the tripod, opened the three legs, and set it up next to the rock where there was a good view of the den. Now all there was to do was wait.

It was almost dark when a strong wind gusted through the treetops. Susan had been examining the den opening through the telephoto lens, checking whether there was enough light to see into it. She sat back from the camera and looked at the huge trees all around her. The wind stopped. The trees stood still. She breathed the word "hush" into the quiet air while holding a finger to her lips, a habit left over from calming fussy children.

Seconds later another blast of wind shook the trees, making a loud rushing sound. The trees squeaked and banged against each other. The air became still and the forest quiet again but only long enough for Susan to take a breath. Then the night erupted in chaos. The wind slammed into the trees, howled through the steep, narrow canyon, and lifted the water in the creek up in waves.

Susan crawled behind the rock with Chance. She sat hunched over, her knees to her chest. The trees whipped in large erratic circles, groaning and screeching. It sounded for all the world like mad beasts had been set loose in the woods. "Please stop," Susan whispered.

Chance pressed against her and tucked his head under her arm. She was unable to think, her mind numbed by the continual thrashing and shrieking of the trees. She was beyond fear, beyond any emotion. Life had closed down to this space behind the rock. Now there was nothing but her and Chance and the wind.

The wind gusted on and off all night. Branches snapped and broke all around them. Late in the night there came a much louder crack very close to them. Susan's eyes flew open. She bent over Chance, wrapping her arms around him. The earth shook with the force of a large tree falling nearby. I'm going to die here, she thought. A tree is going to crush me and Chance.

She formed an image of her children, held onto it as if it were a life raft. All their lives, even before they were born, when they were safe in her womb, she had worried she would lose them somehow. She feared she would turn away at one critical moment and they would be gone. Now she would be the one who was gone because she had come into the woods alone during a windstorm. More than anything else, she was afraid she would make orphans of her children.

Many hours later the wind calmed. For the first time since the wind had picked up, Susan wondered where the bear was. She looked around the rock at the den opening. There was enough light from the three-quarter moon to see that the den was empty. She scooted back under the tree and waited for morning to come.

As daylight entered the canyon, the wind slowed to a soft breeze and then stopped altogether. Exhausted and sore, Susan came out from behind the rock and checked the bear's den. He hadn't come back during the night. She turned in a slow circle, taking in the damage the wind had done. Fallen branches, some as big around as her leg, covered much of the creek bed. Just feet away, a large fir tree lay across the creek, its entire root ball ripped out of the ground.

"Let's get out of here," Susan said to Chance. He was still hitched to her belt. Hastily she gathered her things. She took the Minolta off the tripod, slid the tripod into the side pocket of the backpack and put the Minolta and the telephoto lens in the camera case. She stuffed everything else randomly into her pack and started up the path. She didn't remember to unhook Chance until they were halfway up the steep incline.

He was miles from his territory. He had traveled all day to reach an area he knew would be full of ripe huckleberries. He had been coming here for years, first with his mother and then by himself. As the days shortened and became colder, food was all that mattered. Hunger decided everything.

He was eating mouthfuls of berries when a warm wind swirled around him. Head up, sniffing, he recognized a change in the air.

He continued to eat, stopping to sniff the air as he chewed. At dusk the wind came up hard. It was time to find shelter. He ran, sensing danger in the wind. There was no time to get home. He reached a hillside and used one large paw to swipe at the dirt. He found a spot under an overhang where the dirt was firm and dry. Here he dug with both front paws, throwing dirt under his belly and back between his hind legs. A sense of urgency drove him on.

It had grown dark by the time the hole was deep enough to hold him. The storm had turned into a wild thing, and the fear of it was on him. He curled as far into the bank as he could get. He didn't sleep. He listened to the storm seethe around him. The wind tore large branches off the trees and hurled them against the hillside.

He could hear the loud explosions of trees breaking and falling throughout the forest. He shifted deeper into the hole.

Broken branches and twigs were scattered all along the ridge trail. In one section, a number of small trees had fallen like giant pick-up sticks across the trail, completely blocking the way out of the woods. Branches stuck up from the trees' trunks in a tangled mass. The air carried the resinous scent of freshly cut Christmas trees. Chance scampered over and under the trunks and protruding limbs with ease. Susan followed behind, shoving and pulling her way through the branches. At one point the backpack snagged, held firmly by a redwood limb wedged under the frame. Susan was inching forward in a daze, moving so slowly it took her a second or two to realize that she was stuck. She wiggled backwards and twisted until she broke free.

She wanted to laugh, or maybe cry. Here she was, trapped under the tree rubble by her possessions. She was on the edge of hysteria, too fatigued to think rationally. She shrugged out of the backpack and dragged it behind her until she was clear of the fallen trees and could put it on again, hardly noticing where she was or what she was doing.

By the time she and Chance reached the van, her arms were scratched and bleeding in places. Chance fell into a deep sleep the minute his head touched the seat. Susan's hands were shaking with fatigue, and she fumbled a bit fitting the key into the ignition.

The phone was ringing when Susan opened her front door. She flopped down onto the couch and let the machine answer it. Shirley's voice said,

"Susan, this is Shirley. I wanted to make sure you're all right after that storm last night."

Susan rushed to pick up the receiver. She didn't need Shirley worrying about her again. "Hi, Shirley. Yes, I'm fine."

"Oh, you are there. Did you lose any trees last night?"

Susan sat down and gazed out the living room window. "I haven't been outside to check, but I don't think so. How about you?"

"There's lots of stuff in the yard to rake up, but no real damage. What a storm! We heard on the news this morning that some gusts were over eighty miles an hour. I couldn't sleep at all last night."

"No, I didn't sleep much either." Susan felt punch-drunk. She couldn't focus her eyes, and there was a faint ringing in her ears.

"Oh, I almost forgot. One of your neighbors shot a bear yesterday afternoon. John heard about it at work."

Susan stood up so fast, the room seemed to tip. She moved to the window and stared sightlessly out at her front yard. "Who?" she all but shouted. "Who shot a bear?"

"That crazy neighbor of yours. You know who I mean, Hank something or other? He lives in the blue house about half a mile up the road from you."

"Richardson? Hank Richardson?" Susan asked.

"Yes, he's the one. I guess this bear had been getting into his garbage on and off all summer. He called Fish and Game, and they told him to clean up his garbage situation. Apparently, this wasn't what he wanted to hear. He left some meat out and waited for the bear to show up. Now he's telling people he has bear steaks for the winter."

"Shirley, I've got to go. I'll call you later," Susan said and hung up the phone. She had a history with Hank, knew full well the kind of man he was. Years ago she had sold him a little Nubian buck, a beautiful animal with long, spotted hound-dog ears and a wide, black face. Hank had said he wanted the goat to eat the berry vines in his pasture.

It was from Molly Hampstead, Hank's nearest neighbor, that Susan had learned the plight of the goat. Molly was a large woman, over six feet tall and weighed close to two hundred pounds, most of it muscle. Even with all of that, she was timid. Her voice was so low that Susan could barely hear her when Molly cornered her in the market to tell her about the goat. She told Susan that Hank was keeping the goat tethered on a chain hooked to a spike driven into the ground. Each time the goat had grazed the field in a circle the length of the chain, Hank would pull the spike and hammer it into a new spot.

———

The tense knot of fury. The impatient pacing. The overwhelming desire to do something, anything to make this right.

Susan met Bill at the door when he got home from work that night to tell him about it. "No animal should have to live like that," she fumed. She asked Bill to go with her to get the goat back, to buy him back if they had to.

Bill refused. "Hank bought that goat free and clear," he said. "It's none of our business any longer."

Susan went on ranting about Hank's cruelty, his nastiness, until Bill raised his hands in a surrendering gesture, interrupting her. "Hank's hard to figure. He spent all last weekend working without pay on the boys' softball field. I saw him out there myself, laughing with the kids. Yet he can keep his animals chained up all their lives and not think a thing of it. He has a different attitude about animals than we do, and he can be hotheaded. I don't want you going anywhere near him. Let this one go, Susan. Please."

Less than a month later, Susan was in town when she learned that a pack of neighborhood dogs had killed the goat. The dogs had nipped at the goat, chasing him around and around until the chain was wrapped up tight to the stake and the goat was unable to move. The dogs had torn his neck and belly open.

———

Susan forgot about how tired she was. She was enraged all over again about the poor little goat, and about the bear, Hank's latest victim. She stormed out the door, determined to confront Hank, heedless of the consequences.

Hank was in his front yard, dragging a large broken branch across the lawn. Crab pots were scattered around the yard. The beginning of crab season was weeks away, but these pots were already wet and smelled of fish. Susan suspected Hank might have been poaching.

"Hank," Susan called. She slammed the van's door and strode toward him.

"Susan," he said, as if he had been waiting for her. He let go of the branch and ran his sleeve across his face.

Susan stopped in front of him. "I heard you shot a bear yesterday. Is that right?"

"I don't see how that is any of your business." He shifted his weight from one foot to the other.

"I want to know if it's true. Did you kill a bear yesterday?"

"You should go on home. I'm sure you have some wind damage to deal with. I know I do."

"Hank, please tell me. Did you kill a bear? I have to know." Her voice sounded desperate even to her.

"Listen, I don't want to hear any more opinions about nature's sweet creatures." He leaned closer to her. She could smell the stale odors of bacon and tobacco on his breath. "Nobody wants to deal with wild animals when they threaten my family. So what if I take care of them myself? So what? It's my property, and I want you off it right now, you hear?" He was shorter than her but outweighed her by fifty pounds or more. He thrust his chest forward, scowling.

Susan took a step back. Resisting the urge to run, she turned and walked to her van. She had already climbed halfway in when she saw it, nailed like a rug to the side of Hank's woodshed. The bear had been skinned and the hide cut open at the belly and down each leg. The head hung back, the mouth open, the large canine teeth looking yellow in the sunlight. The bear's empty eye sockets stared right at her.

Susan didn't move, unable to turn away. Hank had followed her to the van. He looked sideways at the bearskin. "Now that you got what you came for, get on out of here. Like I said before, this is none of your business." Susan met his eyes. He glared at her. She looked away and got into her van. She took two deep breaths to stop her hands from shaking and backed out of the driveway.

The minute she got home she called David's number at the college. She wasn't sure if he would be there—she had lost track of what day of the week it was—but he answered on the first ring, saying, "Sharpton here."

"David, it's Susan."

"Susan, good. I got your message yesterday, but I assumed you had changed your mind about going into the woods because of the storm warning."

"No, I didn't hear the warning. I went, but the bear didn't come."

"You went? You were out there in that storm? Good Lord. That must have been quite the night."

"Yes," Susan said, remembering the howling wind, the screeching trees. "It was. But the bear didn't come to his den, and when I got home I found out that one of my neighbors shot and killed a bear yesterday. He'd been complaining all summer about the bear getting into his garbage. I heard he put food out to bait the bear into his yard and then shot it. I'm worried. What if this was...?" She was unable to finish.

David sighed and said, "I hate this kind of thing. So few wild bears get to die of old age. Nearly all adult bears are either shot or poisoned sooner or later, usually sooner." He sounded weary and sad. "Bears have so few cubs to begin with. In low food years they often have no cubs. Any bear killed in a situation like this one with your neighbor is a senseless and tragic loss."

Susan pictured the stuffed bear in the display case outside his office door. She forced herself to ask, "Could the bear my neighbor killed be the one from Woolly Creek?"

"No, not if this bear your neighbor shot had been eating garbage. When we analyzed the fecal samples you collected, there was no sign of garbage—no plastic sacks, no chicken bones, nothing like that. We found grass and lots of berry seeds. In the older samples, we found some deer hair and bird bones, but nothing indicating contact with humans."

Susan sat on the edge of the chair, her throat tight, her eyes burning. Don't cry, she told herself. Don't let this man hear you cry. She steadied her voice and said, "But he didn't come back to his den."

"There are many reasons why he might not come to this den every night. This time of year bears are putting on fat. They will often travel long distances to find food, especially the males. They tend to bed down whenever and wherever they get tired. Assuming this is a male, maybe he got caught out in that storm and holed up somewhere for the night." After a short pause, he added, "And there is the possibility that he smelled you and your dog and abandoned this den." He cleared his throat. "You shouldn't have been out there last night. It wasn't safe. I wish I had known you were going." David exhaled into the phone. Then there was silence. Susan felt the space between them stretch out until she wondered if the line had been disconnected. At last, he said, "Susan." Just that—her name.

She waited, but he didn't say anything more. She gripped the phone tighter and said, "I have to go. I haven't eaten, and I need to get some sleep. It was a long night."

"Yes, yes of course," he said briskly. "You will call me when you're ready to go into the woods again?"

"I will," she said, and gently set the phone's receiver down in its cradle.

She was almost sick with emotions. This was about more than the anger she felt because of Hank killing a bear. Was it how David had said her name? She lay down on the couch and curled her legs up to her chest. She remembered a day shortly after she and Bill had bought this place, the two of them hot and sticky, wrapped in each other's bodies on the old, brown linoleum floor of the kitchen. Wild animal sex is what Shirley had called it when, years later, Susan had told her about that day and the many others like it.

For Susan, it was an exquisite time of uninhibited passion and love. She and Bill would stop in the middle of laying hardwood floors or painting walls and fall together, hands and tongues probing everywhere until they were both sweaty and limp. After Meagan's birth, sex became more of an event by appointment, arranged around naps and babysitters. It was pleasant and satisfying, but it no longer had anything wild or unanticipated about it. It was familiar, predictable, easy sex.

Except for that afternoon about a month before Bill died when he had come home unexpectedly as she was getting out of the shower.

———◆———

Warm steam drifting around her, the scent of lavender shampoo fresh in her hair, the hum of the ceiling fan. Bill standing in the doorway.

Susan jumped. "You scared me," she said. "What are you doing home? Is something wrong?"

"I forgot my Skilsaw." He watched while she wrapped a towel around her damp body, tucking it in above her breast. "You're a beautiful woman," he said.

She was stunned, breathless even, when he came to her, pulling the towel away and wrapping his arms around her waist. They kissed, long and slow. His sandpapery hands caressed her skin. She began to pull at his work clothes with an intensity she had all but forgotten.

They walked, hand in hand, to their bedroom, to their bed. Bill sat on the edge of the bed while Susan undid his clothing—suspender clips, buttons, zipper, bootlaces—tossing each item to the floor, running her hands over his skin as she did. They knew every part of each other's body after more than twenty-six years of marriage. There were no unknown curves, no unexplored hollows.

Now, mixed in with a gentle familiarity, was a new sense of urgency. The pure joy of it made Susan throw her head back and laugh out loud as her body arched to meet his.

Afterward they lay beside each other in the bed, Bill's fingertips lightly stroking her side. A short time later he lifted up on his elbow, kissed her softly on the lips, and said, "Thank you, Miss, but I'm a working stiff and must get back to it."

They laughed about their tryst at dinner that evening. Both of them were a bit shy, not used to this rediscovered sexuality. She asked him what he had told John about being late getting back to work.

"Oh, I told him you and I had a nooner," he answered, smiling sheepishly.

"You didn't?"

"Yes, I did. I don't think he believed me, though. We're old, you know. Old people don't behave like that." He took her hand in his and kissed it gently, a big, boyish grin spreading across his face.

There had also been all those times when she was irritated with Bill in the months before his death. It was nothing he did that caused this feeling, nothing new. It was his mere presence, the noise that surrounded him.

When he was home, Bill took over the usually quiet house with sound from the television or the radio. Sometimes in the evenings when he had the TV on, she would feel overly hot and crowded. She would go stand in the bedroom and breathe in the cool, dark air. Even on the day he had come home early to find her getting out of the shower, she had at first been annoyed. Before he touched her, she had thought: What is he doing home now?

Susan fell into a deep sleep there on the couch. Her dreams were long and complicated. She walked the streets of strange cities, full of beckoning doorways shrouded in dank, clinging vines.

By morning the wind was back, blowing sheets of rain against the house. Susan watched from the kitchen window. The trees beyond the pasture bent and swayed and rain battered the tattered cornstalks. After months without rain, the dry ground couldn't absorb all this water at once. Muddy streams flowed over the top of the vegetable garden and across the pasture, washing away the fertile soil and turning the ground the color of weak coffee.

Susan ran her hand along the edge of the sink. Her eyes roved restlessly from one side of the pasture to the other. What was it she used to do on stormy days when she couldn't be out in the woods? All she could see was a hazy impression of a stranger, a woman who cleaned and gardened and drove children around. She recalled a line from an old folk song: Please don't let me come home a stranger. I couldn't stand to be a stranger. Only the words played through her mind, lyrics without a melody.

She did remember one long, wet winter holiday break when Shawn and Meagan had spent every day running in and out of the house with their friends. All she did, it seemed, was clean up muddy footprints. She had told Shirley that she was sure her children must think she always had a mop in her hands. "Hell, Shirley," she had said, "When I die they're apt to bury me with it as a tribute to how I spent my life."

"There are worse ways to be remembered," Shirley had said.

"There are? What?"

"How about as that strange old goat woman who lives at the top of the hill?"

Yes, there was that, Susan thought now, smiling.

Then the image of the bearskin nailed to Hank's shed came to her. She saw how it would look now, rainwater running out of its empty eye sockets and beading up on its stiff fur.

She couldn't stand being here any longer with nothing to do. She wanted to be in the woods, surrounded by trees. She wanted to see if the bear had come home. She let her mind return to Woolly Creek, felt the cold pressure of the rock on her spine and heard again the fury of the wind. She willed herself to stand up, to look into the bear's den.

The phone rang, shrill and loud. Susan glared at it. On the third ring, just before the machine would answer, she picked up the receiver.

"Hey, Mom. It's your son, Shawn." He always said this when he called, as if she had three or four sons and wouldn't know which one was on the other end of the phone unless he told her.

"Shawn, hi. How are you?"

"I'm fine. You sound sleepy. Did I wake you up?"

"No. I'm sluggish today, is all. It's raining, and I'm feeling a bit closed up inside the house."

"Did you lose your yellow rain jacket?"

"What?" Susan asked, momentarily losing track of what Shawn was saying. In her mind, she was drifting between her house and the forest.

"Don't you remember our yellow rain jackets? You never let a little rain stop you before. We used to go out in the rain all the time on your famous mud walks."

"That was fun," Susan said, remembering Meagan and Shawn dressed in their yellow rain jackets and black rubber boots. They would splash in every puddle, giggling with joy, while she followed slowly behind, keeping a close watch on them.

"Mom, are you there?"

"Oh, I'm sorry, honey. I was lost in the past." Lost. Was that where she was, lost somewhere in the middle of her life?

"I was saying that I bet Chance wouldn't mind a walk in the rain."

"You're right. He'd love it." Chance was lying with his head on her foot, his eyes open, gazing at nothing. Susan wiggled her toe, scratching him under his chin. "And I don't think he'll ever outgrow it."

"Right, mud's not my thing these days," Shawn said. Then, "Mom, I called because I talked to Meagan yesterday. She told me she wasn't coming there for Thanksgiving this year. I wish I could come home. I can't, though. It's such a long trip for a short visit. I can't take time off from classes right now, and I'm scheduled to work on the weekend."

"It's all right, really. I'll be fine here. I'm going over to John and Shirley's." When had it become so easy for her to lie to her children?

"That's good. That should be fun."

To change the subject, Susan asked, "How's school going? You haven't said much about your classes this quarter."

"They're okay. It's not easy being this far away from home. Particularly now."

"I know, honey. I wish we were closer, too. But you have your life there, your job and school, and you have so many good friends. We'll see each other soon. The winter break isn't that far away."

"I'm glad. I'm ready to be home." He paused. "Mom, I'd better get going. I have a study group meeting this morning. I love you."

"I love you too, honey," Susan said.

After placing the receiver back in its cradle, she sat staring at her lap, more troubled than ever. Talking to Shawn and Meagan was so difficult. All three of them kept their sadness hidden, leery of what might be unleashed if they expressed it. Most of the time they didn't mention Bill. They acted as though he were off at work, or maybe away on a short trip. This dance around grief took so much energy.

Then it came to her—Bill died six months ago today. "Six months," she said out loud. Had Shawn remembered this? He hadn't said anything about it.

She didn't want to dredge up the memory of Bill's death but couldn't stop herself. How had that day started? It had been unusually warm for April. She had washed the sheets and hung them outside to dry. And Bill, what had he worn to work that day? She couldn't recall. This troubled her. She wanted to remember forever their last morning together, but there wasn't anything special about it. Bill had eaten breakfast and left for work. There was nothing to make that day stand out from any other until—

Susan faced the window, saw the white sheets floating in the sunshine as if they were there. She felt pulled toward them, her grief unfurling and billowing out in the wind.

She had to stop this. She knew this plunge into depression all too well. She looked anxiously around for anything that would distract her. Her backpack was propped next to the firewood box where she had left it yesterday. Was it just yesterday? It seemed like such a long time ago now.

She dragged her pack into the center of the room and dumped everything out of it onto the floor. How much food and water would it take to stay in the woods for a few days? Gradually the idea took shape. She could go. She could go now and stay two or three days. There was nothing stopping her, nothing she needed to do.

She considered briefly the possibility that David had been right about the bear abandoning his den because he had smelled her and Chance there. She didn't want to believe this, but she couldn't know for sure unless she went back and checked for signs that the bear had been there since she and Chance had left last time.

Suddenly the panic she had felt during the windstorm—the certainty that she was going to die, the sorrow at her children's grief—returned to her. She walked to the window and checked the tops of the trees. They stood motionless, bent and laden with rain. The wind had stopped, and the rain had slowed to a constant drizzle. She could stay home and do, well, practically nothing. Or she could go out in the rain, maybe even another windstorm, and hike back to the bear's den by Woolly Creek.

In the end, she decided to go. "What do we have to lose?" she asked Chance. After all, the windstorm was probably the worst that could happen, and they had survived that.

She rummaged through her kitchen cupboards until she found a large bag of old trail mix stuck way back in the pantry. The small bag she had been carrying with her for the last two times in the woods wouldn't be near enough for three days. She filled six small, plastic sacks with trail mix and threw in an extra one just in case. Chance would also need food. He couldn't go three days without eating. With any luck, the bear would be full of berries and ignore the dog food. She rationed out three days' worth of kibble in plastic sacks and filled the four large water bottles. Chance could drink from the creek, but it wasn't safe for her. Many of the local waterways harbored giardia, which could make her dangerously ill.

When all of her gear and food supplies were in the pack, she sorted through her clothes, making sure she packed several pairs of dry socks, a change of pants, and a warm sweater. She added a half-full roll of toilet paper, wondering how she would deal with this necessity around a bear.

She tossed a couple more rolls of film into the camera case and tested the batteries in both cameras. She put the Minolta, the 50mm and tele-photo lenses, and the cable release back in the camera case and stowed the Nikon under the sleeping bag in the backpack. At the last minute, she threw the daypack in on top of the sleeping bag. It might come in handy to keep food and water close at hand during the night.

With the pack cinched up tight, she put on her dark-green rain jack-et (the yellow one long since gone), her waterproof pants, and her hiking boots. "Are you ready for an adventure?" she asked Chance. He sprang up at the sound of her voice, wagging excitedly.

Susan loaded Chance into the back of her van and slid the backpack and camera case in beside him. She went back inside to make sure she had turned off all the lights and damped the woodstove. The only thing left was to phone David. She had promised to let him know when she went back to the woods. She began dialing his number at the college but stopped before the fourth digit.

The memory of last night's sexual tension—the aching need to be touched, the feel of her and Bill's bodies joining together—was fresh in her mind. It would be better not to talk to David for a while. Let her emotions settle down a bit.

She replaced the receiver and reached for the pen and paper she kept by the phone and wrote: I've gone to the bear's den. If there's a problem, call Professor David Sharpton at the college. She added David's office phone number in case someone needed to know her exact location. She placed the note on the dinner table.

Nearly out the door, it came to her that she should phone Shirley. If for some reason Shirley stopped by here and saw this note, there was no telling what she would do. Susan dialed the number. The answering machine picked up. Susan was relieved that no one was home. At least she wouldn't have to try to explain this to Shirley or, worse yet, to John. When the machine beeped Susan said, "Hi, Shirley. It's Susan. Listen, the rain's getting to me. I'm going on a short trip with Chance to relax and take some photos. I'll call you when I get back. I'm all right, really, just wanting a change of scenery. I'll call you," she said again, and hung up.

This wasn't a complete lie. She was, after all, going on a trip to take photos. She had left out the part about the woods, is all. And the part about the bear.

(4)

Western Screech Owl

At the trailhead, Susan drove her van into the brush to shield it from the road. She didn't want people passing by to be able to see it easily. She was trespassing, after all, and not just for an afternoon but for several days. She let Chance out and shouldered her pack and camera case, groaning under their weight.

The redwood branches over the entrance to the trail hung bent and dripping. The top of her pack hit the lowest branch, knocking loose a cascade of cold water that ran down her neck and under her rain jacket, soaking her sweater and the collar of her shirt. Susan gasped and lurched, causing her feet to slide out from under her. She fell, landing first on her butt and then on her side.

"Great. Just great," she said, her voice echoing off the trees, sounding like it was mocking her. If she had pulled the hood on her rain jacket over her head this wouldn't have happened, but it wasn't raining that hard. She didn't like to use the hood when she was hiking unless it was pouring because it blocked her peripheral vision, making it difficult to see what was on either side of her. She rolled onto her hands and knees and tried to stand up. After a few faltering attempts, she was able to regain her footing. She rubbed her muddy hands on her even muddier pants and glared up the trail. It was now slick with mud. Brown rivulets coursed along the sides, in places overflowing to form large puddles across the trail's entire width. To keep from falling again she would have to walk slowly, which was not her natural pace, and she bristled at the thought of it. For her, the only way to walk was a full-out, long-legged stride. She had tried the easy hip-swaying saunter of her friends when she was in high school but had ended up feeling ridiculous. Her long legs didn't lend themselves easily to a sexy walk of any kind.

Even with the need to pay attention and to move slowly and carefully through the slippery mud, Susan couldn't concentrate on the trail. She kept hearing the way David had said her name on the phone last night, like he cared about her, like he was worried about her. She told herself to stop it. She didn't need this in her life. What she needed was to pay attention to where she was and what she was doing right now. But no matter what she told herself, she couldn't stop replaying the sound of David's voice saying her name. It wasn't until she skidded through a section of clay, almost falling again, that she managed to pull herself together and focus on what she was doing.

It took longer than it had last time for her and Chance to reach the ridge trail above Woolly Creek. Carrying the heavy pack through the slick mud and up the steep grade slowed her down more than she had anticipated. Gray mud covered Chance from head to foot. He looked like a totally different dog, some weird combination of brindle-colored pit bull and floppy-eared pound mutt.

A layer of mist engulfed the trees, filling the forest with the diffused sound of dripping water. The sky was dark gray. The dense, wet curtain of trees on either side of the trail screened out much of what little light there was.

Each time she took a step her right calf burned a little. She might have pulled a muscle when she fell. Her hips had raw spots from where the backpack's belt rubbed on them, and her shoulder muscles were aching. But she didn't want to stop to rest. She needed to reach the bear's den and get her camp set up before it got dark. She hoped the bear wasn't there already, staying out of the rain. She wouldn't know if the bear was there until she was right next to the den. If they did find themselves face to face, it would be entirely up to him what happened next. Other than the pepper spray, she had nothing to use as protection against a startled and possibly aggressive bear.

Susan trudged along, watching the trail in front of her. The mud was less thick here, and she had started to lengthen out her stride when she glanced up and stopped and stared. Ahead of her was the mass of broken branches and trees that had come down during the windstorm, burying a large section of the trail. How could she have forgotten about this? There didn't seem to be an easy way to get around it. The only thing to do was to climb through. She shoved and pulled her way forward, tree limbs banging and scraping the top of the backpack.

When the branches thinned out a bit, Susan picked up the pace, hoping to make up time. Almost instantly the backpack's waterproof cover snagged on a limb, bringing her to an abrupt halt. Cursing under her breath, Susan unhitched the waist belt, hunched out of the shoulder straps, and yanked the pack free, ripping a hole in the waterproof cover.

"Damn it!" she shouted, giving the pack a swift kick. "What was I thinking, bringing this much stuff?" She turned in the direction she needed to go. In front of her was a large tree that had fallen along the length of the trail, blocking one entire section of it. It hadn't been there right after the windstorm, had it? Surely she would have remembered this. It must have fallen since then, weakened by the high winds.

"Now what am I going to do?" Susan asked out loud. Chance, already halfway down the tree's length, turned at the sound of her voice and trotted back to her, moving easily over the rough bark. The fastest way to get past the tree would be to walk along the trunk as Chance had done, but she didn't trust her balance with the big pack on.

There must be something she could leave behind to make the pack lighter. Susan untied the waterproof cover and slid her hand through the tear, wondering if her supplies would still stay dry. The first thing she saw when she lifted the cover off was the daypack she had thrown in almost as an afterthought. It would be much easier to carry just the daypack and her camera case. She could take what food and gear she needed now and come back for more later.

She dumped her supplies out of the larger pack and sorted them into piles on the ground. She loaded the daypack with what she thought she would need for a night and a day in the woods: two bottles of water, two sacks each of trail mix and kibble, tarp, flashlight, pepper spray, spare pants, change of socks, Nikon, tripod, monopod, map, and compass. She rolled the extra sweater up and tied it around her waist under her rain jacket. The sweater she had on was still damp from the water running under her jacket at the trailhead, but it kept her warm enough while she was moving.

The sleeping bag was a problem: it was too big to fit into the daypack along with all her other supplies. She had enough clothes to stay warm without it. If need be, she could always get it later.

The roll of toilet paper had become a white, wet lump from sitting on the damp ground in the mist. Susan bit her lip, holding back a couple of Bill's choice cuss words. Why had she left it uncovered? It was too late now. Leaves and grass could work in place of toilet paper. Who would see her? Maybe the bear, but he wouldn't care. She chuckled at the thought of this. She grabbed up the soggy roll of paper and stuffed it, along with everything else she wasn't taking, into the backpack. She carried the backpack behind a large Douglas fir and stowed it there off the trail.

Walking on the log was a cinch with only the light daypack and her camera case to carry. From that point on she made good time, stopping only occasionally to drink from one of the water bottles and once for both her and Chance to pee. The drizzle had stopped, and shafts of sunlight filtered through the trees. Scores of robins were bathing in the puddles and hopping among the bushes. Others perched on the tops of small trees, which bent and swayed under their weight. The birds chirped and called to each other, forming a noisy symphony in the air around her. When Susan and Chance approached, the birds all fluttered up into the air. Chance glanced at them and trotted on, focusing on the trail in front of him.

At the path leading to the bear's den, Susan called Chance to her and told him to sit. She stood beside him, her head tipped to one side, listening. She could hear the rumbling of the creek far below, but nothing else. She gestured for Chance to go ahead of her down the path. This time, prepared for the descent, she dug in with the sides of her boots, making sure her downslope foot was securely in place before moving her other foot.

She clipped Chance to the leash at the bottom of the path. Together they approached the clearing, staying as far away from the den as possible while still being able to see inside. It was empty. The bear wasn't there.

As they neared the rock, Susan saw a single bear print, sunk about half an inch into the dirt and full of rainwater. She hadn't noticed it on her previous visits. Had she missed it somehow, or had the bear been here since the day of the windstorm? It looked like the footprint of a giant, chubby, barefoot child. She knelt and placed her hand inside the print. It was more than two inches longer and an inch wider than the spread of her hand, larger than any she had seen before.

She knew from David's manual that black bears usually weigh from about one hundred and twenty-five to three hundred pounds, but males could reach a weight of five hundred pounds or more. This was a big one, or at least he had big feet.

She scanned the area around her. The steep canyon walls rose up on either side of the creek bed, closing her in, making it impossible for her to get away from the bear if he charged her. Even if she were out in the open, she couldn't outrun any bear, but especially not one as large as this one had to be. In an effort to calm a growing sense of fear, she took in a deep breath and blew it out slowly. The size of the bear didn't make a difference, did it? "A bear is a bear, right?" she asked Chance. He was busy sniffing around the edge of the bear print and didn't seem to hear her, or maybe he didn't have an opinion about the size of this bear.

The sun had dropped below the tree line and the light in the canyon was fading fast. Susan quickly put the Minolta with the telephoto lens attached onto the tripod and set it next to the rock. She spread the tarp out under the fallen tree and laid the flashlight and pepper spray next to it. She tugged off her raingear and the damp sweater and pulled her dry sweater on over her shirt. Next she fed Chance a sack of kibble, making sure he didn't leave any uneaten on the ground. Then she leaned back in her tree shelter and ate small handfuls of trail mix and waited for nightfall.

The water level in the creek had risen considerably since the rains. Water surged between its banks and pressed down the canyon. Susan thought of the old expression wild and woolly, wondering if this was how the creek got its name. She stretched out and let the forest seep into her, allowing the sound of the rushing water to erase everything else. Gradually she drifted off to sleep.

Susan woke up with a start, confused. Where was she? She blinked and rubbed her hand across her face. Chance brushed her cheek with his nose. Then quivering, saliva frothing around his mouth, he shifted as far over as possible on the short leash, trying to see around the rock. Instantly alert, Susan sat up and took hold of the leash. She signaled for Chance to lie down and put her finger to her lips, telling him to be quiet. He lay with all his weight on his forelegs—his toes spread, his nails digging into the ground, his muscles flexed—and stared at the rock.

Susan rolled onto her chest and peeked around the rock. It was right after sunset, with enough light left to see blurry, colorless forms. And there was the bear! He stood out as a massive dark shape in front of the cave tree. He appeared to be swaying his head back and forth, his nose up. At the sight of him, Susan felt as if her heart had stopped beating. She tucked back behind the rock. "Please, please don't let him smell us," she whispered.

Over the roar of the creek, Susan heard a soft woofing sound. She looked around the rock. The bear turned in her direction. Although unable to see his face in the dim light, she had the impression that he was looking right at her. She didn't breathe, didn't even blink. Finally the bear turned away and dissolved into the darkness of the den.

Susan exhaled slowly and lifted up on her knees to look through the telephoto lens into the den. Even with the long lens, she could barely see the bear's bulky body in the den's charcoal blackness.

Tingling with fear, she ducked back under the fallen tree, pulling Chance with her. She held him close and stroked his neck and back.

She counted her breaths, starting at one and going on until she reached ten, then starting over again—a silent mantra in cadence with the beat of her heart, with the rhythm of her hand moving across Chance's coat. She worried that if she stopped, she would panic. Her leg muscles tightened with the need to flee.

Chance's breathing eased into the deep rhythms of sleep. Susan wiggled closer to him, using his body as insulation against the cold.

The fierce winds stopped as the morning light came. He stood up and shook. Dirt and leaves flew off his fur. Nose up, ears up. Scenting. Listening. The storm was over.

He started for home. He stepped clumsily over large branches and around downed trees. He stopped frequently to graze on the grass that grew in clumps along the trail, chewing while he watched the forest around him. He ate at every berry patch he found. He stopped often and lay down, his head resting on his crossed paws. As it grew dark, he found a dry place under a fallen log and curled up to sleep.

During the night it rained and rained. There was still rain in the morning, and wind was coming hard through the trees. Water dripped from his head and ran off his nose. He moved across the land in an easy, rolling stride. He was close to home when he smelled decaying meat. He snorted and turned toward the scent. He plodded closer. There it was, the half-eaten remains of a dead fawn partially buried in leaves. The scent of a mountain lion was all around it.

Screened by a stand of salal and blackberry vines, he curled his lips, tasting the air for any fresh trace of the lion. There was none. It was safe to eat.

He held the fawn down with one large paw and wrenched the meat free from the bones with his teeth. Blood covered his face and his paws. At times he stopped to lick at the blood on his face—his tongue wrapping around his nose—and to listen.

There was a change in the air. He ears pricked. He caught a slight stirring of movement. Nose up, sniffing. He smelled her, the mountain lion. The scent grew stronger. She was coming his way.

Almost here. Quietly, swiftly, he backed into the undergrowth.

The mountain lion stepped into the clearing. She sniffed the carcass and curled her lips, snarling. He watched, judging her size and speed. Without a sound, he slipped into the forest.

He entered the clearing in front of his den after the sun had set. The scent of the woman and the dog was all along the trail. He knew their scent. It was part of what he understood about the forest. Now it was stronger. He stopped and raised his nose. Was there movement behind the rock? He lowered his head. Waited. Nothing moved. No danger. It was getting dark, and he was tired. He grunted in mild irritation. He entered his den and was soon asleep.

Susan lay beside Chance. He slept with his nose touching her face, his moist breath puffing against her skin. She had stopped counting her breaths but kept running her hand over Chance's back. She envisioned sneaking away with Chance, either along the creek bed or up the canyon walls. But if they woke up the bear and he came after them, they wouldn't be able to outrun him.

Now that she had seen the bear, she knew she had made a serious mistake being this close to him, let alone sleeping near his den. She hadn't thought this through. What a stupid thing to do. Earlier when she had seen the size of the bear's print, she had told herself that size wasn't important. A bear is a bear. Except that this bear was a really big bear.

Next to her the creek hissed and gurgled. The haunting *whu-whu-whu-whu-whu-whu* of a western screech owl floated through the dark trees above her. Closer were the faint scrapings of little forest creatures—mice? beetles?—digging through the dead leaves covering the forest floor. Exhausted, lulled by the sounds of the woods, Susan fell asleep.

Later, in a dream, she and Chance were walking through the forest. She reached up to sweep a branch away from her face. Across from her was the bear. He faced her, his mouth open. She stood petrified, her camera halfway out of the case. The bear ambled toward her in slow motion. Her heart pounded in her chest. She watched the muscles on his shoulders rolling with each heavy toe-in step, saw the bend in his sharp claws. He came steadily closer, his head low, his ears back. She smelled the thick odor of his warm breath and wet fur. She needed to move away from him, tried to move but couldn't. Her limbs were frozen in place. The bear was a mere foot in front of her. Her heart raced and her arm flinched against Chance. He grumbled and moved away from her.

The need for food woke him. He left his den in the gray light of early dawn. He lowered his nose and sniffed. The scent of the woman and the dog was stronger in the damp, morning air. He walked, watchfully, noiselessly. Near the rock he stopped. With his nose and mouth flared open, he breathed in their odor. He took the memory of it with him as he climbed the path out of the canyon.

The dream fading, Susan pressed in closer to Chance. She lay there until her breathing slowed. The sun had cleared the horizon but had not yet reached the canyon floor. The damp ground seemed to have seeped into her bones, making her entire body cold and stiff. She rolled over slowly and looked around the rock at the den opening. The den was empty. She got up on her knees, leaned farther out away from the rock, and looked along the creek bed. There was no sign of the bear. Somehow he had managed to leave the canyon without making a sound or waking up her or Chance.

Susan slid back next to Chance. He sprang up and licked her face. "Do you think we could find him?" Susan asked, scratching behind Chance's ears. Her fear from seeing the bear last night was gone now, replaced by an impatient need to photograph him. Maybe if she hurried, if he was still on the trail above the creek, she would be able to find him. After all, black bears aren't usually aggressive, no matter how big they are. Are they?

Chance pawed at the daypack and whined. "All right. I'm hungry, too. We'll never be able to catch the bear anyway. He's too fast for us." Susan dug around in the pack until she found a bottle of water and what was left of the kibble and trail mix.

After they ate, Susan found her way up the creek bed to a place where she and Chance could pee far enough away from the bear's den that he might not be able to smell it. As she squatted, she ran her hand over the black stems and bright-green oval leaves of the maidenhair ferns that grew under the trees. She had first heard how these ferns were supposed to bring good luck from her neighbor Jean.

———————

The cold bite of a November day; the wild energy of Meagan, not quite four years old; the warm bundle of Shawn, three months in her womb. The pops and clicks of the oven heating up.

Susan was finally feeling well after weeks of morning sickness. She decided as a treat to make chocolate chip cookies. The oven was warming and the butter and sugar were in the bowl when she discovered she was one egg short. She hollered to Bill that she would be back in a minute and started out across the pasture and through the back gate to Jean and Randy's place.

Even on this cold morning, their front door was standing partway open. Jean always left the door open. She wanted people to be able to walk right in without a door to slow them down. Susan knocked on the doorframe and stepped inside, calling out to Jean. A fire blazed away in the woodstove in the tiny living room, making the small house feel like an oven. Susan peeked around the corner into the kitchen.

Jean was there, up on a chair, bent forward with her head buried in a cupboard. Containers of spices, cans of soup, jars of pickles, and assorted envelopes of powdered fruit drinks littered the counter top.

"Doing some winter cleaning?" Susan asked.

Jean stood up straight and turned toward Susan. She looked haggard and a bit crazed around the eyes. Her hair clung to her face in damp, gray ringlets, and beads of sweat coated her upper lip. Without so much as a hello, Jean said, "Robby moved out yesterday."

"Oh," was all Susan could think to say. Robby was the youngest of Jean and Randy's five children, the baby, the only boy, and the last to leave home. Susan knew he was preparing to leave for a job south of here but had lost track of the exact day he would move out.

"There was nothing else to do, and these cupboards haven't been cleaned in years." Jean was back to scrubbing. Her muffled voice echoed slightly from inside the empty cupboard.

The idea that Jean's cupboards had a speck of dirt in them was so unbelievable, all Susan could do was stare openmouthed at Jean's bony shoulder blades. Jean's oldest daughter had once told Susan that she could tell what day of the week it was by what her mother was doing. On Mondays, Jean scrubbed and waxed the floors. Tuesdays were for laundry. Each Wednesday the entire family worked in the vegetable garden in spring and summer or helped split and stack firewood in the fall and winter. Thursdays were set aside for big cleaning projects such as washing windows and wiping out cupboards. Fridays were for shopping and mending. Saturday was family day, the day to attend Little League and basketball games, or go to the beach, depending on the season. Sunday was the Lord's day, the day Jean spent cooking for church socials. Jean had everything organized. This tightly packed house bustled with life, expertly directed by this energetic little woman.

If the cupboards hadn't been cleaned in years, what had Jean been doing on Thursdays? She couldn't have been washing her windows every Thursday. Then it dawned on Susan, today was Saturday—family day. She wanted to tell Jean to leave the cupboards alone, that everything would be all right, but she couldn't get the words out. "Family day," Susan mouthed, pressing her hands on top of her belly. She could feel the warmth of it even through her clothing. The little fetus was heating up all of Susan to keep itself comfortable.

Susan coaxed Jean into leaving the cupboards long enough to fetch an egg and to walk with her to the slated gate that marked the border between their two properties. There, growing in the ditch alongside the gate, was a small clump of maidenhair ferns. Jean knelt and cupped the fronds in her hands. "If you touch them, they're supposed to bring you good luck," she said, smiling at Susan with a bit of her usual I-can-handle-anything attitude. Susan squatted beside her and ran her hands over the fronds. After a moment, Jean stood up, saying she had better get back to cleaning out the cupboards.

Susan cautioned her not to work too hard and waved goodbye. She shut and latched the gate behind her and hurried across the pasture, cradling the egg in one hand.

———◆———

Susan thought about all the things that had changed since that day. Jean had died about five years ago from some rare kidney disease. Randy had sold the place and rented an apartment close to where Robby lived. And now Bill was dead and Susan was alone. She brushed her hand once more across the delicate fern fronds. From this point on, she would need all the luck she could get.

133

Behind the rock, Susan collected her camera equipment and tossed the half-empty water bottle into the daypack. With Chance beside her, hooked to the leash, she started up the path out of the canyon.

The bear's footprints showed clearly in the wet dirt at the edge of the ridge trail above the creek. Susan followed them. The tracks would fade away for some mysterious reason, to reappear again, sometimes on the other side of the trail. Not far up the trail, she came across a fresh pile of bear scat full of undigested huckleberries and grass. A little farther on there was another pile. This one was green and runny with berries and something Susan didn't recognize, a hard, dark lump. She pushed at the lump with a stick, pulling it free from the rest of the scat and examining it closely. It was a deer hoof.

"Did he kill a deer?" Susan murmured. She had read something in David's manual about bears killing other animals. What was it? Oh, now she remembered: David had called black bears opportunistic. They would eat dead animals if they came across them, and they would occasionally kill an animal if the opportunity presented itself or if they were provoked. It was the word provoked that had caught her attention at the time. Exactly what would provoke a bear enough to cause it to kill?

Part of her wanted to turn back, to go home. There was so much here she didn't understand. That was the point, though, wasn't it, to learn about bears? The only way to do that was to stay close to this bear.

Susan followed the bear's tracks for a little over a mile when they suddenly disappeared. She kept going, checking both sides of the trail, but couldn't find where the bear had left the trail. The tracks were there and then they weren't.

She went back to where she had seen the last set of prints, on the side of the trail opposite the canyon. Susan pressed into the undergrowth next to them. The area was full of blackberry vines twisted around old fallen branches and young alder trees. Jagged thorns scraped her face and her arms through her sweater and shirt, caught on her pants, and trapped the leash until she and Chance could hardly move. This couldn't be the way he went. The bear was much bigger than she was. If she couldn't get through the brush, he couldn't. She backed up onto the trail, stepping on the berry vines to pull them free from her clothing.

The bear couldn't have evaporated. He had to have gone somewhere. Susan examined the dense growth that bordered the trail, trying to see an opening of some sort. She couldn't see one. She rubbed at her forehead with the back of her hand. Her hand came away streaked in blood from a thorn scratch above her eyes.

She continued to follow the trail, watching for any sign of the bear. Eventually she gave up. She was out of food and had only a small amount of water left. She needed to return to where she had left her backpack and restock her food and water. They were already heading in the right direction. They simply had to keep going.

The air was still cool, but the sun was shining. It was one of those exceptional days that marked the change from fall to winter. Pacific tree frogs sang in the puddles that had appeared during the rainstorm, their last grand song before winter fully set in. Every time Susan and Chance drew near a puddle, the frogs all through the forest stopped calling. As they moved past, the frog song would start up again. Throughout the day, this loud, intermittent cacophony of hundreds of noisy frogs chorusing accompanied Susan and Chance.

She stopped and drank the last of the water. A hollow gurgling sensation was coming from her stomach. She hadn't eaten anything since finishing off the last of the trail mix that morning. They had made it about halfway from the den to the place where she had left the backpack. If they were going to reach the pack, restock their supplies, and make it back to the creek before the bear returned, they would have to hurry.

Just thinking about walking farther made her stomach growl louder. She stretched, bending forward and backward at the waist. What she wanted to do was sit in the sun and eat a cheddar cheese and tomato sandwich. On toasted rye. With a big dill pickle on the side. But there wasn't a sandwich or anything else left to eat in the daypack, not even a loose raisin or nut. Her only option was to get back to where she had left her supplies.

When they came to the section of trail blocked by the fallen tree, Susan unhooked Chance from the leash: it was safer and easier to walk the length of the tree and climb through the branches without him tied to her. They reached the backpack sooner than she had expected. This pattern of ducking and high stepping over and around the branches was becoming a part of who she was and what she knew of this forest.

She opened the backpack right away and grabbed a bottle of water and a sack of trail mix for her and one of kibble for Chance. While she ate, she thought again about going home, spending the night in her safe, warm bed. What was she doing out here in the woods, sleeping on the ground? It didn't make any sense. None of this made sense. She wasn't a biologist. She was predictable and dependable. She took care of the house and tended the garden. She had no business going into the woods trying to photograph a wild bear, let alone sleeping next to one with only her dog and a canister of pepper spray for protection.

Then, as if it were right in front of her, she saw the bear hide nailed to Hank's shed, its empty eye sockets looking directly at her. At the time, all she had wanted was to get away from Hank, to never see him or the bearskin again. Her outrage at the senseless, needless killing of that bear grew the longer she was in the woods. David had said how so few wild bears lived long enough to die of old age; almost all of them were either shot or poisoned. Susan didn't think anything she did would change that, but she had to try. "All right, we'll go back. One more time," she said, looking up at the trees around her. "But this time I'm taking the sleeping bag."

It was early afternoon when Susan reached the creek bed and harnessed Chance to the leash. She reestablished her camp and readied the Minolta on the tripod. She was determined to stay awake until the bear came back and to be awake again in the morning before he left. The problem was, she had never been able to stay awake all night, even as a teenager. Despite how motivated she was, she always ended up falling asleep, sometimes right in the middle of a late-night movie with her date's arm hot and heavy on her shoulders.

She could easily stay awake until the bear returned to his den tonight, which, if yesterday was any indication, should be around sunset. The real challenge was waking up before the bear left in the morning. Chance wasn't going to be any help; he hadn't made a sound when the bear left this morning. Then she remembered that her watch had an alarm feature. The watch had been an unexpected gift from John.

Bill, the warmth of him; hot steam rising up from the sink; the feel of damp curls clinging to her forehead.

Susan was straining a pan of macaroni noodles with Bill standing next to her, his arm over her shoulder. "Oh, I forgot something," Bill said and headed out the front door to his truck parked in the driveway. When he came back in he was carrying a clear, plastic box with a watch inside.

Bill held the box out to her, saying, "John asked me to give this to you. He figured it might come in handy out in the woods while you're walking. It keeps time and has an alarm. The instructions on how to use it are inside the box."

Susan took the box and turned it over in her hand, examining the watch through the plastic cover. "I don't understand why he would give this to me. And if he wanted me to have it, why didn't he bring it here himself?"

"It's a gift, Susan, that's all," Bill said. "He was looking at them when we were at the hardware store this morning. I said it sounded like something you might enjoy. I was just talking, making conversation. You know how John loves the latest gadgets. Like that blasted answering machine he got for us so I wouldn't miss an important business call. I still miss a lot of calls because hardly anybody but John and Shirley leaves a message. People don't understand what it is. Makes them nervous to talk to a machine. And it's ugly." Bill frowned at the corner of the room where the answering machine was sitting on the table next to the phone. "John's convinced that within the next five years everyone will own one of these. I'll be completely surprised if anyone but John wants one."

"I kind of like the answering machine," Susan said. "If Shirley calls when I'm in the garden, she'll leave a message so I can phone her back."

"See," Bill said. "And I bet you'll like the watch, too, once you give it a try. Probably the reason John asked me to give it to you is that you scare him a bit. You always act like you're ready to pick a fight when he's around."

"Me? He's the one who's always passing judgment on me."

"Is he?" Bill asked. "Are you sure about that?"

"Yes, I'm sure." But she wasn't sure, not really. Maybe she was itching to pick a fight with John. He was always so damn cocky and irritating. So damn sure of himself.

———◆———

For the first time ever, Susan said a silent thank you to John. If she put the watch under the sleeping bag near her head, the alarm should wake her up without making a noise the bear could hear.

Susan set the alarm for four a.m., made sure the pepper spray was within reach, and settled in to wait. Bits and pieces of her life played through her mind: memories of Shawn and Meagan, scenes from her own childhood, recollections of her parents when they were still young and healthy. She stayed away from thoughts of Bill, gently nudging them aside whenever they snuck in.

Close to an hour later, she heard dirt and stones rolling off the hill-side. She looked around the rock, and there he was! The bear was coming down the path. He was much bigger than she had thought after seeing him last night. He had to weigh more than five hundred pounds, with a thick body and legs the size of tree trunks. He appeared to be moving slowly, one lazy step at a time, but he reached the bottom of the steep path in no time. His coat was coal black and shiny, catching the rays of the sun that now lit the canyon as it dropped below the top of the tree line. His head was massive, with small, brown eyes set on either side of a long, tan muzzle.

Chance stiffened at her side. She motioned for him to stay quiet. He lifted his head and sniffed, alert and watchful.

Susan scooted over to the edge of the rock and stretched up to look through the telephoto lens. She couldn't see the bear. She had set the Minolta on the tripod to focus on the den entrance, but the bear wasn't in front of his den. She would have to use her Nikon if she wanted to get a picture of him away from the den.

Carefully she pulled the daypack over and reached inside until she felt the camera. She lifted it out, one painstaking inch at a time, hoping it wouldn't clank against something and alarm the bear. Once the Nikon was free, she looked around the rock. The bear stood at the bottom of the path, his head low, his mouth hanging open. The picture would be clearer if she used the monopod to brace the camera, but there wasn't time to attach it.

She got up on her knees, squeezed her elbows in tight to her sides in order to hold the camera as still as possible, framed the bear in the viewfinder, and pressed the shutter release. The shutter opened and closed, making a loud click by her ear. She crouched behind the rock and grabbed the pepper spray, hugging it to her chest. Her heart was thumping so wildly she was sure the bear would hear it. She counted to ten and then shoved the Nikon up under her sweater to muffle the sound and wound the film forward.

She looked around the rock again. The bear was gone. She checked the clearing. He was right across from her, standing on a flat rock by the creek, lapping at the water. She swallowed back a lump of fear, adjusted the focus, snapped the picture, and immediately dropped behind the rock and clutched the pepper spray again. She counted to five before she shoved the camera under her sweater and advanced the film.

When she looked around the rock this time, the bear was moving toward the cave tree with his back to her. He stopped, turned around and—facing her now—stood up on his hind legs. Susan froze, the

Nikon pressed against her chest, its edges digging into her skin through her sweater.

Walking on his hind legs, the bear backed up to an alder tree and squirmed against the rough bark. With his head up and his lower lip hanging down, he huffed and waggled back and forth and up and down. Susan bit her lip, holding in a laugh that bubbled up in her chest. She was weak with relief and pleasure at the sight of this wild animal scratching his back less than fifteen feet from her. "Look at that. Can you see that?" she whispered to herself. She raised the camera to her eye, blew out one easy breath, and shot the picture. This time she didn't hesitate. She ducked behind the rock and wound the film forward.

Susan leaned around the rock and looked through the lens of the Minolta affixed to the tripod. She could see the bear drop on all fours and move toward his den. She fine-tuned the focus and light setting and pressed the cable release. The bear stopped. He looked over his shoulder at her and pricked his ears. Susan's hand, still holding the cable release, quivered. The rest of her was dead still. The bear tilted his head. Was he watching her? Time stopped. Seconds?—minutes?—later, he turned away and entered the den. Susan sank down behind the rock and breathed slowly in and out.

They were here. He smelled them before he entered the clearing. He stayed away from the other humans and dogs he smelled. This woman and dog were different. They were part of his life.

He drank, the cold clean taste of the water filling his mouth and running down his throat. Then he scratched, the tree's bark rough and satisfying.

He heard a sound, like a twig snapping. It came from the woman. She didn't move. She offered no threat. He yawned and went

to his den, his steps heavy and slow. He had gone miles beyond his normal range, searching for food. Sleep was all he wanted now.

Susan shivered hard enough to make her teeth chatter. The sun had fallen behind the ridge and the temperature in the canyon had started to drop, but it wasn't only the increasingly chilly air that made her shake. Now that it was over and the bear was asleep in his den, the shock of seeing him that close took hold. She shoved the Nikon inside the day-pack and wormed her way into the sleeping bag. She held the side open for Chance, and he crawled in next to her. She nestled up close to him and tried to relax, but she couldn't: her mind was racing.

She was thirty feet from a sleeping wild bear, had been much closer than that when he was drinking from the creek and scratching his back on the tree. And not just any bear. This had to be one of the biggest bears out there. While it was happening, there hadn't been time to feel much of anything. Now, as she relived it, a cascade of emotions rushed through her: fear, excitement, astonishment, and reverence. The sight of him—his power and beauty, the mystery that surrounded him—caused something inside her to shift. For a brief moment, she felt connected to this bear, as if they shared a long-forgotten past.

The feeling faded, and all she could think about was how magnificent he was, from his round, furry ears to the curve of his claws. The whole experience was almost impossible to believe. She had done it, taken pictures of a wild bear. Even though she had come prepared to photograph this bear, she had never truly believed that she would be able to do it.

One thing kept nagging at her: had the bear known she was there? He had looked right at her, at least he had seemed to be looking at her, but he hadn't reacted in any way to her presence. He didn't appear uncomfortable or frightened. He just kept on doing what she imagined wild bears did when they were alone; when they weren't eating or sleeping, they were lapping up water from streams and scratching their backs on trees. Maybe the shadows around the rock had hidden her. There was no other rational explanation as to why he hadn't charged her or run away.

So many questions circled around in her mind: Should she try to follow the bear when he leaves his den tomorrow? How would she be able to stay close behind him without him knowing she was there? Could she trust Chance to stay quiet? What would happen if Chance barked or tried to chase the bear? What would the bear do if he smelled or saw them? Or heard them?

Too tired to stay awake any longer, Susan fell into a restless sleep. Chance curled alongside her, periodically making indistinct whines and paddling his feet, chasing some elusive thing in his dreams.

She was late to class. She ran up the hall, searching frantically for the right classroom. All the rooms were full of students waiting for class to start. Far off in the distance, the late bell started to beep.

Susan's eyes flew open. The bell in her dream revealed itself as the watch alarm under her ear. She fumbled for the watch, found it, and turned off the alarm. Moonlight bathed the canyon around her. Long dark shadows slashed through the creek bed, and a thin layer of icy condensation sparkled on the top of the sleeping bag.

Susan scooted a little way out into the open to be able to see the moon. She was surprised to see that the moon was full. The moon had been almost full when she first decided to try to photograph a wild bear. Had a month gone by since then? The days had slipped by her, especially here in the woods. Here, time had become a flow of days and nights connected together without a clear beginning or ending.

The moon was now touching the tops of the trees behind her left shoulder, shining down into the bear's den. Susan wondered what the bear looked like curled in his den with the moonlight shining in on him.

She sat up abruptly, banging the back of her head on the fallen tree. She bit her lip, cutting off a cry of pain. Was there enough light to photograph the bear asleep in his den? Carefully, she moved to the edge of the rock and peered around at the den. In the moonlight, she could see the bear curled up with his nose tucked into the curve of his hind legs. But when she looked through the lens of the Minolta, it was too dark to see anything other than the shape of the tree.

Photos taken in moonlight hardly ever turned out, but it was worth a try. She set the shutter on the Minolta for time exposure and adjusted the lens opening to the widest setting possible. There was too little light to see if the bear was in focus through the lens of the camera or to see the markings on the focus ring, so she had to guess at the focus based on how far she was from the cave tree: a little over thirty feet. She pressed the button on the cable release to open the shutter and counted off the seconds in her head, one thousand one, one thousand two.... When approximately two minutes had passed, she pressed the button again to close the shutter. She wound the film forward and started over, this time leaving the lens open for two and a half minutes, and once more for a full three minutes. With any luck, one of these exposures would work.

Chance had slept through all of this. Susan lay beside him in their tree shelter and thought about what to do next. She wanted to be ready when the bear left the canyon. First she would have to get the Minolta off the tripod. She and Chance would also need to eat and drink something, and of course they would have to pee. She couldn't start running through the forest after a bear until she had done that.

She pulled the daypack closer and fished around for a sack of trail mix. She crammed small handfuls of the mix into her mouth and ate as quietly as possible. Chance opened his eyes, blinked at her, and shut them again without moving any other part of his body.

Susan couldn't stand it any longer—she had to pee. She shook Chance awake and began to crawl out from under the tree. Chance edged deeper under the sleeping bag, refusing to budge. Susan reached under the sleeping bag and shook him again. He got up slowly with his head and tail low, expressing his discontent about being disturbed before the sun was up. Susan easily found her way in the moonlight to the spot they had used before. She squatted and Chance lifted his leg and urinated along with her. A little pee party, as Susan's mom used to say when they used a public restroom together when Susan was a child. She smiled at the memory.

When they had finished, she tiptoed back to the rock, holding the leash up close to keep Chance right next to her. She checked the bear's den as she went by. The bear was there, curled asleep.

Under the fallen tree, Chance pawed the sleeping bag into a ball, lay down on it, and within seconds was sound asleep. Susan sat down next to him and planned out what she would take with her when the bear left the canyon. She decided that getting the Minolta off the tripod would make too much noise, so she would use her Nikon. She took the Nikon out of the daypack and hung the strap around her neck. She wouldn't need the monopod in open sunlight, and if she put a few rolls of film in the daypack, she could leave the camera case here. She tossed the pepper spray into the pack, just in case. With the daypack ready, she sat beside Chance and watched the sky grow lighter.

Every few minutes, Susan checked on the bear, but he never moved. Would he ever wake up? She fidgeted, trying to stretch her back. She was getting restless and stiff from sitting on the cold ground. Seconds later, Chance stood up, sniffed, and then whined. Susan bent around the rock and saw the bear heading for the path leading out of the canyon. She scooped up the daypack and snuck out from under the tree. Staying low, squatting on her heels, she watched the bear climb up the path. When he was halfway to the top, she ran across the clearing with Chance ahead of her on the leash.

They reached the bottom of the path as the bear was climbing over the edge at the top. Only his rump and hind legs showed below the ridge. Susan climbed as fast as she could, using Chance's pull on the leash to help hoist her up. Close to the top, she motioned for Chance to stay where he was. She lay on her stomach and scrambled forward until she could see along the upper trail. The bear wasn't there.

She said, "Shoot," and instantly clasped her hand over her mouth. What if the bear had heard her? She waited, watching the brush on both sides of the trail. Nothing moved. She stepped out onto the trail with Chance beside her. She bent and studied the dirt, searching for fresh tracks. The mud from the day before had hardened and no new prints showed. Susan sighed. "We might as well eat breakfast. We've already lost the bear."

At the word eat, Chance leaped up and wagged expectantly. Susan poured out a pile of kibble on the trail, and he wolfed it down. Then he fixed his eyes on her as she ate handfuls of trail mix. "How can you eat the same stuff every day? I'm sick of trail mix. Nothing but nuts and raisins. I'd about kill for a salad." She took a long drink from the water bottle and then poured some into the empty kibble sack for Chance. He lapped at it noisily. When he finished, he squatted and defecated on the edge of the trail. Susan didn't need to join him after eating hardly anything but trail mix for the last couple of days. She took a stick and scraped the feces off the trail and covered it with loose dirt and leaves, hoping that the smell of it wouldn't upset the bear.

"What should we do now?" she asked, looking up and down the trail. Chance sniffed at the trail, moving excitedly in small circles.

"Don't pull," Susan said. Chance continued to track the ground, snorting loudly. "What are you smelling?" Could he be picking up the scent of the bear? She squinted into the brush on each side of the trail. Why hadn't she thought of this before? Instead of keeping him in check, she could have been taking advantage of Chance's keen sense of smell. "Come on, Chance, show me where the bear went. Find him for me."

Nose down, Chance weaved back and forth across the trail. Occasionally, he turned back and burrowed his nose in the dirt before moving on again. Farther on, he left the trail and followed a small stream flanked with skunk cabbage, its bitter odor heavy in the air. Chance tried to lengthen his stride into a full run. "Go easy," Susan said. He slowed but kept the leash taut, pulling ahead, following the stream through the woods.

At a spot where the stream took a bend around a rock outcropping, Chance stopped and sniffed the ground, pacing in figure eights in front of Susan. She was ready to give up, thinking he had lost the scent, when he headed away from the stream and bolted through a stand of sword ferns and onto a path winding through a patch of huckleberries. Susan struggled to keep up with him.

Up ahead she saw a fresh pile of bear scat steaming in the cool air. She pulled Chance close and tapped the side of her leg to get him to heel. She leaned sideways and looked up the path, trying to see around a bend. Judging from the steam coming off the scat, the bear had to be very close. Chance whined and looked up at her. She put her finger to her lips, telling him to be quiet, and they cautiously inched forward.

They rounded the bend, and there was the bear. He was off to the left of the path, standing with his side to her, pulling huckleberries free from the plants with his teeth and swallowing them without chewing. Susan stopped. They were too close to him. She took a step back. The bear faced her. Chance curled his upper lip and growled. Susan pulled the leash tighter and gestured for Chance to lie down. Chance dropped down, his muscles tensed, his eyes locked on the bear.

The bear watched them with his head held low, his ears back. He looked away, and then, without warning, he charged at them, blowing hard. The ground thundered under him. Susan couldn't move. She was too frightened to think clearly. After two powerful strides, the bear stopped. He swatted the ground forcefully. Susan sucked in a breath, terrified. Chance vaulted up, snarling, his hackles raised.

"Down, Chance," Susan managed to say. She pulled the leash up even shorter and gripped it tightly in both hands. Chance lunged at the bear, straining forward on the leash, clawing the air and barking, saliva frothing around his mouth.

The bear again raged toward them, his muscles rolling under his skin, his legs pounding the earth. He stopped just short of them. He smacked the dirt again and again, his huge body rocking with each blow. He was so close that Susan could smell the acidic mix of fermented grass and ripe berries on his breath. She grabbed Chance's collar and stumbled backwards, dragging Chance with her. As soon as they stepped back, the bear turned and walked away. He shuffled deeper into the huckleberry patch and resumed eating.

He smelled the scent of their urine when he woke up, but hunger controlled him now. It drove him out of the canyon. Once he was

off the main trail, he slowed. He stopped to drink in a stream. He pawed at a clump of skunk cabbage, stirring up its strong odor.

He left the stream, following a path he had traveled many times before. It led to a large huckleberry patch. He roamed through the bushes, pulling at the few remaining berries with his teeth, swallowing them whole without tasting them.

He heard the woman and the dog before he smelled them. He turned around. They were close. Too close. The stench of their fear was a challenge to him, an invasion. They needed to learn to stay back from him.

He charged at them, blowing. The dog reeked of anger and terror. The woman and the dog didn't move back. He charged again, stopping right in front of them. He rocked and cuffed the ground hard, warning them to get back. The dog growled and clawed the air, drops of saliva spraying around him. Then the dog and the woman backed away. They were no longer a threat.

Now hunger was all there was. He went on eating, checking once to make sure the woman and the dog were not coming closer.

Susan kept dragging Chance back even after the bear moved away. She didn't stop until she was on the other side of the berry patch and behind a tree. She slumped back against the tree and slid to the ground. Chance was still straining against his collar, pulling toward the bear. Susan stroked his head, repeating, "It's okay. It's okay."

Gradually Chance relaxed and lay down next to her. Susan kept a tight hold on Chance's collar as she scooted out from the tree far enough to see the bear. She watched him move through the berry bushes, eating lazily. He shoved the branches aside with his head and reached for the ripe berries, rolling them off with his front teeth. At each bush, he repeated these actions in a smooth, easy rhythm. In spite of his big and ungainly appearance, he didn't break a single branch. He was graceful in an awkward sort of way.

Susan lost all track of time. She saw only the bear: sunlight reflecting off his black fur, the twist of his head as he pulled the berries free, the sway of his large body as he moved through the bushes. The familiar scent of the forest—mold and dirt mixed in with the lemony tartness of fir needles—calmed her. Chance lay with his head on his front paws, watching the bear. Susan drifted, not asleep but not fully awake either.

She came completely awake when she noticed the bear ambling closer to her. He was wild and breathtakingly beautiful.

He stopped with his side to her, his head up, searching for berries. Susan rose to her feet, lifting the Nikon to her eye as she went. She framed the bear in the viewfinder, checked the focus, held her breath, and touched the shutter release. When the shutter clicked open and closed the bear looked at her, his ears cocked. He stood motionless, the fur on his back lifting in the breeze. Susan glanced at Chance. He was still lying with his head resting on his paws, now seemingly untroubled by the bear's presence.

Susan met the bear's gaze. Neither of them moved. She stared deep into his eyes, felt the pull and strength of his wildness, his beauty. For that moment the differences between them slipped away. She became the same as him—an animal in the woods.

It was the bear who turned away. He reached up for a mouthful of berries hanging right above his head. Slowly, as though waking up from a prolonged and intense dream, Susan wound the film forward, raised the camera to her eye, and took his picture.

The bear went back to roaming from plant to plant, sniffing at each one, hunting for berries, eating the ones he found. Susan gave a little tug on the leash to get Chance to stand up, and with him close by her side they stepped away from the tree. She snuck closer to the bear. She found him in the viewfinder, focused the lens, and clicked off photos in rapid succession, pausing only to wind the film forward. When she ran out of film, she shrugged carefully out of the daypack, squatted and rifled around inside the pack, feeling for more film.

With her fingers closed around the film case, she looked up to check on the bear. He was gone. She pivoted around, looking in every direction. He wasn't anywhere that she could see. He had left without making a sound. "Where'd he go?" Susan asked. Chance answered with a soft woof.

What now? She lifted the Nikon from around her neck and put it inside the daypack. She stood up and gazed at the berry patch, thinking about what had happened here. The bear had come close to her and continued eating while she took pictures. Even with the prospect of spending another night sleeping on the cold ground, eating nothing but trail mix, she wasn't ready to leave the woods. "I don't want to go home, not yet anyway," she said, looking at Chance. "One more day, is that all right with you?" Chance sat down next to her and thumped his tail on the ground. She bent and gave him a pat, and together they started through the woods toward the bear's den.

"What?" Susan gasped, taking a quick step to the side, nearly stumbling over the leash. A large, dark eye stared up at her from the ground. She was partway back to Woolly Creek and had been halfheartedly watching the trail for animal tracks when she saw the eye. Chance was out in front of her at the end of the leash, sniffing hard and bristling.

It was a fawn, half buried in leaves. Susan pulled Chance behind her and told him to lie down. She knelt and dusted the leaves away from the fawn. It hadn't been dead long: the blood on its neck was damp, and the ragged hole in its side was still warm.

What had done this? She sat up and scanned the surrounding brush. Then she inspected the dirt next to the fawn. There were no prints close to the carcass, only vague, feathery swirls in the dry areas around it. She told Chance to stand, and with him leashed in close, she walked in an ever-increasing circle away from the dead deer, watching the dirt for tracks as she went. In a damp depression under a small alder tree, she found one print with four toe pads and a heel. It was missing the indentations of toenails. Dogs leave toenail prints; cats didn't. "A mountain lion," Susan whispered.

"Chance, let's get out of here," she said, her voice low and urgent. Chance tugged on the leash, trying to get closer to the fawn, sniffing hard. "No, you leave that!" Susan commanded. "We need to get out of here. Now!"

She headed back the way they had come, looking frequently over her shoulder and listening for the smallest of sounds. She searched her memory for random facts about mountain lions. She had heard stories of people being stalked and killed by them. These were gruesome stories, with graphic details, designed by the media to shock the listening public. And the tales were shocking; there was no denying that.

All her neighbors knew there were mountain lions in the woods around their homes. A couple times a year one was spotted crossing the road. Just last month, her neighbor Pamela Kinsley had shown Susan a picture she had taken of a young male mountain lion in a tree not more than forty feet from the Kinsley's front door. Pamela had seen some of the neighborhood dogs chase the lion up there right in the middle of the afternoon. Being a countrywoman and not afraid of much of anything, Pamela had run out with her camera and snapped the picture. In the photo, the lion looked patient, calmly tolerating his plight. He seemed to recognize that he had no real enemies, that he was at the top of the food chain. He was a beautiful animal, exuding strength and intelligence.

Pamela told Susan that once the dogs had lost interest and wandered away, the lion had climbed down from the tree and simply walked off. Strolled was the word she had used. The lion had strolled out of her yard and into the forest.

There was also that time, years ago, when Susan had lost three baby goats in two days. Each one had been there in the early morning when she let them out of the barn and gone before the evening milking, without any sign of what had happened to them. Bill was sure a mountain lion had taken them. Susan had disagreed. She guessed someone had stolen them. She had no idea who would steal her goats, but the thought of a mountain lion dragging them off was too terrible to consider. At the end of the second day, as unexpectedly as the disappearances had begun, they stopped. No more goats went missing, so that was the end of it.

Recently she had read an article addressing the issue of wild animals in parklands. The author of the article stated that thousands more mountain lions were killed by people than the other way around. Mountain lions, from years of being hunted and killed, had grown to fear humans and to avoid them. Somehow this didn't make her feel any better. She quickened her step.

Close to an hour later, Susan pushed through a small opening on the edge of the trail and stepped onto a wide, dirt road. Immediately she knew she was lost. This had to be Smith and Sons Main Line, the road the timber company used to haul logs to their mill at one end and lumber out to the highway at the other.

Over the years, Susan had heard of the Main Line but had never gotten close to it. When she was practicing with the compass at home, she had seen it marked on the topographical map but hadn't paid much attention. At the time, she hadn't intended to go anywhere near the timber company's main logging roads. Now she had no idea where the Main Line was in relation to Woolly Creek or on which part of it she was standing. She walked to the center of the road and looked in both directions. All she could see was a dirt road cutting through densely forested lands.

"Which way should we go?" Susan asked. Chance was busy scratching behind his ear and didn't seem to care one way or the other about the road. "We could pick a direction and walk until we came out somewhere. My guess is that it wouldn't be anywhere we'd want to be."

The locals all knew that Smith and Sons fined trespassers, sometimes heavily, especially if they found them on the Main Line. She had never worried about this before, as she usually stayed away from active logging roads. Besides, getting fined for trespassing was the least of her worries today: there wasn't a truck in sight.

She sat down on a stump at the edge of the road in the sunshine. This was a good time to take a break. She poured a sack of kibble out onto the ground for Chance and opened a sack of trail mix for herself. After this, there was only one full sack each of trail mix and kibble and a bottle and a half of water left.

"We'll have to go home tomorrow," she said, "but I want to spend one more night with this bear before we go. I think he's starting to get used to us, don't you?" She looked at Chance. He cocked his head one way, then the other, as though trying to find the right angle so that he could understand what she was saying. "Who knows how he'll feel about us in a day or two. This may be the one chance I get to photograph him. All I need to do now is figure out where we are and how to get from here to Woolly Creek."

Susan unfolded the map and laid it out next to her on the stump. She found the Main Line, which ran straight east to west, except for in one spot where it made a dogleg to the north. She had circled the place by Woolly Creek where the bear's den was. Using her finger, she traced a line from there to the Main Line. Then she traced back along her connecting line, searching for the snaking blue marks that indicated small creeks. If she could find the creek they had walked along earlier that morning, she might be able to tell approximately where on the Main Line they were. There were about six or seven little creeks on the map, any of which could be the one she was looking for. She ran her finger along the map from east to west, searching for other landmarks that might show where she was now.

As the Main Line doglegged to the north, there was an area marked on the map as a rock quarry. Susan looked up and down the road. Far off to her left, the road made a sharp bend and disappeared from sight. Could the rock quarry be up there? According to the map, the quarry was located at a bend in an otherwise perfectly straight road. She laid her hand on the map in a line from the rock quarry to the bear's den. "Straight through the woods from the quarry would be the fastest way for us to get back to Woolly Creek," she said to Chance. "Let's go check it out."

Susan stayed on the edge of the road, planning to duck out of sight if a logging truck came by. When she rounded the bend, the rock quarry was there, off the road up ahead of her. "Look at that. I was right. I can read a map." Now maybe she could find her way back to Woolly Creek, and to the bear's den. She hurried toward the quarry.

A small, gray mountain of rock stood well back from the road. Closer to the road were large piles of rocks sorted into various sizes, from boulders to small road gravel. In the midst of the piles of rocks was a gigantic piece of equipment, a type of conveyer belt with large sorting screens fitted into it.

Beside the conveyer was a black lunch pail with its lid open. Susan looked inside. The pail was empty. The quarry had the eerie feeling of a ghost town, where all the inhabitants had gotten up and walked off for some unknown reason.

Susan sat down on a flat boulder next to the conveyer and spread the map out before her. She lined up magnetic North on the compass with the declination arrow and set the compass on the map so that true North on the map and compass corresponded. She read the numbers on the outside ring of the compass that matched the direction of the bear's den: approximately 240° WSW from the rock quarry. If they could stay close enough to that reading to end up somewhere on the trail above Woolly Creek, they should make it back to their shelter by the bear's den before dark.

She gazed out at the trees. This was going to be very different from practicing in her living room.

She had left her watch under the sleeping bag back at the den, but judging from the length of the shadows it was already late afternoon. "We'd better get going," she said to Chance, and together they stepped off the logging road and into the brush.

With the compass pointed at 240° WSW, Susan found a distant tree in the direction she needed to go and plowed her way toward it. Then she found another tree and headed for it. She repeated this over and over again.

The going was tough. Blackberry vines looped and twisted around alders and struggling young redwoods, making it impossible at times to get through. They had to skirt large sections. The leash kept getting tangled up in the undergrowth until Susan couldn't stand it any longer and unhooked it, letting Chance find his own way. Much of the time she wasn't sure she was going in the right direction. Once she followed a brushy trail only to discover she had gone more than three degrees too far to the east.

Along the way, Susan watched the ground for signs of the mountain lion. She flinched at the slightest movement or sound in the brush and continually looked over her shoulder, sure the lion was stalking her from behind. Sharing the woods with a bear was one thing. Knowing a mountain lion was hunting here was an entirely different matter.

What if she saw a mountain lion? What would she do?

She recalled a TV program in which a big-cat expert offered advice on how to behave if confronted by a mountain lion. He had recommended trying to appear as formidable as possible by holding up a stick or raising your arms above your head. He had also said it was important to make loud but non-aggressive noises. This all seemed a bit dicey, as Susan's grandfather used to say. If she waved her arms over her head, would that be enough to trick a mountain lion into thinking she was some giant, deadly creature? And what type of loud sound could she possibly make that a mountain lion wouldn't find aggressive?

In spite of her doubts about the method's effectiveness, and how silly she felt doing it, she tried it out. When she heard (or imagined) an unusual sound, she would wave her arms around in the air above her head and say, "Bad cat. Get back from me," in a deep, measured voice. Each time she did this, Chance looked around as if he were trying to figure out who or what she was talking to.

Hours later, she broke through a scraggly stand of young Douglas firs and stepped right onto the trail above Woolly Creek. "Yes! We did it!" she shouted. With a nod of her head, she added softly, "I did it."

She had new scratches on her arms, and she was weak and shaky. When she licked her lips, she tasted blood from a small scratch on her upper lip. She had done it, though, found her way through the woods with nothing but a map and a compass to guide her. "Time to celebrate," she said to Chance. "You, my friend, can have a little kibble, and I'm going to eat a couple of handfuls of this last sack of trail mix." She ate slowly, watching the sun inch closer to the distant tree line.

The canyon was deep in shadows and cold when Susan and Chance reached the creek bed. She stopped across from the bear's den and bent to look inside. It was empty.

Despite how hard this day had been, Susan knew she wasn't done here. She wanted to learn more about the bear, how he lived, what he thought. Did he have thoughts, or was it instincts that decided everything for him?

She told Chance to stay where he was, and she crept closer to the den opening. It smelled of dirt and leaves and something else, an animal scent, not unpleasant but rich and feral. She breathed in the aroma, memorizing it, making it part of what she now knew of this bear and the forest that was his home.

She wanted to crawl into the den, touch the charcoaled walls, curl up on the dirt floor and sleep there. Instead she moved away, worried that she might have already gotten too close, that the bear would smell her there and—

And what? Leave? Become angry and attack her and Chance in their sleep? Somehow she didn't think he would do either of these things. She remembered how he had charged at her, stopping right in front of her, close enough that she could smell his breath, a heavy mixture of huckleberries and mown grass. If he had wanted to get rid of her, to kill her, all he would have had to do was reach out with one powerful paw and take a swipe at her, but he hadn't. He had shown an enormous amount of restraint. He had scared her. He had meant to scare her, there was no doubt about that, but it was clear he hadn't intended to harm her.

Night was settling in as Susan clipped Chance to the leash and headed for the rock. She lifted up the tripod and Minolta as she went by. She would bring the Minolta with her tomorrow. It was the better of the two cameras, and the one Bill had given her for their anniversary last year. She took the Nikon out of the daypack and set it where she could reach it easily in case she needed it in the morning.

She checked to make sure the alarm on her watch was set and then pulled the sleeping bag over her and Chance. They were deeply asleep when the bear returned to his den.

Susan popped awake. The texture of the fallen log above her was just visible in the pale moonlight filtering through a layer of clouds. What had woken her? She listened intently but didn't hear anything unusual.

Then the air rang with a loud screaming that sounded like a woman or a child in pain or terror. Fear raced through her. Chance was next to her, growling a low warning. She wrapped her arms around him and breathed, "Shush," into his ear. It came again, the shrill, unearthly scream. The mountain lion, Susan thought. She had heard that sound only one other time.

The scent of peppermint, the light touch of Bill's shoulder against hers. And that sound.

"Did you hear that?" Susan asked, her head coming up, her eyes catching Bill's in the mirror over the bathroom sink. "Someone is in trouble, a woman or a child. I can hear them screaming outside."

"It's a mountain lion calling," Bill said through a mouthful of toothpaste. "It's a bit unsettling, isn't it?"

Having a mountain lion prowling outside their house—that scream—was more than unsettling to Susan. It was terrifying. She slept fitfully most of that night, waking up periodically to that wild, horrible sound coming from somewhere out there in the forest.

———◆———

"Shhh, shhh, shhh," Susan said, holding Chance close, the side of her face pressed against his neck. His growl grew lower, more threatening.

The lion screamed again, closer this time. The big cat seemed to be moving along the ridge trail above the creek, coming in their direction.

Now it was silent. This was almost worse than the scream. At least when the lion was calling she knew where it was. Chance wasn't helping. He had stood partway up and was growling and pulling away from her. Susan grabbed hold of his collar, tugged him down next to her, and said in a faint whisper, "Chance. Quiet." He stopped growling and began moaning instead, making a painful, low-pitched sound.

When the scream came again, it sounded like the lion was on the ridge top right above them. Susan cowered back. She ran her hand along the edge of the sleeping bag, searching for the pepper spray. It wasn't there. She got up on her knees and slid her hand under the sleeping bag. She still couldn't find it.

"The daypack," she said. She had left the pepper spray in the day-pack. She groped around for the pack. Once she found it, she blindly pulled out the map and compass, water bottles, rolls of film, spare clothing, and plastic sacks, tossing them aside in her haste to find the pepper spray. Why hadn't she put the spray next to her like she had done before? She had gotten too comfortable in her little shelter and had been careless.

She was no longer concerned about making noise or alarming the bear. She didn't notice that Chance had stood up, bristling and snarling. All she could think about was finding the pepper spray.

"Where is it? Where is it? Where is it?" she repeated, shoving her hand into the pack over and over again.

She was closing her fingers around the canister of spray when the lion screamed again. The sound was still coming from the ridge trail, but now it was farther up the canyon. Susan stopped, her hand gripping the pepper spray. She listened. Minutes passed. The next scream was distant and softened by miles of trees. Even from a long way off, the fierce, eerie cry sent adrenalin racing through her. She gripped the pepper spray tighter and waited. Nothing. Then from so far away that she could barely hear it, the lion called once more.

Susan sagged back against the rock. Chance sprang at her and licked her face. "Chance, no," she said, crossing her arms over her face. She laughed at Chance's silliness and with relief that the mountain lion had moved off and was no longer on the ridge above them.

Change stopped licking and lay down beside her. Susan thought about the bear. He must have heard the mountain lion calling. Why hadn't he reacted? More important, had he heard her? Was he even here? She took hold of the leash and whispered in Chance's ear, "Stay." She peered around the rock at the bear's den. She couldn't see clearly in the thin moonlight, but she had a sense of a darker shape in the blackness of the den. She sat back and tried to remember how much noise she had made. She had whispered to Chance. She might have even spoken out loud. And she had laughed. There was no longer any question that the bear knew they were here. There was nothing she could do about it now, nor did she have the energy to do much of anything. As the fear of the lion settled, all she wanted to do was sleep. She would have to see what happened with the bear in the morning.

The call of the mountain lion woke him, but that wasn't what caused him to lift his head. He had heard the lion call before, knew that she crossed into his territory. He stayed clear of her, only taking advantage of the dead animals she left behind.

It was the sounds of the woman and the dog that roused him. He heard the dog's growl and the woman's voice. He could smell and taste the fear coming off them. He tightened his muscles, preparing to bolt.

The lion passed by, her call coming from far up the canyon. The woman's voice, loud this time. He hunched forward, his shoulders flexed, ready to flee. He waited. Now it was quiet. He grunted once, relaxed, and went to sleep.

Susan fumbled under her to shut off the alarm on her watch. Its persistent beeping had pulled her from a deep sleep. Still half asleep, she strapped the watchband onto her wrist so she wouldn't leave it behind again. She lay listening to the sounds of the creek and smiled as she thought of the bear sleeping thirty feet away, snug and safe in his den.

The sky slowly lightened. She ran her hand along Chance's back and whispered, "Time to pee." She felt her way in the dim light to their usual spot up the creek bed. When they had finished, they walked to the creek. While Chance drank, Susan stooped beside him and cupped her hands in the water and splashed her face. She gasped as the icy water hit her skin. She lifted up the bottom of her sweater and patted her face dry. So much for a bath.

A thin line of light filtered between the trees, changing the eastern edge of the clouds red. Susan recalled the old saying: Red sky at night, sailors delight. Red sky in the morning, sailors take warning. Was another big storm on its way?

Susan snuck a peek inside the bear's den on her way back to the rock. The bear's dark shape, curled against the charcoaled walls of the den, was all that she could see in the dim light.

Behind the rock, she gathered her scattered supplies and repacked her daypack carefully, but she no longer felt the need to remain completely silent. Surely the bear had heard her last night, and he hadn't reacted at all. The smell of food, on the other hand, might be too much of a temptation for him to resist. She and Chance would have to wait to eat until they were farther away from the bear.

When everything else was ready, she checked the film in both her cameras, put the Nikon in the camera case (she would bring it as a back-up), and replaced the cumbersome tripod on the Minolta with the monopod and extended it to its full length. Now all she had to do was wait for the bear to make his move. She sat partway out from behind the rock where she could see the den opening. True to form, Chance curled up and went back to sleep.

The canyon had turned light gray, and a soft drizzle had started to fall when the bear finally came out into the open. Susan removed the lens cap from the Minolta, stepped out from behind the rock, and set the monopod firmly on the ground.

Through the telephoto lens she watched the bear. He sat in front of the hollow tree and licked at one of his front paws, his long, pink tongue slurping noisily between his toes. Susan adjusted the focus, clicked the button on the cable release, and advanced the film. The bear stopped licking and looked at her. Susan shot another photograph. The bear grunted, making a noise that sounded like *humph,* and went back to licking between his toes.

Susan unclipped the leash from her belt. Chance lifted his head. She gave him the signal to stay and moved carefully away from the rock. The bear was now at the creek, hunkered down on his forelegs, lapping at the water. Susan took a few steps into the clearing, set the monopod, focused the camera, and snapped his picture. His thirst quenched, the bear walked in a wide arc around her and headed up the path out of the canyon, keeping his head turned away from her the entire time.

Susan darted behind the rock. She fastened the loose end of Chance's leash to her belt and pulled on her raingear, tugging the pants up over her boots. She quickly closed up the monopod and hung the Minolta with the monopod attached over her shoulder. She swung the daypack and camera case onto her other shoulder and started up the path out of the canyon. She climbed as fast as she could but knew she couldn't catch the bear. Maybe Chance would be able to find him again.

At the ridge top, she didn't wait but stepped directly out onto the trail. The bear was there, up the trail, looking back at her. Susan stood still. The bear turned away and walked leisurely up the trail. Susan followed, making sure to stay a good distance behind him.

After a while, the bear stopped. He pulled up a small clump of grass and gazed around as he chewed. Susan extended and set the monopod, focused the camera, and took five quick shots. The bear moved on. He stopped again to sniff the air. He looked at Susan over his shoulder, stepped off the trail into some berry vines and was gone.

Susan ran until she reached the place where the bear had left the trail. She was certain it was the same place—she hadn't taken her eyes off it—but there wasn't any trace of him. No tracks. No broken branches. The only sign that he had been there was a clump of dark fur snagged on a blackberry vine. She listened for the sound of twigs snapping or something moving through the underbrush but heard nothing. Once more, the bear had simply disappeared.

Susan studied the berry vines on the edge of the trail, running a hand up her arm, feeling the sting of yesterday's berry scratches under her clothing. She felt beat up from stress and lack of sleep and from running through the brush.

In the drizzle, the trail was rapidly becoming a muddy track. Susan poured the last of the kibble out for Chance and scooped the remaining handfuls of trail mix into her mouth. As she ate, she thought about what she should do.

"I want to go home," she said, looking at Chance. "I've had enough of this for now. We can come back, but I want something real to eat, and a nice hot bath, and my own bed. What do you think?" Chance was searching the ground at her feet for any morsel of kibble he might have missed. "Don't have an opinion, huh? Okay. I get to decide, and I say we're going home."

Now that she had made the decision to go, Susan was impatient to get home. She was almost giddy with relief thinking about it. She pictured the bathtub filling with hot water. What about the sleeping bag and the tripod she had left at Woolly Creek? Should she go get them? No. It wasn't worth the energy and time it would take to go back for them. She would come here again soon. She had to. There was no question about that. She could get her gear then. She closed up the monopod and put it and the Minolta in the daypack and started for home.

She walked swiftly, slowed down only slightly by the now-familiar downed tree blocking the path. When she reached the backpack, she shoved the camera case and daypack inside, lifted it on, and started through the labyrinth of fallen trees and broken branches. From there on, she made good time. She was almost to her van when it began to rain hard. Cold, fat raindrops beat on the backpack and ran off her hair and down her face.

He yawned and stood up and moved lazily out of his den and into the clearing. As the days grew shorter and colder, both a yearning to sleep and the need to eat grew in him. For now, the urgent necessity for food was stronger than his desire to sleep. Soon the berries and grasses would be gone and food would be in short supply. Then hunger would slow and he could sleep.

He lowered his nose and sniffed. He smelled the woman and the dog and heard the strange click. He saw the woman standing by the rock. The woman and the dog were part of all that was his, and they did not worry him.

At the creek, he took a long drink and then left the canyon. When he reached the ridge trail, he stopped and waited. He could hear the woman and the dog coming up the path. He was curious about these creatures. Soon they were behind him on the trail.

The smell of a dead deer reached him. He located the direction of the scent and checked to see if the woman and the dog had also smelled it. Did they want to eat, too? He left the trail, moving in the direction of the ripe smell.

The mountain lion had killed again. This carcass lay in an open area next to a small rock outcropping. All that was left of the animal was half the rib cage, the leg bones with the hooves hanging by a tendon, and the head. He poked at it with his nose, raking up the strong smell of old meat and the scent of mountain lion. He scanned the area. The lion was gone.

He clamped his jaw over a leg bone, shook it free, and broke it in half with one bite. He sat down in the damp dirt and held a piece of the bone between his paws, licking at the marrow. The oily flavor coated his mouth. When he had licked the bone clean, he crushed the head with his teeth and licked out the brain tissue. With a deep, satisfied purr, he tore the hooves from the front legs and swallowed them whole.

He sensed a small movement. He raised his head, ears forward, listening. Unable to see through the dense growth, he stood up on his hind legs and watched and listened. Satisfied that he was safe, he dropped down on all fours and sniffed what remained of the carcass, rolling it over with his nose, searching for anything left to eat.

(5)

Double-crested Cormorant

Cold, musty air greeted Susan when she opened her front door. If a fire wasn't kept going all night this time of year, the big, old house got cold and wet and stayed that way for hours, even after she built a fire in the woodstove. She left her backpack inside by the front door and gathered newspaper and kindling to get a fire started. Once the fire was burning, she ran hot water in the old claw-foot bathtub.

She was pouring kibble into Chance's bowl on the kitchen floor when she noticed the blinking light on the answering machine. She pressed the Play button and heard: "Susan, this is David. Please call me when you get in. I have some important information about your project. You can call me either here at the office or at home."

Still wearing her boots and raingear, Susan slumped onto the couch. Muddy footprints began at the front door, went to the firewood box, and from there to the bathroom, where they faded away. She stood up and took her jacket off and let it fall to the floor by her feet. She sat down again and bent to untie her boots. How long had it been since she had taken them off—three or four days? The time in the woods blended together, becoming one long fabric of days and nights. She kicked off her boots and tugged off her rain pants. Then she curled her legs under her on the couch and listened to the water flowing into the tub.

She closed her eyes and pictured David with his graying hair and lined face, his slightly pudgy belly, his gray eyes. Again she heard how he had said her name on the phone the last time they had talked. She ran her hand over her face, trying to clear her mind, but she was too tired to think clearly. With a sigh, she pushed up from the couch and headed for the bedroom to strip off her dirty clothes and get a clean set. David could wait until she had taken a bath. What he had to tell her couldn't be that important.

Susan lay submerged up to her neck in warm water, trying to figure out why she was reluctant to call David. He hadn't done or said anything wrong. He wasn't the problem. She was. There was something about him that had aroused emotions in her she wasn't ready to face.

Even when she was married, she had occasionally experienced feelings of sexual attraction to other men. This made her uncomfortable then and felt especially wrong now, just six months after Bill's death. She slipped her head under the water and let the warmth enfold all of her. Underwater, she listened to the echoes of her heartbeat until she could no longer hold her breath. She surfaced, wiped water off her face with her hands, and reached for the towel on the floor.

Drying off with one foot propped up on the side of the tub, she caught her reflection in the steamed-up mirror on the back of the bathroom door. She watched her softened, liquid image running the towel around her ankle and up the inside of her leg. She tilted her head back and closed her eyes, taking in quick, shallow breaths as she ran the towel further up her thigh. She moaned softly and breathed out the word, "Yes."

At the sound of her voice, her eyes opened, and she stared at her reflection in the mirror. "Oh for goodness sake," she said. She pulled the towel free from her leg and wrapped it around her shoulders, her face burning. Here she was, blushing with embarrassment alone in her own bathroom. What in the world was wrong with her? She picked up her sweatpants and shirt from the bathroom floor and took them with her to dress by the woodstove.

Once she was dressed, and with a firm commitment to keep her mind off sex, she went in search of something to eat. There wasn't much to choose from, just a few cans of soup, half a jar of peanut butter, and a loaf of stale whole wheat bread. She was even out of oatmeal. There were all those beets and beans she had canned, along with a freezer full of other vegetables, but she wanted more than soggy vegetables, especially after being out in the woods for days with nothing but trail mix to eat. A fresh salad and a big slice of spinach lasagna, dripping with mozzarella cheese and spicy tomato sauce, would be perfect. Maybe a piece of lemon cake for dessert. She would definitely make a trip to the market tomorrow. For now, canned soup would have to do.

While the soup was heating, Susan checked the time. It was a little after five in the evening. She should phone David now if she had any chance of reaching him while he was still at work. He might have already gone home, but phoning him there was way too personal.

David picked up on the first ring, answering with his usual greeting, "Sharpton here."

"Oh, David. I wasn't expecting you to be there this late. I was going to leave a message. This is Susan."

"Susan. I'm glad you called. I wondered what was up when I hadn't heard from you. I thought maybe you'd given up on your project."

"No, I haven't given up. I'm sorry I didn't call. I had a...." She couldn't finish.

"Was it something I said the last time we talked?" David asked. "I can be overwhelming at times. I was upset about you being out in that windstorm."

"No, it wasn't you. You've been wonderful. It's me. I'm trying to learn how to live my life on my own. I'm basically muddling along at this point, and I've never been good at knowing what to do when people worry about me." Of course this wasn't the problem, not entirely, but how could she explain why she hadn't phoned to let him know she was returning to the woods? What was she supposed to say: thinking about you awoke a sexual desire in me that I don't want or need right now?

Susan once again felt heat flooding her checks. Before now, she couldn't begin to imagine mentioning her sexual desire to any man other than Bill, let alone a man she hardly knew. If she kept going like this, there was no telling what she would think or say next.

"I see," David said. "Since that's the case, I won't worry about you again. As for being wonderful, I'm rarely that, according to my students. Now that we have that cleared up, I do want to see you. One of my graduate students came across some information that might affect your project. Can you come by tomorrow?"

"Oh. Okay. I mean yes, I can," Susan said, trying to adjust to the quick change in topic. "Will tomorrow afternoon work for you? I have something to show you, also."

"I have a class at four. Any time before that will be fine," he said, and then the line went dead.

Susan held the receiver to her ear for a second or two longer before she realized he had hung up. "I guess we were done," she said and set the receiver down.

In bed that night, Susan lay sweating beneath the blankets. She kicked them aside and covered herself with only the sheet. Chance stood with his head resting on the edge of the bed and watched her. Susan patted the mattress and he jumped up and curled next to her. Once during the night, she got out of bed and slid the bedroom window all the way open and stood there for a while listening to the rain dripping outside.

By 5:30 in the morning, Susan was out of bed and had a fire going in the woodstove. She made coffee, toasted a slice of the stale bread and spread peanut butter on it. She was on her way to the couch, bringing her coffee and toast with her, when suddenly the room seemed to stretch out around her, leaving her small and isolated. The house was too big and too quiet. She hadn't felt like this in the woods. The forest was full of life and never silent. She longed for the night's hooting and scrapings that gave way with daylight to the trilling of birdsong. In her living room, all she could hear were the pops and creaks of the cast iron woodstove and the hum of the refrigerator. She and Chance were the only living things in the house.

The woman and the dog were gone. He knew this as soon as he entered the canyon. He could still smell them, but their scent was now weak, floating in thin drifts above the soil. He drank from the creek and then walked to the rock, sniffing the ground every few steps. Behind the rock, he pushed his head under the fallen tree and breathed in deeply. Their smell was strongest here.

Inquisitiveness overpowered his caution. He hunkered down and rolled his shoulder, trying to reach farther underneath the tree. He used his claws to drag a soft thing most of the way out into the open. He buried his nose in the texture of the thing and snorted in the rich odors of the woman and the dog.

Now he wanted to learn all he could about them. He lumbered across the clearing and up the creek bed to the place where they had left the scent of their urine. He scraped at the dirt and ran his nose over the sour-smelling soil. They had marked his territory, changed what had been exclusively his. Now ownership was the issue.

Their presence did not bother him, but it was essential for him to mark this as his home, to let them know he was the one in charge here. At a large alder tree, he stood up on his hind legs and ran his claws down the bark of the tree, tearing long grooves that showed bright orange in the dying light. He urinated a hot stream over the spot that smelled of them. Satisfied, he went into his den to sleep.

What she needed, Susan decided, was to talk to Shirley. Spending time with Shirley, even over the phone, always helped her feel better, and she really should let Shirley know that she had made it home. She checked the time and reached for the phone. Shirley got up early every day to make what she called a real breakfast for John and the girls. For Shirley this was eggs, pancakes, toast, and fresh-squeezed orange juice. Susan ate oatmeal for breakfast almost every morning and had for years. She couldn't imagine eating something as heavy as eggs and pancakes so early in the day.

The first time Susan and Shirley had gone to breakfast together— the beginning of their Tuesday breakfast dates—Shirley had scoffed at Susan's bowl of oatmeal, saying, "Girl, no wonder you look like a bean-pole, with nothing but oats running through your veins half the day."

Susan tried to picture what Shirley would say if she told her about her time in the woods with the bear. All she could come up with was a cartoon version of Shirley with a flipped pancake frozen in motion about her head and her mouth hanging wide open with no words coming out.

Before this, Susan couldn't imagine anything that would knock Shirley speechless. But the news that Susan had been in the woods sleeping close to a wild bear might do it. Or worse yet, Shirley would shout at Susan, scolding her for her reckless behavior and berating her for making such a dangerous choice. Or maybe Shirley would walk away, telling Susan that she could no longer be her friend since she was willing to risk her life for no reason other than to take a few photos.

Susan dialed Shirley's number knowing that she couldn't tell her closest friend what she had been doing. First she was lying to her children, and now she was having sexual fantasies about David and keeping secrets from Shirley. What in the world was going on with her?

Shirley answered the phone saying, "Yes, what?" There was a loud crash in the background, and Shirley yelled, "Mary Ann, stop that, would you? I'm trying to talk on the phone."

"Hi," Susan said. "Did I get you at a bad time?"

"Oh, Susan, it's you. I thought you were still gone on your trip. I'm glad you're home, though. I missed you. Did you have a good time?"

There was another loud series of bangs and crashes. "Mary Ann, take a break! Right now! Do you hear me?" Shirley yelled.

"Should I call later?" Susan asked.

"No, it's all right. Mary Ann's decided she wants to be a rock star and play the drums in an all-girl band. One of her friends lent her a drum set. Three drums, cymbals, the whole deal. The noise is unbelievable. I'm expecting one of the neighbors to call the police any minute. It's not even seven o'clock yet. How did you ever survive this age with Meagan and Shawn?"

"I didn't survive, not completely. The woman you know now is a mere shadow of the woman I was before raising thirteen-year-olds." Susan shouted to be heard above the background noise. "But you'll miss this when they've grown and moved away."

"Could you hold on a minute?" Shirley hollered into the phone. "I have to go kill my first-born child."

There was another loud crash followed by silence. "Okay, now we can talk," Shirley said when she came back to the phone.

"Did you kill her?" Susan asked. "It's awfully quiet there."

"I was tempted, but no. I threatened her with a month of phone restriction if she didn't stop for twenty minutes. What were you saying? I couldn't hear you."

"I was saying how much you'll miss all this when Mary Ann and Amanda are grown and leave home."

"Right now I can't wait to miss it. There're some days when I wonder what I was thinking having one child, let alone two. Let's talk about something other than children. How was your trip? Where did you go? Tell me everything."

"It was good. I can't wait to tell you about it. I have pictures I want to show you, but they're not developed yet. Can you come over tomorrow? What day is it anyway?" Susan barely listened to Shirley's reply. What had she done? She wasn't going to tell Shirley about the bear or show her the photographs. Shirley would never be able to understand why Susan had done this. Then when she had heard Shirley's voice on the phone, all she could think about was how much she wanted to share this bear and his photographs with her best friend. Susan rubbed her neck and concentrated on what Shirley was saying.

"You must have enjoyed your trip if you lost track of the days," Shirley said. "It's Thursday, and yes, I can come over tomorrow morning after I take the girls to school. Things have slowed down at work, so I'm taking several weeks off to get ready for the holidays and to hang out and be lazy for a change."

"Good," was all Susan could manage to say.

Shirley laughed. "Still a woman of few words, I see. But good works for both things, me taking time off and being able to come over to see your photos tomorrow morning."

After she hung up, Susan paced around the living room, trying to come up with a way to explain to Shirley what happened in the woods. She could only hope that the photographs would help Shirley understand about the bear. Susan checked her watch and dialed *Erick's Photos*. She wouldn't trust anyone other than Erick with these photos.

Erick answered on the first ring, sounding sleepy.

"Erick, it's Susan. Do you have time to develop and print some film this morning?"

"How many rolls are you talking about?"

"Two, one from my Nikon and one from the Minolta."

"Two is all? Are you going to want any special printing or blow-ups?"

"Maybe. I'll have to see the proofs first."

"If you can come now, I can do it right away. I have a wedding to print by tomorrow, but I can fit two rolls in this morning, if it isn't anything too complicated."

"Great. I'll be there in about fifteen minutes." Susan knew Erick hated doing weddings. He felt they insulted his artistic sensibilities.

It took over an hour for Erick to develop the film and make the proof sheets. He and Susan looked at the proofs through a magnifying lens.

"Where did you take these pictures?" Erick asked, all traces of tiredness gone now.

"In the woods, out near my house," Susan answered, moving the lens over the sheet of proofs.

"I can tell it's the woods," Erick said, sounding impatient. "I guess what I meant to ask is how did you get them?" He was unconsciously snapping his fingers, something he did when he was nervous or excited.

"I slept by a bear's den and followed him around."

"You did what?" Erick stared at her, openmouthed.

He so seldom looked directly at her that Susan found it unsettling. She forced herself not to look away. "I went into the woods and got to know this bear. At least I'm starting to get to know him. I took his picture the same way you photograph the crowd at weddings; I tried to be invisible and hoped he didn't notice me."

"Alone? You did this alone?"

"No, I wasn't alone. I had Chance with me." How many times had she said this in the last few weeks? It was starting to become her mantra, something that she chanted every time she heard the word alone.

"Chance? You had your dog with you when you did this?" Erick was running his hand through his short, spiky hair. Susan had seen him do this hundreds of times over the years when he couldn't get the contrast or definition of a print the way he wanted it.

"Yes, Chance was with me," Susan said firmly. "Now let's talk about which of these pictures we're going to print. Can you bring up the contrast on some of them?" Susan didn't want to talk about what she had done in the woods. It had happened, and that was all that needed to be said.

Erick kept on rubbing his hair, making it stand up in clumps on the top of his head.

"Erick," Susan said, pointing to the proofs.

"Oh, right. Sure, we can bring the contrast up, either with filers or a harder gradation of paper. How about size? Eight-by-ten, or what?"

"Let's see if we can get some of them up to sixteen-by-twenty without losing too much definition. Can you do it now?"

"Now?" Erick asked. "Yeah, sure. I don't have anything else to do."

"What about the wedding?"

"That can wait," Erick said over his shoulder. He was already heading for the darkroom.

———————————

Hours later, Susan and Erick had fourteen photographs printed, mounted, and leaning up against the front counter. Most were in standard eight-by-ten format but five were sixteen-by-twenty. In each one, the bear was in a different position.

There were two photographs of the bear chewing on grass and eight of him eating berries from various angles. Of this group, the one Susan had chosen to print in the larger size showed the bear's profile with his head raised and the tips of his small center teeth closed around a branch of ripe huckleberries. Susan liked this one in particular because it captured how delicately the bear plucked the berries from the bushes without breaking a single branch.

Another large photograph was the one Susan had taken of the bear scratching his back on a tree with that goofy expression on his face: head up, eyes closed, lower lip hanging down. Erick had printed the picture so that the bear's black coat stood in stark contrast against the white and brown bark of the alder tree, leaving the surrounding area in shadow. The bear's pleasure leaped off the paper.

The three other larger photographs were close-ups taken with the telephoto lens. One showed the bear from behind and off to the side as he bent to drink from the creek. His long tongue was curled as it dipped into the water, and small beads of moisture shown like diamonds on his chin. The next one was of the bear sitting in front of the cave tree, hunched forward, his head low, his brown eyes looking out with calm intent. A clump of mud was clearly visible below his left ear. In the diffused morning light, his black fur was glistening and streaked with silver.

The last of this group was Susan's favorite. It was of the cave tree in bright moonlight. At first glance, the den appeared as nothing more than a darker area at the bottom of vaguely textured grayness, a study in black on gray. But if you looked closely, and knew what you were looking for, the shape of the bear revealed itself. First it was nothing but a dark form buried in more darkness. Then the curves of the claws on a front paw emerged, then the outline of the bear's face came into focus. Soon it became impossible not to see the bear hidden inside the picture.

"These are beautiful photos," Erick said. "I've never seen anything like them, not here, not anywhere." He walked from one end of the counter to the other, examining each photograph.

"You did a wonderful job," Susan said. "Thank you." She hadn't known what to expect of the pictures, but they were, as Erick said, beautiful. The bear looked wild and at the same time dignified. Each photograph showed him going about his normal, everyday life alone in the woods. They were exactly how she hoped they would be.

Yet something was missing, something more about him that she wanted to show. She examined the photos carefully, trying to figure out what it was that she had felt when she was with the bear that she hadn't captured on film.

She glanced at her watch. "Oh, my gosh. I have to go. I had no idea it was this late." She wrapped each photo in a piece of butcher paper Erick kept in the shop and then stacked the photos together and wrapped another piece of butcher paper around the stack.

"When you have more of these to print, call me right away," Erick said, staring at the floor, his round face growing red. "And be careful out there in the woods."

"I will," Susan said on her way out the door.

David's office door was standing open when Susan got there. She looked in and saw him sitting at his desk eating a sandwich and reading from a stack of papers. Close to his right hand sat a mug with Hug a Fish inscribed on it.

"Hi," Susan said from the doorway. "Is this a bad time?"

"Susan. No, it's fine. Come in." David stood up and wiped his hands on a paper napkin. "Have you eaten? I have another sandwich, turkey with Swiss cheese on rye, and some coffee or juice, if you'd like."

At the mention of food, Susan's stomach growled loud enough that she was sure David heard it: she hadn't eaten much since she had come out of the woods. She put her hand on her stomach and smiled. "A sandwich and some juice would be great."

They ate in silence, sitting opposite each other at David's desk. He looked over the stack of papers while he ate.

Susan ate half her sandwich and set the rest on the paper plate David had given her. She gazed around his office. It reminded her of what she imagined a ship's cabin would be like, with every nook and cranny overflowing with books and papers. There was even a small refrigerator and a toaster oven. The office was comforting in a jumbled sort of way, the kind of place where you could wait out a violent storm.

A framed photograph on the bookshelf behind David caught her eye. It showed two boys standing on either side of a much younger version of David. All three were dressed in jeans and flannel shirts, holding fishing poles and smiling happily.

"Your children?" she asked, indicating the picture.

David turned in his chair and looked at the photograph. "Yes. That's Roger, and that's Derrick," he said, pointing at each boy in turn. "They were eight and ten at the time. We used to go fishing a lot. They're both grown now, with families of their own."

"And your wife? She didn't like to fish?"

David swiveled to face Susan. "When that picture was taken we were no longer married. At that point, neither of us had much interest in being near each other for more than ten minutes at a time."

"I'm sorry," Susan said. She couldn't think of anything else to say.

"We got married too young. It didn't help that I spent so much time at work and too little time at home."

"I see," Susan said, again at a loss for words.

David tossed the remains of his sandwich into the trashcan by his desk and set the papers aside. "You said you had something you wanted to show me."

"Yes, I brought these." Susan reached for the stack of photographs she had set on the floor beside her chair. She unwrapped the pictures and laid them out on a table opposite David's desk. He came from behind his desk and walked to the table. He looked carefully at each picture before moving to the next. When he was done, he faced her, his eyes searching hers. "You took these?"

"Yes."

"When?"

"After we talked last, I went back to Woolly Creek. I stayed for three nights." Unable to meet his eyes, she looked away from him. She stared at his desk, at the residue of his lunch—the mustard-stained paper plate, the empty coffee mug, the crumpled napkin.

David said, "You went back?"

Susan nodded. He was quiet for a long time. Finally he said, "These are outstanding photographs. I can't begin to imagine how you got close enough to this bear to take them."

Susan couldn't help but smile. "I did what you told me. I stayed close to his den at night. I'm not sure how the rest of it happened." She went on to tell him about her time in the woods, from her choice to stay behind the rock, thirty feet from the bear's den, to hearing the mountain lion scream in the night.

She finished by telling him about her last morning photographing the bear. "He knew I was there, he looked right at me, but he didn't react at all. He just went on with what he was doing. Here," Susan said, setting a hand by each of two pictures on the table. "These were taken that morning, this one of him drinking and this one of him looking at me."

David examined the photos. "Remarkable," was all he said.

"When Chance and I followed him up out of the canyon, this same morning, he seemed to be waiting for us." Susan gestured with her hands as she talked, her excitement growing. "He was standing there, right in the trail, looking at us. When we got up onto the trail, he walked off. He didn't run. He sort of moseyed along. He even stopped to graze. Then he left the trail. I lost him in the brush, but before that, before he left the trail, he looked back at us. It was strange, but it seemed like he was checking to see if we were going with him, like he wanted us to follow him."

Susan didn't know what else to say. Here in David's office, the whole thing sounded unbelievable. Without the photographs as proof, it might have been a dream.

David glanced from the photographs to her and again said, "Remarkable." He returned to his desk and shuffled around in the pile of papers he had been looking at while they ate. When he found the ones he was looking for, he held them up. "This is what I wanted to talk to you about. It's a draft of a logging plan one of my graduate students came across. It indicates that Smith and Sons is getting ready to harvest timber in and around Woolly Creek. It includes the area where you found the bear's den."

"They're planning to log close to the bear's den?" Susan asked.

"Yes. They might cut that very tree. I felt you should know about this. I didn't want you to get too committed to your project. I had no idea that you'd been there again, and that all this had happened." David nodded at the photographs.

"But they can't log there. It's his home. He lives there. He'll...." Susan looked away and then back at David. "Is there anything we can do about this?"

"Not that I'm aware of. The head forester for the Woolly Creek area is a man named Jacob Riley. I've dealt with him before. He's careful, follows what few rules there are. You won't find any loopholes in his work."

"Does it say anything in the report about the bear's den? I haven't seen flagging around that area."

"There might not be any flagging for you to see. Smith and Sons hasn't yet submitted a Timber Harvest Plan to the California Department of Forestry for the Woolly Creek watershed, and at this point a wildlife survey is not required."

David gazed around his office, his eyes stopping briefly on the picture of him and his sons. "The sad truth is that when logging plans are drawn up, their potential impact on animals is not taken into consideration. This is especially true of bears. Foresters will tell you that bears thrive in recently logged areas. A bear isn't a logging company's favorite animal to begin with. They destroy trees, especially young trees. They eat them. They even pull off the bark and eat the cambium of fifty- and sixty-year-old trees, basically girdling them. Whether this constitutes a significant problem in a growing forest depends on who you talk to."

"What about near Woolly Creek?" Susan asked. "They can't take trees close to a creek, can they?"

"Yes, they can. The Forest Practice Act of 1973 was set up to pretty much allow timber companies free rein under the guise of providing lumber and other forest products to a growing population, with just a little nod in the direction of watershed and wildlife protection." David leaned back on the edge of his desk and laid the papers down beside him. "Until there are better regulations, there's basically no control of logging in stream and creek beds. Often all the trees down to the high-water line are cut. For now, it's more or less a free-for-all out there."

Susan didn't know anything specific about logging practices. She had lived as a neighbor to Smith and Sons for the last twenty-five years and had seen the timber industry go through major changes during that time. When she and Bill had first moved to Farhaven, timber was the lifeblood of the county. Timber companies controlled almost everything, including what jobs were available and who was elected to public office.

She had become increasingly dismayed at the amount of logging in the area and the ensuing devastation to the land and rivers. She found it heartbreaking that the old-growth redwoods, some of the most ancient trees in the world, were being cut at alarming rates.

A few years ago, somewhere in the mid-70s, the timber industry started to lose its hold on the county. Years of intensive logging had significantly decreased the amount of available old-growth redwood. Now many of the smaller mills had closed down, their employees let go and their lands bought out by larger companies specializing in second-growth timber. Environmental groups were drawing attention to the negative impacts of some logging practices, including mass aerial spraying of herbicides in sensitive watersheds close to residential areas.

Fifteen years ago when Smith and Sons had logged the forest adjacent to Susan's home, she had been horrified at how the land looked when they had finished. The area hadn't been clearcut, leaving some trees still standing. Even so, much of it looked like bombs had exploded there. Most of the trees were gone. In many places, large equipment had driven over the fertile forest floor, turning the topsoil under and creating deep ruts in the sunbaked clay that was left. All of her familiar landmarks had either been demolished or buried under piles of broken branches.

It was hard to imagine trees growing there again, but slowly the land had healed. First berry vines, pampas grass, and mountain lilac poked up through the packed soil. Next came small alder trees, salal, and huckleberry bushes. The few young redwood and Douglas firs left uncut grew stronger, their leaves adding nutrients to the soil underneath them. It wasn't the forest she had known before the logging, and it wouldn't be for a hundred years or more, but it was recovering. Once again it was home to numerous species of birds and other animals, this bear being one of them.

"Can't we talk to the forester?" Susan asked. "Maybe if we show him the photographs, if he knows that a bear lives in this area, he might be able to do something to save this bear's home." She caught herself twirling a strand of hair between her thumb and forefinger, a nervous habit left over from her childhood. She dropped her hands to her side and hooked her thumbs into the front pockets of her jeans to keep them still.

"Probably the best you'll be able to do is find out what percentage of trees they're planning to cut," David said. "Smith and Sons still clearcuts a significant portion of their land, but in the last ten or fifteen years they've been experimenting with a few selective cuts. The objective of a selective cut is to harvest the most valuable trees in a given area, leaving the rest of the trees uncut. I can't venture to guess how many trees they'd leave in a particular area."

He shrugged. "Projected numbers are arbitrary at best. Things can change as they proceed. Often they're unable to leave the required number of trees specified in the Timber Harvest Plan. If a section is too dense, for example, and the young trees stand in the way of cutting the larger trees, the timber company can file for an amendment to cut all the trees—large and small—in a portion of it. This tract is usually not larger than eighty acres, but in some cases it can be well over a hundred acres."

"Doesn't it make more sense to let some of the smaller trees grow instead of cutting everything down to get to a few large trees?" Susan asked.

"Of course it does," David said. "That's the idea behind a selective cut or a thinning. Unfortunately, what makes sense doesn't often play into these decisions. It's important to remember that the mission of the timber industry is to cut trees in the most efficient way possible. Almost anything that stands in the way of that mission is considered an acceptable loss."

Susan gave her head a quick, tight shake, like a horse flicking off a fly.

"All big businesses are the same," David went on. "Their primary goal is to make a profit for their current shareholders. For the timber industry, this means cutting marketable trees now. As a neighbor you have the right to know what the forester's plans are for this area. As I said earlier, the forester for the Woolly Creek watershed is Jacob Riley."

He flipped through a Rolodex on his desk, wrote something down on a piece of paper, and handed it to Susan. "Here's Jacob's work phone number. They won't be doing anything until the rains stop in the spring, so you have time, but the sooner you see him the better. Once Jacob gets a harvest plan approved, he seldom changes his mind."

"Would you be willing to go with me?" Susan asked. She knew she sounded insecure, but this was way out of her league.

"No. I wouldn't be any help. I'd be the opposite of help. Jacob and I have already had some serious discussions about other logging sites. To say we don't see eye to eye on the issue of logging in watersheds is a gross understatement. He knows me, and he doesn't like me. You go. Take these photographs with you. They're compelling. They speak for this bear better than I ever could. Don't expect too much, though. Jacob's paid to provide timber; that's his job, and he's good at it. He's not easily swayed."

He took a small datebook out of his shirt pocket and flipped through it. "I'm going to be out of town most of next week attending a conference in Oregon. I'll call you when I get back to see how it went with Jacob."

"I can't do this by myself," Susan said. "I don't know enough about logging to be able to speak intelligently about this issue, and I don't have a lot of practice speaking in a business setting. In any setting, really. I always say the wrong thing."

David laughed, a deep, joyful laugh that evolved into a low chuckle. After a short, startled moment, Susan asked, "What are you laughing at?"

"You," he said. "You continue to surprise me. I've not met many people who are so right and at the same time so wrong about their own qualities. It's true, you're not a master of small talk, but you're wrong to think of yourself as inarticulate. You have plenty to say when you're passionate about something, and you have no trouble saying it."

All signs of humor were now gone from his face. "You're the best person to speak for this bear. You've been there, I haven't. And you have these," he held out both hands in an expansive gesture, indicating the display of photographs. "Jacob will listen to you. I doubt he'll agree with you, but he will listen, and that's better than nothing."

───────────────

Susan stopped at the local market in Farhaven on her way home from David's office. It was while standing in the checkout line that she made a firm decision to talk to Jacob Riley as soon as possible. In front of her in line was a man she had never met but recognized from seeing him over the years around town. He was one of the many people in the area who lived out in the hills and came into town to shop. They were rugged, independent, hardworking people, usually employed by the timber companies or as laborers for local building contractors.

The man was practically shouting at the clerk as she rang up his groceries. More than likely, years of working around loud equipment had damaged his hearing. "I called the Department of Fish and Game, but they wouldn't do a thing. I told them this bear was coming right up to my front door. Yesterday my wife found some of its fur stuck to the doorframe. She's worried he'll break in someday trying to get food. Those people at Fish and Game told me to clean up my trash, to keep it in the house if I had to. That's all they said, bring in the trash."

The clerk nodded and said, "That's awful."

"Yes, well I told them this bear's getting way too comfortable with people. I said bears don't belong up around people's houses. They belong in the woods. So they says to me that when this bear learns it won't find food around my house it'll head back to the woods. But I'm telling you this bear can't find enough to eat in the woods. Last year the trees behind my house were logged and now there's nothing left, nothing for this bear to eat, and it knows there's food in my house."

"What are you going to do?" the clerk asked. She glanced at Susan and gave her a quick smile.

"I'll try bringing in the garbage," the man said, "but if this bear doesn't go away I'll have to do something. I mean I have kids." He bounced on his toes, his voice carrying throughout the store.

Susan touched his arm. "Yes, ma'am?" His voice dropped a bit as he faced her.

"Where is it that you live?" Susan asked.

"Oh, me and my wife, we have five acres out on the Wild River, about fifty miles from here."

Susan was so relieved that his house was as far away as it was from the bear's den in Woolly Creek that before she could stop herself she said, "Good," loud enough to cause the clerk to look up at her. The man didn't seem to hear her, though. He kept on talking. "Doesn't matter where I live. Bears are becoming more of a problem in lots of places, and I'm telling you, Fish and Game isn't willing to do a damn thing about it." He glanced at Susan. "Excuse my language, ma'am." Susan nodded and smiled thinly.

"Like I was saying," the man continued. "Fish and Game used to catch problem bears and take them out in the woods, but not anymore." He placed his bags of groceries in the cart. When he reached the door he looked back and said in a half shout, "Isn't safe having bears up around the house, that's all I'm saying."

Susan had read an article not that long ago in the local newspaper that addressed the Department of Fish and Game's bear-relocation policy. Some counties live-trapped and relocated bears who were habitually eating garbage and hanging out around houses. This procedure was fraught with problems. The biggest issue was that the process of trapping and relocation frequently resulted in injury to the bear, sometimes severe enough that the only recourse was to euthanize the animal. In other cases, researchers found that they had accidentally relocated a bear into another bear's territory. If this new territory wasn't large enough to support more than one bear, the newcomer and the resident bear often fought to win the territory. The loser would run off, sometimes dying of starvation if there wasn't enough food in the new area for the bear to build up a layer of fat before winter set in.

Another problem was that the relocated bears would often return to their home territories. The article recounted a story of Fish and Game tagging and relocating a young female bear. Later, as she traveled through a neighborhood fifty miles from her home territory, someone shot her. The wildlife biologist working for Fish and Game at the time believed that in all likelihood the bear was not planning to stay around the houses but was trying to get back to her home range in the most direct route possible. Researchers have yet to identify what type of internal homing device bears have. Nonetheless, many bears are able to find their way back to their old territories, even when relocated as far as a hundred miles away.

Right when Susan got home from the market, before she had time to change her mind, she dialed the office number for Jacob Riley. It was late. He might not be there, but she had to take the chance. If she waited until tomorrow, she might lose her courage and not make the call.

"Forestry. Riley speaking," he answered on the first ring.

"Hello, Mr. Riley. I'm Susan Campton. I was hoping I could make an appointment to talk to you about the area around Woolly Creek."

"What's your interest in this area, Ms. Campton?"

Susan didn't know how to answer his question. She should have written something down before she called. What could she say that wouldn't sound ridiculous over the phone?

"Ms. Campton?"

"Yes. I'm sorry." Say something other than you're sorry, she told herself. He doesn't care what you're thinking or feeling. He wants to know why you phoned him.

She gripped the receiver tighter and started, "I've lived close to Woolly Creek for many years now and have come to know much of the land around the creek. I'd like to talk to you about the details of any logging you have planned there. I want some specific information about the location and the number of trees you're planning to cut."

"We haven't submitted a Timber Harvest Plan for the Woolly Creek area. I'm unwilling to listen to public comments until after a plan has been submitted to the Department of Forestry."

"I understand that, but I'd like to talk to you before you submit the plan. Is it possible to meet with you soon?" Now that she had him on the phone, Susan felt more than ever that she needed to talk to him in person about the bear and to show him the photographs. There had to be a way to convince him to leave that section of the forest uncut.

"What is it you want to discuss with me?" he asked. Susan detected the slightest edge of irritation in his otherwise polite voice. She guessed that he had to deal frequently with people who were opposed to cutting trees for one reason or another. But she wasn't another person complaining about logging near their home. She was campaigning to save this bear's home.

"It would be best if we could sit down together and talk," she said. "I also have something I want to show you."

"Some sort of visual aid, huh?"

"Yes, that's right. A visual aid." Susan made an attempt to soften her voice, to sound friendly.

"I have time tomorrow afternoon. Let's see. Can you be here at three-thirty?"

"Yes, that will be fine."

"Come to the main office building at the Salt Lagoon facility. Do you know where that is?"

"Just across from Salt Lagoon, off the highway on the right when driving north?"

"Yes. My office is number seventeen. Ask at the main desk. They'll tell you how to find me."

Susan wanted to shout thank you into the phone. Instead she said, "Fine. I'll see you tomorrow afternoon," and hung up.

That night, Susan again dreamed of the bear. In this dream, when she pushed the last branch aside and faced the bear, she heard a distant buzzing that sounded like a large beehive. As the bear came near her, the buzzing grew in intensity. The bear jerked his head from side to side. Chance drew back on the leash, crouching behind her. She spun around, madly searching for the source of the sound.

Susan woke up, wet with sweat, the blankets and sheets twisted around her. Something was wrong. Her mind was a blank, and her heart was beating as if she had been running for miles. She looked around, unnerved. The dream returned to her and then faded. What's wrong with me? she thought. I've never had bad dreams before, not like this.

She got up and reached for her robe. The clock on the dresser read one-thirty. She should try to go back to sleep, but the sheets on the bed were damp with sweat. She took the quilt off the rocking chair in the living room and stretched out on the couch. Sleep overtook her in stages. She didn't wake up again until early the next morning.

After her morning shower, Susan stood in front of the mirror on the back of the bathroom door and inspected the scratches she had gotten on her face and arms from climbing through the brush in the woods. Shirley was due here soon. Susan didn't want her to see the scratches the minute she came into the house. Neither Erick nor David had noticed them, or if they had, they hadn't said anything about them. Shirley was different; she was more observant, and she worried about Susan. Seeing Susan all scratched up could make everything else Susan was going to tell her more difficult. Telling Shirley about the bear was going to be hard enough. She didn't need a few scratches complicating the issue.

The scratches on her arms were easy to hide with a long-sleeved shirt. The ones on her face were more of an issue. Susan leaned in closer to the mirror. The scratch on her upper lip was tiny and blended in with the color of her lips. Shirley would have to look closely to see it. The one on her forehead was more of a problem. It was healing but was still close to an inch long and bright pink. Susan fussed around with her hair, combing a few strands forward and cutting them a little so that they curled over the scratch. This should work if she could remember to keep her hands off her hair.

Satisfied that the scratches didn't show, Susan went into the kitchen and mixed up a batch of cranberry muffins and started a pot of coffee. She propped the big photographs up against the couch and spread the rest out on the dinner table. Then she stood looking out the front window at the small section of the road visible beyond the driveway, anxiously awaiting Shirley's arrival.

Half an hour later, Shirley swept into the living room, huddled inside a ruby-red wool coat. Her fingernail polish matched the color of the coat exactly. "It's cold this morning," she said. "Seems like we're going to have one heck of a winter." She gave Susan a hug and turned toward the couch, shrugging out of her coat. She stopped with her coat hanging halfway down her arms and stared at the photographs. Susan gently tugged the coat free and folded it over the rocking chair.

"What are these?" Shirley asked, continuing to stare at the photos of the bear.

"The pictures I took on my trip."

Shirley took a step toward the couch and leaned in close to the picture of the bear looking out at her. "Where did you take them? Were you at a zoo or a wildlife park?"

"No. I took them in the woods here on Smith and Sons land."

Shirley stared at Susan. "You took them in the woods? How?"

"Let's sit down, and I'll tell you all about it. I have fresh cranberry muffins and coffee. And there are more pictures on the table." Susan put one hand on Shirley's back, gently guiding her to the table.

"More? You have more pictures?" Shirley walked to the table, her head still turned toward the couch. "This is scaring me. I don't understand how you got these pictures."

Susan poured coffee into two large mugs and set them and a plate of warm muffins on the table. Shirley sat across from Susan at the table, her brow knitted into two tense lines, all traces of her usual playfulness gone. Susan recounted all that had happened in the last few weeks, starting with her first meeting with David and ending with her last day in the woods. What she left out was the sound of the mountain lion screaming and how frightened she had been hearing it. She also glossed over how it felt to be out in the windstorm. That was more than Shirley needed to know. Susan mostly told Shirley about the bear—his size, his beauty, his awkward gracefulness.

Shirley remained silent throughout Susan's account. Neither of them had touched the coffee or the muffins. When Shirley turned, yet again, to scowl at the bear's photos, Susan ran her tongue over her dry lips, and for a brief moment she felt like sticking it out at the back of her friend's head. Why was Shirley being such a pill about this?

"I know it sounds crazy," Susan said when Shirley was again facing her, "but on the last day in the woods, the bear...I guess he had gotten used to us being there, though it felt like something more than that." Susan watched Shirley, trying unsuccessfully to gauge her reaction. "It was almost as if he wanted us to follow him, as if he liked having us around." Silence. "Shirley? Say something."

Shirley sighed. "I don't understand any of this. Why would you want to do this?"

"I didn't understand it at first, either," Susan said. "I thought if people were able to see pictures of a bear in the wild, doing what bears do, maybe they would never consider doing what Hank did. But this project is for me, too. Ever since Shawn and Meagan left home, I've been struggling to find a purpose for my life. Then Bill died, and I felt lost. Not just lonely, but like I'd lost a piece of who I was along with losing Bill."

With a slight smile, Susan went on, "Without a family who needed me, who was I? An empty-nested, middle-aged widow with nothing but a smelly dog for company?" She was trying for some humor, hoping Shirley would crack a smile, but no luck. Now that she thought about it, being a lonely widow wasn't all that funny.

Susan shrugged, embarrassed by her foolish attempt at a joke. There must be a way she could explain to her best friend what she had learned about herself by being close to the bear. "As I spent time near this bear, taking these photographs, getting to know him, I began to rediscover who I am, separate from my family. Do you understand what I'm trying to say?" Shirley nodded, and then shook her head.

"All I know is, it felt right to be there," Susan continued. "Somehow I felt I belonged there. Like I had a reason to be there."

Susan waited. Shirley remained silent, her body rigid. Susan rolled her shoulders, trying to relieve a knot in her back. "When I met with David yesterday," she said, "he told me that Smith and Sons is getting ready to log in the Woolly Creek watershed, right where this bear lives. I have an appointment to talk to the forester later today. Maybe when he sees these pictures, he'll change his mind about logging close to this bear's den."

"Didn't they log here about ten years ago?" Shirley asked, her expression softening somewhat.

"It was closer to fifteen, sometime around 1963 or so, but you're right, it wasn't that long ago." Susan relaxed a little now that Shirley was speaking to her again.

"That's right. John and I had just gotten married. There aren't many trees left, are there?"

"There are some large trees left, especially along the creek. David said they might do a selective cut, taking the biggest trees and leaving the rest."

"That doesn't sound all that bad," Shirley said. "Maybe it won't affect the bears at all."

"If it were a few trees, you might be right, but I'm pretty sure they did a selective cut last time, and you know how that looked. There were hardly any trees left, and in many places there was nothing left of the soil but gray mud. I want to find out what the logging plans are and let them know this bear lives there."

Shirley stood up and looked at the pictures spread out on the table. After studying each one, she went over to stand in front of those leaning against the couch. Susan stayed where she was and watched her friend.

"I like this one best," Shirley said, pointing to the photo of the bear backed up to the tree, scratching. "He looks satisfied, don't you think?

196

It reminds me of John. You know, the way he uses the door frames to scratch his back." A smile flitted across Shirley's lips.

Susan saw the smile, caught her friend's eye, and grinned back at her. "Yes, you're right. He does look a lot like John. Only friendlier."

Shirley laughed, and then frowned. "Don't get me wrong. What you did was foolish and dangerous, and I'm mad at you for not talking to me about this sooner. What if something had happened and I didn't know where to start looking for you?"

Susan tapped the table. "I left a note right here, saying where I was going."

"Oh, you left a note. Great. That's reassuring," Shirley said, pursing her lips.

Susan came to stand next to Shirley. "I'm sorry I didn't tell you about this sooner. I had to work it out for myself first. Once I started following the bear, I sort of got carried away."

"I thought we had a deal," Shirley said. "You'd tell me your important stuff and I'd tell you mine. That's what friends are for."

"I know, and you're right. I didn't want you to worry about me. And I figured you'd try to talk me out of it."

"You're damn right I would have tried to talk you out of it. You are the craziest person I know." Shirley shook her head. "Honest to God, who in their right mind would spend one night sleeping in the woods near a wild bear? And you did this for several nights." She took Susan's hand in hers and swung it back and forth like they were in elementary school waiting in line for their turn at the slide. "You did get some fantastic pictures, though."

Shirley gave Susan's hand a quick squeeze and headed for the kitchen. "Let's make a fresh pot of coffee and eat some of these muffins of yours while we talk about what you're going to say to this forester."

Even after two hours of discussing every possible approach for dealing with Jacob Riley, Susan and Shirley still hadn't come up with a good plan. They finally decided that Susan's best option was to let the photographs speak for themselves. All Susan would need to do after that, Shirley believed, was to point out the location of the bear's den. She was sure that once the forester saw the pictures and understood that this bear lived next to Woolly Creek, he could develop a logging plan that would leave most of the bear's territory untouched.

Susan didn't think it would be that simple. Over the years she had seen many neighborhood groups attempt to negotiate with local timber companies with no success. But she couldn't simply walk away. She had to at least try to save this bear's home.

Before Shirley left, they went outside with Chance to play with him. Shirley loved to throw Chance's old rubber ball for him. She had played softball in high school and pitching the ball for Chance let her show that her arm was still strong enough to throw a runner out at first. Chance loved it, too. He was a full-fledged retriever. To him, life was all about bringing back the flying object.

The first time Bill saw Shirley throw a ball, he had said, "You know, you don't throw like a girl."

Shirley had winked at him and said, "And you, big fella, don't throw like a guy." It was true. For such a tall, strong man, Bill never had learned to direct a ball properly. It almost always ended up either short of where he wanted it to go or way off in the bushes somewhere.

After several throws, Shirley said, "That's it, Chance. I've got to get home." To Susan she said, "You should wear something professional to the meeting. Your tan wool jacket and matching pants would be good. And Susan, honey, don't wear your hiking boots. You have that nice pair of brown flats. They would look great, very sophisticated." Susan chuckled. Leave it to Shirley to come up with the most appropriate out-fit for talking a forester out of logging in the woods.

That afternoon, Susan studied her reflection in the mirror. Shirley was right; the tan pants, jacket, and brown flats did make her look more professional. She was uncomfortable, though, as if she were play-ing at being someone she wasn't. This is not me, she thought. I'm not a businesswoman. I'm not sure what I am, but this isn't it. She settled on a clean pair of jeans, a brown cotton long-sleeved shirt, and her hik-ing boots. At the last minute, she added the wool jacket. A token bit of classiness couldn't hurt.

She placed the photos between sheets of butcher paper in a scuffed, black leather portfolio, a survivor from those long ago photography classes. "Wish me luck," she said to Chance, who watched her from his pillow by the woodstove.

Jacob Riley didn't look at all like Susan had envisioned him. Based on his polite but somewhat curt manner over the phone and David's ac-count, she had expected more of a resemblance to the man at the gro-cery store who was having trouble with a bear. She had pictured Jacob Riley with the same hardened look of someone who has spent years in the woods. Instead, in his tailored business suit and his meticulously combed hair and clean-shaven face, he looked more like a lawyer or a bank manager. When she entered the room, he rose from behind his desk and indicated that she should sit in the chair across from him.

Susan sat, leaned the portfolio against the chair, and tucked her feet back. She buttoned the wool jacket closed across her chest and smoothed the bottom edge down over the top of her jeans. Why hadn't she listened to Shirley and worn her good pants? She could have at least cleaned her boots.

"Ms. Campton, what can I do for you?" Jacob sat with his hands folded on top of a neat stack of papers on his desk.

She began, "As I told you over the phone, I want to discuss Smith and Sons property in the Woolly Creek watershed. I heard that your company is getting ready to log there. Is that correct?"

"Yes, we do plan to log in the Woolly Creek area in the near future, although we haven't submitted a formal harvest plan at this time. What is your involvement with this area? You weren't clear about that on the phone."

Susan hesitated, unsure how much of her history in the woods she should tell him. She had, after all, been trespassing for years. Be succinct, she told herself. Tell him what you want him to know about the bear and nothing more. "In the last few weeks I've spent quite a bit of time in the woods by Woolly Creek. During this time, I discovered a bear's den in a hollowed-out redwood tree next to the creek. I was able to follow and photograph the bear who uses this den. I brought the photographs with me, so I could show you the bear. I'm hoping your company is not planning to log in the area around his home." She reached for the portfolio.

"Let me get this straight," Jacob said. "You followed a bear in the woods and took pictures of it?"

"Yes, that's correct, and I spent a few nights sleeping by his den, getting to know him." She stood up and opened the portfolio, looking around the office. "Where would you like me to set up the pictures?"

"Wait a minute." Jacob sat up taller, his hands pressed on the desktop, causing the pile of papers to shift sideways. "Did I understand you correctly? You said that you slept by a bear's den somewhere along

Woolly Creek? That you followed a wild bear and took photographs of it?"

"Yes. Here, let me show you." Susan took the pictures out of the portfolio and set them, one by one, on the floor opposite his desk, leaning them back against the wall.

When the last photograph was in place, she faced Jacob. He sat with his elbows on the desk and his hands clasped under his chin, staring at the pictures. Susan waited. Jacob got up from behind his desk and came across the room for a closer view. He paced along the wall, looking at each picture for a full minute. When he reached the last one he said, "You'd better tell me what this is all about."

"At first it wasn't about anything." Susan spoke quietly. "I had this vague idea about photographing local bears. I found this bear's den one day on a hike. The rest happened as the bear became accustomed to us. I took these photographs during a three-day period. My dog and I stayed in the woods, slept close to this bear's den, and followed him during the day."

As she talked, Susan stepped closer to Jacob until she was standing right in front of him. She had to resist an urge to step back. She sensed something, almost like a vibration or scent coming off him. This is what a dog would smell, she thought, the scent of strength, power, and dominance.

There was no actual odor, of course, other than that of freshly laundered clothes and a faint aroma of aftershave. It was clear, however, who was in charge here. This was his territory, and she was the intruder.

"How were you able to get close enough to a bear to get these pictures?" Jacob asked.

"My dog and I slept behind a rock about thirty feet away from the burnt-out redwood tree that this bear uses as a den. We were lucky. He seemed to get used to us. He kept doing what he was doing while I took these pictures."

Susan moved closer to the photographs. "These three were taken while I was fairly close to him, out in the open." She pointed to the photographs she had taken on her last morning in the woods. "And these, where he's eating berries, were taken when my dog and I were both there in the berry patch, in plain sight. He knew we were there. He saw us, but he kept on eating like he would if he were alone."

"You're saying you had a dog with you when you took these pictures?" Jacob spoke each word slowly and clearly, as if he had to struggle to keep from shouting at her.

"Yes. But before I did this I conditioned my dog to bears in the zoo. It took some time, several weeks in fact, but he learned to be calm and stay quiet around the bears. Of course it was different in the woods, but other than one time, he remembered what he was supposed to do."

The muscles around Jacob's mouth tightened. He walked behind his desk and sat. "Sit down, Ms. Campton," he said, waving impatiently at the chair across from him. Susan sat. Jacob tapped the top of his desk with his fingertips. "What is it you want from me? About this bear?"

"I want you to leave the trees in the area around his home uncut."

A smile played across Jacob's lips. "Here's something I haven't heard before—leave the trees for a bear."

His face became serious again. "Ms. Campton, I'm unclear as to what section of our lands you're talking about, but if we're planning to harvest timber from the area where this bear's den is, we'll continue with our plans, bear or no bear. Logging doesn't hurt bears. Bears thrive in logged areas. Logging opens the canopy and allows for more grasses and berries to grow, and of course bears also eat young trees."

"This area has already been logged recently," Susan said. "If you have a map, I can show you where I'm talking about."

Jacob selected a map from a rack behind him and, pushing the stack of papers on his desk to one side, unrolled the map on the desk. He set two glass paperweights shaped like redwood trees on opposite corners of the map to hold it open.

Susan came around the desk and looked at the map. "The bear's den is here, next to the creek," she said, pointing to a spot on the map by Woolly Creek. "From what I can tell, all of this is part of his territory." Using her finger, she traced a circle around the area from Woolly Creek to the Main Line, taking in several small streams close to where she had photographed the bear eating berries. "Since much of this area was logged fewer than twenty years ago, there are already patches of berries and open areas of young trees and grasses. If you log here again, this bear will lose his food supply. He'll lose his home. I'm not sure what will happen to him then. I do know that many bears are killed each year when they move into neighborhoods looking for food."

Jacob eyed the map for a long time. At last, he looked up and said, "We are not required to protect habitat for bears. They're not considered endangered."

"Are you planning to log right here?" Susan asked, tapping her finger hard on the map next to Woolly Creek where the bear had his den.

"As I already said, we have not yet filed a Timber Harvest Plan for this area. I'm under no obligation to tell you anything about our plans, but yes, the trees in this area will almost certainly be harvested in the spring or early summer next year."

Susan ran her finger once more around the area where the bear had his den. "Can we talk about how many trees you'll take from this particular area?"

"No. I won't discuss this until we've filed a Timber Harvest Plan. When we do, I will set aside a period of time for public comment. You need to understand that bears will not be a consideration. It's truly not a problem. This bear of yours will undoubtedly leave during the logging operation. He'll probably find a new home. What he does is not my concern. Providing timber is my concern, and the area in the Woolly Creek watershed contains some valuable trees."

Jacob looked at the photographs. "These are beautiful pictures. You're a talented artist." He turned to her. "However, as part of my job as forester, I'm required to remind you that you were trespassing on timber company lands when you took these photos. What you did was dangerous. I strongly recommend that you stay off our lands in the future. If you're found there, you will be cited and prosecuted for trespassing."

Susan walked across the room and collected the photographs. She slid them into the portfolio. There had to be a way to convince him to leave the trees around the bear's den alone. She wanted to plead with him, to shout, even to get on her knees and beg, but none of this would change his mind. In a way, she understood his position. To him, the trees were a crop to harvest. Within a few years after logging, the berries and grasses would start to grow back. But what would happen to the bear before the land recovered, before the berry bushes grew back and the water ran clean again, before the trees grew tall enough to provide shelter and avenues to safety?

Susan was at the door leading out of his office when Jacob said, "Ms. Campton, I'm sorry you're worried about this bear. I want to assure you that he'll be fine. Bears are extremely adaptable."

She glanced back at him over her shoulder and was shocked to see a look of genuine compassion on his face. Was it possible that he had some concern for the welfare of the animals who lived in the woods? Without responding, she stepped out into the hall and shut the door behind her.

She hadn't made it halfway across the parking lot when she started to shake with anger and frustration. She got into the van and gripped the steering wheel, her knuckles white. That compassionate facade of his meant nothing. Nothing! He was going to log the Woolly Creek area regardless of how he felt, or pretended to feel. She was powerless to change that. Her ineffectiveness infuriated her. She hit the steering wheel hard with the palm of her hand. Then hit it again. Her eyes burned with unshed tears. She rubbed at her closed eyelids with her hands. "I will not cry," she said out loud. She took two deep breaths, started the van's engine, and drove out of the parking lot.

At the intersection to the highway, Susan brought the van to a stop. Off to her right, a herd of Roosevelt elk grazed in a large field bordering the highway. There were seven cows and two young bulls with small racks of antlers. Their brown manes lay like cloaks over their tawny chests and backs, making them look regal in the late afternoon light.

For as long as she could remember there had been elk grazing in this field, but she never got over her amazement at seeing them there, so close to such a busy road. Cars and trucks whizzed past, some blasting their horns as they went. The elk continued to graze on the long grass as if nothing unusual were happening.

During the summer months, she had often seen a line of twenty tourists or more standing here by their cars, taking pictures of the elk. Some walked into the field for a closer look. A few years back, she had read a newspaper article about a man who had run next to a large bull elk, terrorizing it by trying to put his young daughter up on its back while his wife attempted to take a picture of them. That man was lucky that no one in his family was injured. Susan tried to imagine the bear there in the field with the elk, peacefully chewing grass. What would he do if a tourist holding a small child ran at him, hoping to get a photograph?

"Adaptable," Susan said, almost spitting out the word. Not that kind of adaptable. Still filled with anger over the possibility of the bear becoming a victim of the timber industry's need for more profit, Susan pressed hard on the gas pedal and skidded around the turn onto the highway.

As she drove along the edge of the lagoon, her shoulders slowly relaxed and her hands lightened their grip on the steering wheel. Here the steel-gray water of Salt Lagoon came almost to the edge of the pavement, separated from it by a narrow strip of brown sand.

Beyond the lagoon, to the west, a wide expanse of wind-rippled beach stretched to the Pacific Ocean. The sun had dropped through a layer of clouds that had rolled in over the ocean, leaving behind a blaze of orange at the horizon. A double-crested cormorant flew over the lagoon, its wing tips skimming the surface of the water—a black silhouette against gray.

If the clouds were any indication, another storm was on its way. As Shirley had said, this winter was likely to be a hard one. Fall was often one of the nicest times of the year on the north coast, sunny and warm, with a touch of coolness to the air. This year the rainy season had already started, and it was much colder than usual for late October.

Susan wondered what the bear would do during the winter, perhaps his last winter next to Woolly Creek. From reading David's manual, she had learned that bears in the Pacific Northwest didn't hibernate in the winter. She had grown up with the idea that all bears hibernated, but that wasn't true. In areas where it seldom snowed, black bears slept longer and more often, but they didn't stop moving around altogether, or stop hunting for food.

As the dark day descended into a darker, colder night, Susan made the decision to go back into the woods in the morning. She wanted to see where the bear went to find food this time of year. More than that, she wanted to follow him while he was still active, before he became sluggish and started sleeping most of the time. She was sure that she had missed a crucial piece of information last time, something she needed to learn about this bear. Or something she needed to learn from him.

Chance greeted her at the front door with his ball in his mouth, as usual. Susan threw the ball across the pasture for him until her arm gave out. Then she went back inside to phone Shirley.

Shirley answered the phone, saying, "It's dinnertime here. If you're selling something, I can't talk now."

"Shirley, it's Susan. I can call later if you're eating."

"Oh, Susan. Good, it's you. No, we're not eating. That's my line for those people selling stuff over the phone. Drives me crazy that they always call right when we're getting ready to eat, but tonight we ate early. Amanda had a basketball game. John took her, and Mary Ann went along. So I'm all alone. How'd it go with the forester?"

"Like I expected it would. He said that bears are not a consideration. Providing timber is. He basically told me that they're going to log around Woolly Creek and there's nothing I can do about it."

"That can't be right. They already logged there. How many trees do they need to cut from one area? Is there something more we can do, or some other reason they might not be able to cut those trees?"

"No, I don't think so. There aren't many restrictions on logging in watersheds, and there are apparently even fewer requirements to protect the animals living there. It wouldn't make a difference anyway, because, like you said, they logged much of this area about fifteen years ago. Any animals needing a mature forest to survive are long gone."

Susan looked out the window at the dark tree line on the edge of the pasture. Her face reflected back at her. She touched the cold glass, let her fingertips rest there for a moment. "I can't talk about this anymore tonight. It's too confusing. I just wanted to let you know what happened, and to tell you I'm going back into the woods tomorrow."

"Tomorrow? I wish you wouldn't, not alone. Do you want me to go with you?"

Susan chuckled at the thought of Shirley behind the rock in her pink pajamas with matching robe and slippers. She would scare the bear away for sure.

"What are you laughing at?" Shirley asked. "You don't think I'm tough enough to sleep out in the forest?"

Susan laughed louder this time. "I'm sorry, but you hate the woods; it's damp and messy, and there's nowhere for you to plug in your blow-dryer."

"I can go a day or two without doing my hair, you know," Shirley said with an audible sniff, which made Susan laugh even more.

"That's enough," Shirley said. "You're starting to hurt my feelings."

"I'm sorry," Susan said again.

"You're right, I'd be more trouble than I'm worth. Still, I don't like the idea of you being out there alone."

"It's a wonderful offer, especially from you, but I have to do this by myself. And I won't be alone. I'll have—"

"Chance, I know, you told me," Shirley interrupted. "And I know you; you'll go no matter what I say. Listen, let me ask John if you can borrow his field radio. You remember that thing he bought from the army surplus store? He carries it with him when he goes fishing, so he can contact me in case there's an emergency. He's working on Saturday this week to make up for the day he missed when you..." Shirley stopped. "Anyway," she went on, "he can drop it off at your place on his way to work tomorrow. That way you can call me if something should happen. It works pretty well as long as you're within about five or six miles as the crow flies from here. It would be better than nothing if you fell and broke your leg or something."

Susan didn't want to carry the extra weight of the field radio. It would slow her down, and it would be close to impossible to carry along with her camera and daypack while she followed the bear through the woods. More than that, she didn't want to have to face John. "It's awfully big to carry in the woods."

"Do this for me," Shirley said. "I'd feel better if you had it with you."

"All right, but I want to leave early tomorrow. It's a long walk, and I have to get there and get set up before dark."

"John can drop it off by 6:30. Oh, and tell me again where you'll be, in case I need to find you."

"I'll be in the Woolly Creek watershed between the Main Line and Fox Road," Susan said. "I'm planning to stay three or four days. That should give me time to see if there's something I missed last time that might help save this bear's home. Please don't worry about me. I'll be fine. I've been walking in these woods for more than twenty years. I'm comfortable there."

"I'm going to worry about you no matter what you say," Shirley said. "Call me when you get home so I can get on with worrying about something else. You know me, I don't feel useful unless I'm worrying about something."

"I'll call you first thing when I get home."

———

Susan spent an hour collecting supplies and packing her backpack. She was glad she had made a trip to the market. The last thing she wanted to eat was more stale trail mix. She sliced a pound of cheddar cheese into large hunks and cut up four apples, putting everything into plastic sacks. She had bought two packages of crackers and a box of chocolate chip cookies, which also went into plastic sacks. She made up several sacks of kibble, two for each day she planned to stay in the woods. After thinking about it for a moment, she tossed in an extra sack of everything.

"You never know," she said to Chance, who watched her closely.

She filled her four water bottles and assembled her clothes, taking her raingear and anything else she could think of that would keep her warm. It was going to be much colder this time and probably wetter.

After that, she checked all her camera equipment. She decided to leave the Nikon and the monopod behind. This would save her from lugging a few extra pounds through the woods. Besides, one camera was plenty, and the tripod was already there by the bear's den if she needed it. She disconnected the monopod and cable release from the Minolta. She put the 50mm lens on the Minolta, stored it and the cable release inside the camera case alongside the telephoto lens, and placed the case inside the backpack. Without the sleeping bag, there was plenty of room for it.

Next, she separated out the supplies she would need for the first day or two in the woods and put them in the daypack, including a change of clothes, a pair of gloves, and the hat with the earflaps. All she would have to do when she reached the windfall was get out the small pack and her camera case, leave the big pack hidden behind a tree, and be on her way.

When everything was stowed in the backpack, she rummaged through the junk drawer until she found some duct tape. She tore off a long strip and used it to mend the tear in the cover of the backpack. "That should do it," she said. Bill had often boasted that he could repair anything with duct tape.

(6)

American Goldfinch

Susan scrubbed at her dinner dishes with greater force than was necessary, working off some of the leftover tension from her meeting with Jacob Riley. The last thing in the sink was the cast-iron skillet she had used to make a stir-fry. It didn't require the strength she was using to scrub at it. It wasn't that dirty. She had only used it to sauté a few vegetables and a handful of walnuts for her dinner. She rinsed the skillet off, crammed it into the drain rack, and said, "Done," to the empty room.

She leaned forward over the sink and stared out the window. The storm front she had seen hovering over the ocean earlier had worked its way inland. The trees at the edge of the pasture tossed and whipped in the wind and heavy rain pounded the kitchen window, striking the glass at an angle, almost sideways.

Everything was ready for her to return to the woods in the morning. Her backpack leaned up against the wall by the front door, the duct-taped cover securely cinched down over the top. Her hiking boots were sitting beside the pack, a pair of wool socks folded neatly inside one of the boots. Susan looked over at the pack and then frowned at the storm raging outside the window.

She didn't want to go into the woods during another large storm, but she didn't want to stay here, either. At home she would be warm and dry and safe, but she had her heart and mind set on being out there with the bear tomorrow. All she could do now was go to bed and hope that the storm would blow over by morning. With a sigh, she headed for the bedroom, shutting lights off as she went.

In bed, with Chance curled up at her feet, she tried to read a novel Shirley had given her but couldn't concentrate on the words. She clicked off the bedside lamp, kicked the blankets down close to Chance, and pulled the sheet up under her arms.

The night had seemed interminably long. Susan slept fitfully, waking up often to listen to the trees shaking and creaking in the wind and the rain hitting the roof above her. By morning the wind had died down to a strong breeze. The rain was still falling hard and steady but straight down instead of at an angle—a slight improvement. She built a fire in the woodstove and then traipsed through the house, peering out one window after another. Chance padded after her, offering an occasional whine.

"I know," Susan said, giving him a good scratch behind his ears. "We'll go when the rain lets up."

By early afternoon the rain had slowed to a light drizzle. Susan couldn't wait any longer. She removed her raingear from the backpack, put it on over her sweater and pants, laced up her boots, and hoisted the backpack onto her shoulders. She called Chance and together they went out the front door.

There, leaning on the porch railing by the door, was the field radio. Susan had forgotten John was bringing it by this morning. Had she missed hearing him knock? Had he come by before she had gotten out of bed? Both of these were unlikely. She had been up before six, and there was no reason why she wouldn't have heard him knocking.

John was a mystery, as was their strained relationship. For whatever reason, the tension between them never eased. Could it be that Bill was right when he had said John was afraid of her? Wouldn't that be an odd twist? Big, old, grumpy John afraid of her. She chuckled at the whole absurd situation. She and John were who they were, and their relationship was what it was. It wasn't ever going to change.

Susan hefted the radio by its strap over her shoulder. It was several pounds heavier than her camera case. What in the world was she going to do with this in the woods? She had promised Shirley she would take it, but it was the last thing she wanted to haul through the brush.

She reached to pull the front door shut and stopped, feeling the woodstove's warmth on her face. She closed her eyes and breathed in the warm, dry air, pictured curling up on the couch with a good book and a hot cup of tea.

With a resolute nod, she closed the door behind her and rattled the knob to make sure it was locked. She stowed the backpack and field radio in the back of the van and held the door open for Chance to jump in. Then she climbed into the driver's seat and fired up the engine.

Chance ran out ahead of her down the slick, muddy trail leading into the woods. Susan followed slowly, walking in a wide-legged straddle, setting her feet firmly in the mud. Whenever possible, she stayed on the edge of the trail where it was less slippery, stepping on the scrubby grass that grew there. There was less mud on the steep grade leading to the trail above the creek, and Susan was able to move faster. She didn't want to fall, but she had to move quickly to reach Woolly Creek before dark.

At the windfall, she slid the backpack and field radio off her shoulders with a sigh of relief. Days of stress and lack of sleep, combined with the energy it took to carry the extra weight of the radio over the slippery trail, were taking their toll on her. "This is harder than it was last time," she said to Chance. He panted happily up at her.

Susan glanced around. The drizzle had given way to a dense curtain of white fog, making it impossible to see more than a few feet in front of her. Tired or not, she would have to hurry. She couldn't trust her footing in the dark with nothing but her flashlight to show the way.

Oh no, she thought. She didn't have a flashlight. The small one was still in the shelter by the bear's den, and she had forgotten to pack another one. "Stupid!" she said, her voice sounding loud and harsh in the quiet of the forest.

Chance, surprised, leaped up and planted his front paws on her chest and licked her face. Susan gently pushed him away and brushed distractedly at the muddy paw prints he had left on her rain jacket. "I can't believe I didn't bring another flashlight. What was I thinking?"

She watched the fog swirling among the trees alongside her. "We've got to get going," she told Chance. He faced the windfall, ready to take the lead. Susan took the daypack and camera case out of the backpack and dragged the large pack behind a group of trees.

With the daypack and camera case across her shoulders, Susan reached for the field radio but stopped. It was too big and too heavy to carry all the way to the creek. She would be fine. If she needed it, it would be here. But what if she couldn't get back here?

"No," Susan said, shaking her head. She didn't have time to worry about that right now. She didn't need or want the what-if warning the radio carried with it. She took it behind the trees, shoved it inside the large pack, and secured the cover. Then she motioned for Chance to go ahead of her through the windfall.

From that point on they made good time. The trail had become so familiar that Susan moved faster each time. Even so, it was almost dark by the time they reached the path leading down to Woolly Creek. At the top of the ridge she stopped and called Chance to her. She told him to lie down. She wasn't sure if she should clip him to the leash. They had never gotten here this late in the evening before. She didn't want Chance running ahead of her—possibly right into the bear—but being tethered to him while climbing down the steep, darkened path would be dangerous for both of them.

Even though it was risky, she decided she needed to keep Chance close to her. She hooked one end of the leash to her belt and the other to Chance's collar, and they started down. She hadn't taken more than three steps when Chance heaved ahead, pulling so hard on the leash that Susan lost her balance and fell onto her hands and knees.

"Chance. Go easy," she said, her voice low but firm. She braced herself with her hands and struggled to stand up. Once standing, she reined Chance in close to her and took his face in her hands. "Go easy," she said again. She held onto the leash with one hand, using the other to grab onto tree limbs as she half skidded, half stumbled the rest of the way down to the creek bed.

When they reached the bottom, Susan stopped and listened for any sounds that might indicate that the bear was there. Since the last rainstorm, the creek had risen about a foot and was coursing with greater force, crashing over rocks and boiling around the tree that had fallen across its banks during the windstorm. The roar of water buried every other sound. She scanned the ground for fresh scat or new prints but couldn't see anything clearly in the dim light. The clearing in front of the den wasn't visible from where she stood, but she could see along the creek bed. The bear wasn't there. Chance was lying quietly at her feet. She took this as a no-bear-in-the-area vote.

Susan and Chance crossed the clearing. She stayed as far away from the cave tree as she could while straining to see if the bear was in his den. When she was directly in front of the den, it was too dark to see inside.

With night coming on, the fog had become denser, the damp air chillier. Susan was anxious to get in her little tree shelter and curl up inside her sleeping bag. She stepped behind the rock and stopped. There was the sleeping bag, lying halfway out in the open.

"Damn," she whispered. Somehow she must have inadvertently left it that way. She pressed her hand on top of the sleeping bag. The nylon fabric squished and water pooled around her fingers. It was soaked. How would she get warm now? She reached under the tree and felt the part of the sleeping bag that had stayed covered. It was dry, but there wasn't enough of it to do any good. She dragged the sleeping bag out from under the tree, bunched it up, and shoved it close to the rock.

By now the sun had set and the half-moon hadn't yet cleared the tree line. That, along with the thick fog, made it dark enough that it was almost impossible to see anything, and the canyon was getting progressively colder. Susan was damp from sweat under her rain jacket and starting to shiver. She had to clamp her jaws shut to keep her teeth from chattering. This wasn't good. Right now, quickly, she needed to find a way to get warm. Chance followed as she climbed under the tree. The tripod and her wet sweater from the last trip were there where she had left them. Using her feet, she pushed them down by the rock. She squirmed out of her raingear and damp sweater and into a dry sweater from the daypack.

The tarp was all she had to pull over her as a cover. The thin canvas didn't offer much protection from the cold, but it was better than nothing. She lifted one edge for Chance. He crawled under it and curled up beside her. Susan tucked the tarp around them both and draped an arm over Chance. The warmth of their bodies slowly heated the space under the tarp, and Susan finally stopped shivering. She didn't think about setting her watch to wake her up in the morning. The rhythmic lifting of Chance's rib cage under her arm and the puffs of his warm breath on her face soothed her. She relaxed into a deep sleep.

The cold weather marked a change in him. Everything was harder, each step closer to his den heavier. When he reached his den, sleep was all he wanted.

The sound of the woman and the dog coming down the path woke him. He blinked and yawned. There was no reason to move. Even curiosity could not rouse him. He curled up, tucked his nose into the curve of his hind legs, and went back to sleep.

He slept undisturbed until awakened by the cold morning air. He left his den, responding to an increasing hunger. He drank at the creek and then lumbered across the clearing, sniffing the ground as he went.

Partway across the clearing, he stopped and inhaled with a snort, pulling odors from the moist air. He turned toward the rock. Now he was alert, aware, and interested.

Close to the rock, he breathed in through his open mouth. He stretched forward toward the rock. It was their smell, the smell of the woman and the dog that drew him in.

Susan jolted awake, sensing something near. She listened. All she could hear was the flow of water in the creek and Chance's snoring. The hair on the back of her neck prickled. Something was there, on the other side of the rock. She was sure of it.

She was afraid to move and give away her position. At the same time, she didn't want to lie there and do nothing while a large animal snuck up on her, possibly the bear or worse yet, the mountain lion. She needed to do something, but what? At least she needed some sort of protection. Where was the pepper spray? Was it in the daypack? Where had she put the daypack?

Carefully, she lifted her head and looked around. One of the pack's blue shoulder straps was sticking out from under the tarp down by her feet. She couldn't reach it and get the spray out fast enough if an animal attacked.

Stop this, she told herself. Just look. See if something really is there. She rolled over and peeked around the rock. There, a foot away from her, was the bear. His head was low, even with hers. She gasped involuntarily, but she didn't pull away. For a crazy minute she thought about saying: Oh, it's you. You scared me.

The bear looked almost comical, with his neck stretched out long and his lower lip hanging down. She had to hold back from leaning in closer and sniffing him, as he had obviously been doing to her. After a long, silent moment, he turned away and ambled across the clearing. He looked over his shoulder at her before starting up the path out of the canyon.

Susan's heart was racing. She couldn't believe she had been almost nose-to-nose with a wild bear. With this bear. She sat behind the rock and ran her hand along Chance's back. He grunted and nuzzled closer to her. He had slept through the entire thing.

How could Chance not have known the bear was that close? Or maybe it wasn't that he didn't know. Maybe he didn't care. Maybe Chance no longer considered this bear dangerous. And the bear, what was he thinking? Why had he gotten so close to her? He hadn't been angry or upset. He had seemed more curious than anything else. Was that possible? Was he curious about her and Chance, wondering about them in the same way she wondered about him? Or was it merely that he had smelled their food?

There wasn't anything in David's manual about bears' curiosity, but there was a whole section on their unceasing hunger and continuous drive to eat. Susan assumed that all animals were inquisitive to some extent. Was there something in this bear's history that made him more inquisitive than others of his kind?

She thought about following the bear. If she got going right now, she might be able to catch up with him. She stretched her legs out in front of her and flexed her thighs. She didn't want to move fast, wasn't sure she could even if she wanted to. Her hips and shoulders were stiff and all her muscles were sore from sleeping on the cold ground. Besides, she and Chance needed to eat something, and she had to find a way to dry the sleeping bag. "Come on, Chance," she said, crawling out from under the tree. "Time to get a drink and pee."

The bear's footprints were all along the bank of the creek. Susan also found long scrape marks where the bear had clawed the ground. It looked like the bear had been scratching over the area where she had been urinating. Why would he do that? Was he trying to rake up the scent of her urine, or cover it up? Chance had already lapped at the water in the creek and raised his leg in his usual spot. She pulled down her pants, squatted, and peed right behind where the bear had clawed at the ground. She leaned forward and ran her fingernails lightly along the length of the claw marks, feeling the damp earth on the tips of her fingers.

Until that time on the ridge trail when the bear had apparently been waiting for her and Chance, she hadn't given much thought to what he was thinking. But seeing him there then, standing down the trail peacefully watching her, she had begun to suspect that something other than pure instinct controlled his behavior.

Now she realized that she wanted to know more about the bear than what he did with his time. He was an individual with a unique personality, not just a collection of hard-wired instincts that determined his behavior. To get to know him, she would need to spend more time with him. She would need to pay attention and be patient. And she would definitely need a dry sleeping bag. She and Chance headed back to their shelter behind the rock.

Although the fog had lifted during the night, the over lapping canopy of branches above the creek allowed only dappled sunlight to reach the canyon floor. If she wanted the sleeping bag to dry, she would have to carry it up to the ridge top and hang it in a sunny spot. First she needed to go through her daypack. She had been scared this morning when she couldn't find her pack and easily reach for what she needed. She pulled the tarp out into the open and arranged her supplies in neat piles on top of it, all the while seeing again the bear inches in front of her, feeling his warm, grassy-smelling breath on her face.

It wasn't until Chance started to paw at the sacks of dog kibble that she remembered they hadn't eaten. She poured out a sack of kibble for Chance and opened one sack each of apples and cheese for her. She sat beside him and slowly ate her breakfast. As usual, Chance devoured his food in less than a minute. "You know, you'd enjoy your breakfast more if you'd chew it," Susan told him.

The air was already warming up. Columns of vapor drifted up from the sides of the canyon. Susan breathed in the damp air. She could feel the trees settling in around her, could imagine them pressing their roots deeper into the earth, pulling their sap inward, preparing to wait out the long, cold months ahead.

She dug her hands into the wet, leafy loam. She pictured thin, rust-colored roots growing from the tips of her fingers down into the soil, anchoring her to this spot. She saw herself growing old alongside these lofty giants, living the rest of her life among them, accepting the strong winds and heavy rains as they did, protected and buffered by each other. Then she remembered her talk with Jacob Riley, saw what logging would do to Woolly Creek and the land surrounding it—most of the trees gone; the earth raw and slashed; gray clay bleeding into the creek, transforming it into a muddy torrent.

Susan pulled her hands free from the dirt and looked at the treetops far above her. She felt connected to these trees, a part of them. Her cells were made of the same stuff as theirs. To survive, she needed nutrients, water, air, and light, as the trees did. She took in a deep, long breath and let it out slowly. She stood up and unhooked the leash from Chance's collar, shoved the loose end into her pocket, and reached for a stick. "Come on, Chance. We need some time to play."

Chance leaped up, planting his large feet on her chest and licking her face. "Keep off me, you silly dog," Susan chuckled, pushing him away. She cocked her arm like a pitcher in the big playoff game and flung the stick across the creek. Chance sprang into the water. He swam a few strokes, raced up the opposite bank, seized the stick, and swam back. He dropped the stick at her feet and shook a spray of icy water around him. Susan jumped away from him, laughing. "Chance, stop that, you're getting me all wet." Still laughing, she grabbed the stick, ran a couple of steps up the creek bed, and tossed the stick across to the other side again.

The woman came from behind the rock. He held his ground, unafraid. Curiosity kept him there, but soon hunger pressed at him.

He left the canyon, expecting them to follow as they had before. He waited at the top of the ridge. They didn't come, so he started back down the path to the creek to check on them. He was most of the way down when he heard them. He stopped and listened, rolling his head to one side and pulling his ears forward. He heard the woman's voice and a loud splash and her voice again. He stood on his hind legs and looked over the undergrowth to the clearing below. There, along the edge of the creek, he saw them, the woman running and throwing a stick and the dog swimming.

Something stirred within him. He saw a roll in the leaves and a playful chase through the creek, felt a gentle shove and an easy nip on his neck. These memories lingered briefly with a deep sense of loss and sadness, and then they were gone.

He dropped on all four legs and followed the path to the ridge above. Now all he knew was hunger.

Susan stopped mid-throw. She glanced over her shoulder and then scanned the canyon walls, sure that something or someone was watching her. Her mind filled with an image of the bear. She could see him hidden halfway up the canyon as clearly as if she were standing next to him. A strong, almost overwhelming feeling of sadness and longing flowed through her as a vision of a mama bear and her cub came to her. They were playing here beside the creek, right where she and Chance were now. They were frolicking in the water, gently nipping at each other's necks and rubbing their shoulders together tenderly.

Susan gave her head a quick shake. Was this a hallucination or just her imagination getting away from her, which it seemed to be doing a lot lately?

Something was happening to her, but she wasn't sure what. Was she losing her mind from being alone so often with only Chance and illusions of this bear for company? Had she created this idea that she had some connection with this bear out of a sense of loss and loneliness?

Susan again shook her head. The picture in her mind of this mother and her cub playing was so clear to her, but she couldn't possibly know what this bear was seeing or thinking. Besides, bears don't grieve for a past memory based on something they were seeing now. They can't make that kind of connection. They return instinctively to a safe place to sleep and to the best berry patches. They know when mating season is and can search out a mate. Apart from that, they are solitary animals without strong attachments to others of their kind. David said as much in his manual. Bears don't experience longing or desire for a lost loved one the way humans do. Or do they?

Susan once more ran her eyes over the canyon walls, searching for the bear. As far as she could tell, he wasn't there. It was hard to see much of anything through the thick undergrowth, but surely she would be able to see the bear if he were there. He was big and black. He would stand out against all that green.

When she looked back at the creek, she saw the muddied water, the trampled and broken plants. Chance was madly digging at the bank, making a deep hole, and her and Chance's prints were everywhere along the creek bed.

"Look what we've done," she whispered. This was the bear's home, and they had trampled all over it. She let the stick fall to the ground and called to Chance. She clipped him to the leash and started for the rock, watching where she set her feet. They had done enough damage already; she didn't want to do any more. Silently she vowed to be more careful, more respectful from now on.

She rechecked the sacks of food. There wasn't enough to last two full days, even if she stretched it. She would need to stay in the woods much longer than that if she wanted to learn something more about this bear. She should have brought all the food and water with her, but she hadn't wanted the daypack to be too heavy. This might be the best time to go back for the rest of her supplies.

She slid her arms through the straps on the daypack, hung the camera case across one shoulder and the sleeping bag and her two damp sweaters over the other, and headed up the steep path. She left the sleeping bag and her sweaters draped over a small tree on the ridge top in the sunshine. She didn't want to spend another night sleeping under the tarp. Its musty odor permeated her clothes. She could even smell it on Chance.

The day was clear and sunny, warm enough to take off her sweater. Susan saw this day as a special gift before the endless rains of winter began. She set the camera case and the daypack down and pulled off her sweater and tied it around her waist. She lifted her chin, basking in the feel of the sun's warmth on her face. It reminded her of being a kid, growing up in the desert around Tucson. The land there had shimmered with heat, the hot sun as much a part of her life as the air she breathed.

Smiling at the memory, Susan gathered up the daypack and camera case and started down the trail. Her long strides matched Chance's pace exactly. They had adapted to walking connected by the short leash.

Even on this warm day that reminded her fondly of her childhood home, she couldn't completely relax. The bear was somewhere out there, but it wasn't the bear that caused her to continually peer through the brush or turn her head to check the trail behind her. She suspected the mountain lion was hunting nearby. The thought of its silent presence was unnerving. Having Chance close to her helped her feel a little more at ease. The two of them together might make a mountain lion think twice before attacking. Susan didn't unhook Chance from the leash until they reached the downed tree that blocked the trail.

Walking on the fallen tree no longer required any conscious effort. She placed one foot at a time around each upright branch and swung through, hardly slowing from her normal pace. At the windfall, she climbed over and under the tangle of tree limbs with ease, using her hands to protect her face and leaning into the dying branches with her shoulder.

Bill used to tease her about how competent she was in the woods, saying she must have been born there, calling her his wild, forest woman. She wasn't wild, though. She knew this about herself, knew the secret shyness that kept her from making friends easily or feeling comfortable in groups of people.

Here in the woods, the animals didn't care about her shyness. All that mattered to them was that she was a human, and therefore they were wary of her and stayed hidden most of the time. Oh, they were here. There was no question about that. Over the years she had seen their signs in footprints and scat but rarely saw more than that. They were experts at staying soundless and out of sight, only showing themselves in startling, unexpected moments, offering nothing but a quick glimpse before they were gone. Even this bear had shown how good he was at vanishing completely when he wanted to.

It was close to noon when Susan and Chance made it to where she had hidden the backpack. The minute they stopped, she realized she needed a bathroom break. She moved into the brush and Chance squatted down right next to her. Susan used some leaves to clean herself and buried both piles in tree duff.

She pulled the backpack out from behind the trees and emptied everything out of it and the daypack onto the ground. She touched each item, calculating its importance before she stowed it in the daypack or put it back in the backpack to leave here.

When she was done, the only thing left on the ground was the field radio. She really did not want to take it with her. It was like an omen of impending disaster from the unnatural, human world, a world precariously balanced on a false sense of security. It didn't belong here. It was good enough that she had brought it this far. "Or bad enough," she said out loud. She crammed it inside the backpack, cinched the waterproof cover over the top, and dragged the pack behind the trees. With the daypack and camera case over her shoulders, she started off.

She took her time going back, stopping often to check the trail for animal tracks and to watch the birds. What a splendid day it was. The warmth and beauty of it caused her to forget her fear of a mountain lion lurking nearby and simply relish the day.

The birds were flitting about and calling to each other in a great many different songs, most of which Susan had never learned to identify. She did recognize the short trills and thin twitters that made up the American goldfinch's song. These little birds, closely resembling yellow canaries, hopped through the hydrangea bushes outside her bedroom window most of the spring and summer. She had spent many hours watching them early in the morning while the rest of her family slept. Now one perched near her atop a thistle, singing out its unique *potato chips, yip, yip* call. Susan's hand lifted of its own accord, moving toward the little bird. She longed to feel its silky, yellow feathers and the racing thump of its heartbeat against her palm. The bird was close enough that with one flick of her hand she would have it. She let her hand fall empty to her side and walked on.

By the time Susan reached the ridge above the creek, a thin layer of fog had drifted in and it was getting colder. The sleeping bag that had been in the sun that morning was now in the shade. "Shoot," Susan said, running her hand along the bag, feeling the damp fabric under her fingers. She couldn't use it to stay warm tonight, not with it still being this wet.

Her two sweaters had dried. She untied the sweater from around her waist and put it on. She then pulled one of the dry sweaters on top of it to help keep her warm. She stuffed the other sweater in the daypack and rolled up the sleeping bag and hung it over her shoulders. Maybe she could use it under the tarp to provide some protection from the cold ground. She unclipped Chance for the descent. Carrying the sleeping bag, camera case, and the full daypack down the steep path was hard enough. She didn't need Chance pulling on her.

Susan sidestepped and slid down the path. The sleeping bag kept slipping off her shoulders and bunching up around her legs. She tripped over it in a couple of the steeper spots. By the time she reached the canyon floor, dirt covered almost the entire bag. Some forest woman I am, Susan thought, rubbing at the leaves and dirt on her pants.

Chance was waiting for her at the bottom of the path. His ability to adapt to what she expected of him continually amazed her. "Good dog," Susan said and clipped the leash back onto his collar. She checked the den as they went by. It was empty.

It was darker and colder in the deep shade of the canyon floor. Susan used what remained of the fading daylight to organize her gear, feed Chance, and eat her meal of cheese and crackers.

The fog was thicker now, gliding in ghostly swirls along the canyon walls. As Susan watched, there was a minor fluctuation in the light.

Then in a flash, the entire canyon turned bright pink. She whispered, "Oh," and the light was gone and the canyon dark. Nightfall! She had heard that term all her life, but this was the first time she had a true sense of what it meant. Did this happen on other nights, this complete and instantaneous change from light to dark? Had she missed it all these years by not paying attention at this exact moment?

The temperature dropped sharply. Susan spread the damp sleeping bag in the tree shelter and folded the canvas tarp in half and flattened that on top. She lay between the folds of the tarp with Chance next to her and tucked the edges around them both. She started to set her watch to wake her up in the morning but decided against it. She didn't like the startling feeling of waking up to the alarm, and she wasn't even sure the bear would come back tonight.

It took her a long time to fall asleep. She kept listening for the sounds of sliding stones and leaves that signaled the bear coming down the path or a grunt as he relaxed into sleep. She never heard him. Eventually the usual night sounds eased her into slumber.

It was still dark when Susan woke up, but before long a thin line of misty, yellow sunlight started to show through the trees at the edge of the canyon. She rolled her shoulders and tried to stretch out her arms, feeling tight and stiff with two sweaters on. She pulled the top one off and laid it next to her. When she moved, Chance lifted his head and grunted in protest. All she could think about was how hungry she was. She wasn't simply hungry. She was craving one specific thing: chocolate chip cookies. The thought of them was driving her wild. She sat up and reached for the daypack.

David had cautioned her about opening the food sacks and eating close to the bear, especially anything sweet or that made noise when eaten. She shouldn't have brought something as sweet and crunchy as a cookie into the woods with her, but she had wanted something other than trail mix to eat. If dried oatmeal, nuts, and raisins were all she had to eat, she would…well, she couldn't do it, that's all there was to it. So she had packed the cookies, and now they were practically shouting at her from inside their plastic sacks. She would be careful, take one out and seal the sack up immediately afterward. She leaned around the rock to look at the bear's den. It was still too dark to see inside. She decided it was worth the risk. For all she knew, the bear wasn't even there.

She pulled one sack after the other out of the daypack, fingering each until she found one that held the round cookie shapes. She sat back and ate, chewing with her hand over her mouth, trying not to make noise. This was worse than when Meagan and Shawn were little. Back then, she used to lie in bed eating forbidden foods while the children slept in their bedrooms across the hallway. They were experts at sniffing out cookies or ice-cream at night. More often than not, they would show up at the bedroom door, rubbing their eyes and asking what she was eating. Susan hoped the bear didn't show up now, wondering the same thing. She stifled a giggle, imagining reaching around the rock to hand him a cookie and telling him, as she had her children, "You get just one, and then you have to go back to bed."

He woke up to a sweet, unfamiliar smell. It called him out of his den early.

As the days became shorter, he slept longer, usually waiting until it was light in the canyon before he left to forage for food. His movements were slow, following rhythms buried deep within him,

patterns that flowed with the seasons. He would continue to travel through his territory during the cold rains of winter, eating and drinking, but he would seldom go far.

Today he combed the air, trying to identify this new odor. He knew it was coming from behind the rock. The stronger scent of the woman and the dog was all around him, layered on top of the fainter, sweeter smell.

The sweetness was not enough to keep him here. The time had come to travel to the last berry patches of the season.

With one last sniff, he started up the path to the ridge top. He knew the woman and the dog were behind him. He could hear them. This was what he expected. When he reached the ridge trail, he stopped and waited for them.

Susan heard the bear move as she was swallowing the last little bite of cookie. She looked around the rock and saw him heading up the path out of the canyon. So he had been here all along. As she rolled back over, she caught her foot under the tarp, flipping it up. The sacks of food she had strewn about in her search for the cookies bounced off onto the dirt. Cursing silently, she scooped up the sacks and her spare sweater and stuffed all of it into the daypack. She hung the pack over one arm, grabbed the camera case by its strap, and dashed out into the open with Chance close behind her. They ran, connected by the leash, across the clearing. Susan struggled into the daypack straps and slung the camera case across one shoulder as she went.

With Chance ahead of her now, Susan scrambled up the path and onto the ridge trail. The bear was a short way up the trail, looking at her and Chance as he had done before. Then he stepped into the brush and was gone. Susan ran for the spot where he had left the trail, the pack thumping against her spine. Even though she knew this was the right place, she couldn't see a way through the brush. The plants had closed in around him.

She leaned her shoulder into the thick brush and pushed until she broke through to a narrow path. And there was the bear, standing less than six yards ahead of her. When he saw her, he turned and headed up the path, slowly, as if he were taking a casual morning stroll.

He really is waiting for us, Susan thought. Not just at the ridge top. He had done that before. That might have been because he was nervous when he heard us coming up behind him out of the canyon. This was different. Once hidden in the underbrush, he could have kept going, as he had the last time. Yet here he is, walking up the path right in front of me and Chance, looking back at us every few steps.

Chance took advantage of the fact that they had stopped and raised his leg, making a small puddle on the side of the path. At the sound of his urine splashing onto the dirt, Susan felt a painful urge to empty her own bladder. She checked the bear. He had stopped a short way ahead of them and was rooting at a rotten stump.

She stepped partway into the brush, pulled her pants down, and squatted. The bear turned in her direction, his nose quivering. All of a sudden it seemed like a very bad idea to be squatting with her pants around her ankles this close to a bear. She stood up—the last of her urine running down her legs—and tugged up her pants.

The bear snorted, his head low, his mouth open. Instinctively, Susan flexed the muscles in her legs, getting ready to run. The bear sniffed and went back to the rotten stump. His long tongue flicked out at the crumbling wood and, covered in bugs, curled back into his mouth. Susan removed the Minolta from the case, adjusted the light setting, focused on the bear, and snapped his picture. The bear thrust his tongue into a crack in the stump. He held it there long enough for her to take another picture. He was getting to be a real camera ham.

The bear continued poking and sniffing at the stump, pulling bugs out with his tongue. Susan edged closer, hoping to get a better picture of his face. She had taken three steps when the bear faced her. He slammed his right front paw so hard against the ground that Susan could feel the earth shake under her feet. He flared his upper lip and blew fiercely.

Surprised by this change in the bear's behavior, Chance rocked forward and yipped, loud and shrill. The bear blew another warning. Susan wrapped the leash tightly around her hand and began slowly to back away. The bear turned and attacked a small clump of pampas grass growing beside the path. He hit the grass again and again, snorting with every strike. Pieces of grass flew around him. Chance yipped again and strained against the leash.

The bear stopped. One large paw hovered motionless above the grass, the power of the arrested blow vibrating in the air. He looked at Chance. Their dark eyes—so much alike—met and held. Neither animal moved. Then, with a grunt, the bear meandered back to the stump and prodded deep into the rotten wood with his tongue.

It was wrong for the woman and the dog to come near him. They should know not to come so close. He slapped the ground and snorted a warning.

The woman and the dog stepped back. Anxiety still pulsed in his veins. His muscles tensed, and he felt his jaw tighten. He attacked a clump of grass, swatting at it, grunting his displeasure. Strength and power raced through him. When the dog barked, he stopped and turned to him, studying him, learning him. Knowing him.

I got too close, Susan thought. He was telling us to behave ourselves, to keep a polite distance. "You don't have to tell me twice," she whispered, her voice trembling.

The bear acted like he had all day to poke at the stump. Finally, after one last reach of his tongue, he lifted his head, glanced at Susan and Chance, and started up the path. Susan followed, making sure to stay well back from him.

He rambled along, stopping here and there to pull at tufts of grass. He would stand there, chewing contentedly, and gaze around him, blades of grass hanging from the sides of his mouth. Susan clicked off several photos of him chomping grass with a faraway look on his face.

The calories from her breakfast cookie were wearing off. Her hands were shaking, and she felt lightheaded. She hadn't fed Chance yet, either. They needed to stop, but she didn't want to lose sight of the bear.

She stayed with him for another half hour, getting hungrier and shakier with each step. At last, the bear stopped at a pulpy log on the side of the path. He dug at it with his paw until it broke into pieces. Then he went to work licking out termites and sowbugs as they scurried about, trying to escape.

Susan checked the distance and decided she was far enough back from the bear to safely open the food sacks. She put the Minolta back in the camera case and took a sack of kibble out of the pack, peeled it open, and stopped. Bears love dog food. She looked at the bear. Chance pushed at the sack with his nose. The bear faced them, sniffed once, and then went back to licking up bugs.

Susan held the open sack out to Chance. He ate at his usual break-neck speed. When finished, he ran his tongue all around the inside of the sack, licking up the last traces of food. He looked so silly that Susan chuckled out loud. She instantly covered her mouth with her hand, afraid that she might have alarmed the bear. He didn't seem to notice. He kept pulling at the log and licking up bugs as if she hadn't made a sound. Susan held back another laugh. Chance and the bear looked so much alike, pushing and probing for the smallest scrap of food. This was their life, eating and sleeping. They were creatures made from the same pattern, with the same desires. The main difference between them, as far as Susan could tell, was that domestic dogs appeared to have, if not love, at least deep affection for the people they lived with.

Susan stared at the bear. Was it possible that this bear was feeling some form of emotional attachment to her and Chance? She looked down at Chance. He gazed up at her, his tail sweeping from side to side in the dirt. She had heard stories of wild animals forming attachments to people, especially if the animals were in captivity. Susan always assumed this was an affection based on need: in captivity, the animals would die without the food and shelter provided by the people caring for them. But this bear wasn't in a zoo. He was free in his home here in the woods. He didn't need her to take care of him. He didn't need her for any reason at all.

Susan poured water from her bottle into the empty sack and held it open for Chance to drink. She watched the bear as Chance drank. She had to be careful not to make assumptions based on nothing but a few encounters. This was a wild bear, not a pet. He would always be a wild bear. How he behaved and what he did in his life had little if anything to do with her.

When Chance had finished drinking, Susan raised the bottle to her lips and squeezed it, swishing the plastic-tasting water around in her mouth to rinse off her teeth before swallowing. She stored the bottle and sack in the pack and rummaged around until she found a sack each of cheese and apples.

Just as she was taking the sacks out of the pack, the bear moved off. He was no longer ambling but was now walking in long, purposeful strides. Susan wanted to call out, Hey, wait. I haven't eaten yet. Instead, she crammed the sacks back into the pack and shrugged it and the camera case on while jogging to keep the bear in sight.

The bear went along the narrow path, brush snapping and rustling at his sides. Susan had to turn sideways, with Chance behind her, to fit through long sections where berry vines and young alders grew into the path. Sometimes she would catch a hint of the bear's bulky rear end disappearing around a bend. At times she was sure she had lost him, but then she would again catch a glimpse of him up ahead.

Farther up the path, Susan rounded a bend and stopped so suddenly that Chance ran into the back of her legs. The bear was right in front of her. He was looking at her, not over his shoulder this time, but directly facing her. She was close enough to him that for a second she thought about reaching out and running a hand through his black fur, petting him like a large dog.

Of course she knew better than to touch him. She had to move back, and do so quickly. Chance had stopped at an angle in the path as he collided with her. Susan shoved backward, wanting to create more distance between them and the bear. She wasn't sure if Chance had looked past her and seen the bear, but he could surely smell the musky, oily scent coming off him. Either way, Chance didn't react. He merely leaned his side against her legs as she pressed into him.

The bear grunted and shook his head. Susan could feel the air between them move, could have sworn she felt stray bits of his fur fling against her face. She kept trying to step back, but Chance refused to budge. He acted like this was a new game and matched her increased pressure. Susan turned and was reaching for Chance's collar to yank him out of the way when she felt the bear leave the path.

Though this had all happened within seconds, it seemed much longer. Every detail replayed in her memory: seeing the bear; the pressure of

Chance's body on her legs; the bear's up-close smell; the stirring of the air between them; and the last, sensing the bear's departure while she was looking the other way.

Now, Susan hurried to follow the bear through a break in the foliage and down a gentle embankment to a small streambed. She no longer questioned whether the bear had been waiting for them. It was obvious that he was waiting for them. What she didn't understand was why he would do that.

The bear stopped to drink in the stream. Susan watched from the bottom of the embankment. He lapped at the water for a while before sauntering up the streambed, sniffing here and there. When he found a good spot, he pawed at the ground and lay down. He opened his mouth in a wide yawn and closed his eyes.

He's taking a nap, Susan thought. He's sleeping right here, with Chance and me this close to him. No one will ever believe this.

Chance, evidently unimpressed by what the bear was doing, lay down and also went to sleep. Susan settled down next to him and—at last—took the sacks of apples and cheese out of her pack again. She opened them and ate, savoring each bite. When done, she watched the bear sleep.

Time became irrelevant, replaced by the rhythm of the bear. She didn't feel the weight of the camera case over her shoulder or think about photographing him. Her breathing slowed to match his, her chest rose and fell in time with his. The forest wrapped around them, weaving them together.

Her eyelids fluttered shut and her head drooped and then popped back up, bringing her out of her trance-like state and fully awake. This wouldn't do. No matter how tempting it was to join in on naptime, she didn't want to fall asleep and miss the bear leaving. She couldn't be absolutely certain that he would wait for them every time. She sat up taller, flexed her shoulders, and stretched her neck from side to side. Her back ached. She stood up and arched backward, pressing her hands into her lower back.

Chance lay curled on his side. The bear had also turned onto his side and curled into a big, furry ball. Susan took the Minolta out of the case, knelt close to Chance, and snapped his picture. She replaced the lens with the long one and focused on the bear. She held her breath to keep the camera steady and took the bear's picture. She was advancing the film when the bear sat up and yawned, his long canine teeth glinting white in the light. He stood up and shook, and with a quick glance at Susan, waded across the stream and started up the opposite bank.

"Come on, Chance, we're moving again," Susan said. She jammed the Minolta down into the case and snatched up the daypack. The bear was already out of sight. Susan and Chance splashed through the shallow stream and ran up the slope onto an overgrown trail in time to catch a glimpse of the bear rounding a bend on the right.

He no longer appeared awkward to her. He looked strong and formidable. Now Susan understood why David had said she could never outrun a bear. Just moving at an easy lope, this bear covered ground so fast that she could barely keep him in sight.

She couldn't keep going at this pace much longer. She could walk for many miles, but it had been years since she had done any running or jogging. She hated it. It had never come naturally to her. Here she was, already huffing and puffing for air. The daypack banged against her back and the strap of the camera case rubbed on her shoulder, feeling heavier with each step. It had also gotten hotter, and she was sweating heavily under her sweater.

Chance was hardly panting. He trotted happily along at the end of the leash, glancing back at her now and again. "Showoff," Susan gasped between breaths.

When the bear disappeared over a rise in the trail, far ahead, Susan stopped. She would never be able to catch up with him, and it didn't look like he was going to wait for them this time. With a sigh, she dropped the daypack on the ground and carefully set the camera case down beside it. She pulled off her sweater and tied it around her waist. Sweat ran down her chest and back and stained her shirt where the straps of the pack had been.

She stood there, hands on hips, looking around her. Nothing was familiar. Where the heck were they? There were no recognizable landmarks above the line of foliage growing on each side of the trail, or behind or ahead of her, nothing that would help her find this location on the map.

Susan took a deep drink of water and poured some into an empty plastic sack for Chance. While he lapped at it, she pondered their predicament. They could go back the way they had come, follow the trail and look for the stream. If they were lucky, from there they could find the other trail that led to Woolly Creek. Or they could continue to go in the direction the bear had gone.

"We probably won't see him again today," she said. "But we might as well keep going. Maybe we'll break out of this trail up ahead and be able to figure out where we are." She hated to backtrack, a trait that was unquestionably akin to the stubbornness David had accused her of. She felt driven to see what was around the next bend, over the next hill. And she didn't think she was really lost. She was right here. She just didn't know where here was yet.

Hunger urged him on. He was no longer thinking about the woman and the dog. He was heading to a berry patch, one he knew to have ripe berries late into the season.

The scent of people grew stronger the farther he went. It surrounded him, moving with him all along the trail. He grew more fearful with each step. He had already slowed when he heard human voices.

The wide trail was right there, on the other side of a large, treeless space. He had crossed it every year, but never with people this close. He clicked his teeth together and rocked back on his heels. He knew the woman and the dog were behind him. Their scent was growing stronger. Silent, watching, he waited in the shadows of a large pile of dead trees for them to come.

He saw them. The woman and the dog were coming toward him.

The trail ended in a large clearing, an old log landing, cluttered with piles of slash mixed in with gray mud. Across the clearing was a wide, dirt road. This had to be the Main Line. Susan didn't know of any other logging roads this size cutting through the forest. She looked around, hoping to find some sort of landmark that would help her determine where on the Main Line they were this time.

It was on the second pass through the area that she saw the bear. He was standing about twenty feet from her, behind one of the larger slash piles. His black coat acted as camouflage, blending in with the shadows cast by the pile of tree limbs.

He was looking right at her, staring at her, in fact. Susan stood quietly with Chance, watching the bear, shifting her gaze away occasionally so as not to make him uncomfortable. This went on long enough that Susan began to wonder if he could see her clearly. If so, did he recognize her? She had read in David's manual that, contrary to popular belief, bears can see and detect objects and color quite well at close range. If that was true, why was he staring at her like this?

When Chance noticed the bear, he pawed at the ground and barked, his tail wagging excitedly. "Chance, quiet," Susan said. Chance stopped barking and sat down at her side, his tail sweeping the ground. He looked back and forth between Susan and the bear.

The bear turned toward the road. All at once a loud rumbling and banging erupted close by. Was the noise coming from the rock quarry? Had they ended up by it again? Was someone using the large rock sorter? Why hadn't she heard it sooner? She couldn't have missed it, even from miles away. It must have just started up. Had the bear known it was here? This had to be what was bothering him. He was scared of the machine and the people who were running it. Had he been waiting to warn her about this?

Susan cautioned herself not to read too much into this. Most likely the bear was waiting because he was afraid with the workers and the machine so close. That was all there was to it.

The bear folded his ears flat against his head and looked toward the sound. He pawed at the dirt; the muscles in his back and legs tightened and released in one long shudder. Her heart ached to see him this way.

She was getting ready to yell out to the workers to be quiet, to shut off the machine and let the bear get across the road, when she remembered Jacob Riley's threat that she would be prosecuted for trespassing if found here. Trespassing wasn't a serious crime. It usually didn't involve more than a fine. Still, she couldn't stop thinking that she would be in serious trouble if these men saw her here. Probably the bear's fear was affecting her. For whatever reason, it seemed essential to stay hidden from the workers.

Suddenly the air seemed to split open with an ear-piercing screech. Instantly the machine stopped. Susan's ears rang in the silence. Off to her right she could hear a distant murmur of voices and a man's hearty laughter. The bear was looking in the direction of the voices, his ears forward, his upper lip flared out.

After a quick glance at her, the bear moved cautiously around the slash pile and out into the open. He bounded through the exposed area and stopped behind another pile of slash. He sniffed the air and broke out into the open again. This time he stopped behind a Douglas fir tree on the edge of the road.

Susan, with Chance close to her, ran through the open space and hunched down behind a stump close to the bear. From where she was now she could see part of the rock quarry and the edge of the conveyer. Two men were bending over it with their backs to her. She cocked her head and listened. She couldn't understand most of what they were saying. She did hear one man yell, "Damn thing is…."

She shifted her attention back to the bear. She would go when he went. Together they could make a break for it, run across the road and into the forest beyond.

The bear faced her, his head rocking from side to side. Then he looked straight ahead, charged out from behind the tree, and lunged toward the road. He moved so swiftly, it took Susan a second to react. By the time she leaped out from behind the stump, the bear had already made it across the road.

Susan sprinted across the road, her boots thudding on the packed gravel surface. Chance ran in front of her, pulling her with the leash. She didn't look toward the men at the quarry but heard one of them shout, "Hey, did you see that? It looked like a woman and a dog running across the road." She was already up the embankment on the far side of the road when the other man answered, "George, you horny old cuss. Now you're seeing women in the woods."

Susan and Chance ran hard. She didn't see the gouged soil beneath her feet or feel the heat beating down on her. She didn't notice the gray mud splattered on the piles of dead tree limbs. Fueled by adrenaline, she was running as if her life depended on it. She was running behind the bear.

The shriek in the air tore at his ears and sent fear racing through him, tightening his muscles and causing his heart to beat faster. All he wanted was to get away from the assault of the noise and the stink of men. He bolted across the wide trail and up the other side. He didn't stop until he was far away from the sound and smell of people.

Everything around him was wrong. How could this be the same place? All the trees were gone, and the ground was nothing but baked mud. Warped branches and small tree trunks torn from the earth lay buried in clay. Mud oozed in the shadows and collected in small dark streams in the deeper ruts.

He wasn't lost. His destination was a part of him. It didn't require visual orientation. Now everything he remembered from this place was gone: the coolness of the forest, the clumps of grass, the small stream, the berries. All were gone. He pawed at the ground and waited for the woman and the dog.

Susan breathed in a raw lungful of air. Sweat streamed down her face, and a searing pain stabbed her in the side below her rib cage. She slowed to a walk and then stopped. She leaned over, hands on her knees, and tried to catch her breath and ease the pain. After a couple of shallow breaths, she raised her head and checked for the bear. He had slowed to a walk but was farther away all the time. Susan didn't want to lose sight of him. She had no idea where they were, other than that they were somewhere in the woods. Without the bear, she would be completely lost.

Still bent over, she massaged her side with her fist and scanned the area. All around her was a ruined landscape. She knew this was the aftermath of a clearcut logging operation. Even though she had never seen one up close before, she had seen sections of clearcuts from a distance while driving on the highway. They stood out like large, bald scars on the hillsides.

The logging near her home hadn't left the land looking like this. At the time, Susan had thought it was the worst possible thing that could happen to the forest. But at least there a few trees remained uncut, including some large ones, and sections of the soil were relatively undamaged. Here, all of the topsoil had been scraped up and plowed under by heavy equipment, leaving a layer of clay exposed. Branches and small tree trunks, half buried in clay, littered the ground. Slick, gray mud seeped into deep grooves left by the machines.

Susan wondered idly whether the slash would be burned at some point, or left to rot, becoming mulch to nourish young plants. If left alone, this area could once more become a mature forest. But that wouldn't happen. This was timber company land. Their job was to harvest trees as soon and as efficiently as possible. Once the trees were a marketable size, the loggers would return with their machines and cut them down again.

The pain in her side was gradually easing. She stood straight. The sun was now low in the sky and shining right at her. She shielded her eyes with her hand and looked where she had last seen the bear. There he was, standing about forty feet ahead, facing in her direction. She could have sworn he was farther away when she had stopped. She remembered seeing his dark shape moving off in the distance. Had he come back? Even if she was wrong about how far away he had been, even if he hadn't come back, it was clear he was waiting for her and Chance now.

A low grumbling came from her stomach, and once again she felt lightheaded. She needed to eat. The few bites of apple and cheese she had eaten earlier were nowhere near enough to sustain her. For a few years now, she had needed to eat more often to keep from becoming weak and shaky. Another symptom of getting older. If it wasn't one thing, it was another. I would be better off following behind an old, crippled bear, she thought. At least then we might travel at the same speed.

She checked the bear again. He wasn't moving. This looked like a good time to take a break. She drank and then gave Chance his share of water. When he was done, she put the water bottle back in the pack and took out a couple of sacks of food.

While eating, Susan looked around at the devastation logging had caused to this part of the forest. Most people had no idea what this type of logging looked like or what it did to the land. Maybe she should show them. She crammed the food sacks into her pocket, got out the Minolta and focused on the bear. The telephoto lens brought him close enough that she could see the gray clay oozing up between his toes. He now stood with his side to her, emptiness all around him.

She took four pictures of the bear, changed lenses and took four more pictures of the bleak landscape. She looked over at the bear. He was moving again, this time not at a run but in a steady walk. Susan put the Minolta away in the case and swung it and the daypack over her shoulders. With Chance out ahead of her on the leash, she followed behind the bear.

The sun was dipping below the distant tree line when they left the clearcut behind. The transition from a dead land to a living one happened just like that. One minute they were walking through exposed clay soil and broken branches and the next they had crossed over into a young forest full of berry vines and small stands of skinny trees.

This area had been logged recently, probably within the last ten or so years, but it must not have been done as a clearcut. Much of the leafy topsoil remained. Young, straggly brush now grew in the ruts left by the large equipment, and blackberry vines were already growing over the piles of slash. And there were trees, most of them young Douglas firs, not much taller than Susan, but here and there a circle of redwoods grew around an old stump. Wild rhododendrons poked up through the berry vines, their leggy branches reaching high above the ground.

Susan and Chance followed the bear into a shady patch of huckleberry bushes. The plants were heavy with ripe berries. The bear had stopped and was busily stripping berries off the bushes. He rolled his eyes at them but didn't stop eating. Susan was so relieved to have stopped that she thought only briefly about how unusual it was to find a patch of ripe berries this late in the year.

Her feet were throbbing, and her neck and shoulders ached. She plopped down onto the ground and laid the daypack and camera case beside her. Chance stretched at the end of the leash, mouthing huckleberries off the bushes. Susan plucked a handful of berries and let them fall one by one into her mouth. They tasted sweet and tart. They tasted of the forest.

She leaned back against an old stump and relived the day's journey, trying to make sense of it. The bear had traveled, using some sort of memory or instinct, to arrive here when these berries were at their ripest. She gave up attempting to explain this. It had happened. Here they were, and that's all that mattered.

The only sounds in the quiet of the late afternoon forest were the faint smacking noises of Chance and the bear eating berries. This young, recovering forest felt like home to her. She extended her hands, palms against the ground. Maybe if she remained quiet and held still long enough, if she allowed herself to open to it, she would feel the new life growing and moving in the soil beneath her.

———————————

Susan woke up to a darkening sky above her and the sound of Chance's snoring beside her. She had nodded off. How long had she been asleep? Daylight was almost gone, and the air was several degrees colder. She untied the sweater from around her waist and put it on. She looked for the bear. He had wandered farther into the patch of berries and was still eating. It hadn't occurred to her until now that they might not be going back to Woolly Creek. Other than on her first night in the woods, the night of the windstorm, the bear had always come to the cave tree when it was dark.

As Susan watched, the bear sniffed the air once, walked in a big half-circle around her, and headed away from the huckleberry patch, deeper into the trees. She grabbed her things and jumped up. "Chance, let's go." Chance grunted but didn't move. "Come on, Chance, let's go," she repeated. He sighed, rolled over halfheartedly, and stood up. "I know, it's been a long day, but we have to go. I don't want to lose this bear."

She went as fast as she could while still being careful not to trip in the fading light. The bear plodded onward, looking straight ahead. He seemed to know exactly where he was going. He went in a direct line through a small grove of Douglas fir and across a gully to a rock outcropping partially screened by alder trees. He stopped in front of the rocks, glanced back at her, and vanished.

Susan approached the rocks cautiously. She didn't want to frighten the bear by getting too close. She didn't notice the cave until she was standing right in front of it.

Two large slabs of rocks had fallen into each other, forming a type of A-frame. Susan bent and looked inside. There the bear was, curled into a tight, cozy ball. It was too dark to see if he was sleeping, but it was clear he wasn't planning to go anywhere else anytime soon.

Great, Susan thought. He's got a place to spend the night, but what about us? Night was coming on quickly and getting colder by the minute. She could see the smoke-like puffs of her breath. Cold as an Alaskan night, as Bill used to say. Cold enough to freeze to death.

She set the daypack and camera case down and groped around inside the pack for the flashlight. She couldn't feel it. She tipped the pack over and dumped the contents out onto the ground. She ran her hands over each item. Not there. Susan wanted to shout at herself. Why couldn't she remember to bring that stupid flashlight? What was it with her and flashlights?

She pulled on one of her extra sweaters, tugged on her gloves, and yanked the hat with the earflaps onto her head, flaps down. She put everything else back in the pack, slung it and the camera case over her shoulders, and turned to face the rock outcropping.

Susan felt along the edge of each rock, searching for an indentation that might offer some protection for her and Chance during the night. It was too cold to spend the night out in the open, and if the cold didn't get her, the mountain lion might.

After a while she felt a narrow opening, not tall but big enough for her to duck through. She stuck her head into the opening and sniffed. She smelled dry earth and decomposing leaves, nothing more. "Hello?" she called, not as a greeting but to use her voice to hear how large the cave might be. The sound resonated back at her, giving her the sense of a small, enclosed space.

"This is probably our best bet," she said to Chance. She ducked inside with Chance close behind her.

The cave was bigger than it appeared from the outside, high enough for her to sit up in and deep enough for her and Chance to lie down side by side. When they were inside, Chance buried his nose in the fabric of the pack and snorted. "Hungry?" Susan asked him. "Me too." Dinner was kibble for him; apples, cheese, crackers, and cookies for her; water for both of them. Now only one bottle of water and a couple of sacks of food and kibble remained, enough to last one more day, maybe a little longer if she rationed carefully.

Susan rested against the rock and thought about their situation. The bear had obviously been here before. He knew where the huckleberry patch was, and he had walked right to the cave in these rocks. Could this be his winter home? David had said that male bears have large territories. With such a territory, did a bear have multiple dens?

Thoroughly exhausted, she lay down and snuggled up close to Chance, but she couldn't quiet her thoughts. A barrage of questions kept plaguing her: What if the bear didn't return to Woolly Creek tomorrow? How would she ever find her way back there without him? What if she couldn't find her way out of the woods? What would happen to her and Chance? She wanted to get up and check the map, see if she could figure out where they were, but it was too dark to see. Once again she chastised herself for forgetting to bring that damn flashlight.

It took a long time for her to fall asleep. Close to her were the little cracking and popping sounds of a small creature stirring about. Farther away, she was sure she heard the rustling of a bigger animal moving around. Every sound seemed unusually loud; every sound spoke of danger.

Sometime during the night, she fell into a restless sleep and dreamed of the bear. He was walking ahead of her through an unknown and darkly distorted landscape. Stunted, burned trees covered in a layer of black ash twisted up from the ground. With each step he took, the bear stirred up a swirl of cinders. Susan followed behind him, breathing in the black dust. Finally the bear stopped at a large deformed tree, its branches gone; only a burned-out, hollow trunk remained. He snorted the foul air and, looking over his shoulder at her, stared deep into her eyes. He turned and took a step closer to her and—

Susan's body jerked and her eyes flew open. Chance was whining and leaning into her, his nose touching her face. "What is it?" she asked, pushing him away, trying to pull herself back from the dream. Daylight was streaming in through the opening in the rocks.

"Oh no," Susan said, checking her watch. Eight o'clock. How had she managed to sleep so late? She grabbed the daypack and camera case and crawled out of the cave with Chance close beside her.

The instant they were out in the open, Chance lifted his leg beside the rocks. Susan followed suit, squatting next to him. From there she looked along the face of the rock outcropping at the bear's cave. She couldn't see much from where she was, but she guessed the bear was already gone.

With Chance clipped to the leash at her side, she headed for the bear's cave, being careful to stay back from its opening: she didn't want to startle the bear if he was in there sleeping. She peered inside. The cave was empty.

"Now what?" Susan said, stepping back from the cave. With no landmarks to guide her and no bear to follow, she was utterly and hopelessly lost. She felt a thin edge of panic move through her. She wanted to run—anywhere, everywhere—looking for something she recognized. No. She couldn't do that. She had to stay calm. Running around willy-nilly wasn't going to help anything.

Some years ago she had taken an aerobics class. The instructor had been a big fan of cleansing breaths, saying they helped calm the soul.

Susan tried it now, breathing in deeply while sweeping her arms above her head and exhaling as her arms circled down to her sides. Nothing happened except that she felt slightly dizzy. Maybe she was doing it wrong. She hadn't stayed in the class for long. All that Spandex and loud music had given her a headache.

Chance nudged at the pack with his nose. "You think we should eat, huh? Well, I agree." If nothing else, eating would slow her down and keep her from doing something stupid.

A layer of frost coated the ground along the edges of the rocks, but in the sunny patches it was already warm enough for her to take off the hat and the gloves and her top sweater. She sat on a rock in the sunshine and ate her meager breakfast. Chance had finished his ration already and was now sniffing the ground for any tidbit she might have dropped.

The thought that she may never find her way out of the woods kept plaguing her. There were many stories out there about lost hikers who wandered around aimlessly until they were too exhausted to go on. This made it extremely difficult, if not impossible, for the search and rescue teams to find them. Susan pictured the field radio lying useless in the backpack, miles from here. Even now, she was glad she had left it behind. If she hadn't, she might be tempted to use it to call for help.

"We can figure this out," she said, looking at Chance. "Right?" He gazed up at her and nodded; at least it looked like a nod. Susan scratched him under his chin. "I'm glad you agree."

She unfolded the map and found the rock quarry adjacent to the Main Line. She tried to remember which way they had gone after crossing the road, but she couldn't. She really had no idea. She wasn't even sure how long she and Chance had run behind the bear before they reached the clearcut. The sun had been shining directly at her when she had stopped to catch her breath, so at that point she was heading west, but that wasn't enough information to go on.

There was nothing on the map indicating recent logging sites, or any other landmarks that she recalled seeing. Susan cursed and slapped her hands on top of the map. Chance, excited by her sudden movement, sprang up and barked.

"I'm sorry," Susan said. "I didn't mean to startle you. It's that I'm... I'm lost." She nodded her head. "Yup. We're lost."

She took one last look around and then gathered up her belongings and headed back the way they had come yesterday. If they went back to the huckleberry patch, she reasoned, she might be able to find a few of their footprints heading in the direction of the clearcut. From there, maybe she could find her way back to the Main Line and then to Woolly Creek and the bear's den.

Tracks covered the wet soil at the bottom of the gully. Mixed in with a slew of deer prints were hers and Chance's heading in the direction of the rock caves. What made Susan want to break open a bottle of champagne (if one were to magically appear) was a set of bear prints, not leading toward the rocks but away from them, in the direction of the berry patch. With a tremendous sense of relief, she ran toward the patch.

"Please let him be there," she whispered. As she neared the berry patch, she stopped abruptly, pulling Chance to a halt. She closed her eyes and said one more time, "Please let him be there." She opened her eyes, took a few more steps, and there he was, wandering through the plants, pulling berries off as he went. "Oh, thank God," she said softly.

She moved closer. The bear must have been there all morning. Many of the plants covered in ripe huckleberries yesterday now held only a few scattered here and there.

How long was the bear planning to stay here? There really was no way to tell. It could be days, maybe even weeks. Susan had just enough food and water to last through the day. Unlike the bear, she and Chance couldn't live on bugs and berries, not for long anyway. And there was Shirley to think about. She would have a posse out combing the woods if she didn't hear from Susan before tonight.

Susan checked her watch. It was almost nine. If they didn't leave soon, they wouldn't reach Woolly Creek before dark. Maybe she could find more of their footprints to help guide her back there. Barring that, there must be a major creek or large hill she could locate on the map to use to plot a course.

For now she stayed, watching the bear. She might not ever see him again. It might be impossible to find him. If he had an additional cave here, he could have others throughout his territory, however expansive that was. She hoped it was large enough to support him if his home on Woolly Creek was lost due to logging.

What about the clearcut they had come through yesterday? Had that been part of his territory, too? Had he already lost some of the food supply he had always counted on to survive?

Susan readied her camera. She wanted one more picture of the bear before she left. She approached slowly and stopped when she was close enough for the shot. The bear faced her as she was adjusting the focus. He's getting nervous about me being close, Susan thought. She clicked the picture and took a step back.

The bear glanced behind him before facing her again. Susan wound the film forward and lifted the camera to her eye. The blurred, black shape of the bear filled the viewfinder. She stumbled back, her finger involuntarily pressing the shutter release.

The bear was less than a foot away from her. He stretched his neck toward her and sniffed at the camera she now held against her chest.

With her free hand, Susan took hold of Chance's leash, willing both of them to stay calm.

Chance inched nearer and sniffed the bear's front leg. The bear lowered his head until the two animals were nose to nose. Susan wrapped the leash around her palm, getting ready to pull Chance away.

Now the bear lifted his head to Susan. He again stretched toward her and sniffed along her chest, stopping for an instant at the camera before moving up to her face. Puffs of his warm breath tickled her cheeks.

Her mind flooded with pictures of wild things, things she could not know and had never seen: mother bears with their cubs, rolling in tall weeds; two burly male bears standing face to face on their hind legs, swatting at each other, mouths open. She saw patches of ripe, wild berries and fields of tender spring grasses. She saw streams alive with spawning salmon.

She stood silent and unmoving while the bear ran his nose over her face. This lasted for a lifetime, and yet was over in a heartbeat. The bear exhaled softly, stepped away, and walked deeper into the berry patch.

Susan's legs gave way under her. She fell to her knees. Chance sniffed her face, following the traces of the bear's nose on her skin. She longed to stay here with the bear, to never leave. A wild black bear, both feared and revered, creature of stories and legends, had touched her.

What would it be like if she never left the woods, never went back to her house? She would grow old here—her gray hair long and snarled, matted with leaves and twigs. She pictured herself following the bear through all the days of his life, seeing him mate, grow old, and die. Chance would die also, long before she did, leaving her with the bear and his children, and eventually his grandchildren, as her companions.

In this future, Susan saw Meagan and Shawn and Shirley going crazy with fear. They would search for days, maybe weeks, before giving up, never knowing what had happened to her. They would find the backpack and field radio tucked safely behind the tree. Later, by Woolly Creek, they might find her sleeping bag and the flashlight she never seemed to remember to bring with her. But they would not find her.

Susan knew she couldn't survive in the woods. She wasn't equipped, as the bear was, with extra layers of fat and the ability to slow her metabolic rate. She would die of starvation or exposure. Late one night as she slept, the cold northern winter would steal her life. Then the raccoons and foxes, and yes, even the bears, would consume her flesh and gnaw her bones. The beetles and maggots would return what little was left of her to the earth.

Susan stood up and put the Minolta in the camera case, letting her hand rest briefly on the camera before closing up the case. "It's time to go home," she said. Chance looked up at her, and then he walked away from the berry patch, pulling her with him.

The woman and the dog stayed close, running behind him across the wide trail and through the damaged land. This land used to be a shady forest with cool water flowing through it and rotting stumps full of bugs. He had stopped to eat and drink here every year when the daylight became less, the nights longer. Now that the forest was gone, there was no reason to be here. He slowed only so that the woman and the dog could stay with him.

He was very hungry when he reached the huckleberry patch full of ripe berries. He ate, letting the sweet berries run down his throat. He ate without stopping until it was dark.

He moved away from the berry patch to the safety of his den, one he had shared with his mother before she left him. The woman and the dog came with him out of the grove, through the trees, and

across the gully of muddy water. They did not come into his den. He slept all night, rising as the sun was clearing the tree tops.

As the day grew light, the woman and the dog were again in the berry patch. Now he was curious. He wanted to know them, to see and smell them up close. He knew to be wary of humans and dogs, but these two were different. They were his. He took the risk and moved closer to them.

First he reached out to the woman, but then he bent close to the dog. He sniffed the dog, breathing in his unique scent, and the dog sniffed him back. He returned to the woman and smelled her, understanding her, knowing her. He knew the stench of aggression. It smelled of power and anger mixed with fear. Neither the woman nor the dog smelled of it. Their scent was as he knew it would be, as it always had been, a soft mixture of fear, curiosity, and gentleness.

The woman and the dog left the berry patch. He watched them go without sadness or sense of loss. They always returned. Now he needed to eat. He left the berry patch and headed for a field of winter grass.

Susan followed Chance, forgetting to watch for prints in the dirt. Her thoughts were with the bear. She kept replaying the sensation of his nose on her face. She could still feel it: cold and wet like a dog's. All traces of sadness about leaving the bear were gone, replaced by the pure joy of a wild animal accepting her, something she hadn't felt since she was a child living in the desert outside of Tucson.

She was about eight years old when she had first stumbled across a natural oasis. She had been exploring around the saguaro cactuses, hunting for lizards, when she found herself at the edge of a sandy pond.

There, in the shade of tall, drooping trees—the likes of which she had never seen before—she had discovered frogs and tadpoles and long-legged birds. She lay in the damp sand at the water's edge with these creatures all around her, oblivious to her presence. She became a part of that cool, secret place. Frogs leaped close to her face. Birds stepped right on top of her fingers with their leathery, sharp-nailed feet.

Susan had never felt that way again, not until today. Before the bear touched her, she had always assumed that a wild creature's acceptance of a human was a gift reserved for children.

The sound of Chance drinking from a muddy puddle brought Susan back to where they were for the first time since they had left the berry patch. They were on the rim of a wide, smoothly sloping canyon with a forested ridge beyond.

Susan turned in a circle, taking in her surroundings. She had no idea where this canyon was or how they ended up here. Why hadn't she been paying attention? She had walked along blindly behind Chance without once checking to see where they were going.

The canyon below and the opposite ridgeline shimmered in the midday sun. Across the canyon, the nearly leafless branches of alder trees stood out like purple smoke against a dark line of conifers. Susan saw a snaking line of sparkling blue green close to the canyon floor. A creek? Could that be Woolly Creek?

She traced the easy drop of the canyon with her eyes. Off to her right, at the top of another hill, was the edge of a clearcut. Below that, visible between the trees, was the brown line of a logging road. Was that the Main Line? If so, how had she and Chance ended up this far over? She looked at her watch. It was twelve-thirty. They had been walking for over three hours. All that time she had been lost in her own thoughts.

It seemed to Susan that they had only two options: They could head for the road. If it turned out to be the Main Line, they could probably find the rock quarry and from there get to Woolly Creek through the forest the way they had before. Or they could hike down into the canyon to the creek and follow it. With any luck, it would be Woolly Creek and lead them to the bear's den.

Susan got out the map and compass. Holding the compass in her hand, she took a sighting on the logging road. She took another reading in the direction of the clearcut and one more toward the creek. On the map, she followed the Main Line with her finger and traced from there to Woolly Creek. None of it made any sense.

The map showed several ridge lines above Woolly Creek, but there were also ridges above two other creeks. Any one of these could be where she was standing. She folded the map, put it in the pack, and hung the compass around her neck. Surveying the canyon and ridge top, she ran through the options once more. One choice wasn't any better than the other. Susan started into the canyon, heading toward the creek.

The descent was fairly easy. Chance trotted at the end of the leash at a fast clip along a narrow trail. Susan, struggling to keep up with him, caught her foot on a blackberry vine snaking across the trail and almost fell. She reined him in close to her and said, "Chance, slow down. You're going too fast. What's gotten into you?"

Chance slowed but not by much. Every once in a while he would give a little skip like he was going to leap into a full run. Then he would glance back at Susan and slow down again.

The trail ended in a half-circle of tangled brush. It was as if the animals who used it had gotten this far when they decided to turn around and go back the other way. It reminded Susan of a turning circle at the end of a suburban cul-de-sac. Chance pushed into the brush, dragging Susan with him. She planted her feet and pulled back on the leash. "I can't go that way, Chance. We'll have to go back and see if we can find another way."

She checked the compass. They were still heading roughly in the direction of the creek she had seen from the ridge top. Her boot had come untied, and as she bent to retie it she noticed that the forest had become unusually quiet. Nothing moved in the brush, and the birds had fallen silent. Even the distant rapping of a woodpecker she had been listening to all along the trail was gone. Something was wrong.

Susan tilted her head and listened. Silence. She tapped her lips with her fingertips and peered into the brush on either side of her. There was nothing there that she could see. Then, as suddenly as it had fallen, the silence was broken. Once more the air was alive with the chirping and calling of birds. Susan blew out a sigh of relief.

If a predator had caused the forest to grow silent, it was gone now. Susan pushed aside the thought that perhaps she and Chance were the intruders, that they had startled the birds into silence. When it had gone quiet, the mountain lion was the first thing that came into her mind. Then it occurred to her that it might have been her imagination playing tricks on her, making her hear a break in the birds' songs when none was there. She believed she belonged in the woods, that her presence was accepted. But here, where she had never walked before, the forest was watchful, unsure of her intent.

Susan and Chance started back down the trail, looking for a way through the brush. Chance repeatedly lurched into the dense undergrowth on the side of the trail. Susan pulled him back each time, saying, "No, Chance. I can't go that way." They had gone about a quarter of a mile when Chance again tugged Susan to the edge of the trail. This time there was a small opening in the brush. It wasn't exactly a path, more a thinning of the underbrush. "This looks like our best choice," Susan said, and she followed Chance through the opening.

She was no longer thinking about where they were going. Walking became a rhythm, a type of ballet made up of the movements of her long, thin body and the tug of Chance on the leash. It was the cold bite of the air that brought her attention back to her immediate surroundings. The sun had dipped below the tree line and dusk was closing in.

"Chance, let's stop for a minute." She took a sweater out of the pack and put it on over the one she was wearing. Then she checked the compass. They had veered away from the creek. Up ahead, another trail intersected with this one. If they went to the left on this new trail they should get back on course.

It was obvious they weren't going to make it back to Woolly Creek before dark. Susan wasn't worried about spending another night out in an unknown section of the woods. If they were going to spend the night here, that was how it was going to be.

For most of her life she had planned for every possible outcome. She made lists and checked things off as she went. She liked to be in control. She wanted to believe that if she planned carefully and took every precaution, she could guarantee her family's complete safety. Now she understood that there were some things she couldn't control or prepare for. All she could do was try to deal with whatever came her way.

The air was becoming increasingly colder. Susan pulled her sweaters more tightly across her chest and gazed around her at the forest. What would Bill have thought of her revelation? She could almost hear him laughing. He used to tell her that she worried too much. "Hey, things happen," he had told her more than once. "You've got to relax and enjoy the adventure."

Susan smiled at the memory of Bill. Her sorrow over losing him wasn't gone, and never would be, but it was softened by a lifetime of memories, some good, some not so good. She breathed in the cold forest air. Bill was dead and she was not. It made no difference what had brought her to this place in her life. All that mattered now was going on.

She stepped behind Chance out onto the cross-trail. There, off to her right, a large tree lay along the length of the trail with a tangle of windfall sticking up behind it.

"Good thing we don't have to go that way," Susan said. She turned left on the trail and stopped. She looked again to the right. Wait a minute. Is it—? Can it be—? She moved closer to the downed tree and saw that it was the same section they had come through each time they had entered or left the woods since the windstorm. She stared at the road home, unable to believe what she was seeing.

She knelt and took Chance's head in her hands. "How did you do this?" They had ended up right where they needed to be after traveling through a part of the forest they had never been in before. Was Chance able to smell this place, or did he have some other way of knowing, some form of navigation unknown to humans? Whatever it was, even if Chance had no idea where he was and ended up here by some kind of miraculous mistake, Susan was so happy to be here that she felt like singing and shouting for joy, maybe doing a little jig in celebration. She didn't, though. She merely unclipped Chance and said, "Let's go home."

When they reached the backpack, the first thing Susan did was get out the field radio, extend the antenna, and call Shirley. It was almost dark. If she waited until she got home to make this call, Shirley would be frantic.

When Shirley answered, Susan depressed the talk button on the radio and said, "Hi. It's me." She released the button so she could hear Shirley's response.

The connection was full of static, but Susan could still make out Shirley saying, "Oh, thank God. Where are you? Are you okay?"

"Yes, I'm fine. I'm leaving the woods now. I didn't want to wait until I got home to call."

Again static and Shirley's voice saying, "I'm glad you're safe. I can't wait to hear all about it, but don't tell me now. Get home; it's almost dark. You must want a bath and something hot to eat. Call me later. I'll be home all night."

"How about I call you tomorrow morning? I'm beat. And you're right, I do need a bath and something to eat." Susan was more tired than she had ever been in her life.

"Okay, phone me in the morning. Thanks for calling now. I've been waiting all day. I was worried about you."

"I know. I was fine, though. I'll tell you all about it tomorrow." In truth, she had no idea how she could ever explain what had happened in the woods. Now, even to her, it seemed like a dream.

(7)

Snowy Egret

Susan stood in her front doorway, taking in the cold rush of damp air that greeted her when she opened the door. She had expected the cold, musty feeling of the house: it was that way much of the year if a fire wasn't constantly going in the woodstove. What stopped her with her hand resting on the doorknob was how empty the house felt. In the woods, life and energy surrounded her: trees, berries, flowing water, birds, and bugs everywhere. And there was the bear, of course, but she couldn't think about him now. Just the thought of him made her feel too lonely.

"Good grief," Susan said. "Could I be any more depressing?"

Chance had slipped by her through the doorway and was heading for the couch. At the sound of her voice, he looked back at her and said, "Woof." Then he jumped up onto the couch and stretched out, looking extremely content.

Susan laughed. "Okay, you're right; it is comfy here. All I need to do is get the house warmed up." She started a fire in the woodstove and fed Chance, but after that all she wanted to do was go to bed. She didn't even have enough energy to eat or take a bath. Nevertheless, she forced herself to do both, knowing she would feel better afterward. While the tub was filling, she heated up a can of vegetable soup and toasted a slice of whole wheat bread. She ate quickly, bathed, and fell into bed. She was asleep within minutes.

In the pale light of early morning, with the sound of light rain tapping on the roof above her, Susan snuggled deeper under the blankets. The gloominess of yesterday's cold, empty house was gone now, replaced by the comfort of this warm, familiar bed. In the trance-like state between sleeping and waking, she traveled with the wild bears, free in the untamed land that had come to her with the bear's soft touch. The images were veiled and foggy like old and much-loved home movies. She was with the bears, rolling in fields of grass, feasting on plump berries, roaming on and on through an ancient forest. She knew she had not imagined this place, these bears. They existed, if only in a collective animal memory.

Susan yawned and stretched. "Time to get up," she said to Chance. She could lie here for hours, sleepily romping around with black bears, but it was already almost seven o'clock, and she had things to do. She clomped around in the kitchen in her bathrobe and floppy slippers, making coffee, cooking oatmeal, and feeding Chance.

She brought her coffee and bowl of oatmeal with her to the phone table and dialed Shirley's number. Mary Ann answered. When Susan asked to speak to Shirley, Mary Ann yelled, "Mom, it's Susan. Don't talk long. We're going to be late for band practice."

When Shirley came on the line Susan said, "Is this a bad time? I can call back, or you can phone me later."

"You must have slept in. You usually call earlier than this. I'm anxious to talk to you, but yes, I'll have to phone you later. We're on our way out. There's no school today. It's one of those teacher workshop days, but Mary Ann still has band practice."

"I didn't know she was part of a band."

"Remember that drum session a week or so ago? She wouldn't let loose of it, kept pestering me about wanting to play the drums. John and I couldn't stand it any longer, so we checked into it and, as it turns out, they needed a drummer for the marching band at her school. I'm telling you, miracles happen. Now she gets to play the drums, and I don't have to listen to it at home. And you won't believe this, but she's good at it."

"That doesn't surprise me. Remember when she was a baby and she'd bang the spoons on the highchair when we met at the diner for breakfast? She made such a racket, I used to think they'd change the OPEN sign to CLOSED when they saw us coming with her." Susan laughed at the memory, seeing little Mary Ann's chubby hands, each gripping a spoon and banging away furiously on the highchair's tray, her bare legs kicking underneath in time to the beat.

"Gosh, I'd forgotten all about that. Funny I'd forget that," Shirley said. In the background there was the sound of a door banging shut. "I'd better go. Mary Ann has the car keys. If I don't get out there, she's apt to drive off without me. I'll call you later. Will you be home?"

"I'll be gone most of the day. I want to get the photos developed and talk to David. Let's plan to meet tomorrow morning. Then you can see the pictures, and I'll tell you everything that happened."

Erick was in his darkroom when Susan arrived. He opened the door to her knock and stepped aside, inviting her to enter. His shirt and pants were more rumpled than usual, and his hair was shorter than when Susan last saw him. It looked like he had cut it himself: it was about an inch long in some places and half that in others, and it was standing up in disorderly clumps. Susan noticed specks of gray showing around his temples. This surprised her. She had always seen him as a kid, so much younger than she was. Yet here he was with his hair turning gray. Inside the dark room, Susan thought about their longtime relationship.

How long had they known each other? It must be close to twenty years now, and all she had ever known about him was this, his work. Were his parents still alive? Did he have brothers or sisters? Pets? A girlfriend? She knew he wasn't married. He had told her that much, let it slip out accidentally one day when he was finishing up prints for a wedding. "I could never make a commitment like this," he had said, sweeping his eyes over the pictures of the bride and groom. He didn't elaborate, and she hadn't pressed him. At the time, she had been amazed he had revealed even that much about himself.

He knew most everything there was to know about her family, though he had never met them. He had seen their likenesses emerge and change in his darkroom from year to year. He had even seen Chance grow from a puppy to an adult dog in photographic images.

When Bill died, it was Erick who had helped design the announcement for the memorial service. Susan wanted something personal, something that would show who Bill was in his life, not just what he had looked like. Erick stood close by while she searched through all the pictures she had taken of her husband over the years.

———

A tight sadness in her chest. Bill's face shining up at her from stacks of photographs.

There were too many. How could she select the right one? "I can't do this," she said. "I can't choose one."

"Okay. Let's use more than one," Erick suggested. "We can make an arrangement of three or four on the front of the announcement. We can even put a couple of pictures on the inside. There aren't any rules about how many pictures you get to use."

So that's what they did. They printed a grouping of photographs showing Bill in the different phases of his life: as a young man, straining behind the tiller, dirty and sweaty, the muscles in his neck and arms tensed in effort; as a father, reading a storybook on the couch with a sleepy child cuddled under each arm; as a middle-aged man, squinting into the sun and beaming like a boy, a big basket of freshly picked blackberries in his hand.

———

Here in the darkroom, Erick looked up from a tray of printing solution and found her staring at him. He shifted his gaze past her right ear and asked, "Is something wrong?"

"Oh," Susan said, caught off guard. "I was thinking about how long we've known each other and how little I know about you. You know a lot about my life, those things that can be shown in pictures anyway, but I don't really know anything about you."

Erick's entire face, from his neck to his hairline, grew pink. He ran his hands through his hair and turned his attention back to the developing photograph. Using a pair of rubber-tipped bamboo tongs, he lifted the photo out of the stopping bath and placed it into the fixing solution.

"This is the last of these," he said, without looking up from the tray. "When it's done we can get started on yours."

Susan had seen him do this before, pretend that he hadn't heard her and go on as though nothing had happened. It was a tactic he used to keep from divulging anything personal.

In a little over six hours, Susan's photos were mounted and leaning up against the front counter. Susan studied the prints. Something was still missing from them. She would never be able to capture on film what she had learned about the bear. She couldn't show how he had been inquisitive and come close to her, first when she was behind the rock and again when he had brushed her face with his nose on that last day in the woods. She had even asked Erick to print the picture she had inadvertently snapped that last day when the bear sniffed her. It didn't matter that it showed an out of focus, unidentifiable shape: it was a souvenir just for her.

"This one is my favorite," Erick said, pointing to a close-up of the bear's face. "He's eating grass, isn't he? Some of it is sticking out of his mouth." Susan said that, yes, the bear had been eating grass.

Erick leaned closer to the photographs. "These of the logged area are terrific. They really show how barren the land is. We should make one of them larger. We can get it up to sixteen by twenty, maybe larger, without losing clarity. You can pick which one you want and leave it with me. I'll get to it later today. You can hang it by this one of the bear standing in the same area. In fact, you should display this whole group together when you set up your show. They make an impressive statement." He nodded as if agreeing with himself.

"My show?" Susan asked.

"Yes, your show. You have to exhibit these somewhere. You can't just hang them up in your living room where nobody will see them," Erick said, gesturing toward the photos with a sweep of his hand.

"I've never shown any of my photographs publicly before. I don't even know how to find a place that would be willing to show them."

"I know, but these are good, too good not to share. They say something about this bear. I never thought much about bears before. After the last set we developed, I've been thinking about them all the time, wondering how many are out there in the woods, how they survive, that type of thing. These photos are also about what's happening to the land around here. They're important. I'm sure any gallery in town would be happy to display them."

"I'll think about it." Susan stacked the photographs between sheets of butcher paper and placed them into her portfolio. "Thank you again for all your help. Without you, these wouldn't be as good as they are."

Susan was halfway out the door when Erick said, "Susan, listen, about what you said earlier, about not knowing anything about me. I want you to know that I think of you as a friend. I'm glad I've gotten to see your family grow up through their photos. I feel like I know them." His face turned beet red. "These pictures of the bear, they're the best I've ever worked on. You see, that's the thing; my life is about photographs. Pictures, that really is all there is for me." He shrugged. "Maybe someday I can show you my work. If you're interested. When you have the time." Erick's eyes skimmed across her face and darted around the room.

Susan wanted to hug him, or at least lay her hand on his shoulder, tell him how much his friendship meant to her, but she knew that would make him extremely uncomfortable. It was somewhat amazing that he had said as much as he had. So she settled on, "Thank you for being my friend. I couldn't do this without you. And I'd love to see your photos.

Next time I'll call ahead so we can arrange a time for you to show them to me."

Susan opened the door to David's office to find him seated at his desk across from a young woman. She was willowy thin, with strawberry-blond hair pulled severely back from her face and tied in a ponytail at the base of her neck; no unruly hairs poked out anywhere. She was leaning toward David, talking, her long, elegant hands open and held out in his direction, palms up. David motioned for Susan to come in. Without even a glance in Susan's direction, the young woman continued speaking, saying to David, "You don't know how long I've worked on this. I can't do it over. I won't. It's done."

David said, "Susan, good to see you. This is Magdalene Doran. She's in my Biology 410 class." He indicated with a wave of his hand that Susan should sit in the chair beside Magdalene's.

"Why don't I come back later," Susan said from the doorway. "You're busy. I'll call, and we can set up an appointment."

"No, sit down," David said. His eyes held hers. "Please," he added. "Magdalene and I have finished for today."

Magdalene stood up and looked at Susan through narrowed, brown eyes. She turned to David and said, "We haven't finished this yet, Professor Sharpton. We need to resolve this issue."

"Fine. Make an appointment with the secretary in the Biology office, and we'll continue our discussion then." David nodded in the direction of the door. Magdalene left, shutting the office door firmly behind her.

"I'm sorry," Susan said. "I should have called first."

"No. Believe me, I'm glad you came when you did. That young woman has been a burr under my saddle for the last three semesters.

She's a dedicated student, but she's belligerent, and she wants everything to be easy, every time."

He came around to the front of his desk and leaned back against it, facing Susan. "Okay, enough of that. Tell me what happened with Jacob. What did he say about the plans for logging around Woolly Creek?"

"He said they're planning to log where the bear has his den. He also said that bears are not factored into logging plans, that what happens to this bear is not his concern, providing timber is."

"Unfortunately, that's true. Many people think there are already too many bears out there. There are growing numbers of reports of nuisance bears around people's homes."

"Are there that many wild bears left?"

"Hard to tell for sure," David said. "No one has done an accurate count in this area. Based on what little research has been done, there aren't as many black bears out in the forest as most people think." He frowned. "I had a man call me about a month ago claiming he'd seen three or four bears prowling in his neighborhood, a newer housing tract outside of Holtenville. Do you know where I'm talking about?"

Susan nodded. She was familiar with the area he was referring to. In the past few years, housing developers had bought out many of the old farms and privately owned forest lands around the township of Holtenville. Susan had once joked with Shirley about this uncontrolled growth, saying that the schools had better hire security guards for their playgrounds or some developer would build a housing tract on them when no one was watching.

"According to the man who phoned," David said, "these bears have been knocking over garbage cans and getting the dogs barking at night for over a month now." Susan smiled, trying to picture a whole herd of bears marauding through this otherwise quiet suburb.

"I know," David said, returning her smile. "It is a funny thought, all those bears getting together to check out the garbage in this man's neighborhood. Makes you wonder what types of foods these folks are throwing away. Must be something tasty." His smile faded. "More than likely, all of these sightings were of the same bear as he traveled in what used to be his territory. Bears adapt quite well and seem to be perfectly happy feeding off garbage and fruit trees when they lose their native foods. It's not bears who are having trouble sharing their space, it's people. And it's people's attitudes about bears that will ultimately affect the outcome of these encounters. If this case is like most others, this bear's days are numbered if he keeps showing up around these houses."

David exhaled and said, "I'm sorry. I'm ranting. It's just that it's close to impossible to make people care about protecting bears when they see these big animals causing trouble in their neighborhoods, when they are worried about the safety of their families."

There wasn't anything to say to this. Susan unconsciously ran her hand over the top of the portfolio leaning against the leg of her chair.

"Do you have more photographs?" David asked, nodding at the portfolio.

She didn't think she needed to explain her choice to return to the woods, but she did want to reassure him that she hadn't gone off without telling anyone. "While you were gone, I went back to the bear's den."

David raised an eyebrow. Susan quickly added, "I let a friend know where I'd be. I even took her husband's army field radio with me."

"Good," David said. Then he smiled. "A field radio. That must have been hard to lug along with you in the woods."

"Yes, well I didn't take it the whole way."

"Ha!" David barked. "I would have left the damn thing behind a tree somewhere. Now let me see your photographs, and you can tell me what happened."

Susan spread the photographs out on the table. Words came easily as she described her journey following the bear to the rock quarry, then across the Main Line and through the clearcut, straight to the patch of ripe huckleberries and a second den. When it came to finding the right words to express what mattered most about her experience, Susan faltered. She took the blurry, up-close shot of the bear's face from her portfolio and laid it on the table next to the other photographs.

"What's this?" David asked.

"The bear," Susan said. "His face. I took it on our last day together, right before I left."

Both eyebrows went up this time. "Did he charge you again?"

"No. He came up to me, right up to my face." Susan held her hand up, almost touching her face with her palm. "His nose was this close to me. He sniffed me. I could feel his breath on my skin. Before that, he did the same thing to Chance. Their noses touched." David watched her closely but said nothing.

"He seemed curious about us," Susan continued. "I guess he wanted to learn more about us." She knew this didn't fully explain what had happened, but there was no way to explain the intense closeness of those moments. How could she begin to describe what she had seen and felt when she was that close to the bear, how for a short time she had been a part of his past and his future. She didn't understand it herself. All she could do was tell his story with her pictures. She would never be able to tell the rest of it. She glanced at the photographs. Her eyes rested briefly on the blurry close-up of the bear when he had sniffed her on that last day in the woods, mixing his wild, grassy scent with her smell.

Looking back at David, she said, "After that he walked away. He went back to eating berries as if nothing unusual had happened." Susan perceived a subtle shift in David's posture, a slight relaxing of his shoulders. Perhaps he felt relieved that the bear had moved away from her.

"Before this last day," she said, "he continually waited for us to catch up with him. He could easily have run off at any time. But instead of trying to run away whenever Chance and I fell behind, he slowed down, sometimes stopping altogether. When there was a fork in the trail, he waited until he could see us before he went on."

David returned his attention to the photographs. It was so quiet that Susan could hear the muffled voice of another professor lecturing somewhere in the building.

"Now what?" David asked.

"I don't know," Susan said. "Things are so easily misunderstood. I don't want anyone to think of bears as approachable or friendly, or worse, as pets. They're not. If I had tried to force some type of contact, none of this would have happened. All of this was on his terms, in his time, in his home."

"Yes, of course some people will misinterpret this," David said. "There's no way around that." He paused, his eyes searching hers. "After our second meeting, I figured you'd have some degree of success photographing a bear. You were determined. As a matter of fact, you were more than determined, you were fearless, and stubborn."

He smiled at her before continuing. "However, I never quite believed you would be able to follow a bear through his territory; that in itself is close to impossible. You were able to do that and more. Somehow you managed to get this bear to accept you, something few people, even the most seasoned biologists, have accomplished with a wild animal. What's more remarkable is you did this with a dog leashed to you."

In an attempt to make light of his compliment so she wouldn't start to blush, Susan said, "Next time I might take a house cat and a trained monkey with me, see how that works out."

David chuckled. "If anyone could pull that off, you could." He walked around the table again, studying each photograph. When he reached the last one, he said, "First, in case I forgot to tell you before, these are remarkable photographs."

Remarkable, Susan thought. That seemed to be his favorite word. Even so, no matter how hard she tried not to, she blushed at his praise.

"I'll keep talking so you won't get too embarrassed," David said. "These pictures reveal more about the life of a wild black bear than all the research information I've compiled over the years. Not many people read my research; it's dry and boring. But people will look at these pictures and learn something about bears and what's happening to the land they live in." David lifted the picture of the bear standing in the clearcut. He held it at arms' length, examining it. Then he turned it so that it faced Susan.

She looked at the photograph. He was right: letting people see the pictures of this bear might help them appreciate wild bears, might in some way help the bears. "Erick, the fellow who develops and prints my photographs, suggested I exhibit these at a gallery in town."

"Good idea. Do you have a gallery in mind?"

"No," Susan said. "I'll have to think about it, check with a few, see if they'd be interested." Wait a minute. There was something Julie had said. What was it? She had said something about how she hoped that seeing the bears in the zoo might help people understand wild bears better. The problem was that bears in zoos weren't wild bears, not any longer. Having humans taking care of them had socialized them, made them more domesticated than wild. What if people could watch up close how the bears in the zoo behaved and then see the photographs of this bear on his own in the woods, living his normal life without human interference? Would that help them gain a better understanding of wild bears?

"Maybe we could display the photos at the zoo," Susan said. "Near the bear enclosure, if possible. That way, people could observe the bears in person," she grinned, "or in bear, I should say, and also see photographs of a bear in his natural habitat."

David nodded. "Are you thinking of a permanent exhibition? Something that would stay at the zoo?"

"Yes. That would be the best option, if it's okay with Julie."

"Let's do it," David said, turning to reach for the phone. "I'll call Julie right now, see what we can arrange for a gallery set-up. We'll also need to schedule an opening reception."

Susan touched his hand, stopping him. "Let me go see Julie first. That way I can give her time to consider all her options. She's a bit in awe of you. She may not be able to say no to you, even if she thinks it's a bad idea." Susan tried in vain to catch his eye. "You have that effect on people."

Somewhat abruptly, David said, "Okay, you talk to her. Let me know what you two decide and when the reception will be. I have some people I'd like to invite."

"About the reception," Susan said. "I'm not good at that sort of thing. Maybe you could give a talk or something."

"You have to let people see you. You're the artist. More people will come if they can meet the artist. That's the point, isn't it, to get people to look at the pictures, and you can answer questions, talk about the bear."

"Yes, okay," she said. "I'll do the reception if it'll get more people to come to the zoo, encourage them to think about wild bears. But how will I explain about the bear, about the way I was able to take these pictures? What if people get the impression they can follow bears around in the woods and everything will be fine?"

"You'll come up with the right thing to say," David said. "You really are better at getting your point across than you think you are. Or maybe you won't have to say a word, simply smile and be aloof. That should do it. Most people believe that artists are all sort of strange to begin with."

Susan laughed with relief and in disbelief. Praising the quality of her photos was one thing, but he had also called her an artist. He had said it more than once. She had heard him.

She wanted to throw her arms around him and thank him for everything he had given her—his support, his encouragement, his help—but she couldn't. They had never touched, not more than a brush of a hand or shoulder. There had been no real intimacy, only the sexual tension she had felt that one night over the phone, the night after the windstorm. Just thinking about that night made her feel hot and damp.

"I should go home," she said. "I haven't spent any time there in days." She gathered her photographs together and slid them inside the portfolio. At the door she turned to him and said, "David?"

"Yes."

"Thank you for your help."

He gave a little wave of his hand as if to say it was nothing.

Instead of going straight home, Susan pulled onto the highway and turned in the direction of the zoo. With a bit of luck, Julie would be there and they could talk right away. While she drove, Susan thought about how she would hang the photographs. Chronological order would be best, except for those she had taken in the clearcut. Those would go last. The final photo would be of the bear standing toe-deep in gray mud, surrounded by the treeless landscape. That would finish her statement, and the bear's.

Suddenly she saw again the bear hide nailed to the side of Hank Richardson's shed. It had been haunting her on and off ever since she had first seen it the day after the windstorm. This was the one picture missing from her collection, the photograph she still needed to take. She would have to go back soon, some time when Hank wasn't around, and see if the hide was still hanging there. She had no idea how long it took to cure a hide, or how long Hank would leave it nailed up outside.

Maybe she could talk to Hank about this instead of sneaking around his place when he wasn't home. She could reassure him that she wouldn't show anything else in the photograph, nothing that would indicate whose shed it was. She didn't want this to be a negative statement about him personally.

No, it was too late for that. She had already made her attitude about killing bears clear to him. Hank would never knowingly allow her to photograph the hide, especially if he had any idea how she intended to use the photo. She would have to take the picture when he wasn't home.

Did she really need the picture bad enough to risk another confrontation with Hank? Yes, she did. The unnecessary killing of bears was an important part of what she wanted to say with her photographs. This would be the final picture in the series, with the bear in the clearcut next to it.

As Susan pulled into the zoo's parking lot, the sky darkened and a spattering of raindrops hit the windshield. She ran toward Julie's office, holding the portfolio of photographs wrapped in her jacket up close to her chest to keep it dry. She didn't quite make it to the office door before the sprinkle had turned into a heavy downpour.

When Susan entered, Julie looked up from behind her desk and said, "Susan. What a nice surprise." She came around the desk to greet Susan, saying, "Goodness, look at you. You're all wet. Would you like a towel?"

"No, thanks. I'm fine, a little damp is all."

"I've been wondering how your project in the woods was going," Julie said, "and how Chance was doing. I've missed seeing you two here at the zoo."

"The project was different from what I had expected, different and better. So much happened. I have a lot to share with you and something to ask of you. Do you have time now, or should I come back another day?"

"Of course I have time," Julie said. She drew up two chairs in front of her desk. The two women sat across from each other, their knees almost touching, while Susan described her experiences in the woods with the bear. Julie listened attentively, periodically asking a question, once or twice leaning forward to touch Susan's hand.

"What an extraordinary experience," Julie said when Susan had finished. "Were you able to get any photographs? That was what you had originally wanted to do, wasn't it?"

"Oh," Susan, said reaching for the portfolio. "I was so eager to tell you about the bear that I forgot about the photos. I brought the ones I took during my last few days in the woods. I have more at home, earlier ones."

Susan handed the photographs, one at a time, to Julie, with the exception of the blurry close-up of the bear's face. She wouldn't be displaying this one to the public, and she didn't want to explain again how she had taken it.

Julie examined each photograph before setting it aside on her desk and reaching for the next one. Holding the last photo, Julie said, "These are wonderful photographs. In this one, you can see the bugs on his tongue. The way he has his eyes rolled toward us, it's like he's saying, 'Do you mind? I'm busy'." She set the photo down and pointed to the group taken in the logged area. "These break my heart. The bear appears so lost among all that mud." Julie sat quietly, studying the photographs. When she looked up, she asked, "You said you have more?"

"Yes."

"What are you planning to do with them?"

"That's what I wanted to ask you. Would it be possible to display them here at the zoo?"

Julie agreed instantly, obviously thrilled with the idea. In addition to making the bear photos available, the exhibit would be one more way to encourage people to come to the zoo. After a short discussion, they decided to have the opening reception here, in Julie's office. It was large for an office and could easily hold thirty or more people at a time. Donations collected at the reception would go toward building a permanent display case close to the bears' enclosure. The photographs would remain here, in Julie's office, until the case was completed.

They set the reception date for the Saturday after Thanksgiving. "That's a good time for fundraising," Julie said, with a sly grin. "People are usually generous that time of year."

On the way home from Julie's office, Susan stopped at a deli and ordered a cheddar cheese, avocado, and tomato sandwich on rye bread to go. She cranked up the van's heater and ate as she drove. Her shoulder and neck muscles felt tight, and she had the beginning of a headache. She was excited about exhibiting the bear's photos, but the more she thought about the opening reception, the more her head hurt. She wasn't comfortable around large groups of people. She always ended up being self-conscious and tongue-tied. The ability to make small talk eluded her completely.

Snowy egrets were fishing in the natural estuary bordering both sides of this section of the highway. They stood as still as statues on thin stilt-like legs, their graceful necks curved, their long beaks poised above the water. How tranquil they were. How nonchalant. They seemed unaffected by cars whizzing past: they continued to fish and glide over the water as their kind had more than likely done in this very spot for centuries, long before humans arrived here.

Crescent Bay lay to the west of the wetlands, and expensive homes scaled the first hills to the east. Past the houses the forest began. Timber companies owned thousands of square miles here. Many of the hills that Susan could see in the distance had the patchwork look of recent clearcutting.

With these beautiful, white birds so close and the forest spreading out beyond, Susan felt drawn into her fantasy about escaping to live in the woods forever. She could abandon her van right here, on the shoulder of the highway, wade past the egrets, and stride through the neighborhoods and into the forested hills. Among the trees, her lack of social skills would pass unnoticed. There would be no need to speak; she might even forget how. She would remain forever lost in the woods. No, not lost. She would find who she was in the woods. "Found," she said softly.

Maybe this had already happened. She had learned a great deal about herself out there with the bear: her stamina, her courage, her relationship with nature. More than that, she had found a connection to this bear and to the land he lived in. For a few brief moments during her time in the woods, she had been able to slip through the thin veil that separates humans from other living creatures and become a part of this bear and his forest.

Susan knew what she had to do now. She would finish what she had started with the bear, all of it, including the reception. Who knows? She might enjoy it. After all, she was the artist.

The answering machine was blinking when Susan opened her front door. She expected it to be Shirley. Instead, when she pressed the Play button, she heard Jacob Riley's voice saying, "Ms. Campton, this is Jacob Riley, the forester you spoke with the other day. I called to let you know that I went to the area you mentioned in our meeting, the one in the Woolly Creek watershed. I thought it might put your mind at ease if you knew that we will not be cutting the tree you identified as a bear's den. We will be taking many of the surrounding trees, about fifty percent of the canopy, but not that specific tree.

"While I was there, I retrieved the items you left behind. I can have them brought to you, or you can pick them up at my office. Give me a call and let me know what would work best for you.

"I also wanted to talk to you about your photographs, the ones you brought with you to our meeting. I was wondering if you might be interested in selling copies of some of them. I'd like to hang them here in my office. Maybe we can talk about this when you call to make arrangements for getting your camping gear. Thanks. Bye."

What was that all about? She knew what cutting fifty percent of the trees meant. It didn't mean taking every other tree. It could mean cutting all the large trees, leaving the small ones or the damaged ones, like the bear's hollowed-out tree. The most valuable trees were usually the first to be cut. Making a profit was the timber company's top priority. Jacob Riley had told her as much. What was surprising was the fact that he had gone out in person to inspect the land around the bear's tree, and that he had taken the time to call her about it. Not only that, instead of having her arrested for trespassing, he had brought her belongings back and was arranging to return them. And the last, wanting to buy copies of her photographs. That was truly surprising.

He was on his way to his home next to the creek when he smelled the stranger. The scent swirled and floated all along the ridge trail. He moved down the hill toward the creek, stopping often to sniff and listen, his mouth hanging open, his head low.

In the clearing, the unfamiliar stench was everywhere. He lunged halfway back up the hill and stayed there, hidden.

He combed the air with his nose and mouth. Where were they? There was no trace of them, of the woman and the dog, just this rank new smell. He hung his head and rocked on his heels. Then he climbed the rest of the way up the hillside, leaving the creek bed behind. There was no reason to stay here. Everything about it had changed. This was no longer his.

It was time to phone Meagan and Shawn to tell them about the bear. She had been putting this off, but now she was ready to tell her children the truth about what she had been up to in the woods.

First she called Meagan. "Hi," Susan said when her daughter came on the line. "Is this a good time for you to talk, or should I call back later?"

Meagan launched into a rapid-fire accounting of her life. Susan listened politely, adding an occasional, "Mm hmm," or, "Yes, I see." After a while, she interrupted, telling Meagan that she had phoned to let her know how her photo project in the woods had gone.

Meagan said, "Oh," and then fell silent. The silence rang with Meagan's impatience to get on with what she was saying and her annoyance at her mom for interrupting her.

Susan started with the day Chance had chased a bear through the woods. She went on to tell her daughter everything that had happened with the bear in the last several weeks. Meagan listened without comment or interruption. Susan finished by telling her about the plans for the photo exhibit at the zoo and her idea of raising money to help preserve the habitat of wild bears.

When Susan stopped, Meagan said, "You're telling me this for the first time now? What if something had happened to you while you were out there, and I didn't know where you were?"

"I know I should have talked to you, but I didn't want you to worry. And I needed to do this on my own."

Meagan's reply began with an exasperated sigh. Susan could picture her daughter's face the way she had seen it so many times during Meagan's teenage years: her lips firm and unyielding, her eyes narrowed in defiance. Now Meagan said, "For heaven's sake, Mom, you're all Shawn and I have left. We're a family. We need to talk to each other. Especially about something as important as this."

Susan wanted to tell her that yes, they were a family, but Meagan and Shawn were building their own lives, lives that didn't include her except for phone calls and occasional visits. She couldn't live her life for her children any more than they could live their lives for her. And it was working out. She was finding her way. She no longer felt so lost. Instead she said, "I want you to trust me. I can take care of myself."

"It's not that I don't trust you," Meagan said with another exasperated sigh. "It's that I love you. I don't want anything bad to happen to you. Plus, I'm interested in what you do with your time. Including this." She went on to ask a few questions about the photography exhibit and reception. She and Peter wouldn't be able to attend the reception because they would still be at Peter's grandmother's house in Nevada. Susan agreed to send her one of the flyers and any newspaper articles pertaining to the event. Meagan and Peter would see the exhibit when they came in December.

The last thing Meagan said before hanging up was, "I still can't believe you didn't tell me about this sooner."

All Susan could think to say was, "I'm sorry," although she wasn't sorry. She was glad she had done this on her own without involving her children until now. They didn't need to know everything she was up to any more than she needed to know every little thing about their lives.

Next Susan phoned Shawn, knowing that this would be the easier of the two conversations. He had always been more relaxed about life than his sister, and his reaction to her narrative and her news was true to form: he didn't seem at all upset at the idea of his mom wandering around in the forest with wild animals. He was too young, and too preoccupied with his own life, to worry about what might be lurking in the woods, or anywhere else for that matter. He merely said, "That's wonderful, Mom. I can't believe you did this. It'll be fun to see the pictures when I get home."

Susan woke up to the gray light of early morning filtering in through the bedroom window and the sound of light rain falling on the roof. She had slept almost ten hours. She yawned and stretched and thought about how nice it would be to spend a long, lazy day at home.

She fed Chance and then made a pot of coffee and her usual breakfast of oatmeal. She was in the kitchen washing up her few dishes when the front door swung open and Shirley's voice sang out, "Hello? Anybody home?"

Susan came from the kitchen, wiping her hands on a dishtowel. "You're up and about early," she said.

"I had to drop Mary Ann off at a band practice, so I thought I'd come by. I couldn't wait a minute longer. Tell me about what happened with the bear this time before I burst."

Susan and Shirley sat across from each other at the dinner table. For close to an hour, Susan described in great detail her latest encounters with the bear, showing the photographs as she went. Again she struggled with finding the right words to explain that last day in the woods, how the bear had come close to her, touching her. She ended up glossing over it and moving on to the planned exhibit at the zoo.

"Wow," Shirley said. "That's great news."

"Yes, it's good, except for one thing," Susan said. "To raise money for the permanent exhibit, I've got to go to this reception."

"I know," Shirley said, "you would rather be out there face-to-face with a bear, but you've done that. Time for your next challenge."

"I suppose," Susan said, setting the reception aside for now. "I have another challenge. One more photograph I want to take." She went on to tell Shirley about her plan to photograph the bear hide at Hank's.

"You're not going do this by yourself," Shirley said, shaking her head. "I won't let you. Not this time. Hank's crazy. I don't want to think about what he'd do if he caught you there. I'll go with you. I can be the lookout, drive the getaway car. When should we do it?"

"I'm not sure. It has to happen soon, though, and when he's not home. I'm not even sure if the hide is still there."

"Let's go right now. If he's there, we'll leave. We'll go in my car, he won't recognize it, and if he sees it, he'll think we're lost or something." Shirley stood up, plucked her purse and keys from the table, and in an instant had her hand on the doorknob, ready to go.

"Let me think about this for minute," Susan said, stalling for time. Going to Hank's by herself was one thing; taking Shirley there was out of the question. Hank truly was crazy, not just quirky or eccentric, but potentially dangerous. More times than she cared to remember, he had discharged his revolver when he suspected a thief was prowling in the bushes behind his place. It was impossible to guess what he would do if he found her and Shirley there uninvited. "I'm not dressed yet," she ventured. "And it's raining."

"This isn't much of a rain, more a light drizzle. Don't think about it. Throw on your clothes and get your camera and let's go."

The air inside the car was electric with excitement and anxiety during the short ten-minute drive. Shirley slowed the car as they neared Hank's place. When they had passed it, she drove to the stop sign at the end of the road and made a U-turn.

On the second pass, she pulled the car over across from Hank's house and stopped. "It doesn't look like anyone's home," Shirley said. "There isn't any smoke coming from the chimney, and I don't see that old, rusted-out beast of a truck of his, either, do you?" Susan shook her head.

"You stay here," Shirley said. "I'll go up and knock on the door. If someone answers, I'll pretend I'm lost. I'll ask for directions to—"

"To where? The hospital? The morgue? Shirley, this isn't a good idea. What if he—"

"Recognizes me? He won't. I've only seen him around town, only met him face to face once, and that was years ago. If he does recognize me, so what? Locals get lost, too. He won't connect me to you." She touched Susan's arm. "Relax."

Before Susan could protest further, Shirley had opened the car door and was outside and moving briskly toward Hank's front door. Susan turned in the seat and craned her neck, trying to keep her eyes on her friend, as though this could somehow keep Shirley safe. It seemed like hours, but Shirley was back in less than two minutes.

"Come on," Shirley said. "No one's here, and I saw the bear hide. It's still nailed to the shed. It looks awful, though. The fur's falling out in places, and there's dried blood and some type of gunk mixed with dead flies in the eye sockets. It's spooky, but it's there. Let's go before Hank comes home." Shirley took off at a run, her strapless shoes crunching on the graveled road.

Susan pulled the Minolta free from the case and jogged behind Shirley across Hank's front yard and around the side to the shed. She came to a dead stop when she saw the bearskin. Shirley was right; it looked terrible. Large bald patches of dried skin covered much of the hide, and what little fur remained was dull and stiff. Empty, crusted sockets were all that was left of what once had been this bear's eyes. Dark streaks of rainwater dripped off the hide and onto the ground at Susan's feet.

"Hurry. Take the picture and let's get out of here," Shirley hissed in Susan's ear.

Across the yard, a large mixed-breed dog chained to Hank's front porch yawned awake. At first he stared at them, seemingly baffled. Then he sprang toward them, jerking the chain, barking and snarling. They cringed away from him.

"Hurry," Shirley said again, digging her fingernails into Susan's arm.

Susan took three shots: two of the whole hide and one close-up of the dead bear's head, its empty eye sockets blankly staring right out at the camera. Then she said, "Let's go."

Together they ran to the car and jumped in. Shirley floored the gas pedal, gunning the engine and spinning the tires in the loose gravel. She grimaced. "Terrible. The hide, I mean," was all she said.

"Yes," Susan answered.

When they were safely out of sight of Hank's house, Shirley brought the car to a stop at the side of the road. Her face was pale, the dark circles under her eyes standing out in sharp contrast. "Why do you suppose Hank killed that bear?"

"I don't know." Susan watched the trees outside the window drip moisture from their heavy branches.

The two women sat in silence. After a few minutes, Shirley gave Susan a mischievous grin and said, "You have to admit, it was kind of fun sneaking into Hank's yard. And that dog! I thought he was going to break loose and kill us."

Susan shook her head. "You call that fun? And you say I'm the crazy one."

"When can we get the pictures developed?" Shirley asked. "Can we do it now? I want to see them."

"Now? I was at Erick's most of the day yesterday," Susan said. When she saw the look of disappointment on her friend's face, she relented. "Okay, yes, we can probably do it now. If Erick's not too busy, I'm sure he'll do it for us. It's going to take three or four hours, though. Don't you have something else you need to do?"

"Not a single thing. You see before you a free woman."

———

Four hours later, Susan and Shirley were on their way back to Susan's house with three new photographs lined up on the back seat of Shirley's car. Susan had the strange sensation that they had three decomposing bears as passengers, a crowd of ghosts watching them from behind.

Shirley pulled into Susan's driveway and shut off the engine. They sat staring out the front windshield.

"Oh, I forgot to tell you," Susan said, "Jacob Riley, the forester I spoke to about the Woolly Creek logging, called and left a message on my machine. He said he had gone personally to inspect the area around the bear's tree and that they wouldn't be cutting that particular tree."

"That's good news, isn't it?" Shirley asked.

"Yes and no. He said they were still planning to cut fifty percent of the trees near the creek. It's hard to know how that will affect the bear. We'll have to wait and see. But get this, he also said he'd like to buy some of my photographs of the bear to hang in his office."

"Now that's interesting," Shirley said. "I wonder why he would want to hang pictures of a wild bear in his office. They don't fit in with the theme of logging, do they?" Susan shook her head no.

"Are you going to sell them to him?"

"I'll have to think about it. This whole thing with the photographs is taking on a life of its own. Maybe I will. I could donate the money to the zoo for the display cases. Or…." Susan gazed out the side window. It was no longer raining, but the air still felt heavy and wet. "What do you think about starting a fund for the restoration of bear habitats?"

"A fund to restore bear habitats? Do you mean you want to give money to land owners to set aside some of their property for bears? Or provide money to help educate people about the needs of bears—public service announcements, school programs, that type of thing?"

"I don't know. I haven't given it much thought. Probably not that many of my photographs will sell, but if they do, I could use the money to set up a fund that will benefit wild bears in some way."

"We'd have to work out the details," Shirley said, "but you're right, it sounds like a good idea. Your photographs are wonderful. I know people will want to buy them the minute they see them. I'll be the first to buy one. I want the one of the bear scratching his back on the tree to give to John for his birthday next month. He'll love it." She glanced at the pictures in the back seat. "I'd also like to help with the project to protect the bears' homes. Maybe I can do the bookkeeping or research or something?"

"Let's think about it, take our time," Susan said. "We don't have to decide right now." Her mind was spinning. She needed a break from thinking about bears. When all those weeks ago in David's office she had said she owed something to the bears, she hadn't known how much time and energy paying that debt would take.

She stepped out of the car and retrieved the photographs from the back seat. She opened the front passenger-side door again and said to Shirley, "Thank you for being there today. I couldn't have done it without you. I mean that dog and the bear hide and the fear of Hank showing up. I would have run away if you weren't there."

Shirley laughed. "That's me, always the brave one."

Susan smiled at her friend and said, "I'm serious. I'm glad you were with me today. We'll figure out what to do next. First I have to get through this photo exhibit and reception. I'll need your help with that for sure, if you're willing to help. If you have the time."

"Of course I'll help. Now go in and get some rest. You've had a busy week, and it's going to get busier."

The next few weeks passed in a blur. Susan and Shirley agreed to skip their usual Tuesday lunch date and instead concentrate on the photo exhibit. Susan threw herself into preparing for the exhibit. She figured if she kept busy, she wouldn't have time to worry about the reception. She drove to town so many times she lost count. She dropped the photographs off to be framed and made another trip into Crescent to pick them up and deliver them to Julie's office at the zoo.

Several times she met with Julie to discuss the layout and choose the photographs for the advertisement announcing the opening reception. She spent one entire afternoon working with Erick on the design of the brochure to be handed out during the reception. The brochure would include a small sampling of her photographs and a request for donations to help build a display case to house the photos permanently at the zoo. They also drew up an insert for the brochure. At the top of the insert was a simple statement in bold print telling people how to purchase copies of the bear's photographs. Centered below this was the photo of the bear in the clearcut, and below that was one sentence stating that all of the profits from the sale of the photographs would go into a fund for the preservation of black bear habitats.

Near the end of the first week, Susan drove to Jacob Riley's office to pick up her camping gear. He wasn't there. She left a note telling him that she would be pleased to sell him copies of her photographs. She included Shirley's name and phone number, as she would be the one in charge of taking print orders.

Susan had been relieved when Shirley offered to handle all the print sales. Susan couldn't begin to picture herself talking to strangers about the price of her photographs. Shirley, on the other hand, would be good at it.

True to her word, Shirley was also helping in other ways. She spent two weeks researching the legal and financial aspects of a nonprofit organization. Even though she was grateful for Shirley's help, Susan assumed this would be a waste of Shirley's time: not many people would want to buy her photographs.

Erick suggested that Susan number and sign all the prints and sell only fifty copies of each one. "It's called a limited edition," he said. "People will feel like they're getting something unique, and you can charge more for each one."

Susan thought often about the bear. Right in the middle of cooking dinner or preparing for bed, she would close her eyes and there he would be, standing in the huckleberry patch or looking back at her from up the trail. She wondered if he had gone back to Woolly Creek or stayed in his rock cave near the huckleberry patch. Maybe he was in a different part of the forest by now, sleeping in another den.

Each evening she stood on her porch and watched as day gave way to night. She was waiting for that instant when the sky would suddenly change from bright pink to black, as it had that night in the woods, but it never happened here. The light always faded little by little until it was gone.

It rained for days, backing off to a drizzle before starting up at full force again. Late Monday afternoon, five days before the opening, Susan was home after spending the day at the zoo, helping Julie paint her office walls a shade called *Light Eggshell Brown*. The two of them had agreed on this color as the best backdrop for the photographs.

Susan was now sprawled on the couch, absently petting Chance. He lay with his head and chest across her legs. A strong wind was blowing torrents of rain against the house. Although bone-tired, she couldn't stop thinking about her time in the woods and wondering about the bear.

Finally she got up and laid the map of the Woolly Creek area out on the dinner table. She ran her finger along the Main Line and tried again to determine where she had been on that last day in the woods, but it was impossible. She had no way of knowing where the huckleberry patch was or how Chance had led them from there to the windfall.

She touched her face lightly with her hand, reliving the feeling of the bear's breath on her skin. I have to go back to Woolly Creek, she thought. I have to. I'll go after the reception. I need to see if he's been there. The decision made, she felt more relaxed than she had in days.

She returned to the couch, wiggled her legs back under Chance, and fell asleep.

Susan and Shirley spent most of the next day hanging the photographs on the newly painted walls of Julie's office. Susan already knew the order in which she wanted to hang the pictures, but Shirley was obsessed with height and spacing. They had moved each picture a little to the right or left and up and down about a hundred times. Why did Shirley have to be so picky? Wouldn't people be viewing the pictures, not the spaces in between?

Shirley finally stepped back, saying, "There, now they're perfect." Susan had to agree, they did look good, but at that point she was so relieved to be done with this project that she would have agreed to anything. They could have laid the photos out on the floor for all she cared.

On Thursday, Thanksgiving Day, Susan loaded Chance into the van and drove inland, away from the coast. Shirley had wanted Susan to spend the day with her, John, and the girls, but Susan had declined the invitation. This was her first holiday without Bill, and without her children. She didn't want to spend this day around another family. She wanted to do something she had never done with Bill, to create a totally different holiday, one that didn't hold the sad reminders of how she used to spend this holiday.

When their children were still young enough to enjoy such outings with their parents, Bill and Susan had often taken Meagan and Shawn to a swimming hole on the North Fork of the Hawkins River. Susan had never been farther inland than that. Today she drove past their old swimming hole and made the turn at Paulson's Bar, following the road to New Camp. She had heard about the abandoned gold-mining town along the Madrone River, a tributary to the Hawkins River, and found the idea intriguing. Today she would get a chance to see it.

The narrow road snaked along the mountainside, climbing almost a foot in altitude for every five feet it traveled forward. Soon Susan was higher than the tops of the giant Douglas firs and Jeffrey pines growing in the river valley below. She half expected to see bald eagles soaring by the van's windows.

When she reached the township, she was disappointed. She had driven up for miles with nothing but treetops and visions of eagles to keep her company. Then, off to her right on a flat above the river, appeared a whole group of homes—almost a small subdivision—smacked right up against each other. She had been anticipating something more romantic than these slapped-together little houses. She couldn't see any signs of people living in these homes now. No smoke was coming from the stove pipes or lights showing in the windows, although many had children's toys scattered around outside, and one had a large ham radio antenna attached to its side. Maybe these were summer homes. It would be difficult to live all the way out here in the winter.

A bit farther up the road on the left was a group of older buildings, constructed from whole logs and long wooden planks. Susan guessed these might have been part of what once was the town of New Camp, maybe the mercantile or the school.

On the way back down the hill, she noticed an empty campground. The sun broke through the cloud layer as she pulled into a parking space adjoining one of the campsites. Bear-proof garbage cans and graying picnic tables shone silver in the soft, misty rays of sunlight.

Susan let Chance out and followed him on a trail that led through a small stand of trees, ending at a sandy beach on the edge of the Madrone River. Here was the romance she had been wanting. The river roiled over large rocks, frothing up rainbows in its wake. At a spot where it cut in close to the bank, a deep pool had formed. The water was emerald green and so clear that Susan could see the rocks on the bottom.

Mesmerized, she felt almost as if she had driven high enough to reach heaven. She stayed for a long time, watching the river. Chance dropped a stick at her feet and pranced and pawed at it. Susan barely noticed. He eventually gave up asking her to play and waded at the edge of the swimming hole, snapping at floating leaves drifting on the water.

The sun slid behind the clouds and the rain started up again. Susan stood in the rain and threw a stick for Chance half a dozen times: it wasn't fair to come all this way and not toss a stick for him. To Chance, playing meant fetching; that's all there was to it. If there was water involved, better yet.

On the way home, Susan toyed with the idea of finding a restaurant that was open and getting dinner, maybe turkey with all the fixings. As she entered town, she changed her mind. She would eat alone in a restaurant someday, possibly even enjoy it, but her first holiday without her family wasn't the right time for this. She didn't want to be alone in a crowd. She drove home without stopping. When she arrived, she fed Chance and made her same old simple, familiar dinner—stir-fried vegetables, walnuts, and brown rice—about the furthest thing from a turkey dinner there was.

The evening of the reception, Susan took her time getting dressed. She decided to wear the black silk dress she had worn to Bill's memorial service. It was the only nice dress she owned. On that day, nearly eight months ago, she hadn't cared what she looked like. Come to think of it, she couldn't remember having chosen or buying this dress. Had Shirley picked it out? Bought it for her? Probably. Susan would have selected something that fit looser and was less revealing.

She turned this way and that, examining her reflection in the bathroom mirror, noticing how the dress flattered her curves, hugging her waist and flowing down over her slender hips to just past her knees. She hardly ever wore a dress and it was strange to see herself in one now, but hey, she looked pretty darn good. "Not bad for an old widow," she said, turning in a slow circle in front of the mirror.

Around her neck she wore an elegantly crafted, small silver bear hanging from a thin chain. This had come in the mail three days ago, a present from David. Inside the box was a folded note, saying simply, For Good Luck.

Right before she left, Susan coiled her hair at the nape of her neck and fastened it with a silver barrette that had belonged to her grandmother. Her dark curls fanned out below the clip, touching her shoulders. The shorter parts that she had cut to hide the scratch on her forehead had grown out a little and now made a soft frame of curls around her face.

Julie's office was already hot and crowded by the time Susan arrived. The second she walked through the door, two television reporters and their camera crews surrounded her. They shoved microphones at her and bombarded her with questions. She squinted into their glaring lights, trying to see who was asking, and answered as best she could.

The reporters eventually ran out of questions and went off to examine the photographs. David came to stand beside her. "Look at you all dressed up," he said. "You look stunning."

She touched the silver bear hanging from the delicate chain around her neck. "Thank you. For the compliment, and for this."

He nodded and leaned in close and said, "Quite the crowd. Julie sure knows how to stage an event." His cheek brushed hers. Susan didn't move. She wanted to hold onto the feeling of his skin against hers, a reminder of how it felt to have a man touch her. David took a half step back, breaking the contact.

From that point on, waves of people came up to her, asking her questions, leaning near her in an attempt to be heard, telling her how impressed they were with the photographs. Susan nodded, smiled, and tried to answer their questions. It didn't make much difference what she said: it was impossible to hear anything specific above the noise of so many people talking at once.

Shirley waltzed amid the crowd, the pleated skirt of her green satin dress twirling around her knees. She was obviously enjoying herself. She loved mingling at parties, meeting new people, and she was good at it. In most situations, her soft Georgian accent had all but disappeared, but in large gatherings it became more pronounced. This, along with her natural social skills and intelligence, made her a cordial and interesting hostess.

John, on the other hand, stayed only long enough to look at the photographs. As he was leaving he came over to Susan and shouted above the noise, "These are good. You did a good job." Susan was speechless. Had she heard him correctly? As far as she could remember, this was the first time John had complimented her on anything.

"Friend of yours?" David asked.

"No," Susan said, watching John walk away. Then, "Yes, maybe."

Halfway through the evening, Susan caught sight of Jacob Riley. He was the last person she expected to see here. She nudged David with her elbow and nodded in Jacob's direction. David raised his eyebrows and shrugged. When Jacob's eyes met hers, he lifted his right hand to his forehead in a quick salute. What could that mean? Was he congratulating her on the exhibit or recognizing a worthy opponent?

Four hours passed before the room began to empty. Susan was mentally and physically exhausted. She wanted to go home. David had remained beside her all evening, introducing her to many of his students and co-workers and fielding questions. Now he moved closer to her and spoke softly, saying, "I think it's safe to leave. I'll walk you out, if you want."

Susan nodded. She said goodbye to Julie, thanking her with a hug for all she had done. She then put her hand on Shirley's shoulder and said, "I'm going." Shirley whispered in Susan's ear, "We've already sold sixty prints of your pictures." Susan smiled, genuinely pleased and surprised. Who would have thought?

Outside, standing by Susan's van, David said, "Quite the shindig, eh?" Susan agreed, smiling.

David cleared his throat and gazed around before meeting her eyes. "When this project is over," he said, "I'd like it if we could still see each other."

"I don't think this project is going to be over anytime soon, if ever," Susan said. "I hope you and I will be working together for a long time. I still have a lot to learn about black bears, and so much to do to help them keep their homes."

"Of course," David said. "But I meant besides work. In addition to."

Susan looked down, studying her shoes, as though they were now the most fascinating sight around. She had always assumed that she was the only one having fantasies about the two of them. Had she missed something? It was possible; she was pitifully out of practice in the romance arena.

The mere thought of a romantic encounter with David made the idea of sleeping alone again tonight almost unbearable. What if she were someone else, someone altogether different, a woman who could throw caution to the wind, do whatever she wanted in spite of the consequences? She was in the process of changing much of what she believed about herself, building a new concept of who she was. Why not this? Why not go home with David right now? What difference could it make? She was no longer a married woman. Bill was dead and David was here, alive, interesting, and kind of cute.

She saw clearly how her and David's naked bodies would look together, entangled and sweaty, his slightly paunchy belly fitting nicely into the hollow below her ribcage. She almost chuckled out loud at the image. She could feel herself straining toward the undercurrent of his passionate, physical energy. But she didn't want to be with David just to keep from being lonely. If she had an intimate relationship with a man, she would want it to be a long term one. Now wasn't the right time for something like that. It was far too soon after Bill's death. She had to learn how to live alone first, to take care of herself.

"David," she said, her voice gentle. "I'm not sure what you had in mind, but I hope you'll understand when I say that I'm not ready for a relationship with a man, other than that of a working partner and friend." She glanced at the main entrance to the zoo. People were leaving, holding flyers from the reception in their hands and talking softly among themselves. "It hasn't even been a year since my husband died, so I need to take my time. I can always use another good friend, though, if that would be all right?"

There was a short, uncomfortable silence before David said, "Yes, friends. Of course, as friends. Maybe we could go for a hike in the forest. I'm stuck inside so much of the time now, I don't get to be out among the trees as often as I'd like. Or maybe I could cook a meal for you. Lunch to start, and dinner and wine when you're feeling brave." He smiled and quickly put his hands out in a wait-a-minute gesture. "Don't get me wrong; you don't have to be brave to eat my cooking. I love to cook, and my friends tell me I'm good at it."

Susan was grateful for the muted lighting in the parking lot—provided by a hooded lamp mounted on a post in the center of the lot—otherwise he would be able to see her blushing again. Why was she always thinking about sex around him? The thought of being wined and dined by candlelight (her imagination added this part) didn't help.

"That would be nice," she managed to say.

"Good," David said. "I'll call you in a day or two, after you've had time to recover from tonight, and we can decide what we'd like to do, hike or eat. Or maybe both. I'd love to meet Chance, and of course you must meet my cat, Angel."

"That would be nice," she said again. She searched for something more to say. She wanted to be as understanding and gracious as he was being, but she settled for her usual approach to conversation: saying whatever popped into her head. "Oh, I almost forgot. I'm going to Woolly Creek tomorrow, just for one night. I have to see if the bear has been there. I really want to see him again."

David cocked his head and stared at her the way children often do when they can't quite figure out what is going on with the adults in their lives. Then he said, "Of course you should go and take a look." He reached around her and opened the van's door. "While you're at it, you can see if Jacob's crew has been out there flagging the area."

She got into the van and fiddled with her keys. "I'll call you when I get home. From Woolly Creek, I mean. Not tonight."

"Right," he said, nodding. He stood there watching while she backed out of the parking space and drove away.

That night, in her own bed, alone, Susan couldn't sleep. Voices, questions, faces, random scenes from the reception cluttered her mind. What had she said to the reporters? Who was that man who had shouted at her about bears eating his garbage? What had he said? Something about a new way to make garbage cans bear-proof. And there was David, the smell of him—spicy aftershave mixed in with a hint of the salty odor of sweat—and the feel of his face against hers.

Thinking about David brought a deluge of questions and feelings: Would she ever feel at ease showing her naked, middle-aged body to a man other than Bill? What if she never had sex again? Would David want to have sex with her at some point? What if he didn't? Or worse, what if he did? And if he did ask her, what would she say?

"Yes," she whispered, running her hand across the cold sheets on the side of the bed where Bill had slept. She would say yes.

Susan was awake by six the next morning and felt surprisingly good after such a restless night. She threw off the covers. Might as well get up and get an early start. With the nights coming on so much earlier, she would need the extra time to reach Woolly Creek before dark.

Icy puddles, shining like small, silver lakes, overflowed the low spots in the trail. The endless days of rain had given way to cold sunshine. Susan was glad she had brought the sleeping bag. She had intended to leave it behind—having it tied to the bottom of the daypack made the whole thing cumbersome—but seeing a layer of ice on the van's windshield, she had gone back inside and tied it on. Along with the sleeping bag and the rest of her usual gear, she brought just enough food and water for one night.

Chance ran ahead, his hind legs kicking up as he frisked through the puddles, breaking the ice into long shards. The cold didn't bother him. His thick undercoat offered protection, and the Labrador's trademark enthusiasm didn't allow for hesitation. He was pure, boundless, in-the-moment joy. Susan stayed close behind him. She was as thrilled as he was to be back in the woods. Her legs reached out in long strides, her boots crunching through the fern-patterned ice right next to Chance's footprints.

She stopped only long enough to clip Chance to the leash when they were past the windfall. She was anxious to get to Woolly Creek to see if the bear had been there. Maybe he was there now, curled up in his den, lazy on this cold day.

Farther along the ridge trail, Susan saw two slender pieces of white-and-red striped plastic tied to a large Douglas fir. She lifted the ends of the ribbons and ran them through her hand. So the loggers had been here marking the trees.

From that point on, orange plastic ribbons hung from every fifth or sixth tree. Some of the larger trees had single stripes of blue spray paint around their trunks. Susan wanted to rip off the ribbons and rub out the blue paint, but this wouldn't stop the logging. It might make things worse. She didn't know what the different colors meant. Maybe some of the trees had been marked to be left uncut—the ones with the blue stripes or the orange ribbons. Or maybe both, she thought wishfully.

At the path leading down to the creek, Susan unleashed Chance. At the bottom, she stopped and looked around. Not much had changed here. The timber company's markings hadn't come this close to the creek yet.

She leashed Chance and walked past the bear's tree, leaning to check inside the den as she had done so many times before. The bear wasn't there. The den looked cold, dark, and empty. Above the opening she spied a yellow metal triangle. Susan walked closer. Nailed to the tree, the yellow sign announced, in bold, black letters:

WILDLIFE
LEAVE TREE
SMITH AND SONS
TIMBER COMPANY

Was this Jacob's way of protecting the tree? He had said that his company wouldn't be cutting this tree. He had also stated clearly that bears' dens were not a consideration when planning a logging operation, that existing laws governing logging did not protect bears or their habitats.

She had never seen a sign like this in the woods before, and it was hard for her to imagine what animal a timber company would be willing to protect. Maybe a bald eagle. She stepped back and looked up into the living branches high above her. There was nothing but silence and tree limbs. If an eagle had a nest here, it was well hidden.

Susan set up camp under the fallen tree, smoothing the sleeping bag out on top of the canvas tarp and setting the flashlight next to it. The flashlight had become her own private joke. The fact that she had remembered to bring it pretty much guaranteed that she wouldn't need it.

She settled down to wait, stretching out inside the sleeping bag, glad she had brought it. Chance lay beside her and was asleep the second his head touched his front paws. Susan thought about how amazing it was that dogs could fall asleep practically the minute they stopped moving, and then she too was asleep.

Soon afterward, Susan woke up in the twilight, alive with expectation, positive she heard something moving down the path. She looked out from behind the rock. Nothing was there. She waited. Still nothing. Then came the distant sound of pebbles rolling off the canyon walls. Something was coming down the path. "Please let it be him," Susan whispered. But it wasn't. The bear never entered the clearing.

Susan heard the faint clinking of small rocks sliding down the canyon walls intermittently for about two hours. Most likely it was a bird or a mouse poking through the undergrowth, knocking stones loose while searching for food.

The sky grew dark, the light leaching away bit by bit. Again Susan curled up in the sleeping bag alongside Chance and fell asleep. Throughout the night she drifted in gentle dreams of trees and ferns and elusive animals—but not the bear. He didn't come during the night to his den or to her dreams.

In the morning, Susan woke up certain that she wouldn't see the bear again that winter. Fleetingly, she considered trying to find the way to the bear's cave by the huckleberry patch. If she went to the Main Line and found the rock quarry, she could cross the road and go through the clearcut section and find the berry patch and then the cave. She had already run this through her mind many times, and each time she knew it wouldn't work. Even if she found the clearcut, she had no clue as to which direction to go from there. She could wander around for days and still not find the cave. Or, she thought, I might walk right to it. Stranger things have happened. She looked at Chance, remembering how he had miraculously led her to the trail home during their last time in the woods when they had seemed so lost.

She would come back but not during the winter. She would wait until spring, just as the trilliums were starting to bloom. She would again walk by the chorusing tree frogs. This time, frenzied with their instinctual need to find a mate, the frogs would continue their loud songs as she and Chance splashed through the puddles right beside them. The entire forest would be heavy with the need to procreate. Even the plants would be full of sexual desire, pollen coming off them like sticky, yellow dust.

On that day in the spring, Susan would walk straight across the clearcut until she came out on the other side. If she didn't find the huckleberry patch, she would start again. She would keep trying, not leaving until she found it, until she knew whether the bear was still there.

For today, she was content to be here. She leaned against a tree beside the creek. The water flowed past her on its impatient rush to the ocean. From somewhere in the woods, she heard the high whistle of a hawk. Her mind emptied of the harried confusion of the last few weeks. Now there was nothing but this creek and the forest. She waited until the sun had moved far over in the sky. Then it was time to go home. She gathered her gear and, right behind Chance, she climbed out of the canyon.

Acknowledgments

Warm thanks to the following people for reading various drafts of this story over the years and offering valuable help and suggestions: Dan Berman, Mike and Marcie Cavanagh, Lauren Lester, and Sonja Manor.

Special thanks to my team of readers who underlined and penciled in and used sticky notes to help me find what I needed to fix. Without their tireless and careful attention to detail, this story would never have gotten past the first draft: Reta Austin, Michele Francesconi, Sandra Healy, Matt Hinton, Rebecca McEwing, Monika Newman, and Anda Webb.

I owe more than I can say to Jesse Ralston, who had the task of pointing out those areas that needed work. His innate skill for the pacing and rhythm of a story made this a better story and me a better writer.

To Dave Bitts, I offer up my sincere gratitude. At first he hesitated when I asked for his help, and then he said he'd give it a try. In the end, he not only gave me his excellent skills as a proofreader but also his joy for this story.

A big thank you to Dylan Berman for allowing me to use a passage from his poem, "What, you ask, is Nature."

Last but not in any way least, I am thankful for my husband, David Ralston. He read several drafts of this story, cheered me on, and told me in no uncertain terms that I needed to get this one done and out there for people to read. He is always and in every way supportive of my work and of me.

Author's Note

Even though this story takes place in the late 1970s, the plight of black bears living in Timber Company lands hasn't changed. The main goal of these companies is to make a profit by providing lumber and other forest products to a growing population. The laws that govern timber harvesting are there primarily to support this goal. The impact of these policies on watersheds and privately owned forest lands is becoming painfully obvious as more and more animals relying on clean streams and rivers and a mature forest to survive are now on the endangered species list.

The black bear in this story is an imaginary bear, but his situation is similar to all black bears living close to human activity. Every year black bears enter neighborhoods that border forest lands in search of food after intense logging or encroaching housing developments have taken over what once was their home. There are numerous stories of black bears breaking into chicken pens, damaging fruit trees, or tipping over garbage cans while scavenging for food. Fear and misunderstanding drive these stories, which are repeated and often embellished. More times than not, this leads to a disastrous outcome for the bears, who were doing nothing more than taking advantage of the food so temptingly offered up by humans.

I strongly encourage anyone living close to black bear territory to learn more about these animals and their behaviors. Listed under Research are the names of some of the best-known black bear experts. If you are interested, you can find much of their work online.

Research

I consulted the following sources in order to write a fictional story that is as accurate as possible where fiction crosses into fact. Everything I got right is because of these experts and their research. Anything I got wrong is my own fault.

Black Bears:
"Black Bear Facts," Lynn Rogers, PhD, Wildlife Research Institute
"Language and Sounds of Black Bears," Lynn Rogers, PhD, Wildlife Research Institute
"Communication of Black Bears," Get Bear Smart Society
The Great American Bear, Jeff Fair

In addition, I listened to hundreds of stories about black bears: everyone living in bear territory has a bear story to tell. Besides being wildly entertaining, each of these stories helped me learn more about black bears and how they behave.

Timber Harvest:
"Timber Harvest and Water Quality," December 2002, California Senate Office of Research
Z'berg-Nejedly Forest Practice Act of 1973
Jim Adams—Forester, Humboldt County, CA

Photography and Camera Equipment:
Matt Hinton of Matt Hinton Photos, Humboldt County, CA
Minolta SLR Camera & Accessary Guide, Minolta Corporation, 1985

Birds:
Gary Lester—Bird expert, Humboldt County, CA
Secrets of the Nest—The Family Life of North American Birds, Joan Dunning

About the Author

Glory Ralston lives with her family in a small, rural community in far northern California, with the Pacific Ocean on one side and what remains of the redwood forest on the other. The extraordinary beauty and challenging personal and environmental issues of this area form the backdrop for her stories.

Other Works by This Author

While the Music Played, a novel

Some Things Are Obvious, a novel

Made in the USA
San Bernardino, CA
20 August 2019